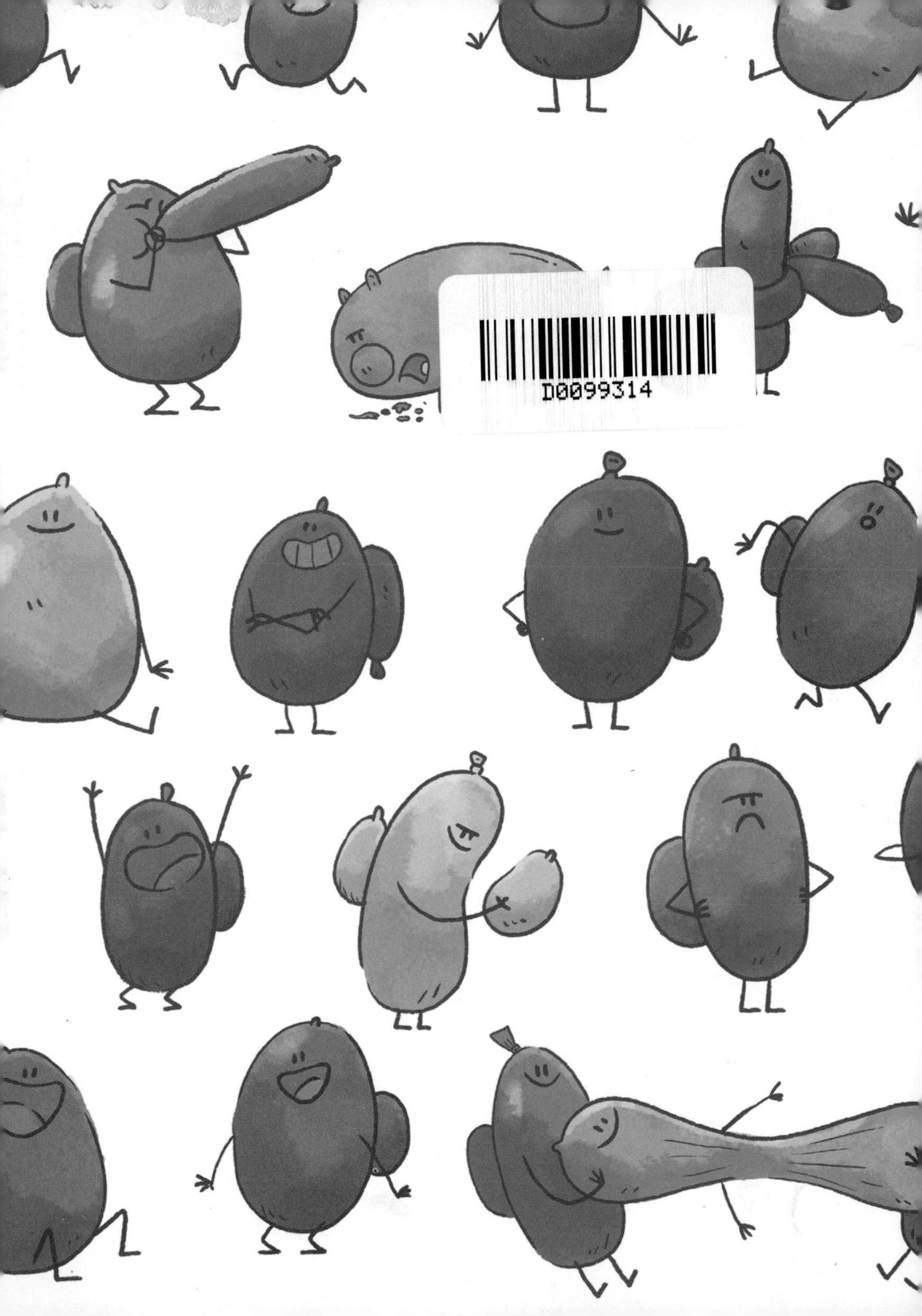

Blue, Barry & Pancakes

ESCAPE FROM BALLOONIA

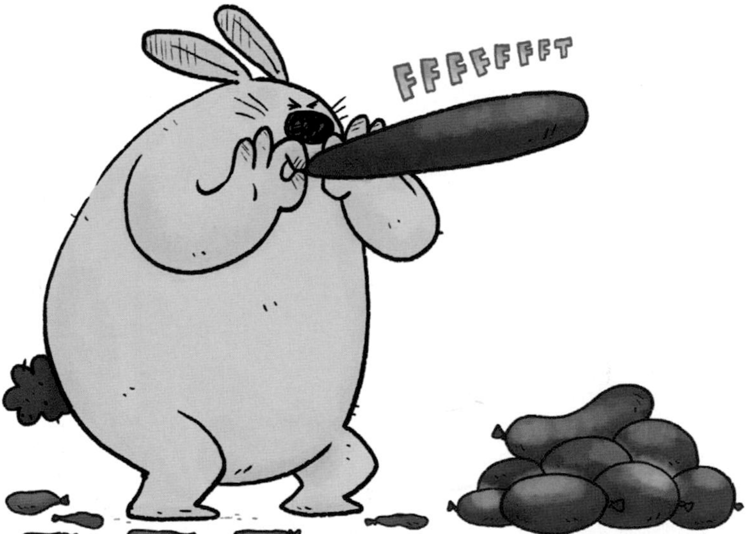
FFFFFFFFT

Barry & Pancakes

ESCAPE FROM BALLOONIA

:01

First Second
New York

by
Dan & Jason

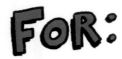

FOR:

Lindsay, whose loving support and nonstop balloonian wrangling made this book possible. —D.A.

Catherine, who's taken me on all the best adventures of my life! —J.P.

:01
First Second

Published by First Second
First Second is an imprint of Roaring Brook Press,
a division of Holtzbrinck Publishing Holdings Limited Partnership
120 Broadway, New York, NY 10271
firstsecondbooks.com
mackids.com

Library of Congress Control Number: 2020918356

Our books may be purchased in bulk for promotional, educational, or business use. Please contact your local bookseller or the Macmillan Corporate and Premium Sales Department at (800) 221-7945 ext. 5442 or by email at MacmillanSpecialMarkets@macmillan.com.

FIRST EDITION

First edition, 2021
Edited by Calista Brill and Alex Lu
Cover design by Jason Patterson
Interior book design by Sunny Lee

Dan & Jason draw mostly in Photoshop on a Wacom Cintiq. They clean up the drawings, paint the environments, and add the text and word balloons. The font is a unique Blue, Barry, and Pancakes typeset created specifically for these books.

Printed in China by RR Donnelley Asia Printing Solutions Ltd., Dongguan City, Guangdong Province

ISBN 978-1-250-25556-3
10 9 8 7 6 5 4 3 2 1

Don't miss your next favorite book from First Second! For the latest updates go to firstsecondnewsletter.com and sign up for our enewsletter.

BY ART WE LIVE

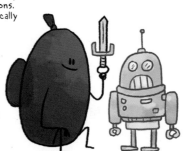

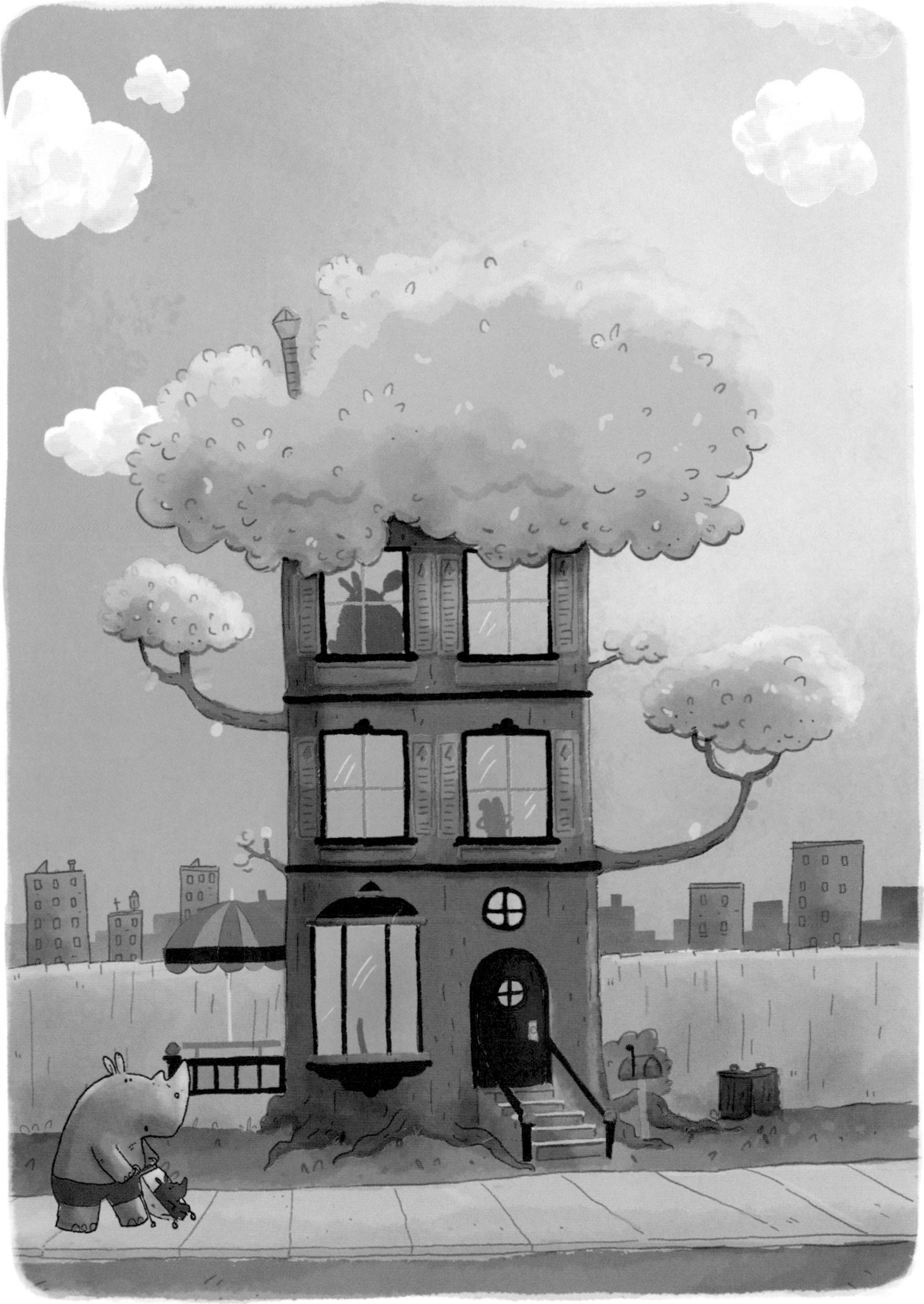

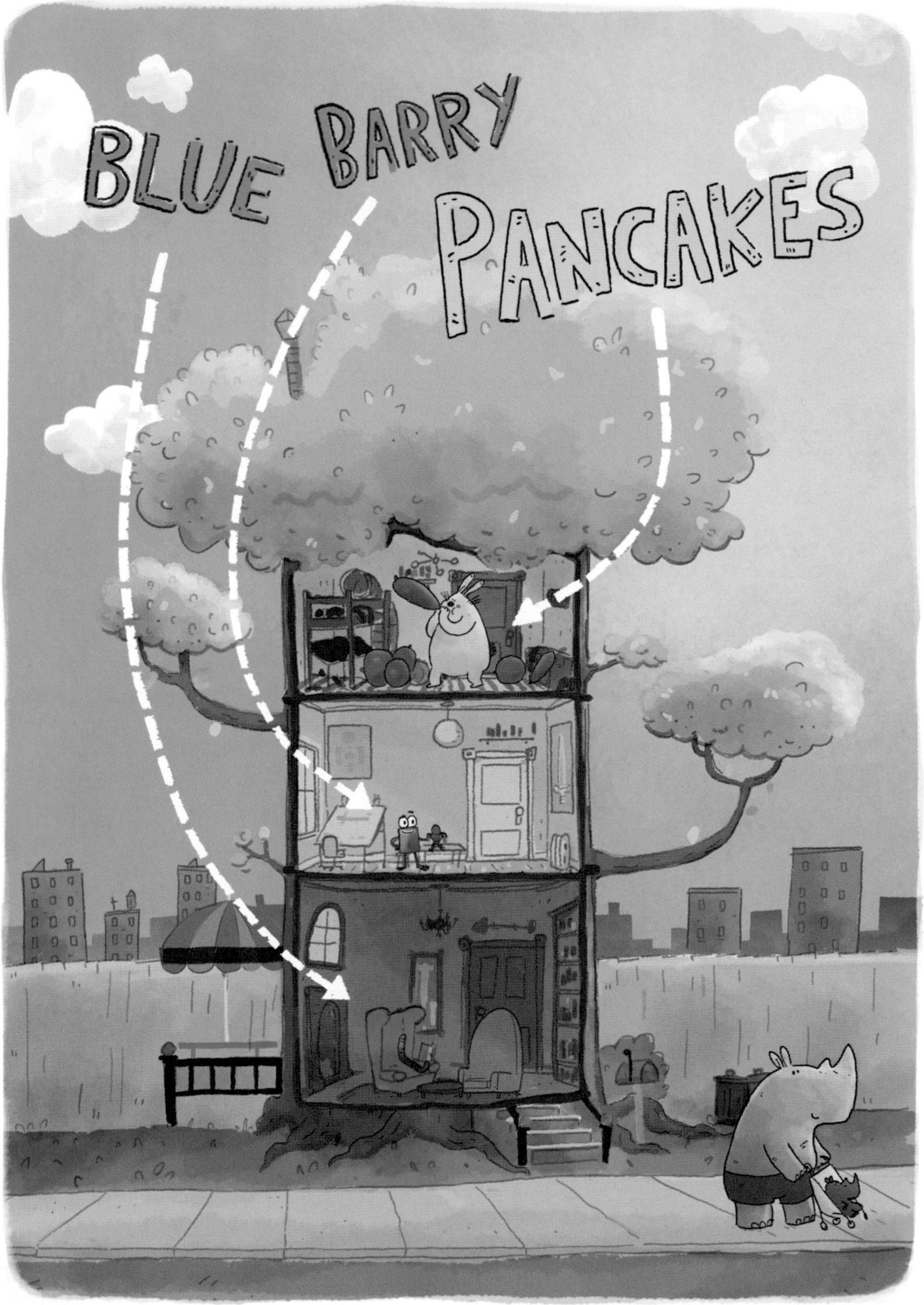
BLUE BARRY PANCAKES

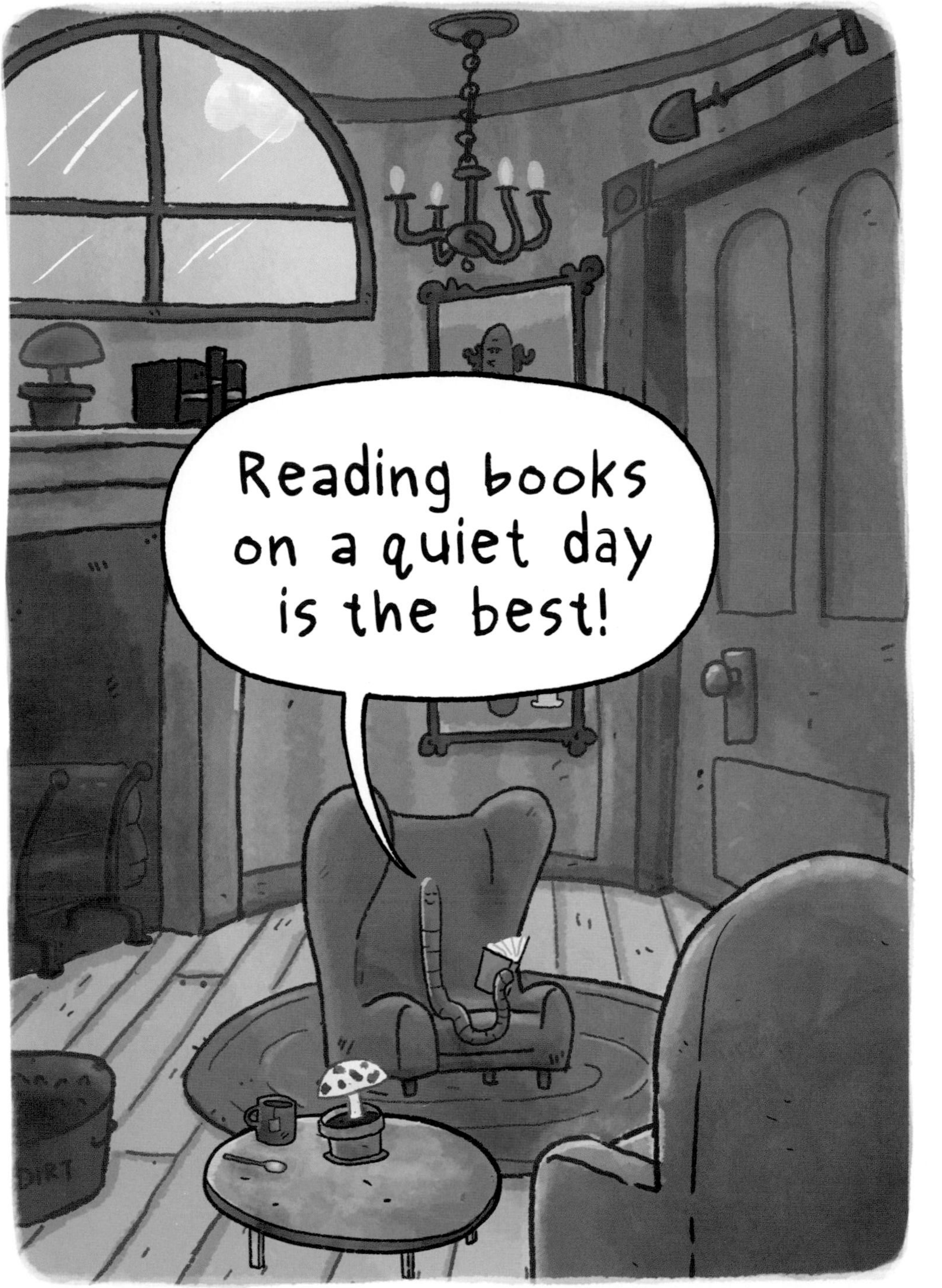
Reading books on a quiet day is the best!

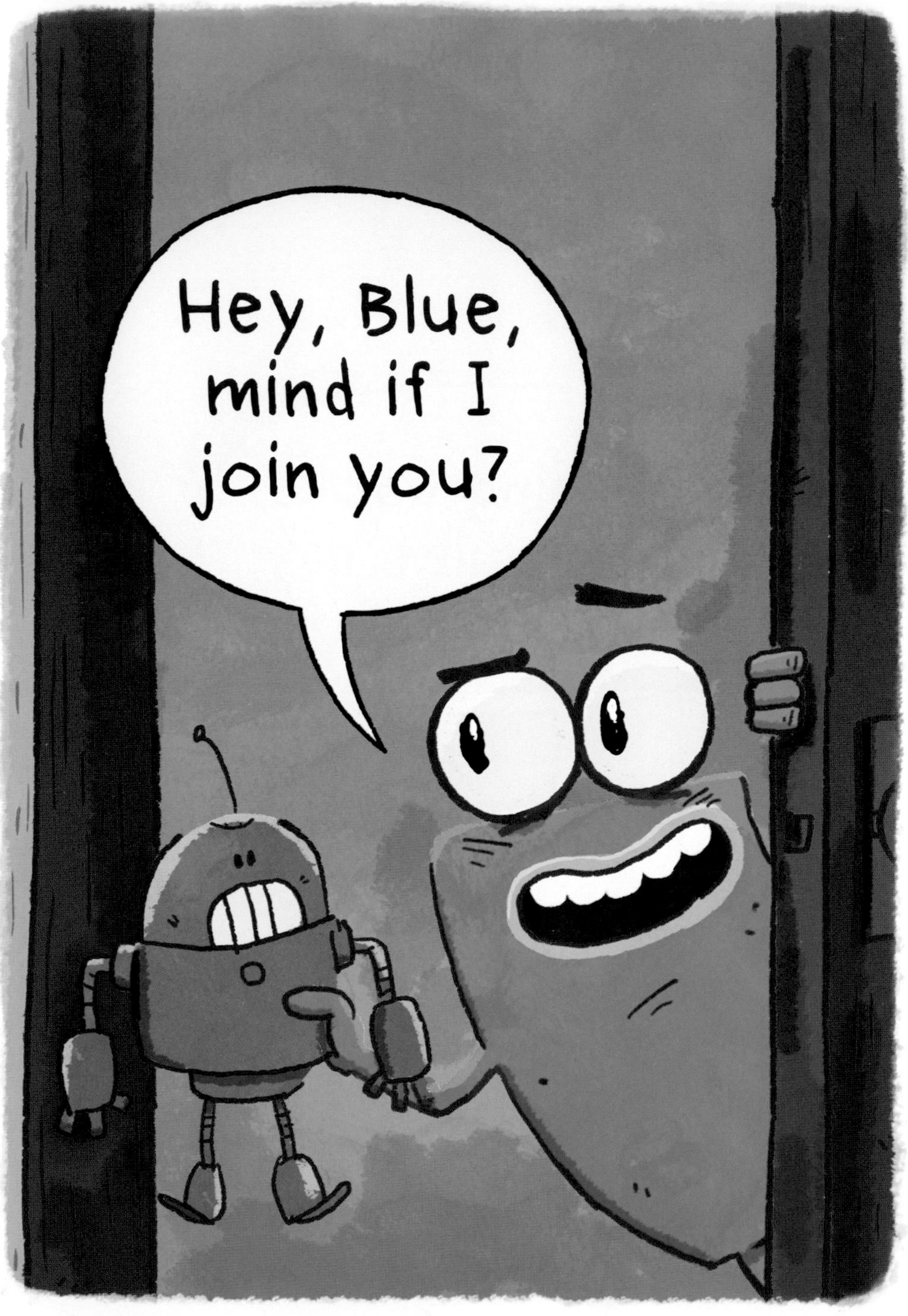
Hey, Blue, mind if I join you?

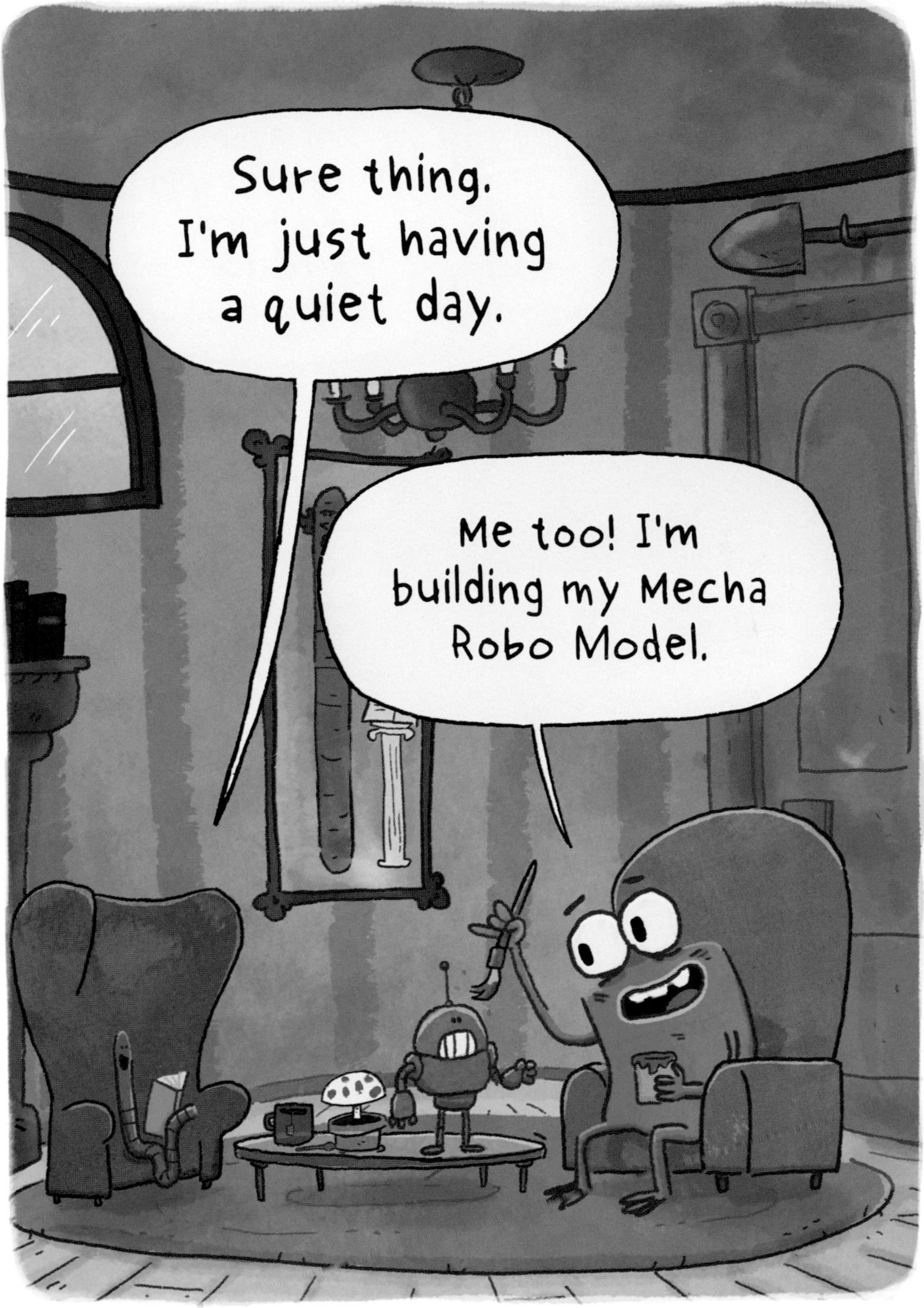
Sure thing. I'm just having a quiet day.
Me too! I'm building my Mecha Robo Model.

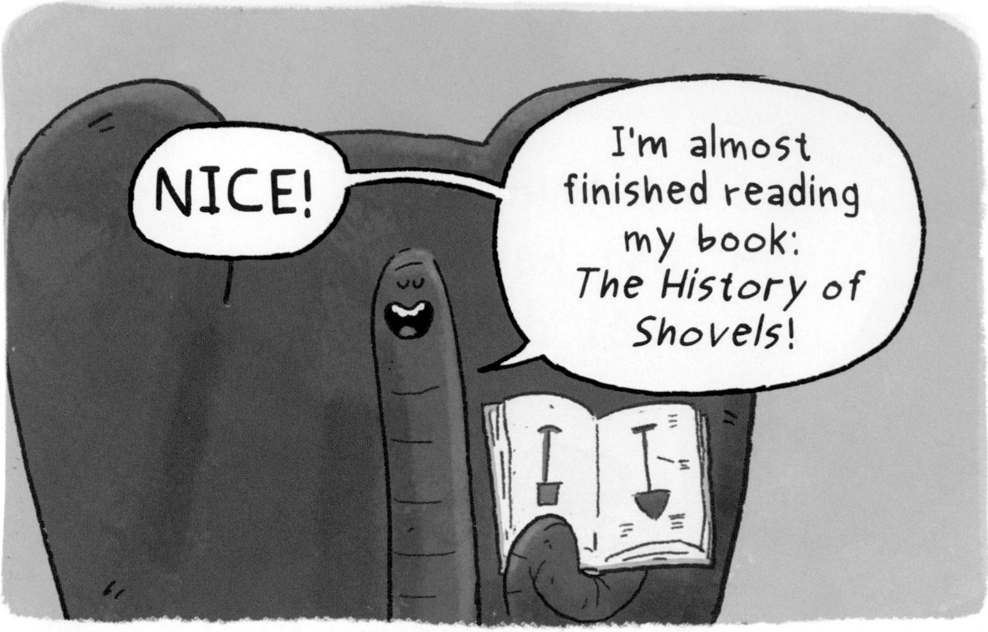
NICE!
I'm almost finished reading my book: *The History of Shovels*!

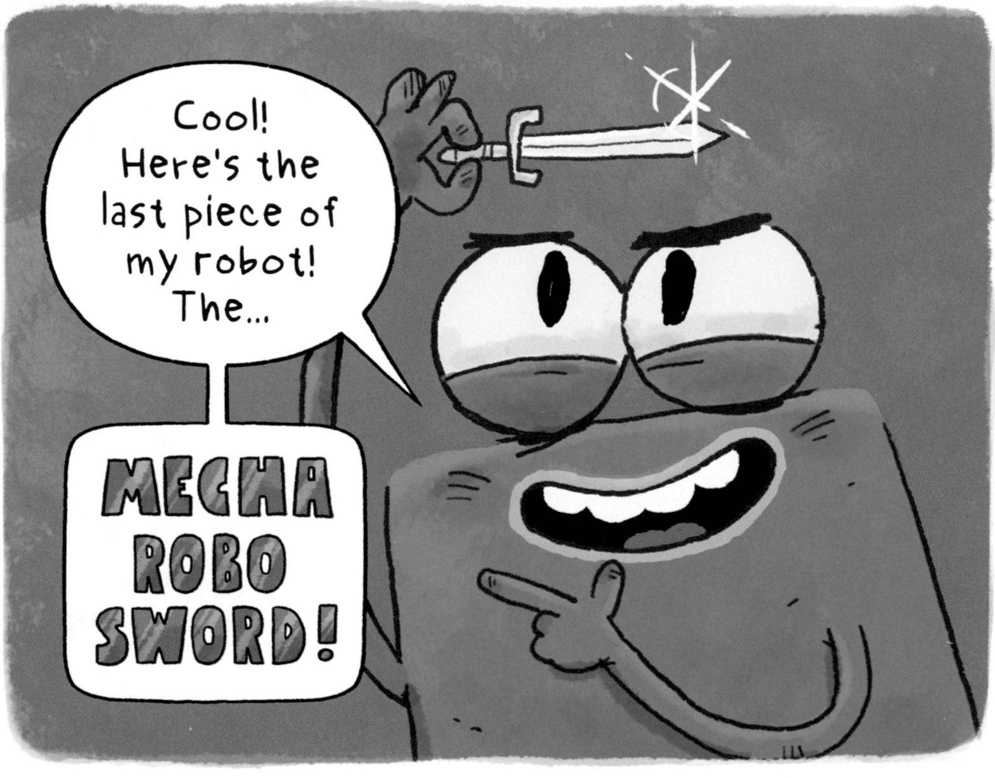
Cool! Here's the last piece of my robot! The...
MECHA ROBO SWORD!

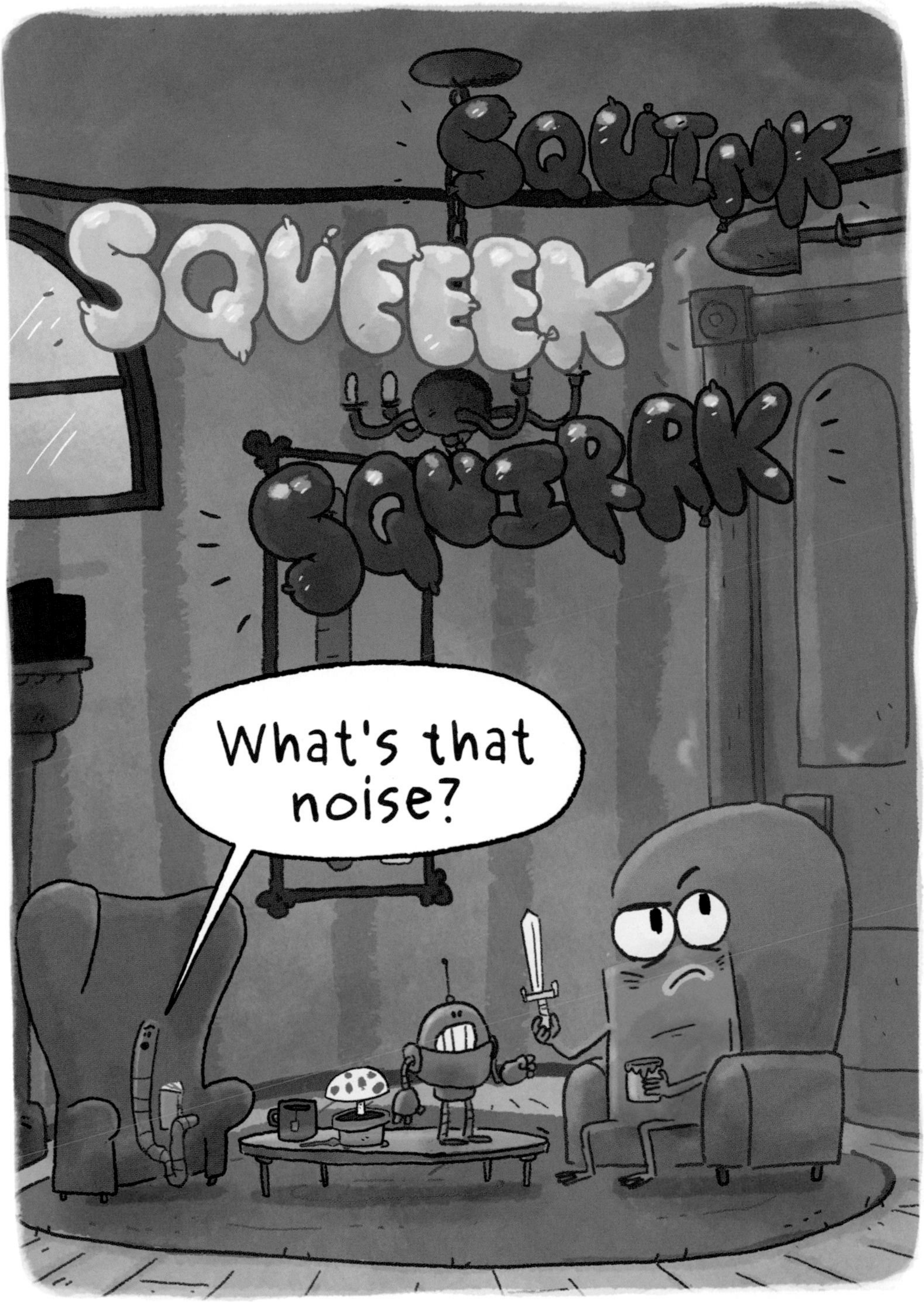
SQUINK
SQUEEK
SQUIRRK
What's that noise?

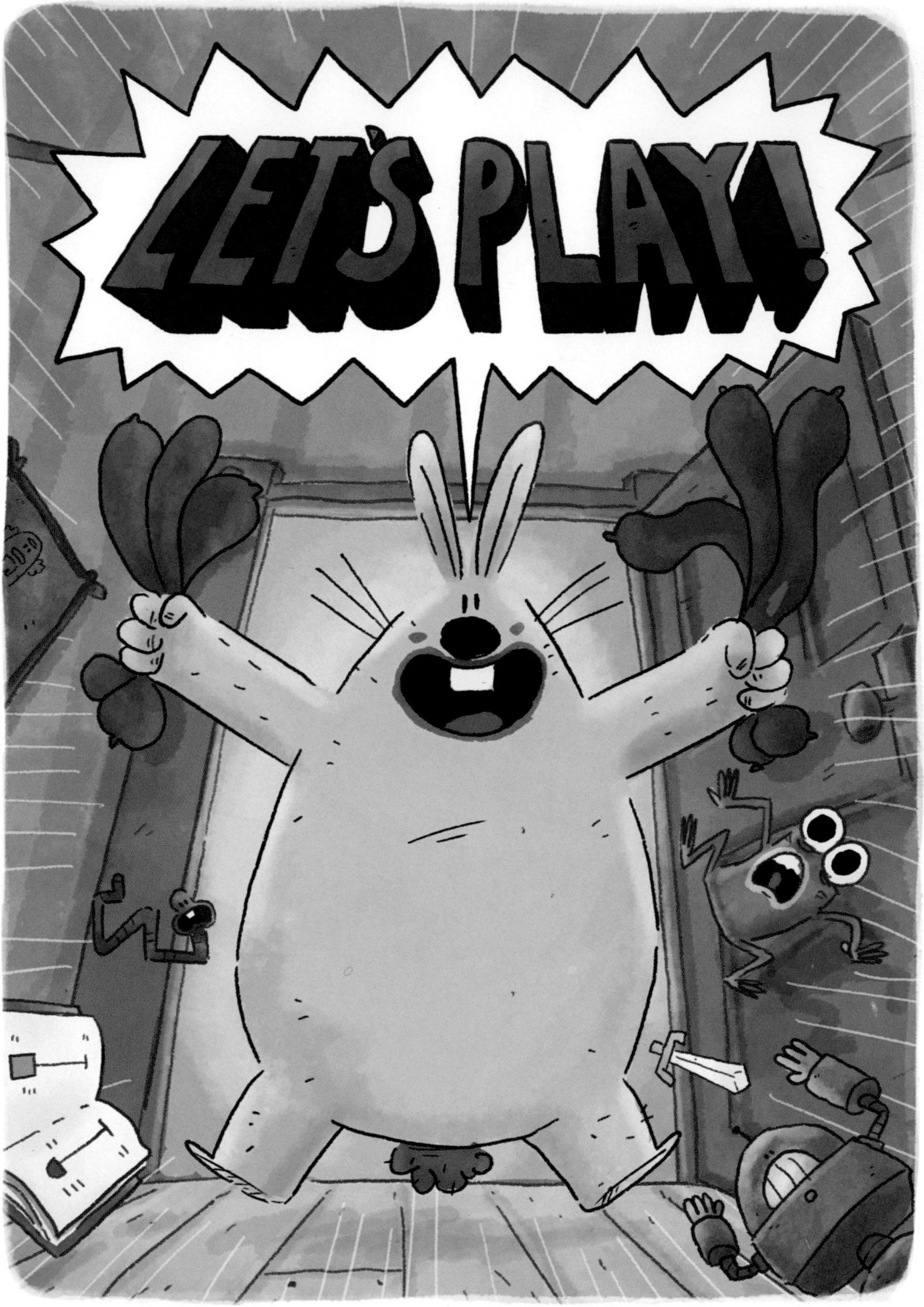
LET'S PLAY!

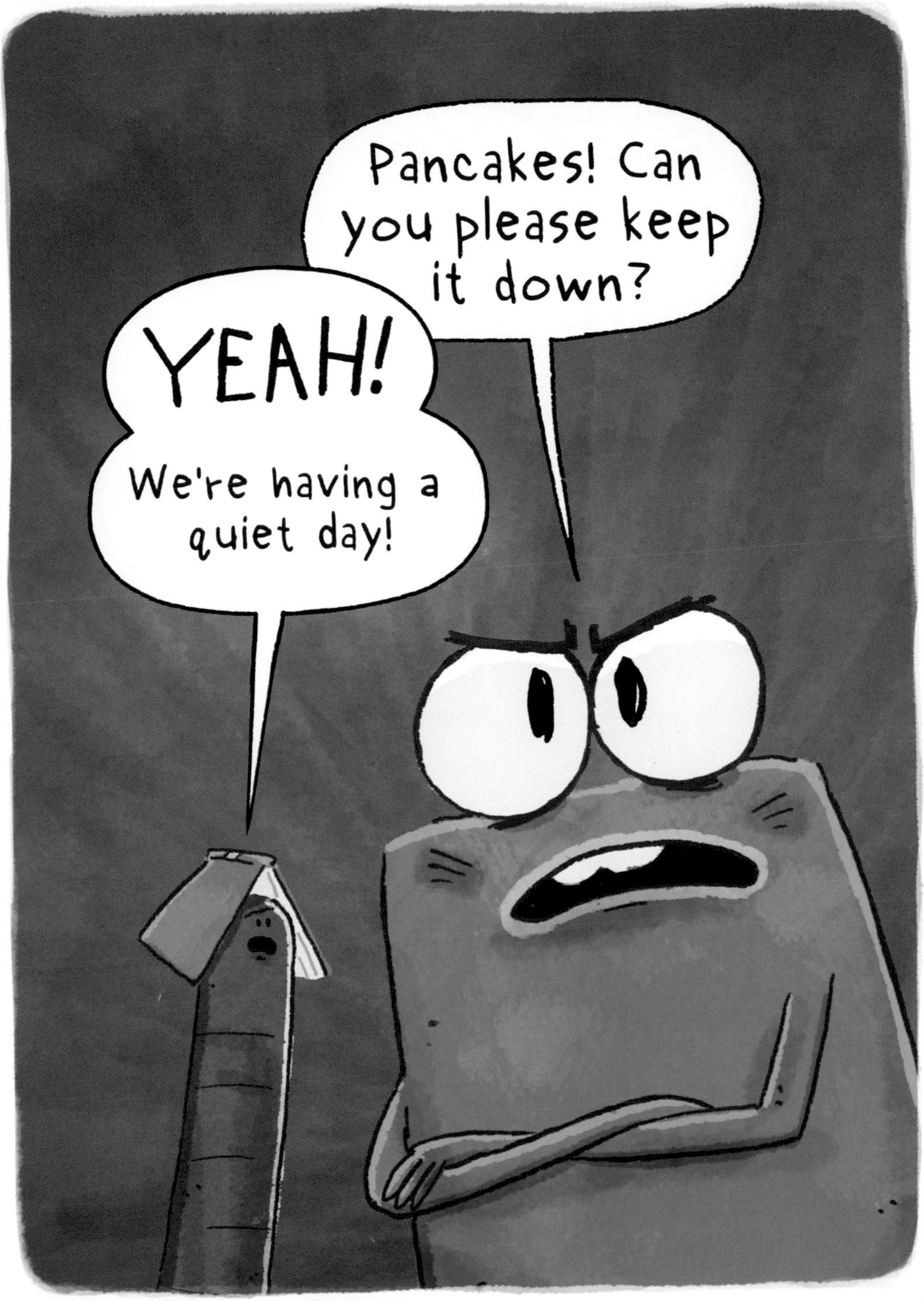
Pancakes! Can you please keep it down?
YEAH!
We're having a quiet day!

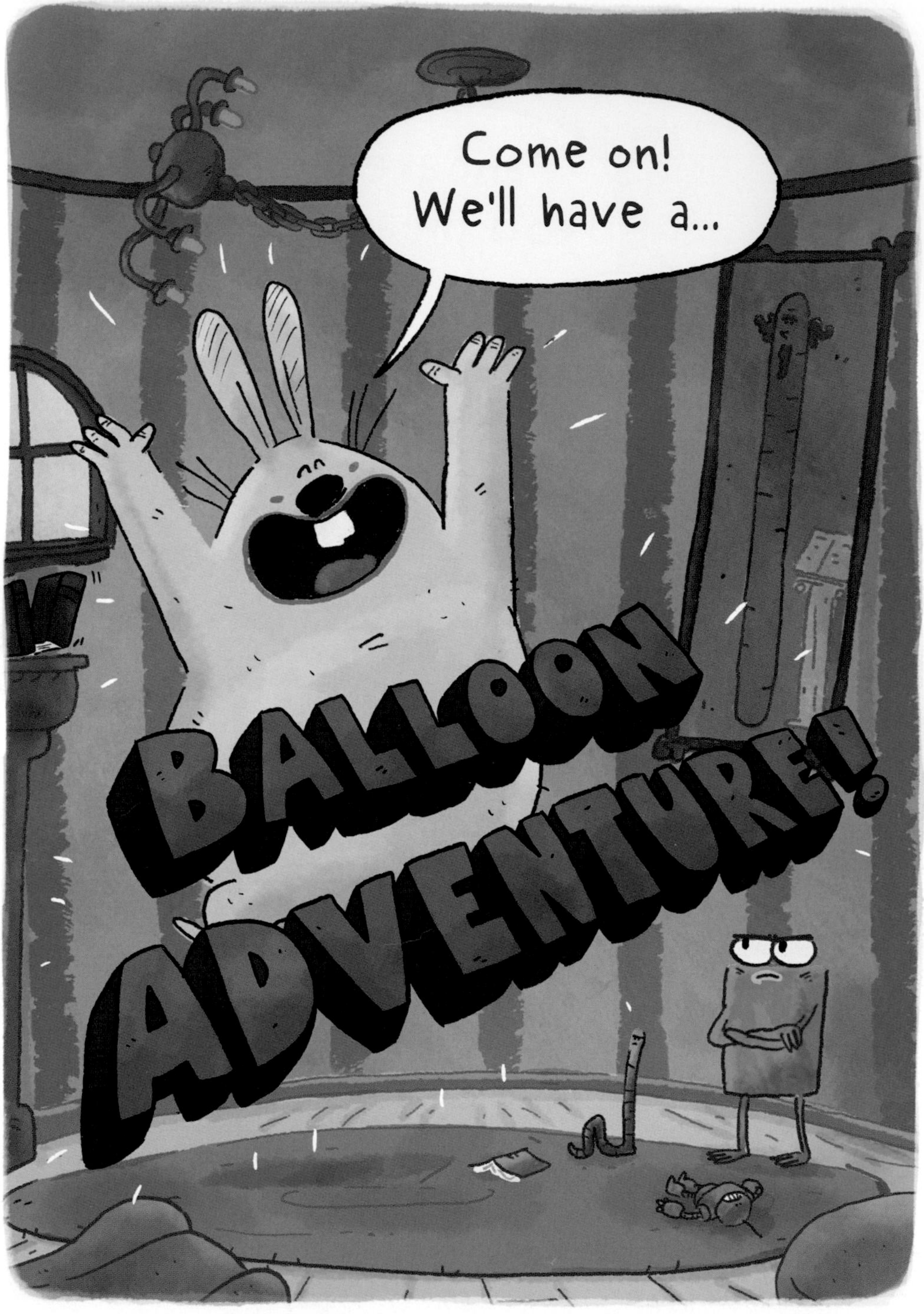
Come on! We'll have a...
BALLOON ADVENTURE!

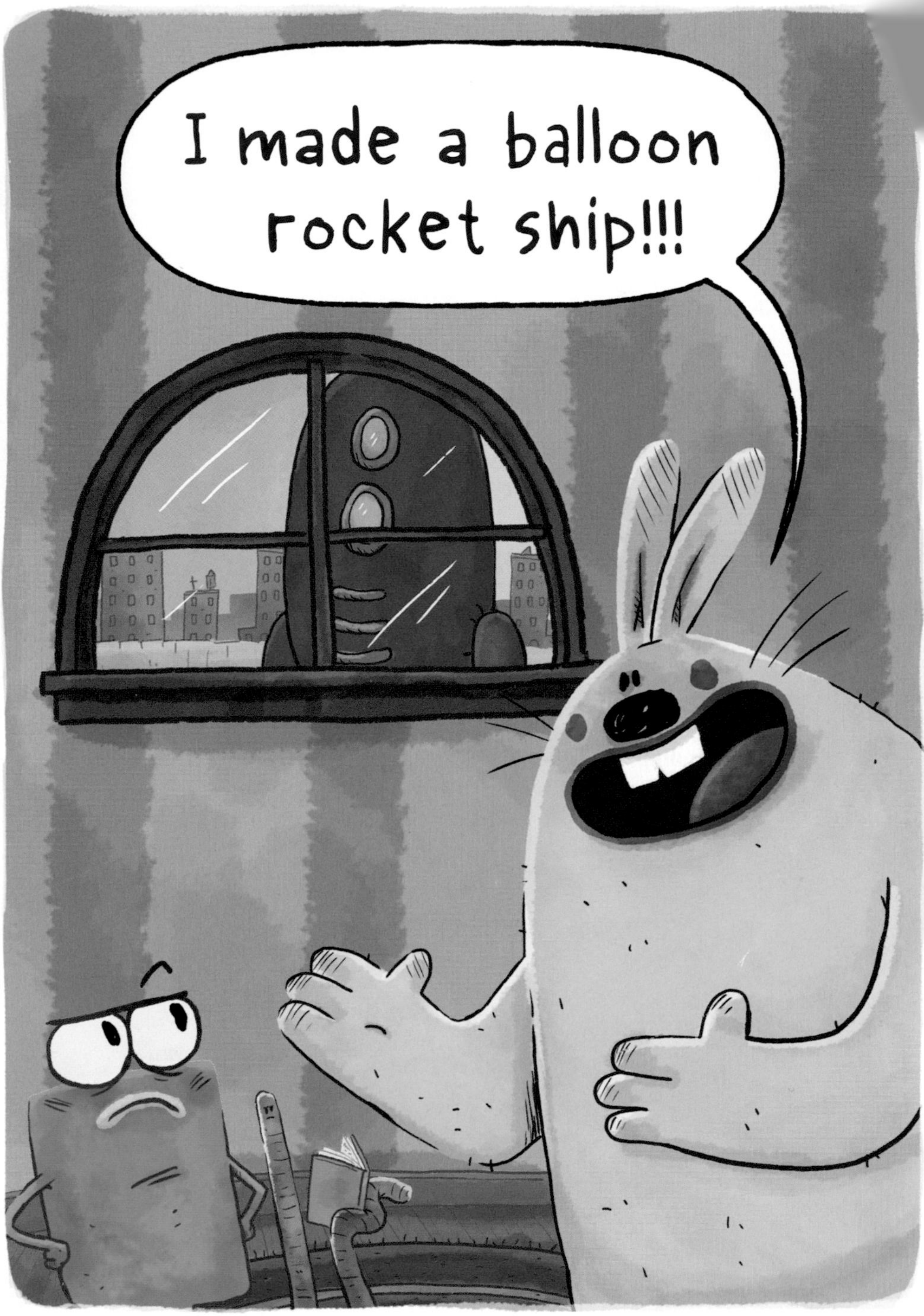
I made a balloon rocket ship!!!

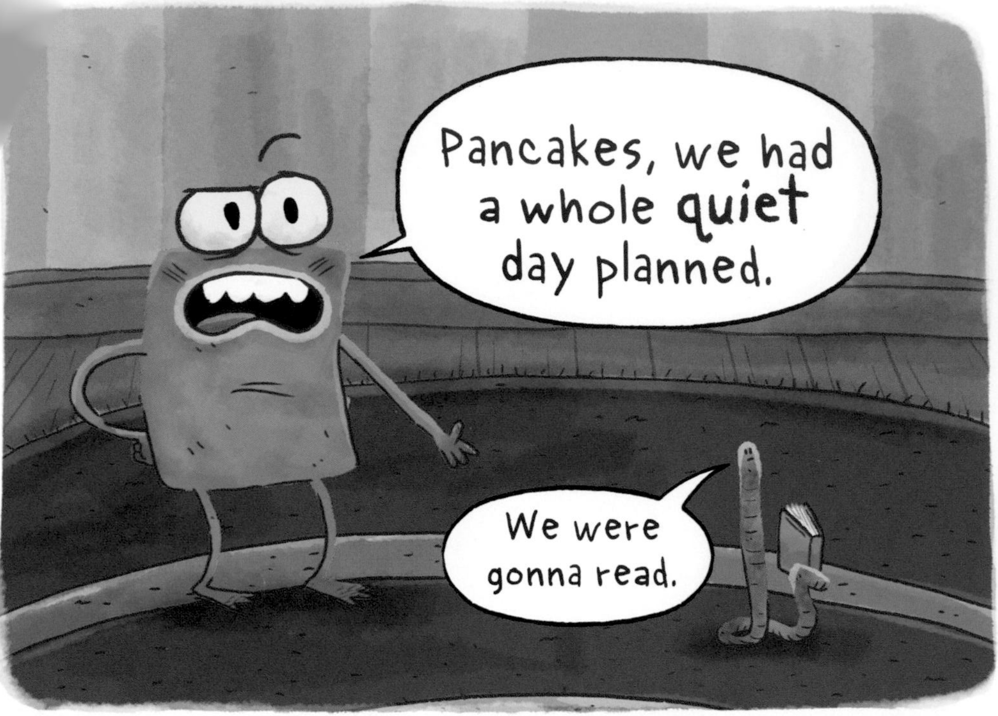
Pancakes, we had a whole quiet day planned.
We were gonna read.

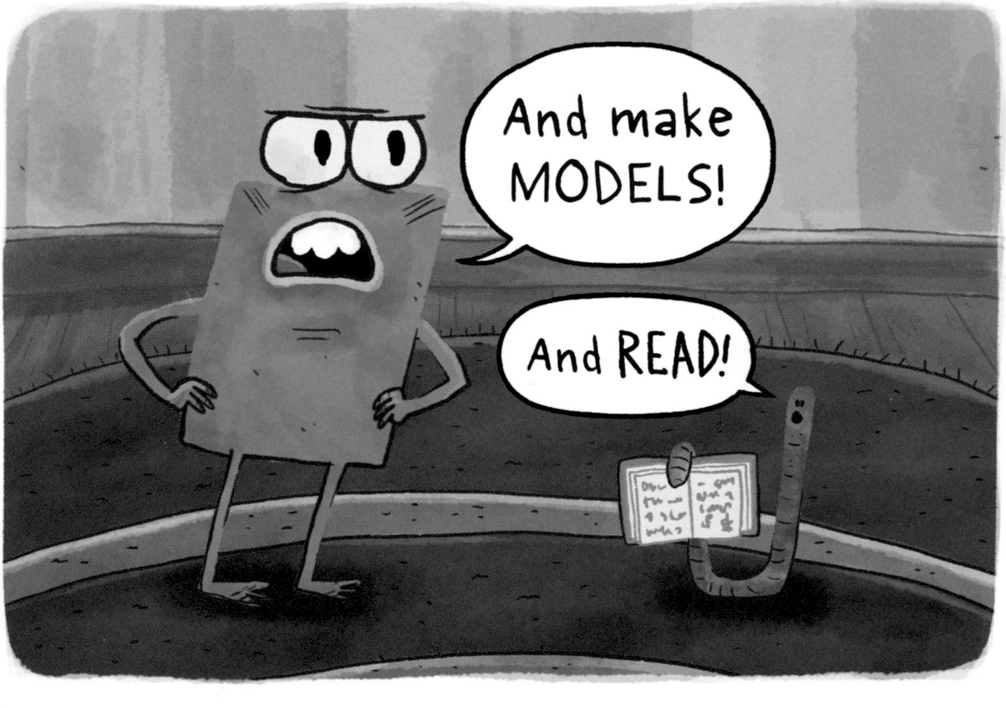
And make MODELS!
And READ!

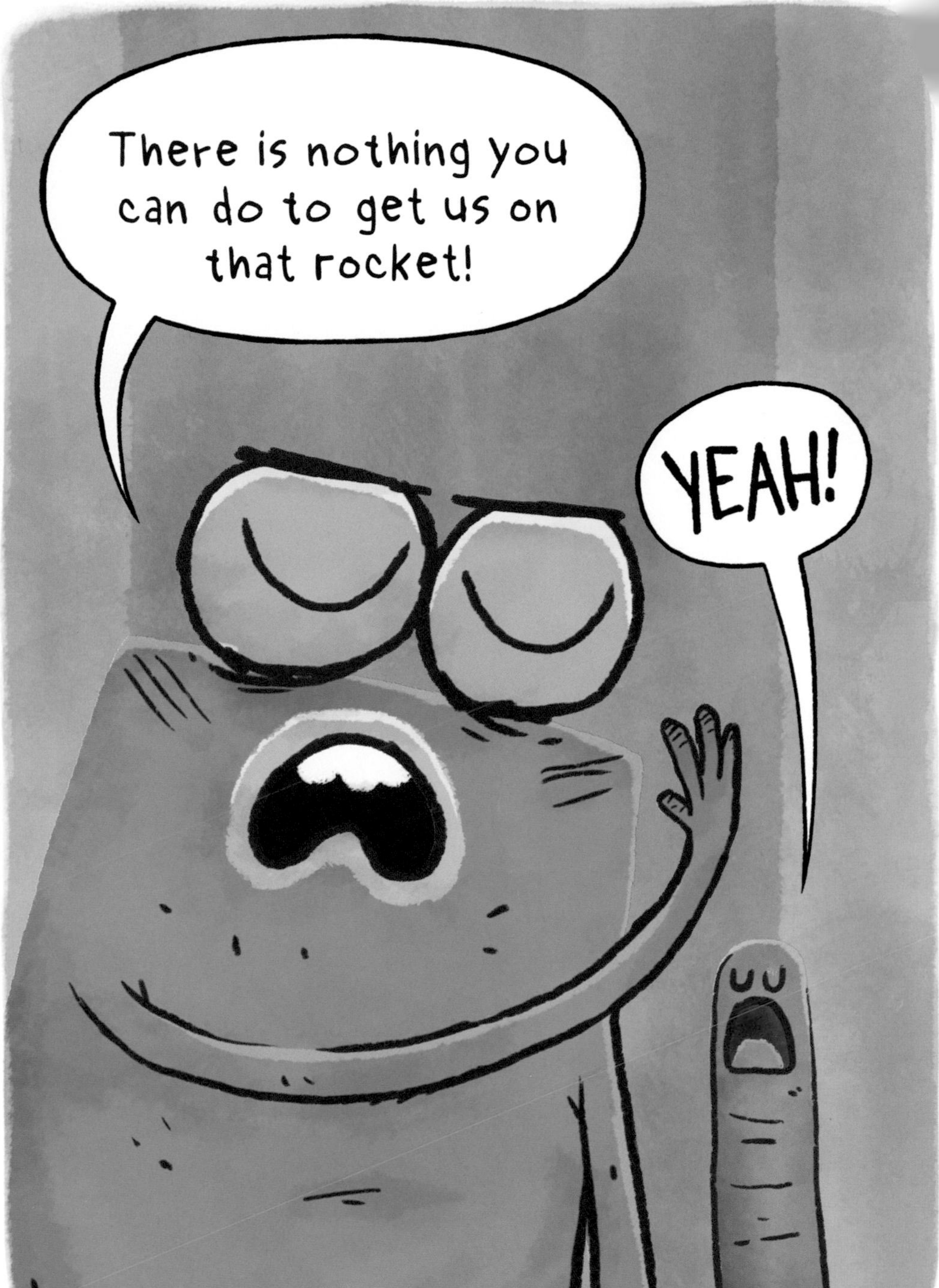
There is nothing you can do to get us on that rocket!
YEAH!

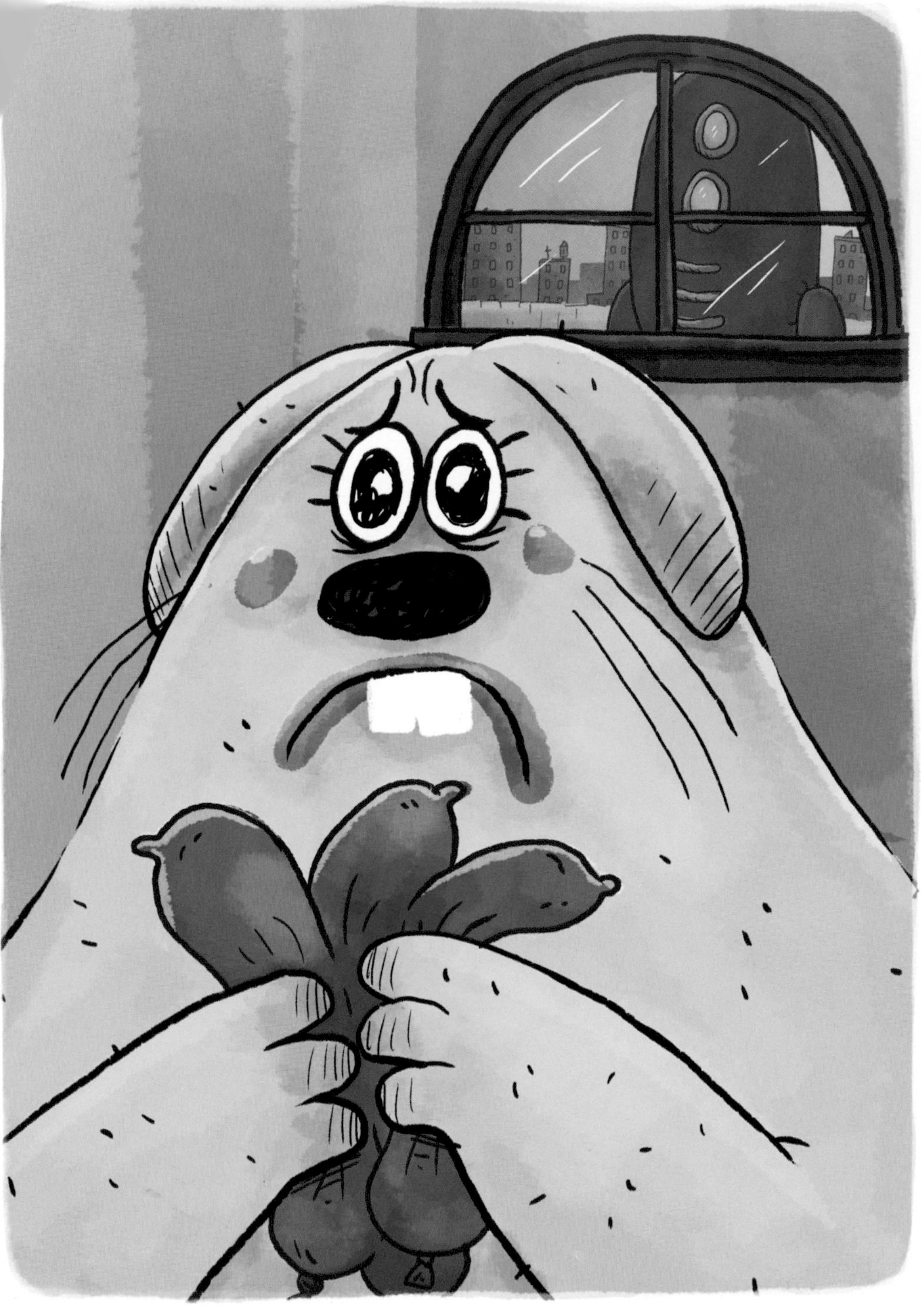

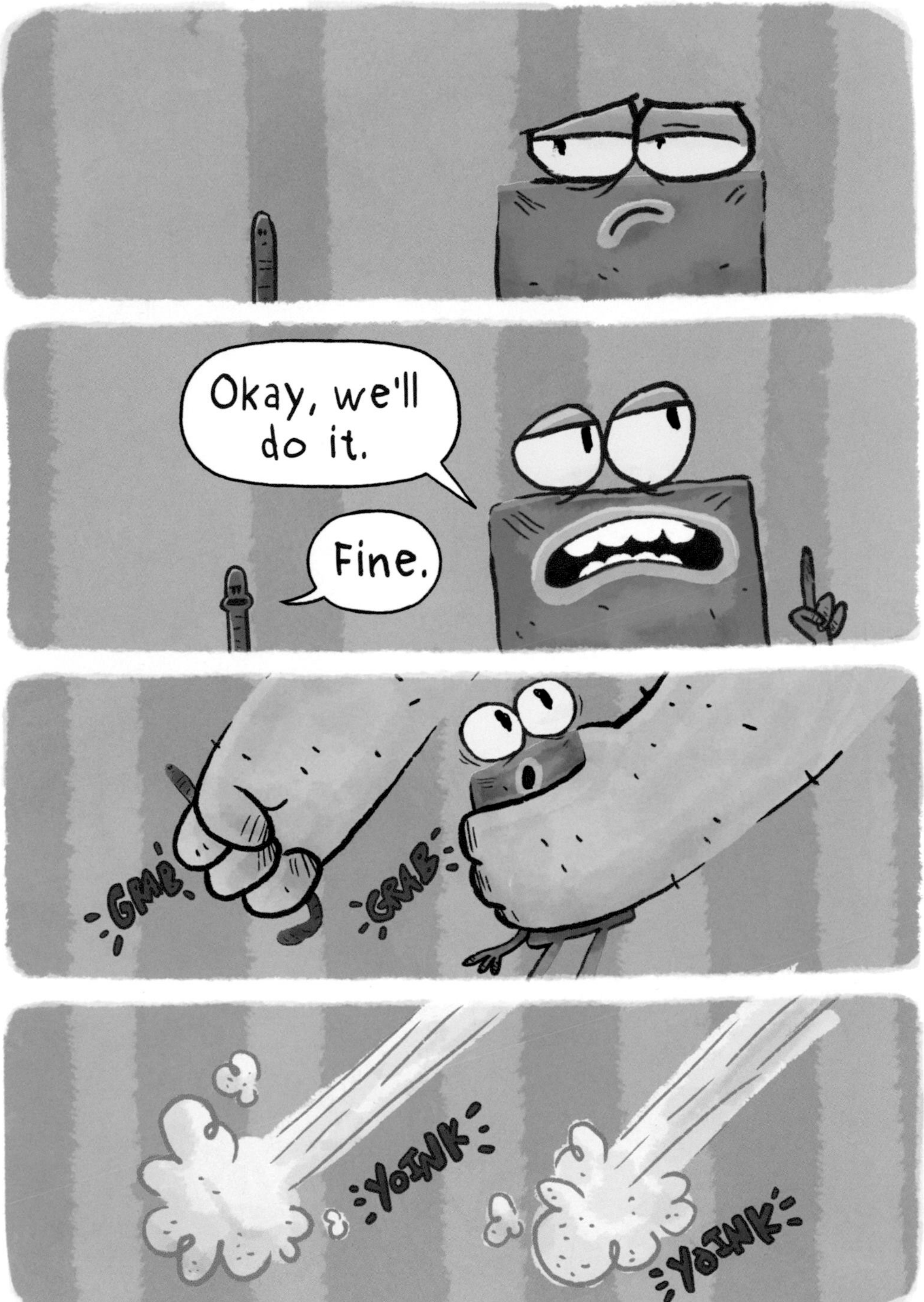
Okay, we'll do it.
Fine.
GRAB
GRAB
YOINK
YOINK

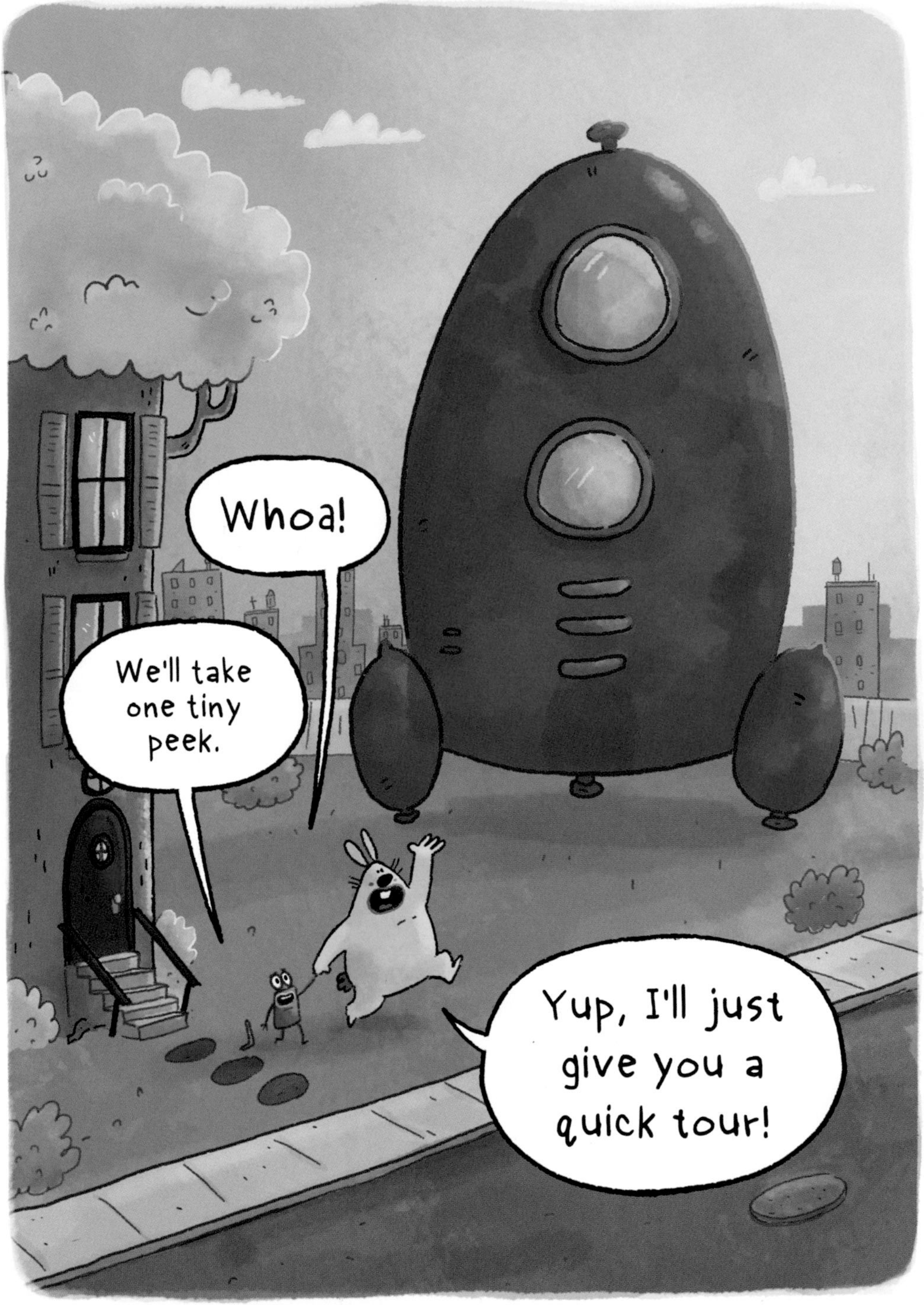
We'll take one tiny peek.
Whoa!
Yup, I'll just give you a quick tour!

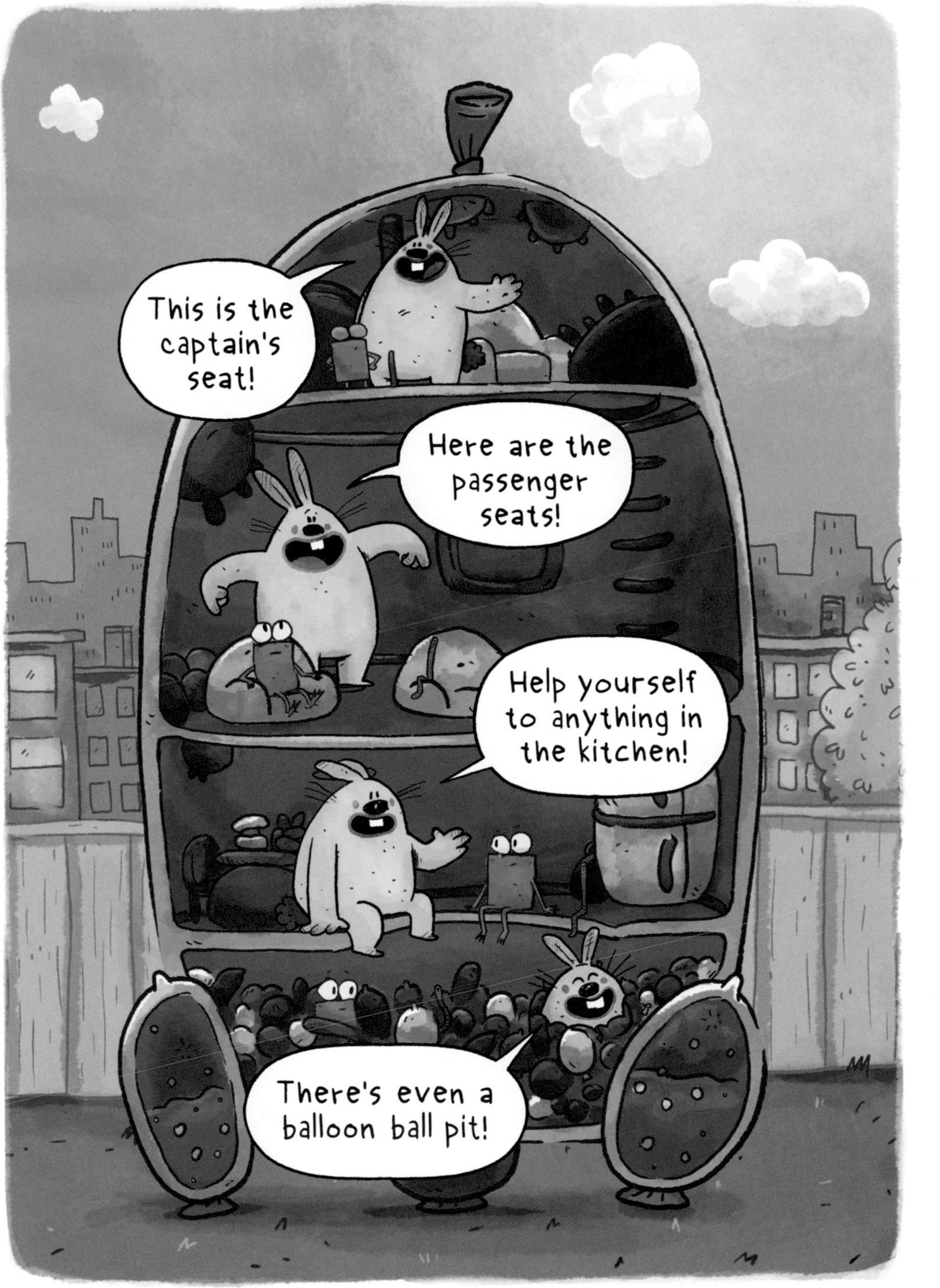
This is the captain's seat!
Here are the passenger seats!
Help yourself to anything in the kitchen!
There's even a balloon ball pit!

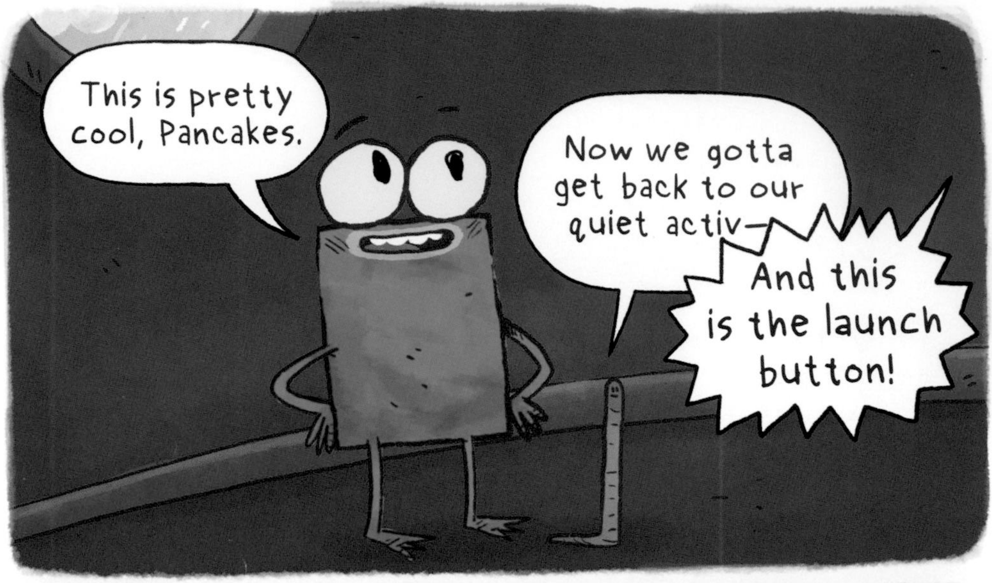
This is pretty cool, Pancakes.
Now we gotta get back to our quiet activ—
And this is the launch button!

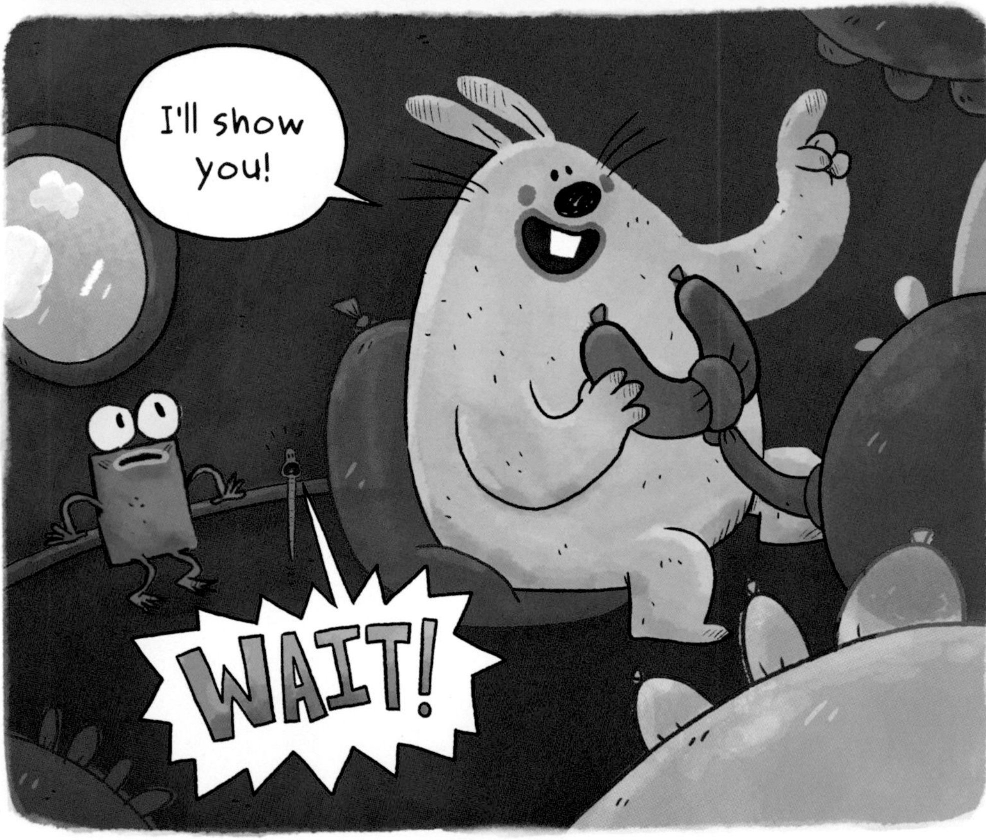
I'll show you!
WAIT!

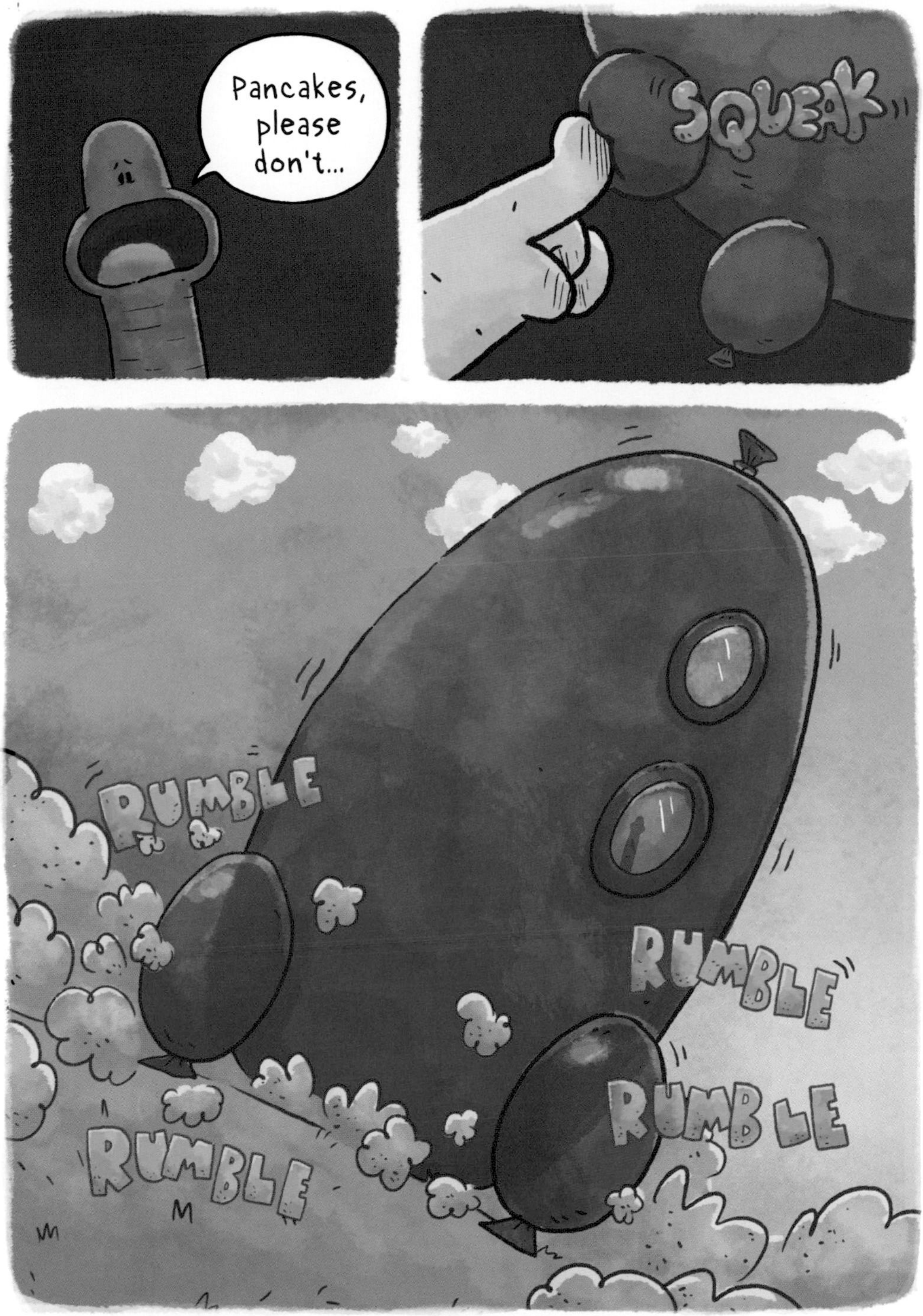
Pancakes, please don't...
SQUEAK
RUMBLE
RUMBLE
RUMBLE
RUMBLE

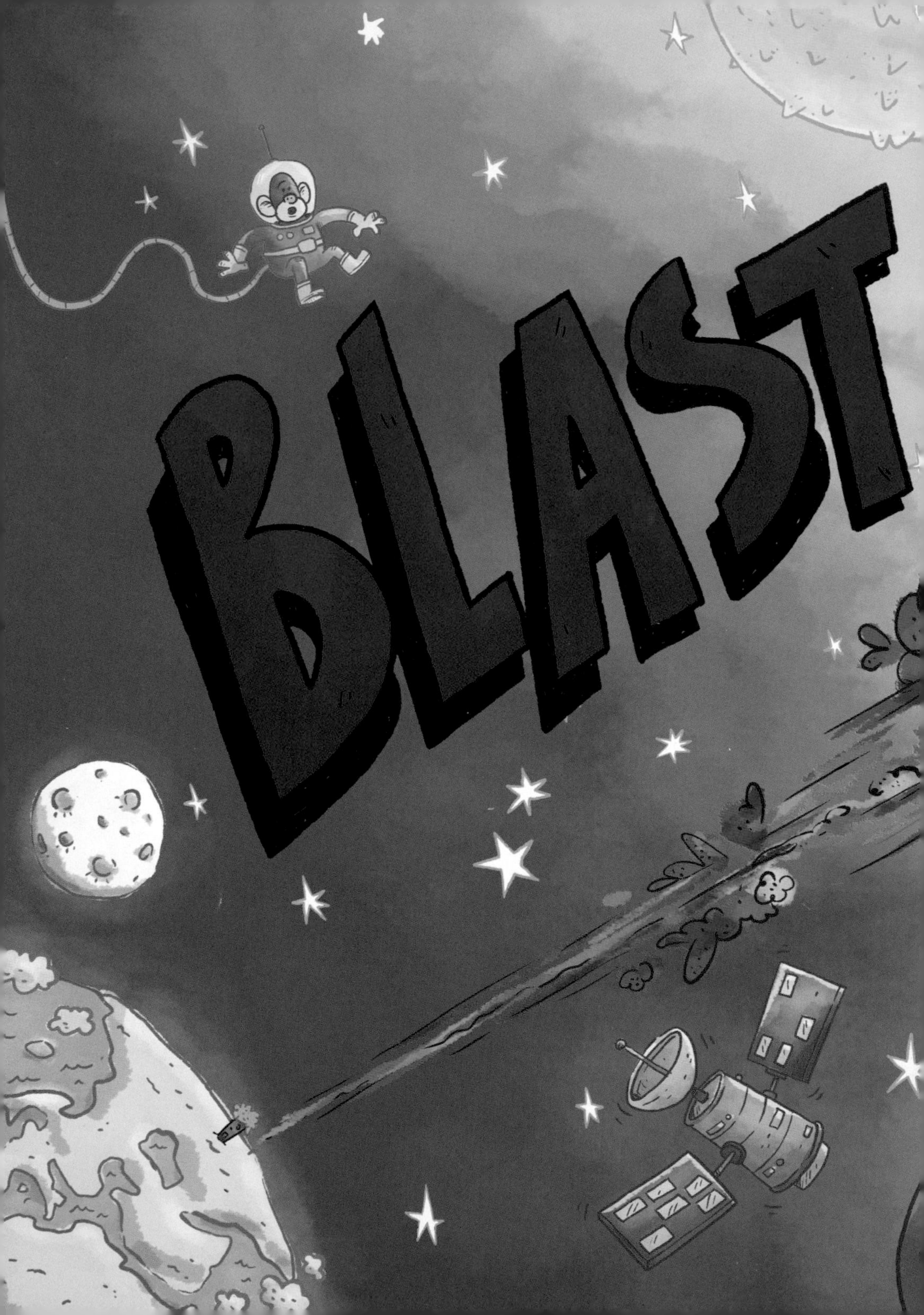
BLAST

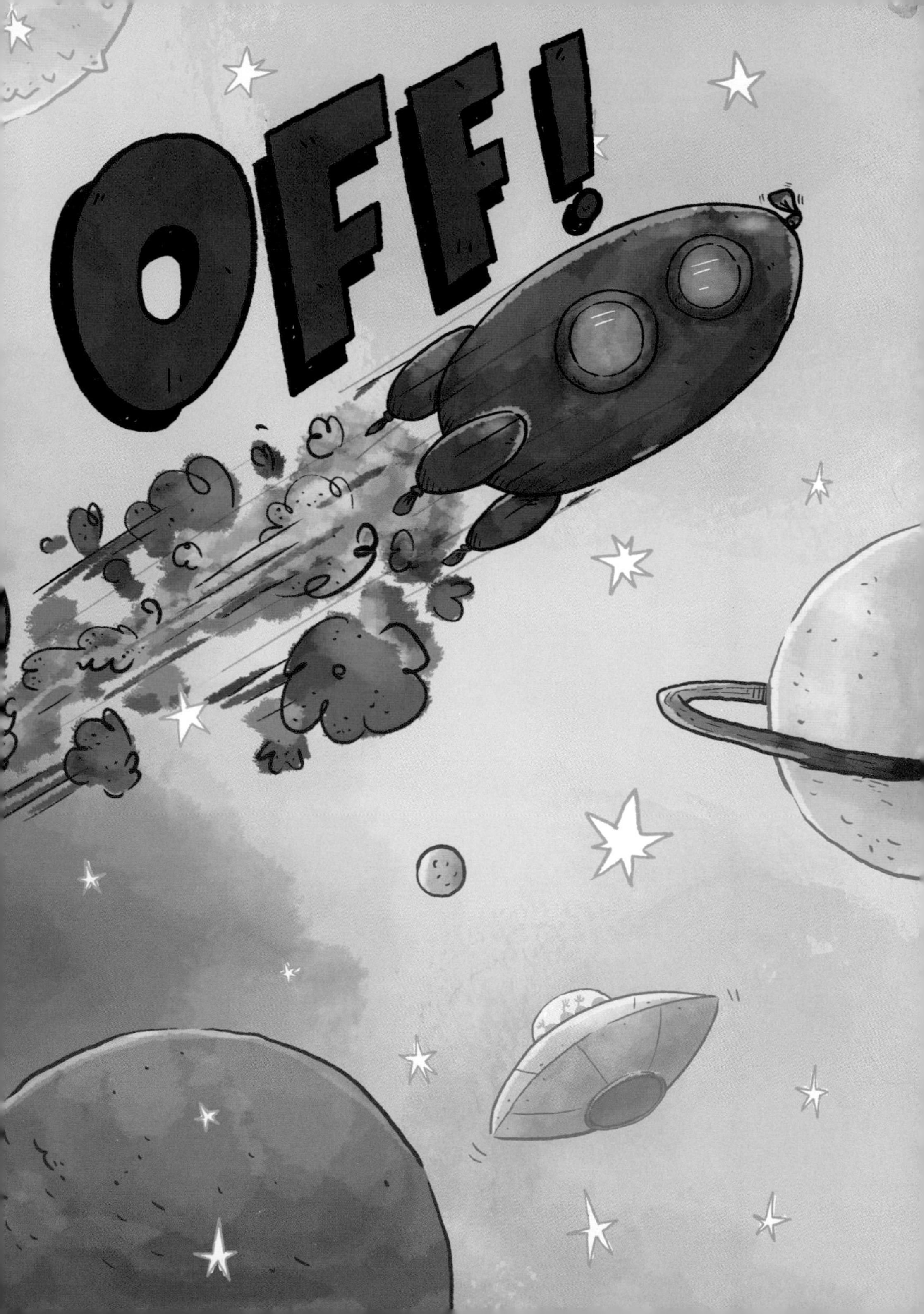
OFF!

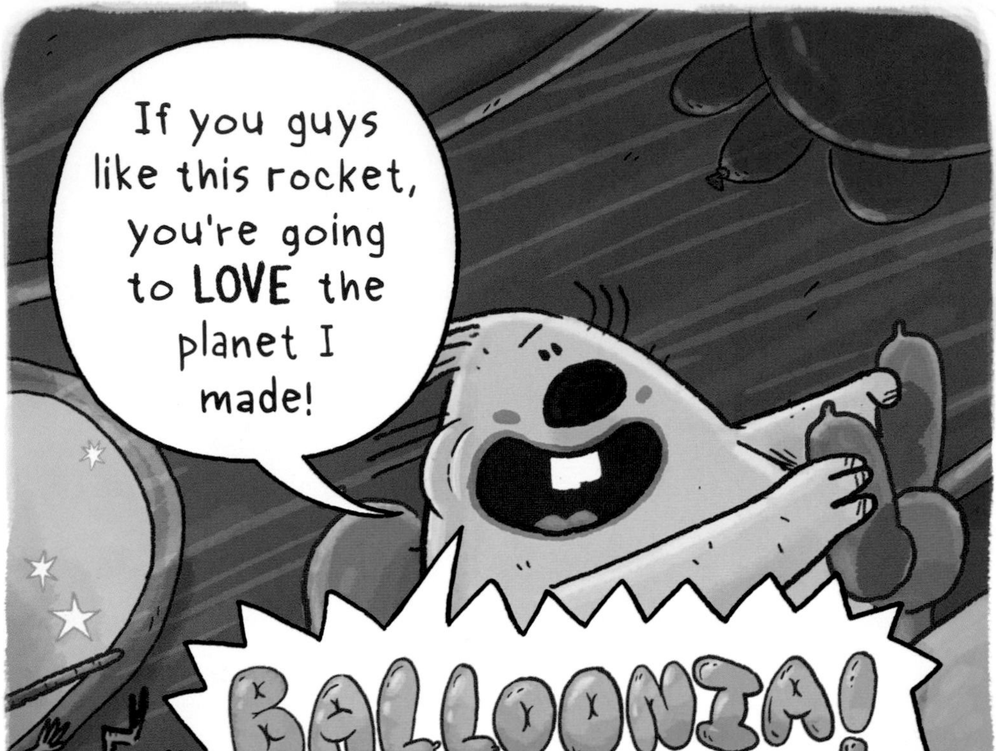

If you guys like this rocket, you're going to LOVE the planet I made!
BALLOONIA!

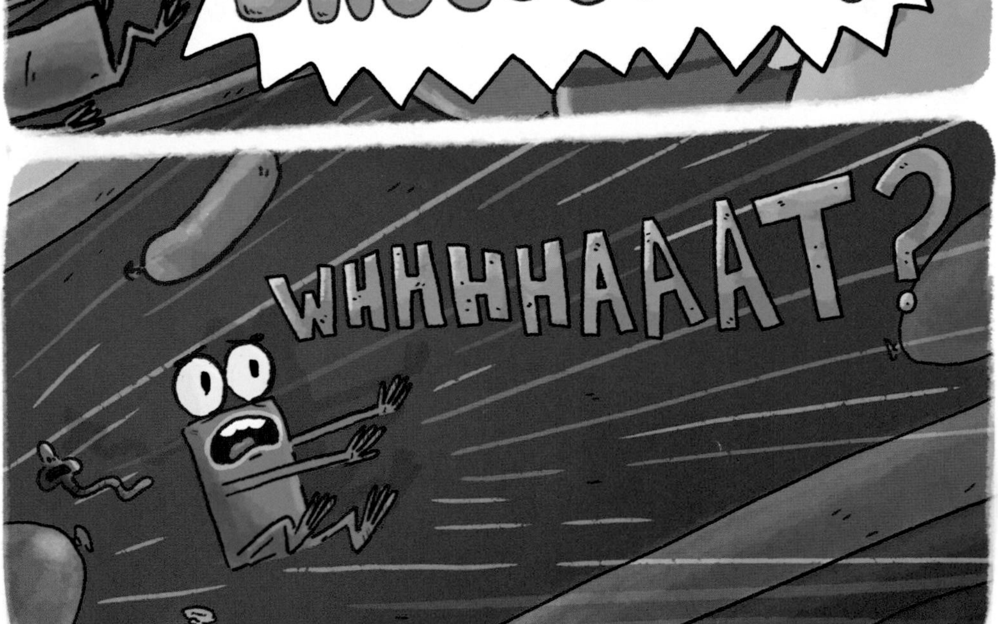

WHHHHAAAT?

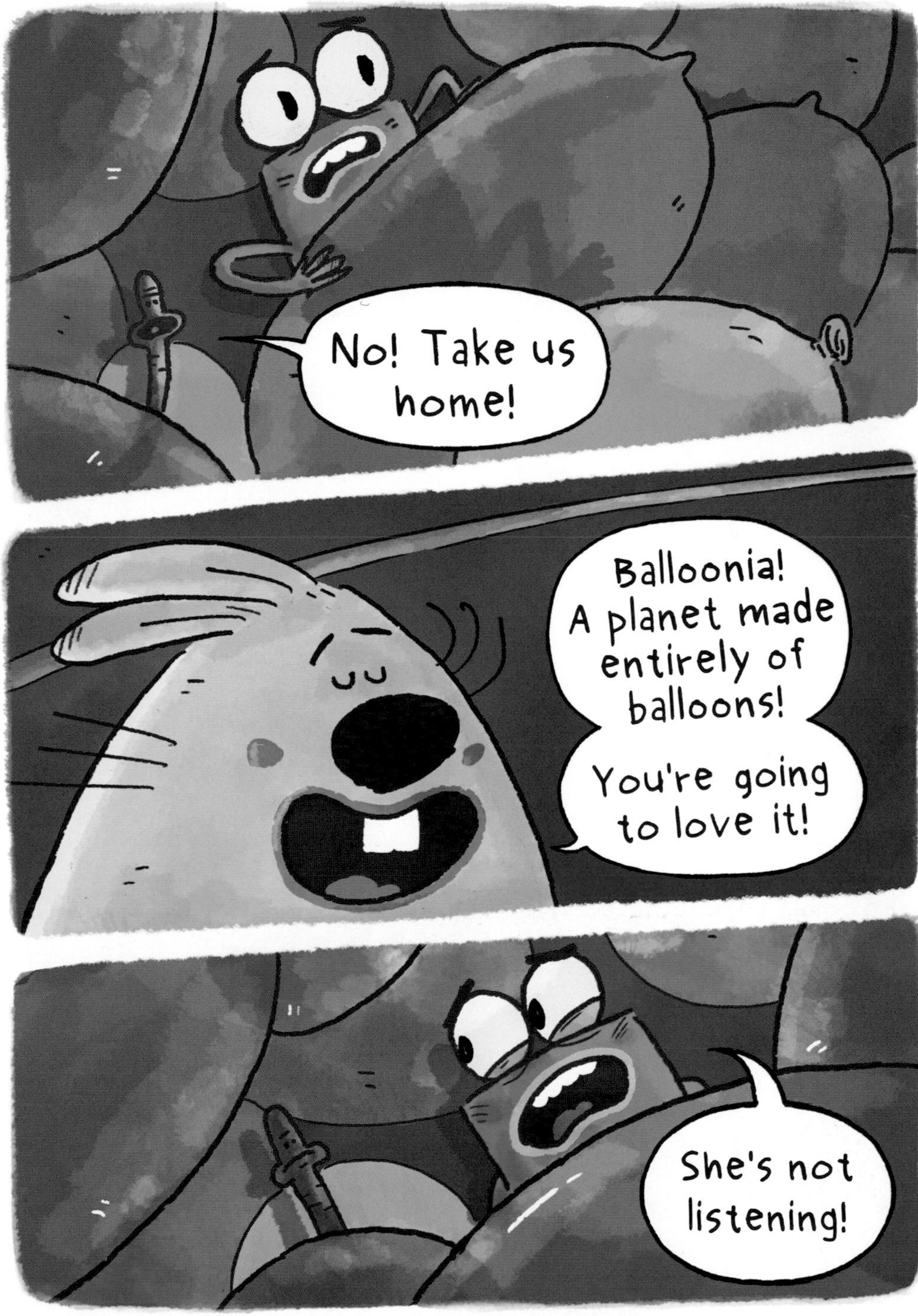
No! Take us home!
Balloonia! A planet made entirely of balloons!
You're going to love it!
She's not listening!

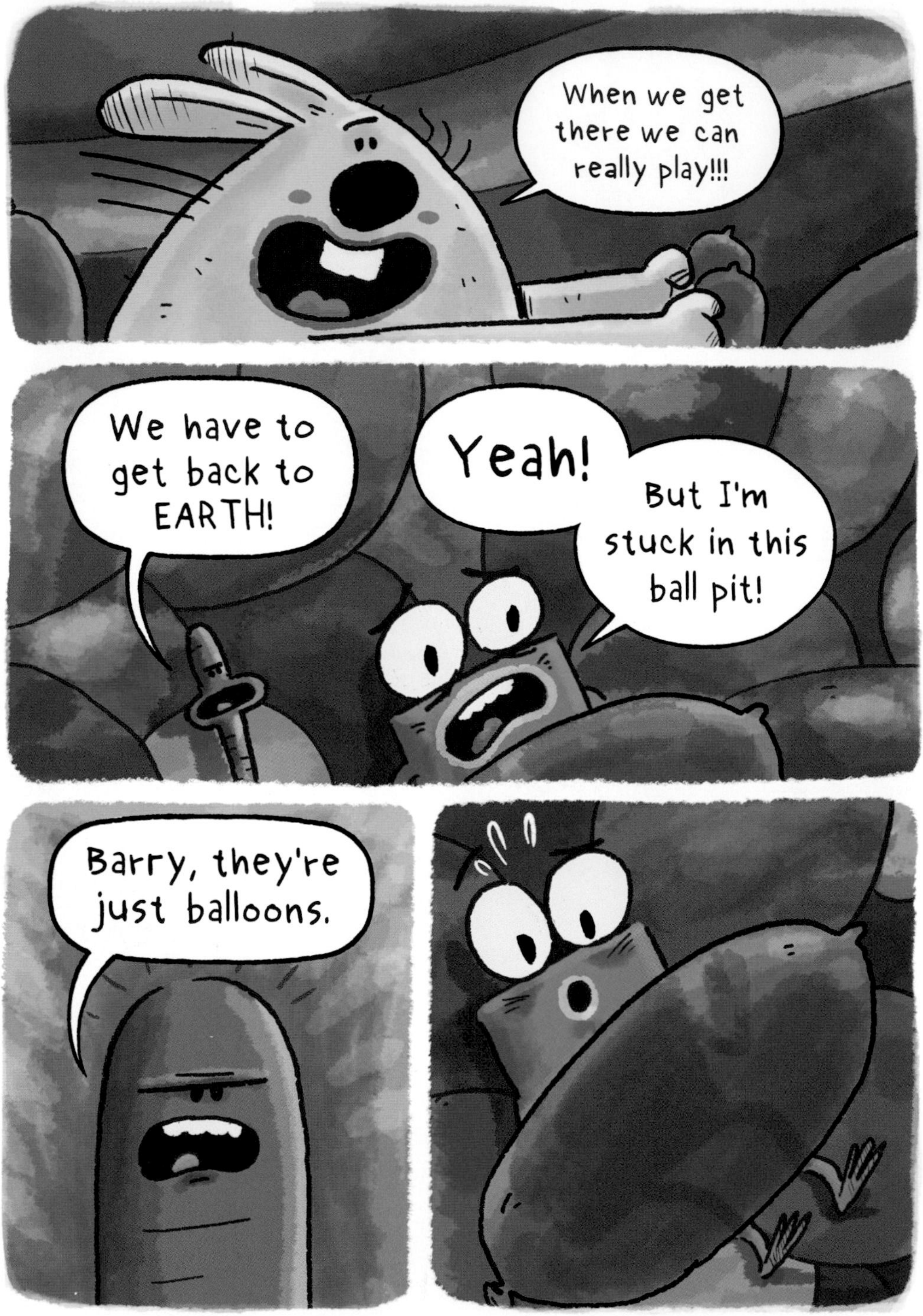
When we get there we can really play!!!
We have to get back to EARTH!
Yeah!
But I'm stuck in this ball pit!
Barry, they're just balloons.

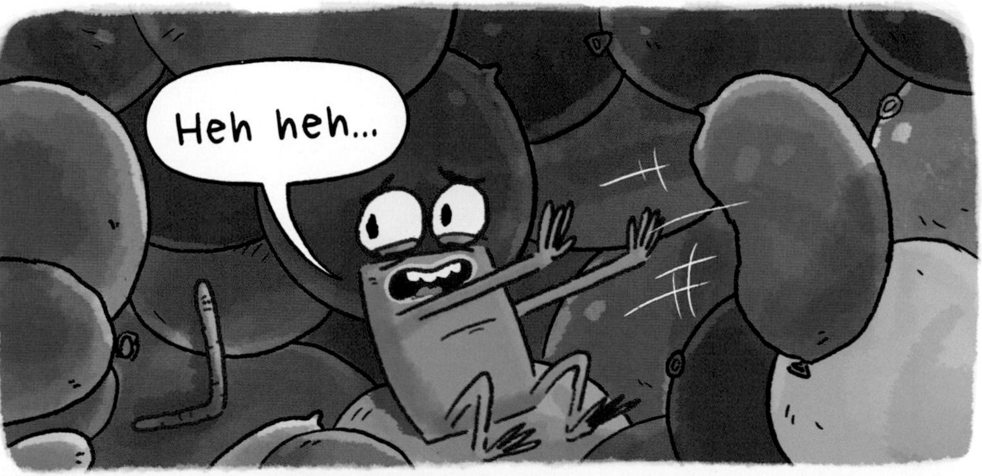
Heh heh...

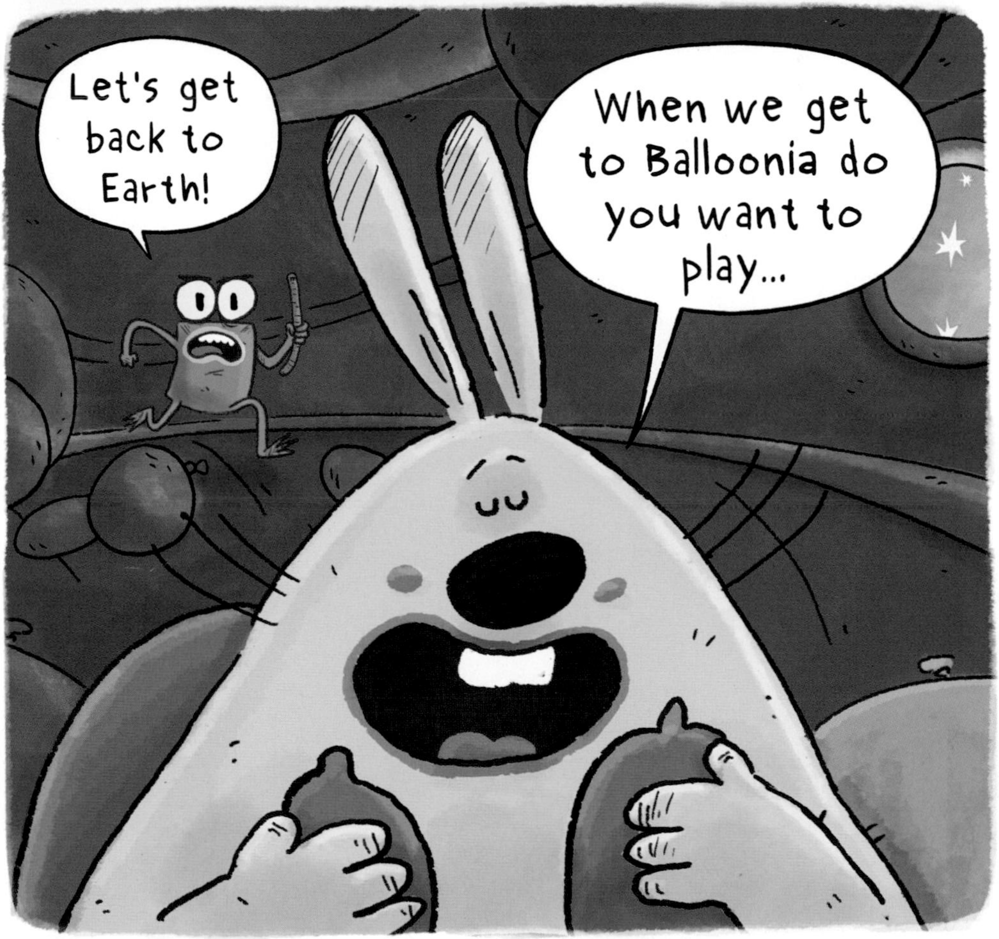
Let's get back to Earth!
When we get to Balloonia do you want to play...

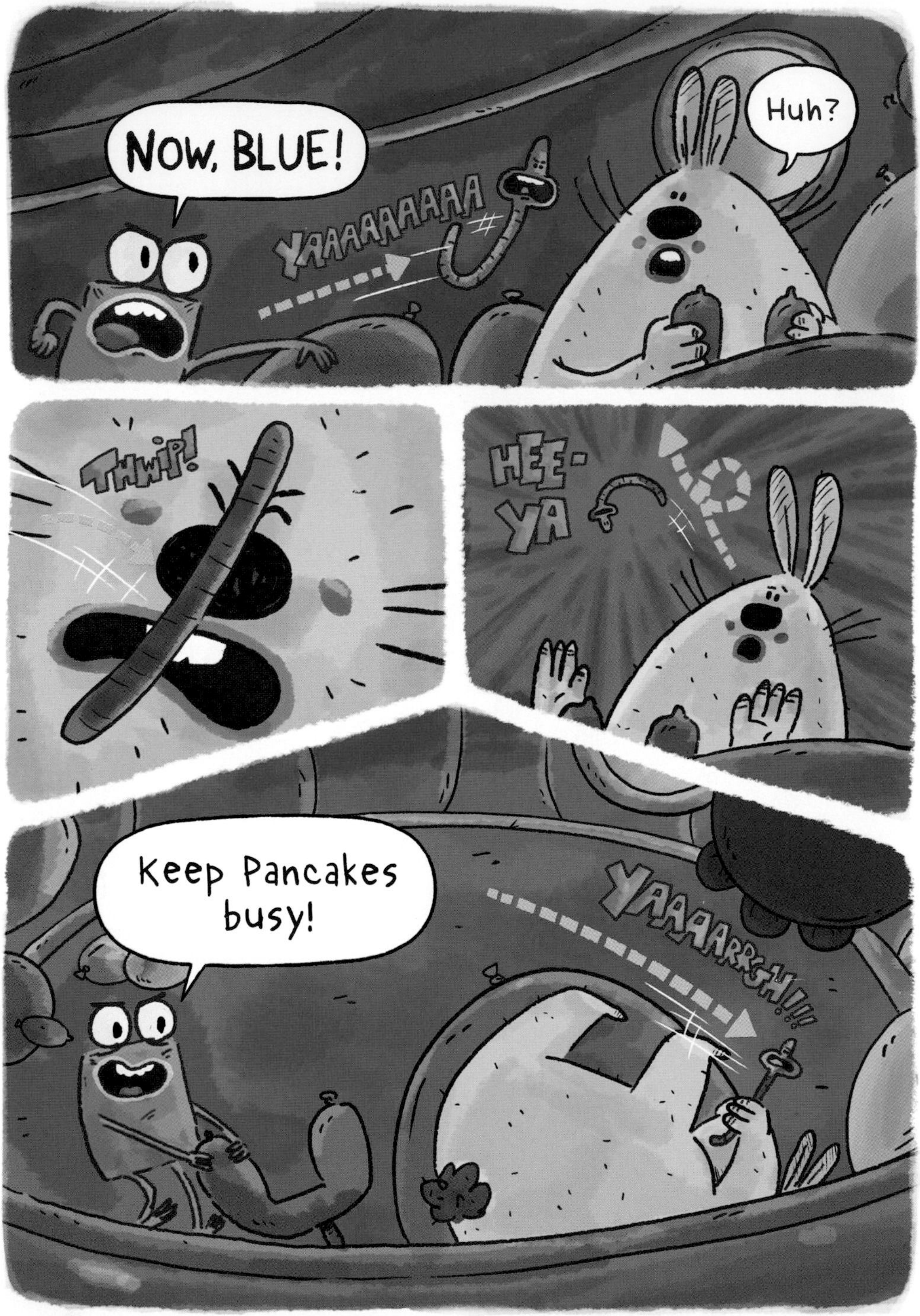
NOW, BLUE!
YAAAAAAAAA
Huh?
THWIP!
HEE-YA
Keep Pancakes busy!
YAAAARRRGH!!!

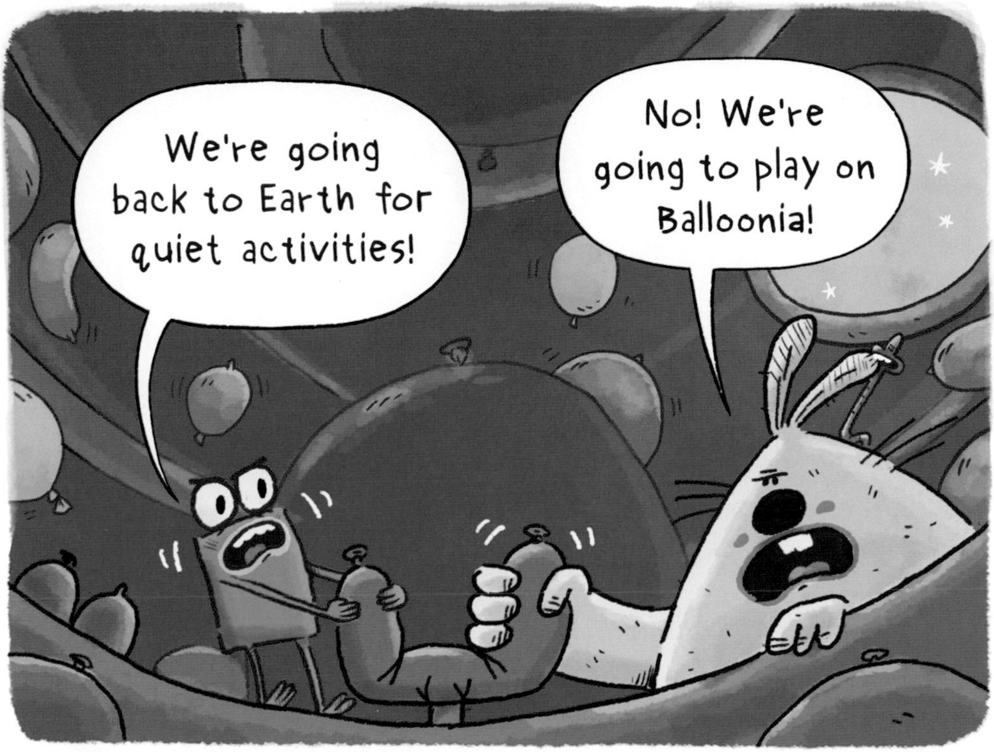
We're going back to Earth for quiet activities!
No! We're going to play on Balloonia!

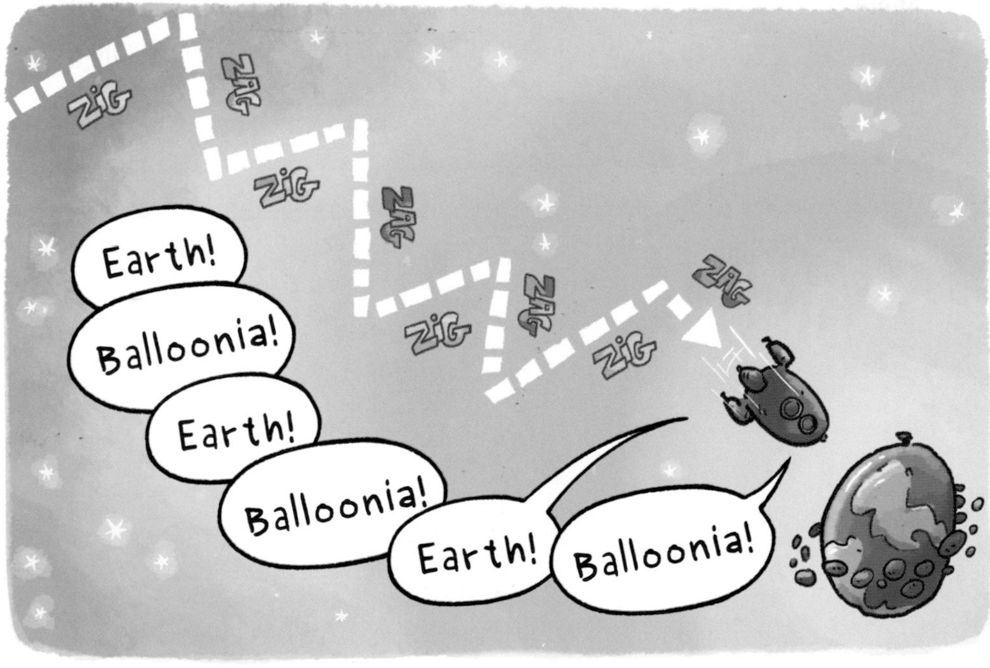
ZIG
ZAG
ZIG
ZAG
ZIG
ZAG
ZIG
ZAG
Earth!
Balloonia!
Earth!
Balloonia!
Earth!
Balloonia!

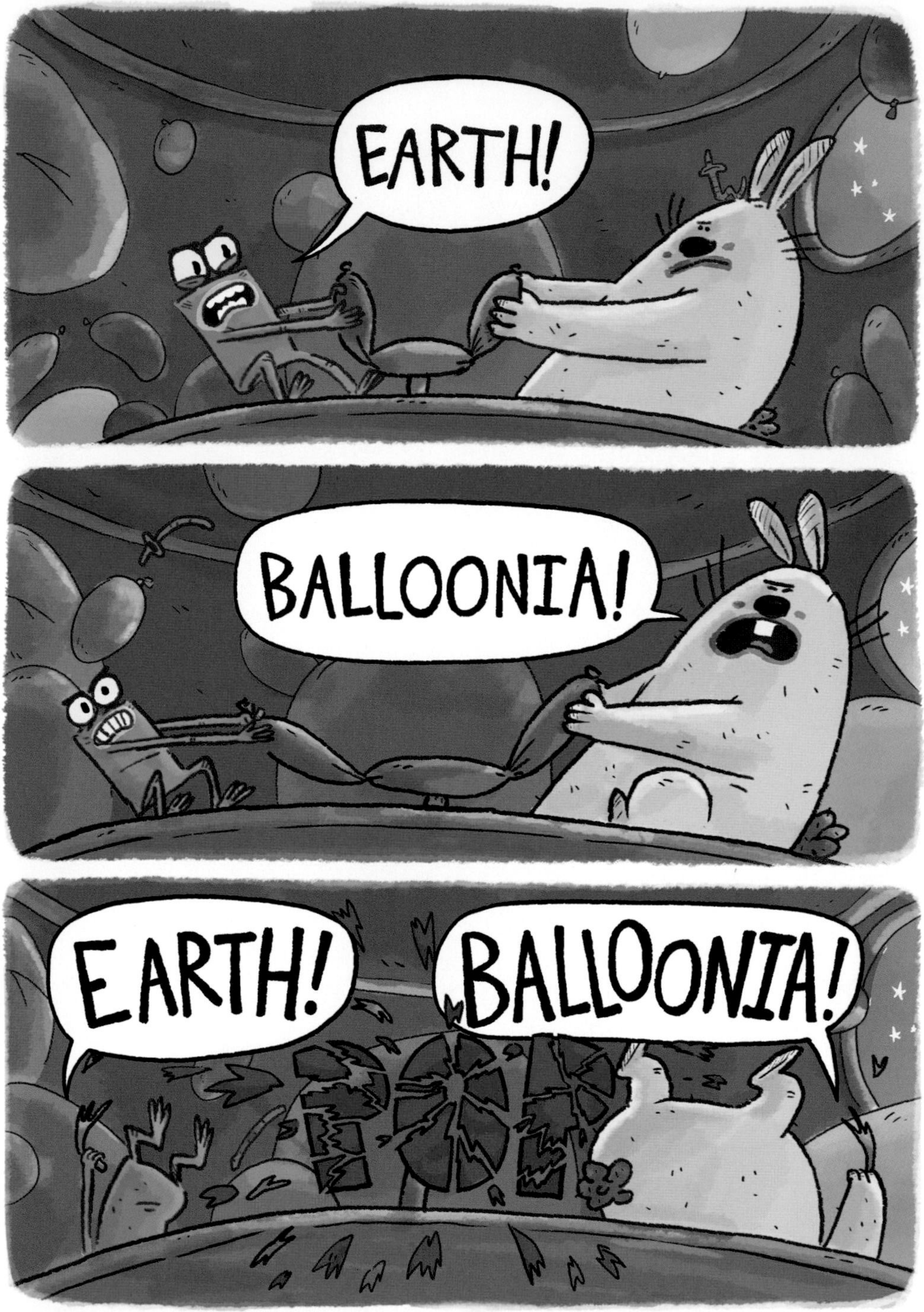
EARTH!
BALLOONIA!
EARTH!
BALLOONIA!

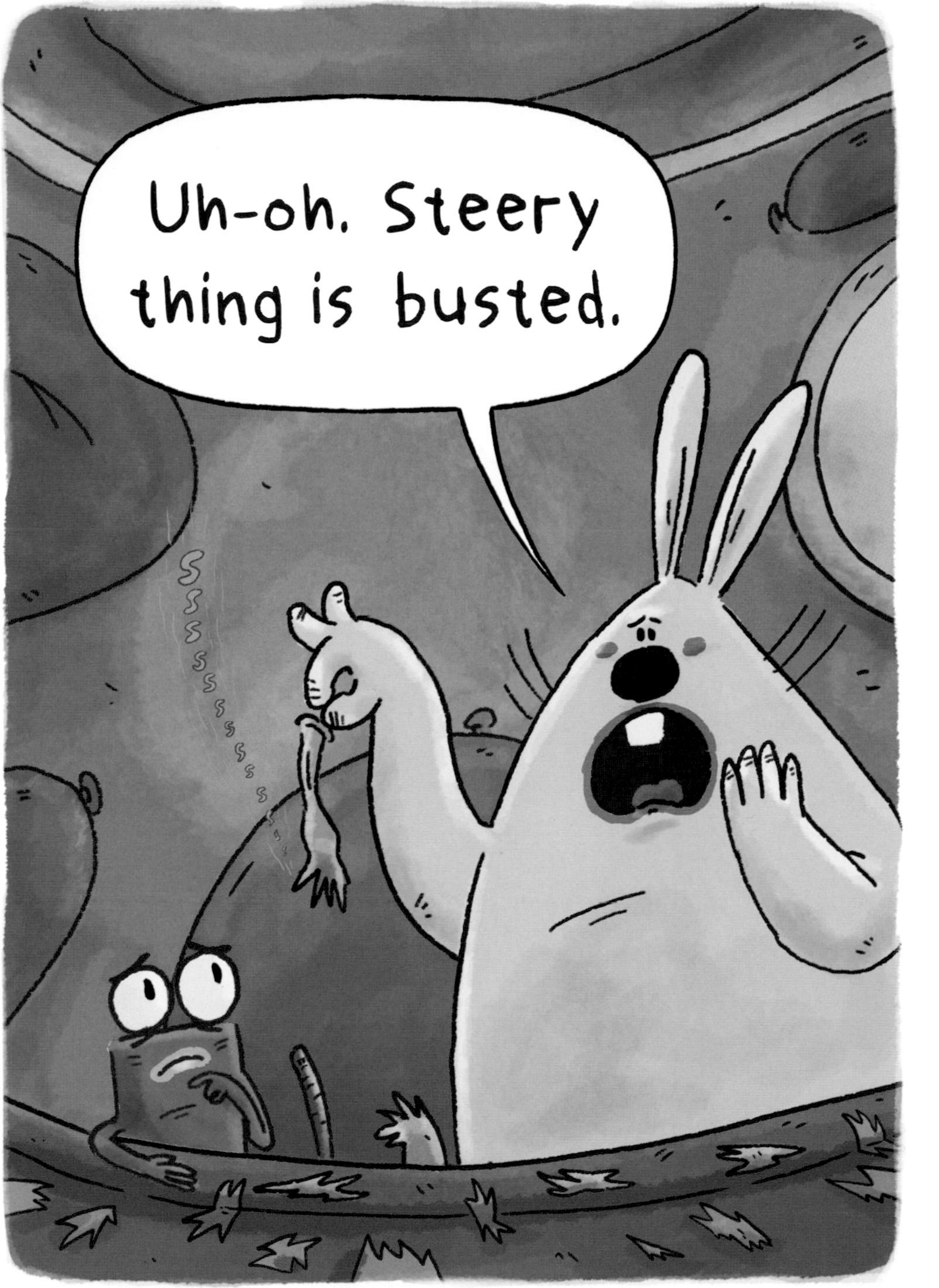
Uh-oh. Steery thing is busted.
SSSSSSSSSSS

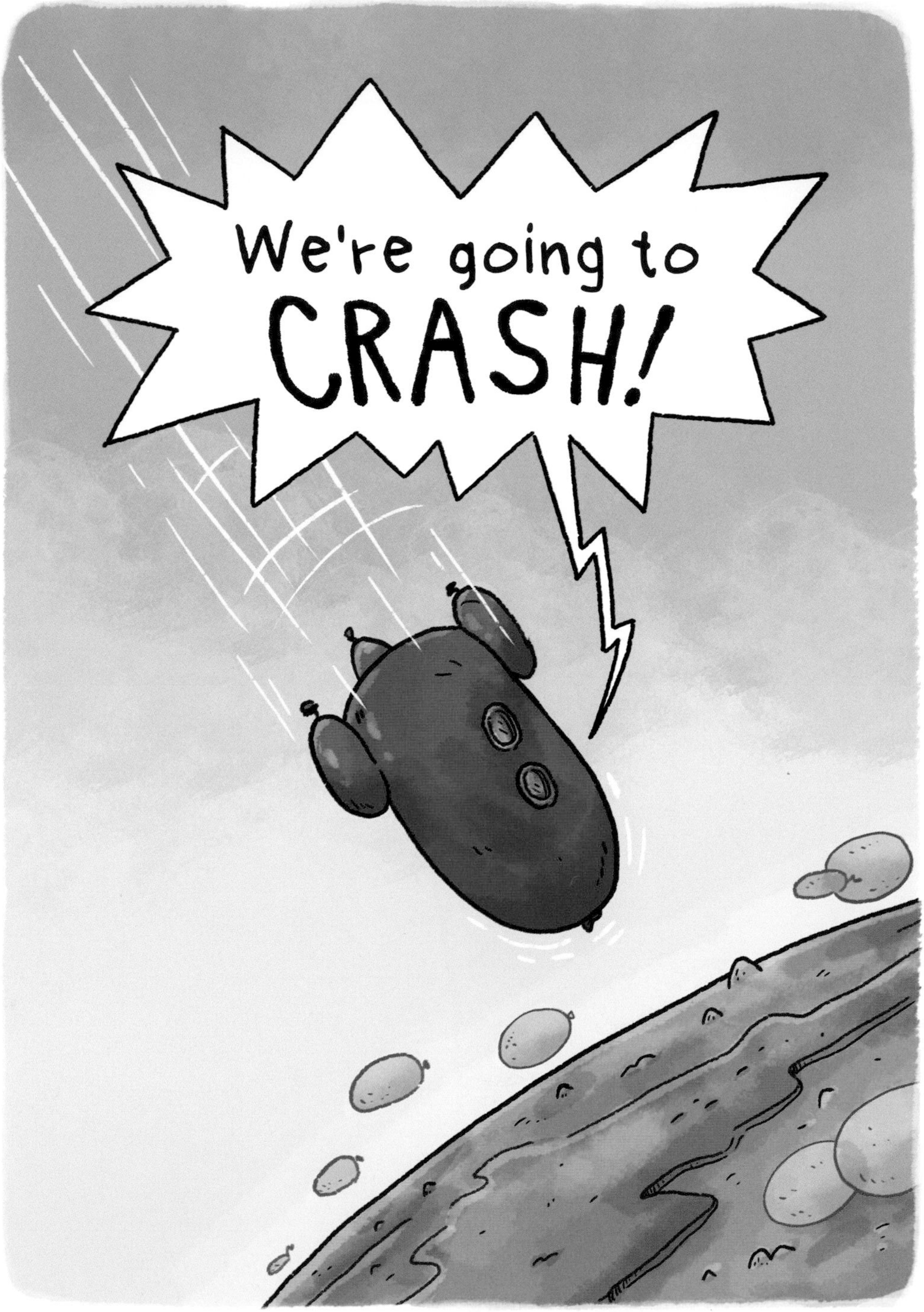
We're going to CRASH!

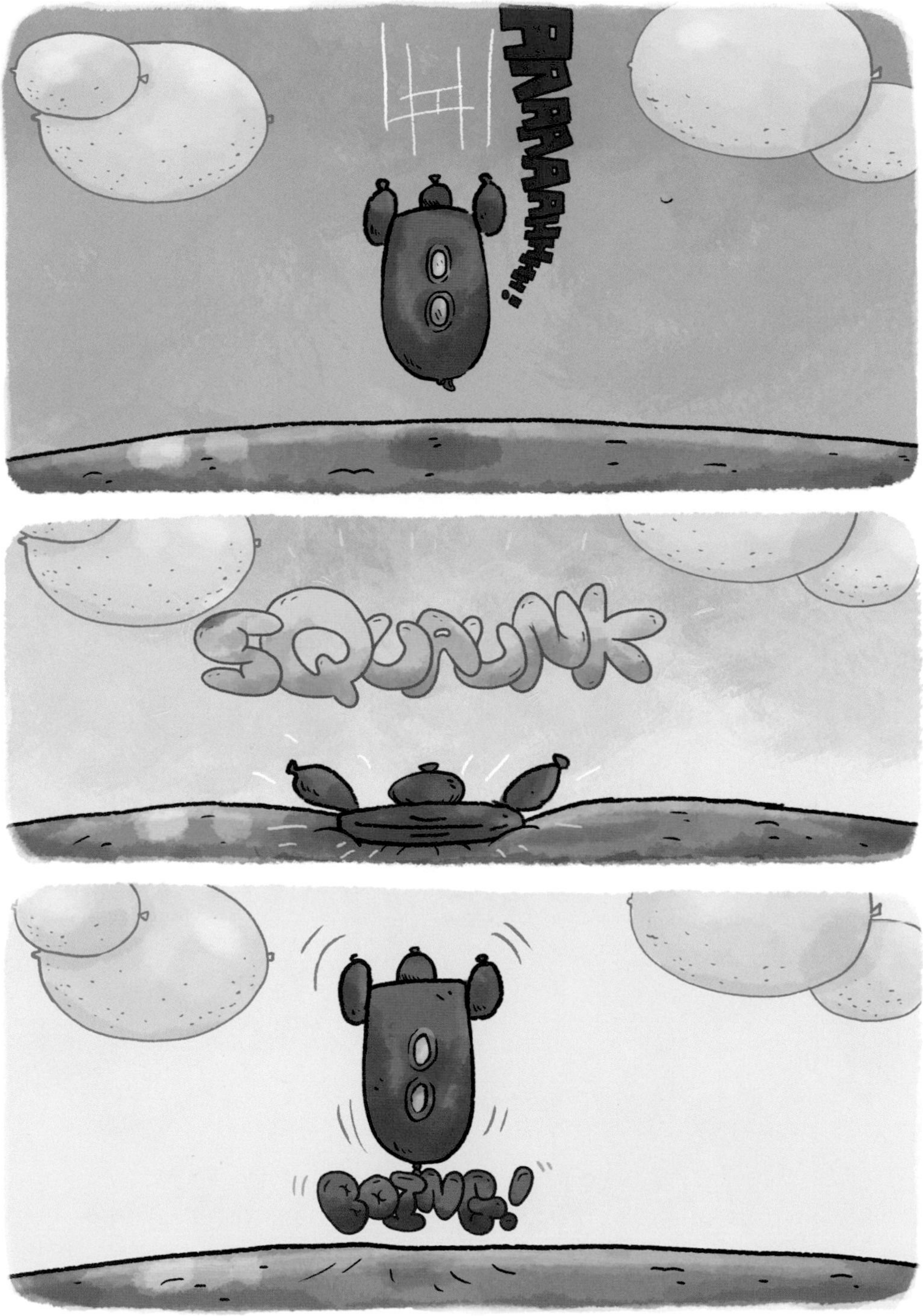
AAAAAAHHHHH!!
SQUAUNK
BOING!

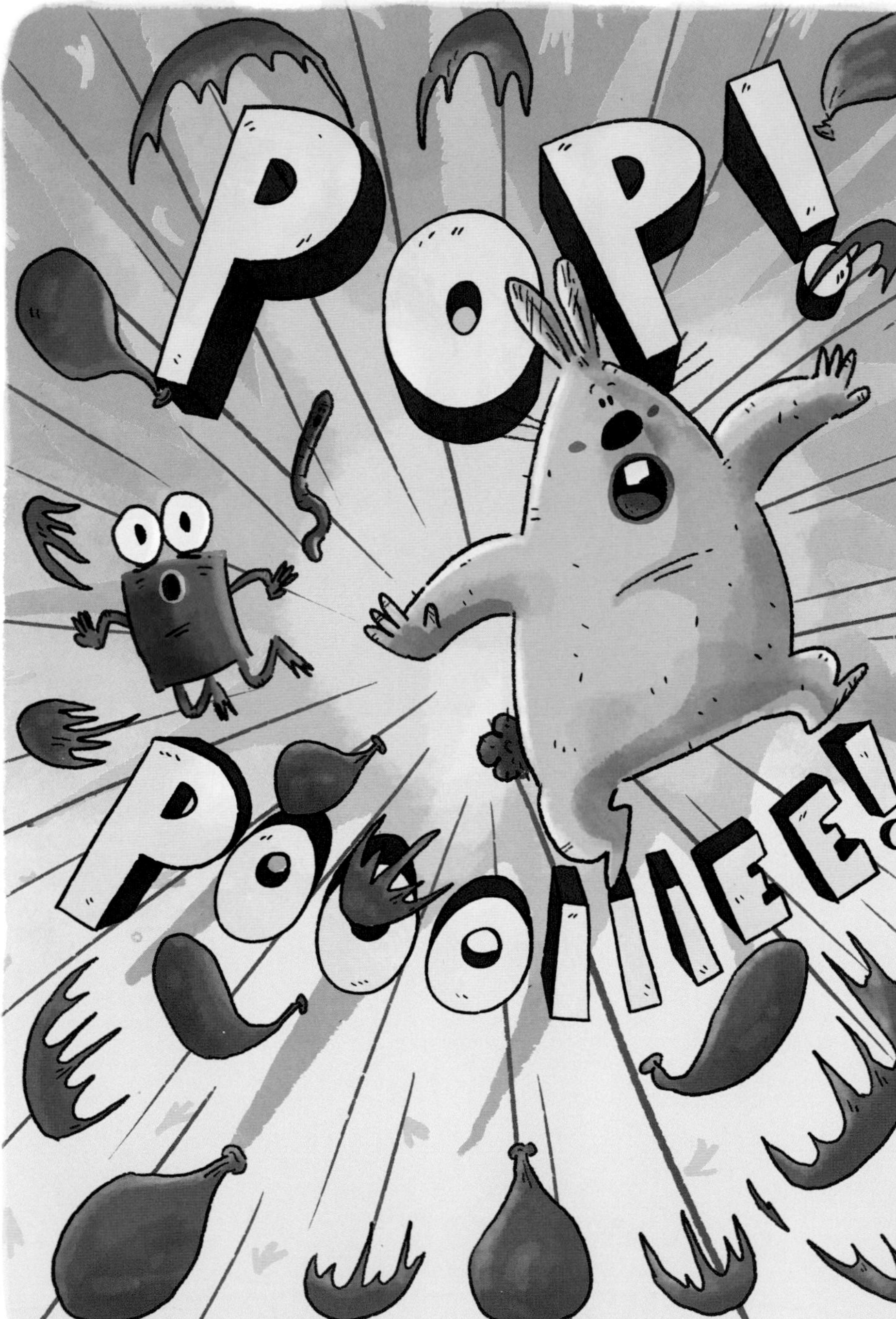
POP!
POOOOIIIEEE!

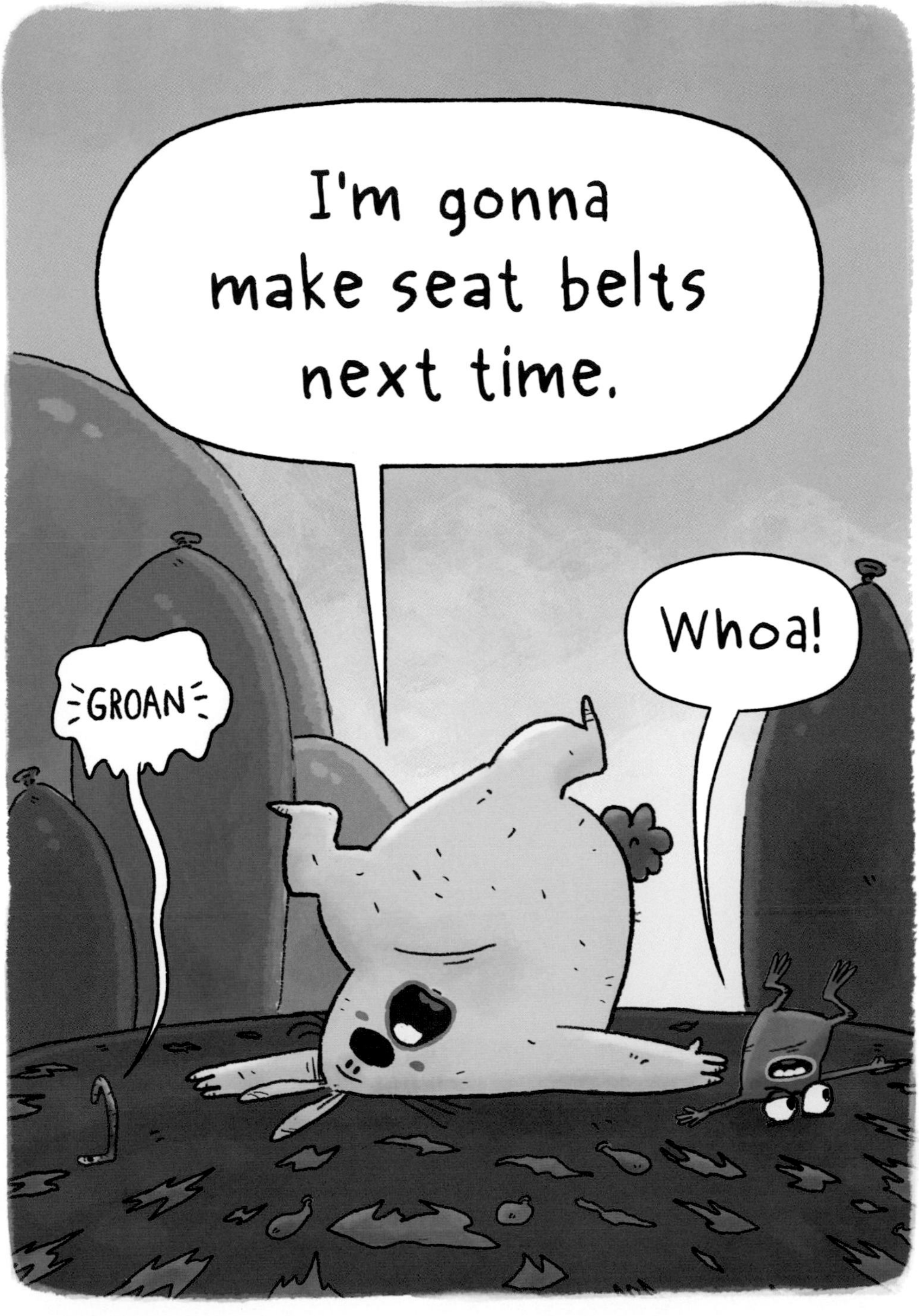
I'm gonna make seat belts next time.
GROAN
Whoa!

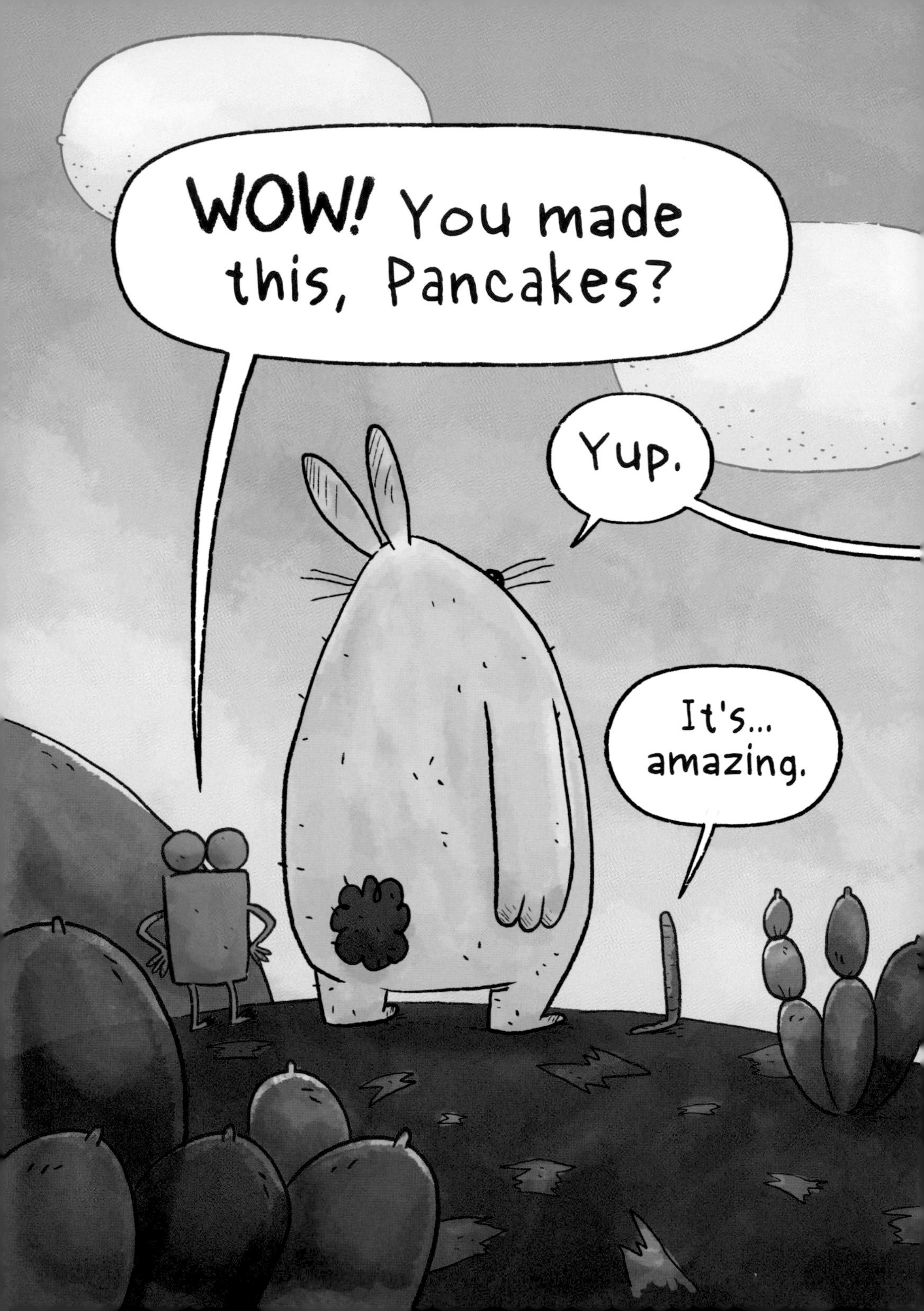
WOW! You made this, Pancakes?
Yup.
It's... amazing.

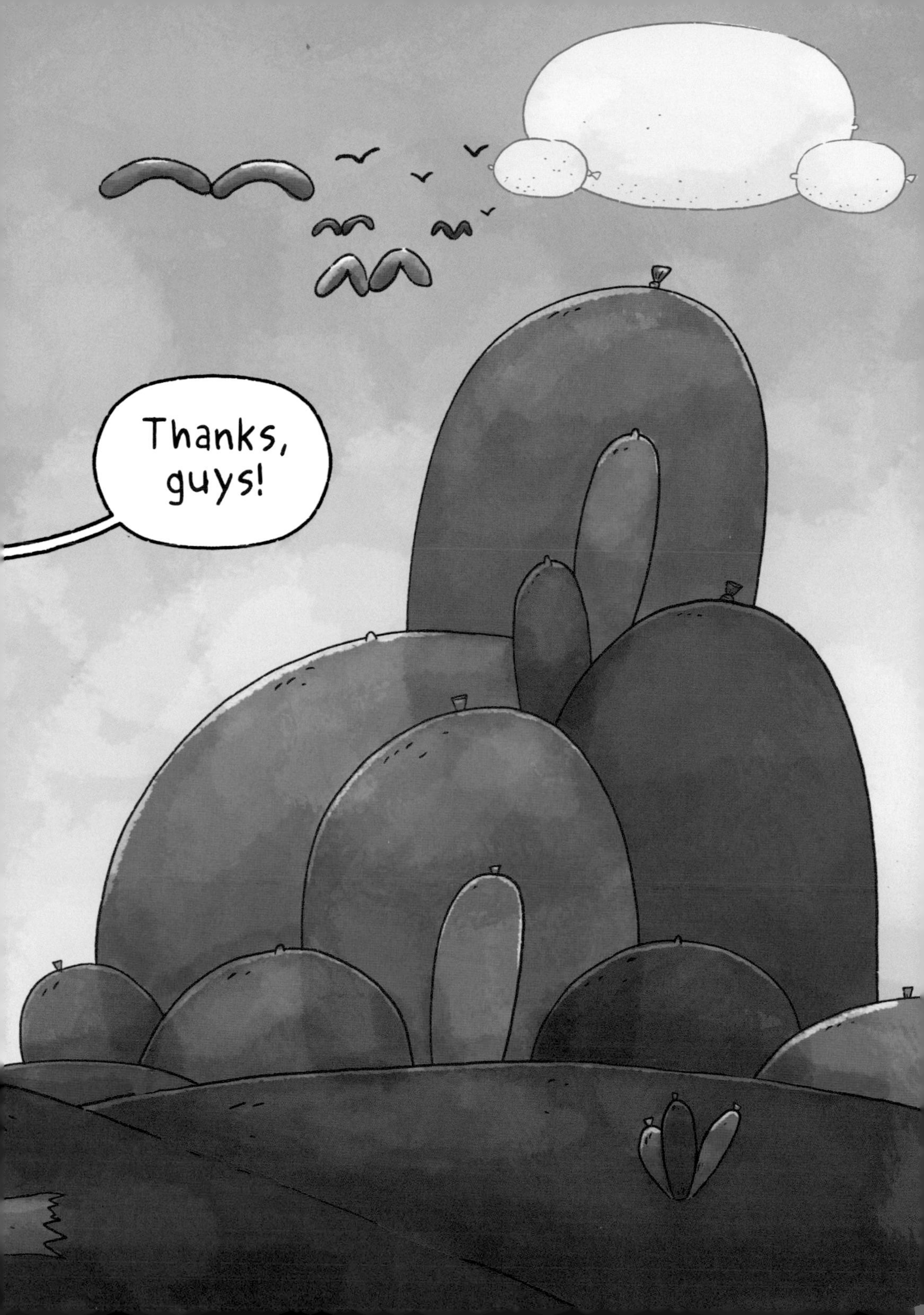
Thanks, guys!

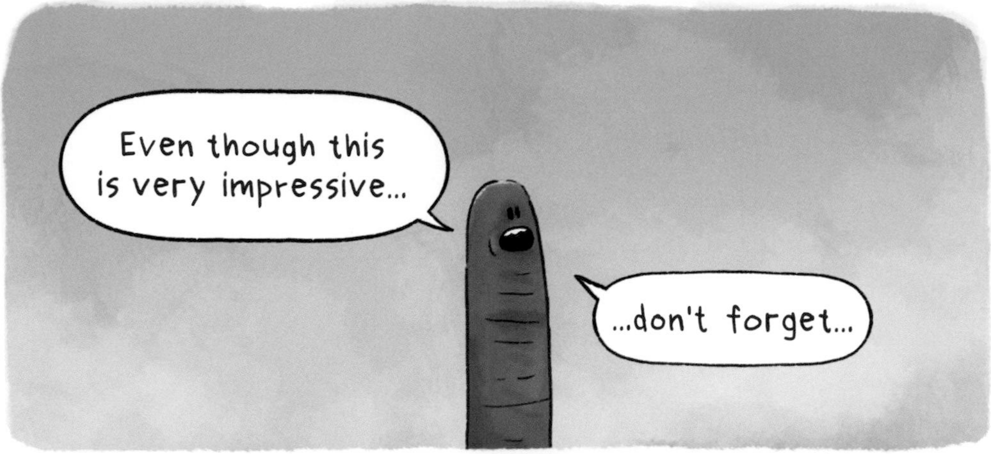
Even though this is very impressive...
...don't forget...

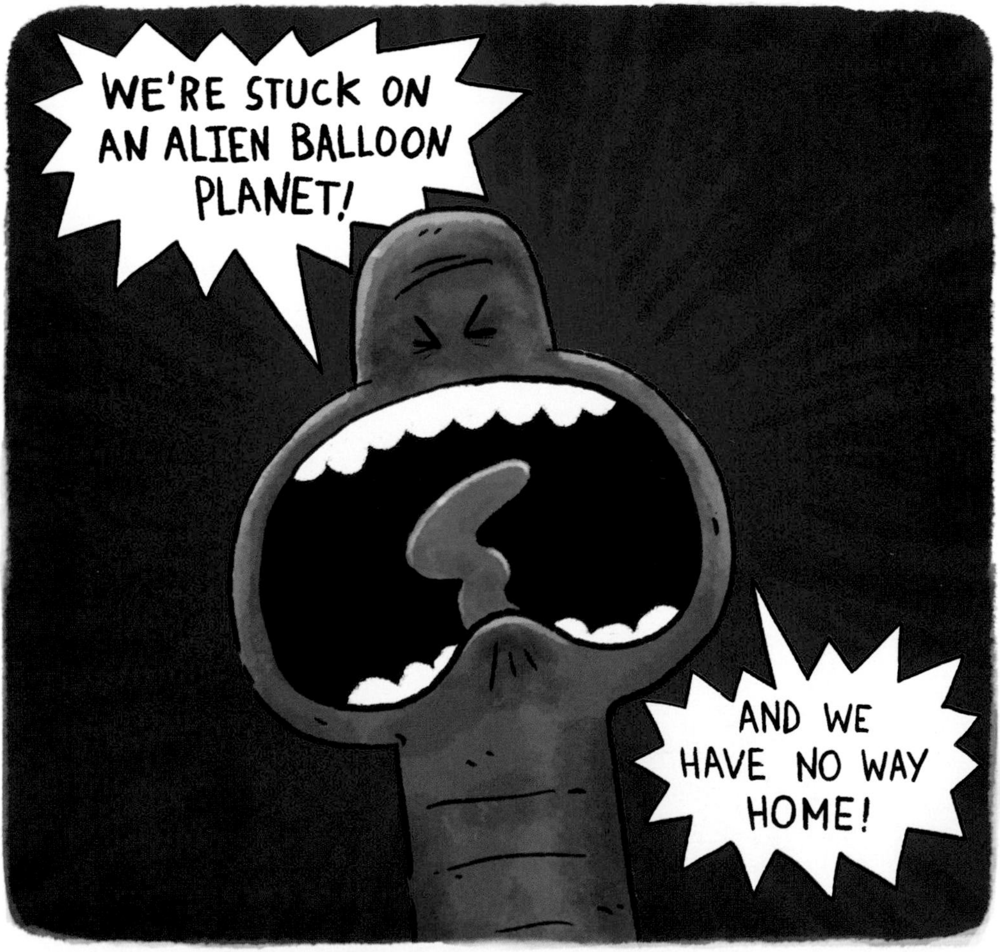
WE'RE STUCK ON AN ALIEN BALLOON PLANET!
AND WE HAVE NO WAY HOME!

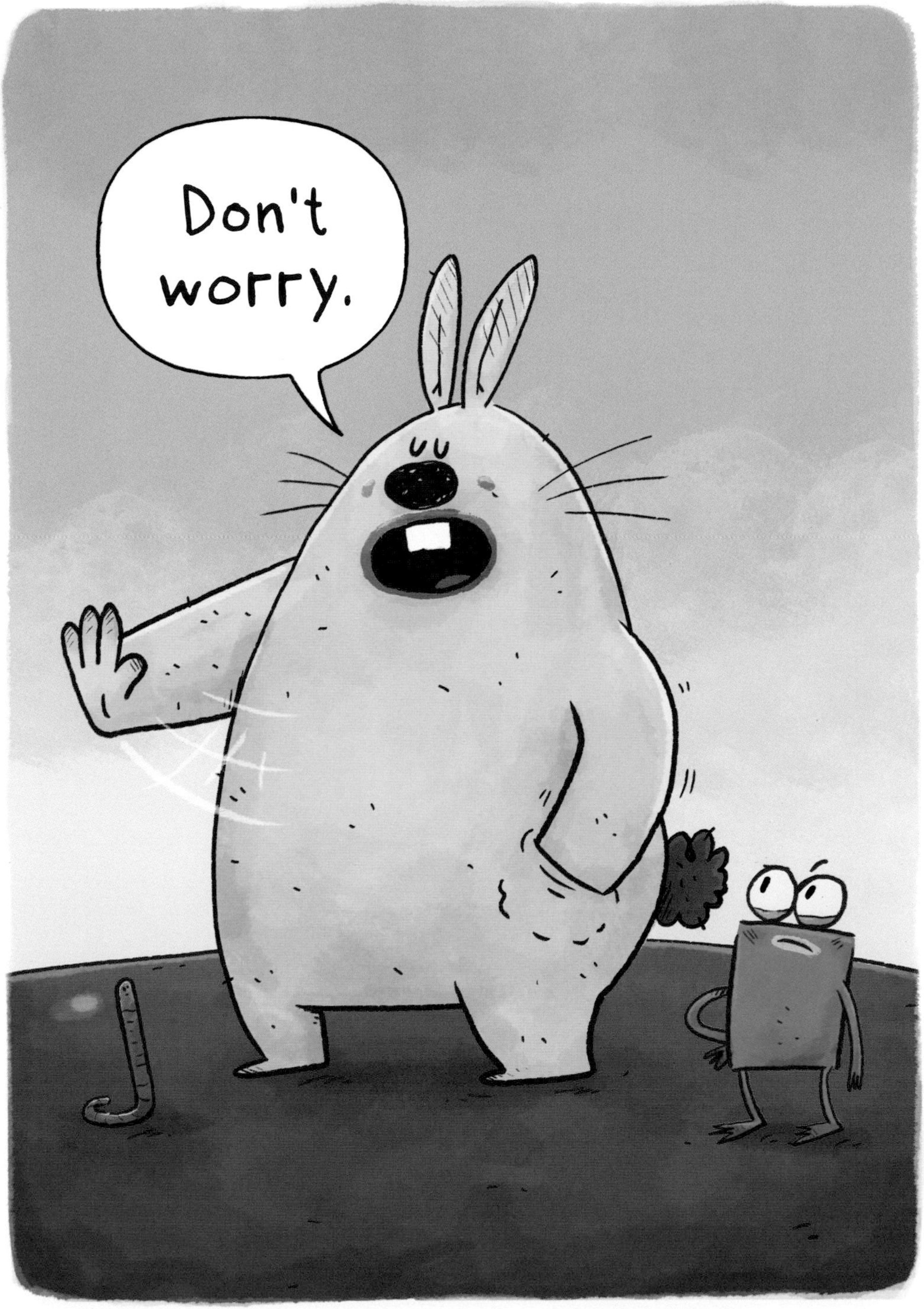
Don't worry.

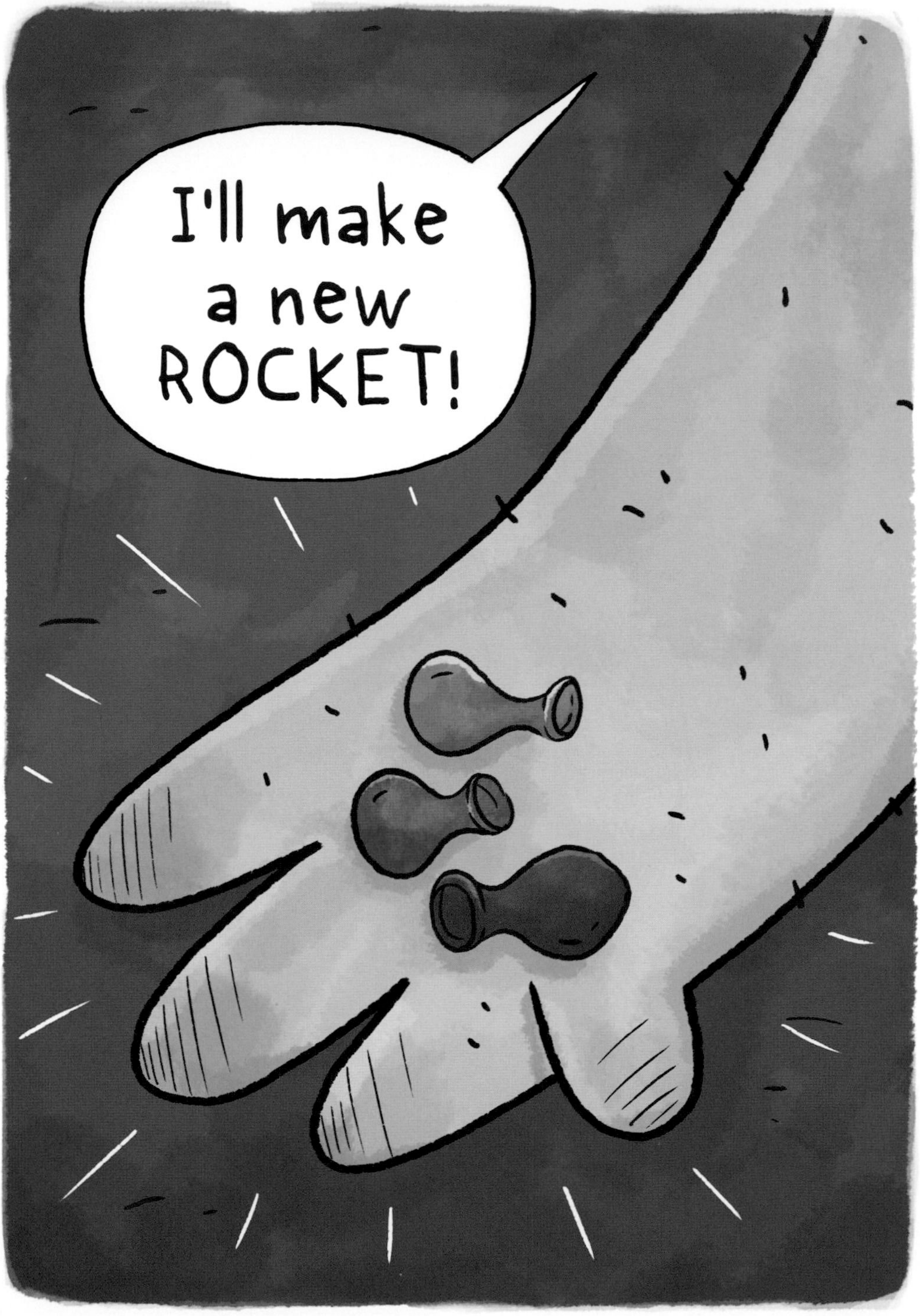
I'll make a new ROCKET!

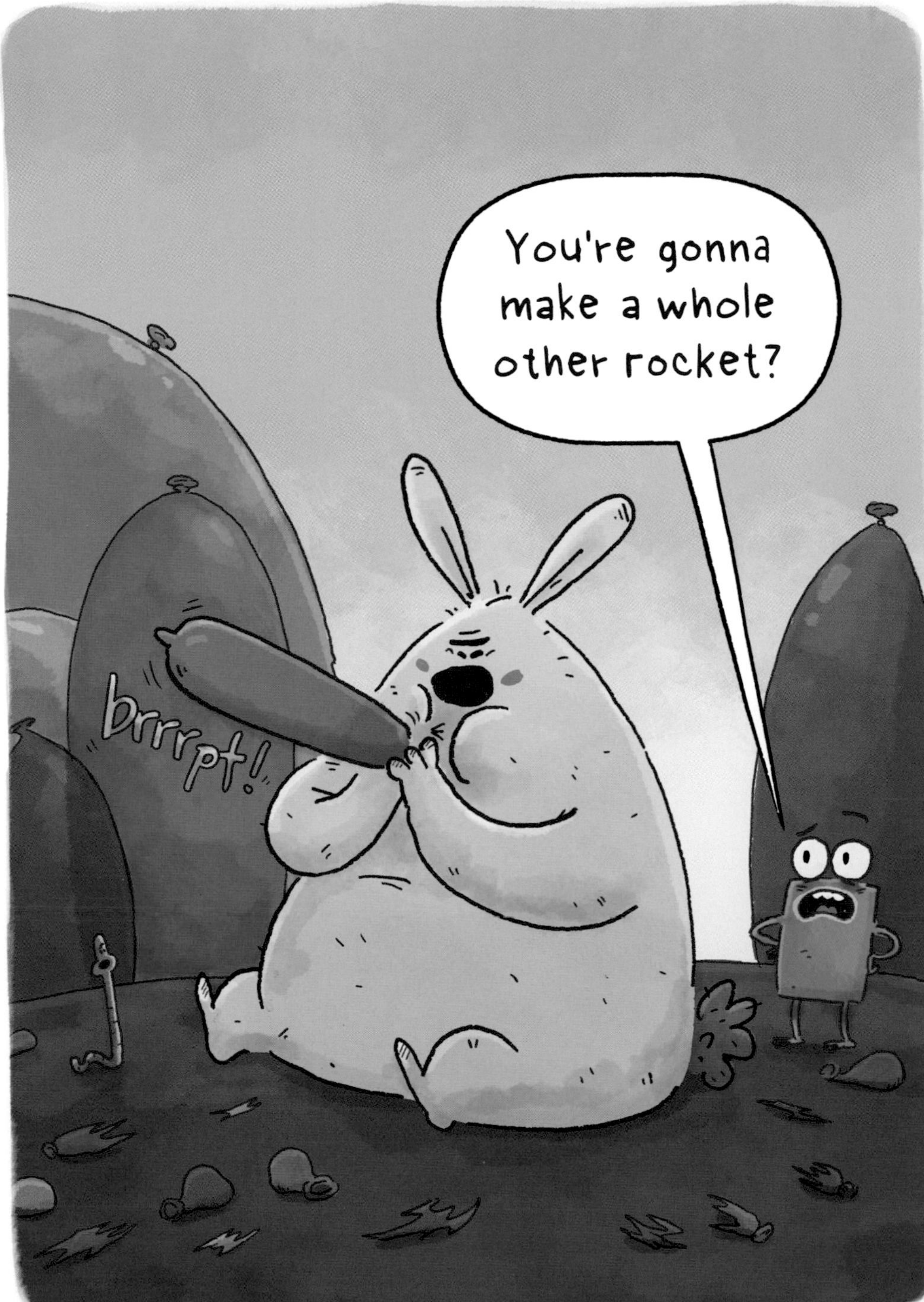
You're gonna make a whole other rocket?
brrrpt!

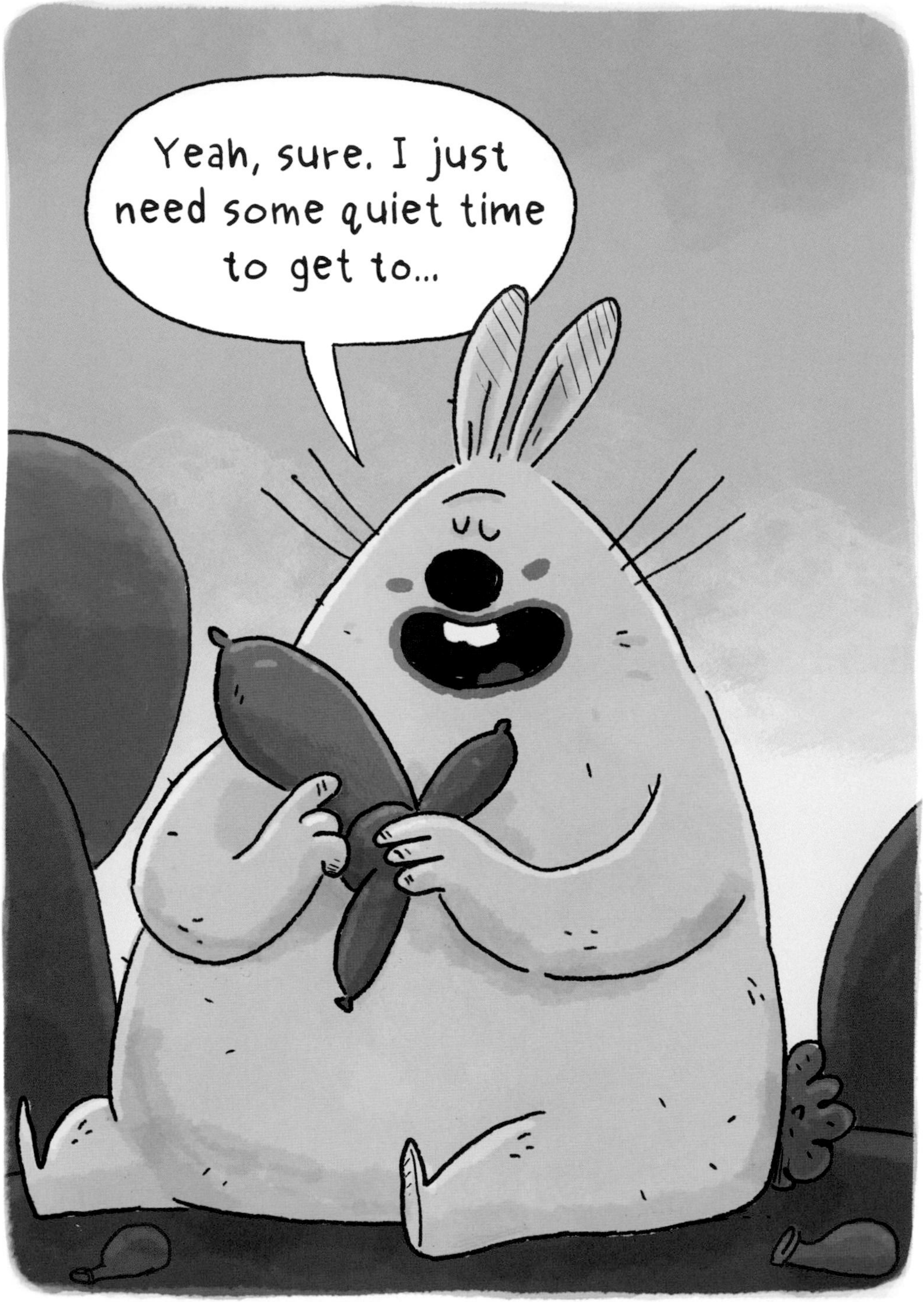
Yeah, sure. I just need some quiet time to get to...

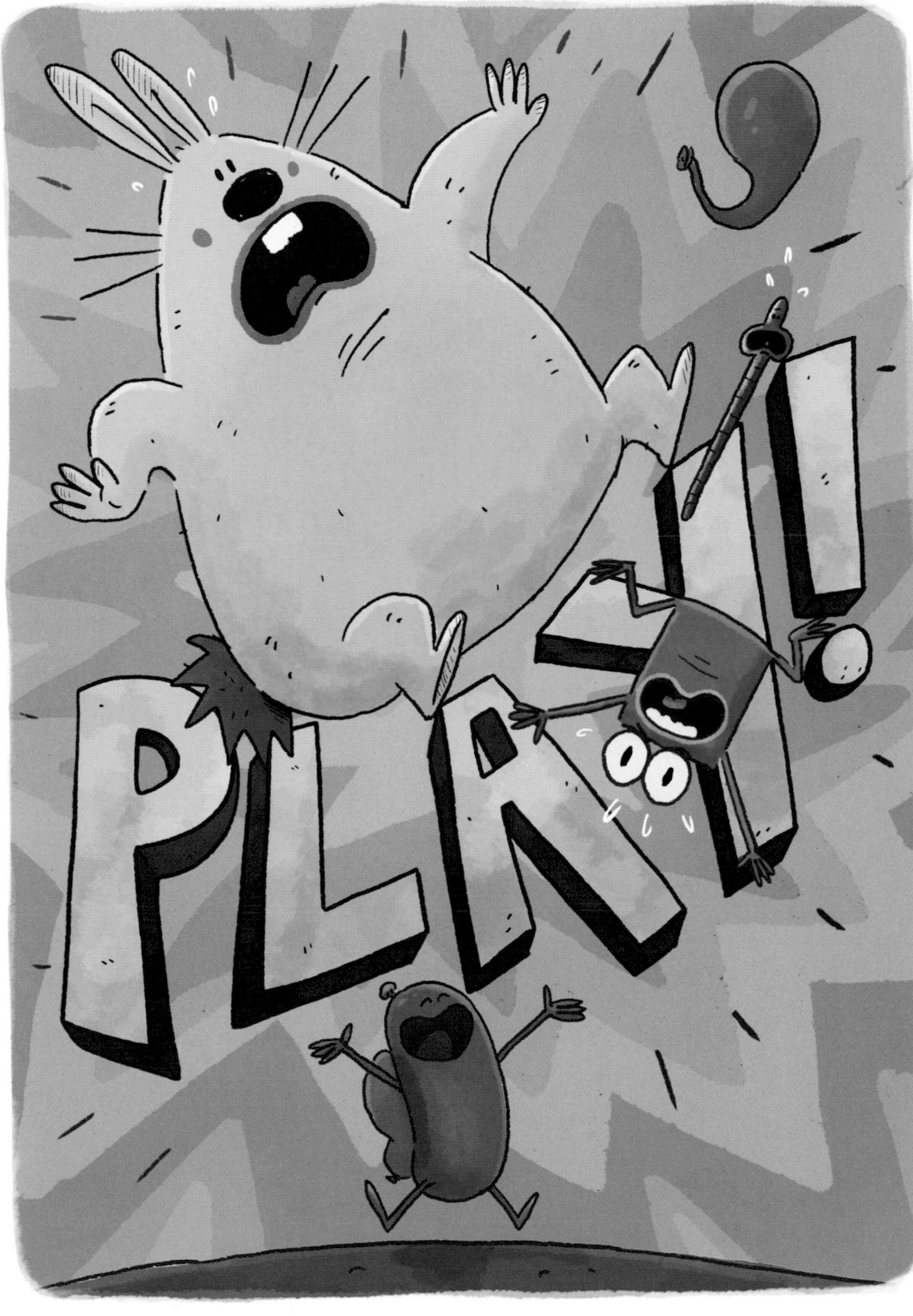

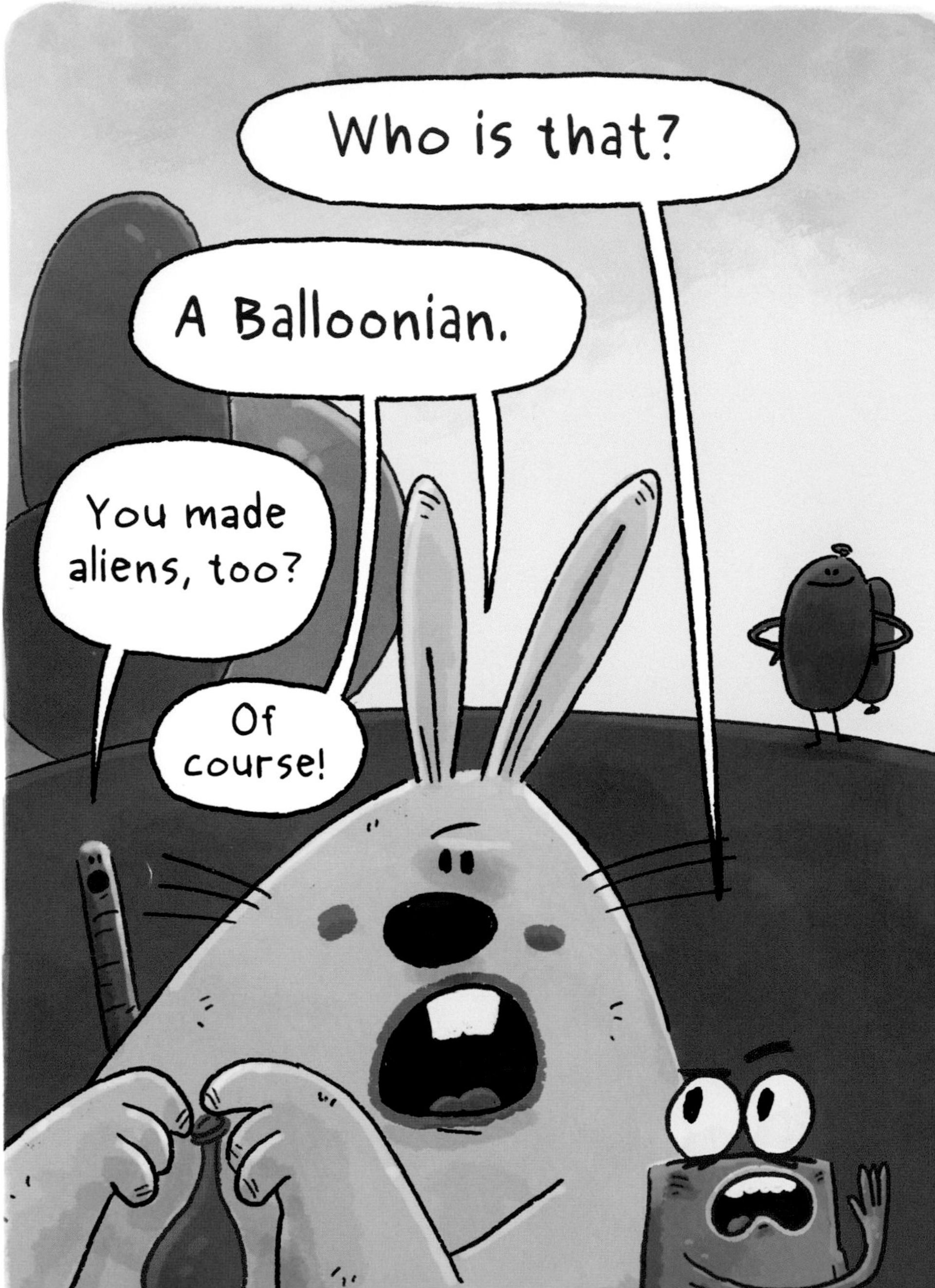
Who is that?
A Balloonian.
You made aliens, too?
Of course!

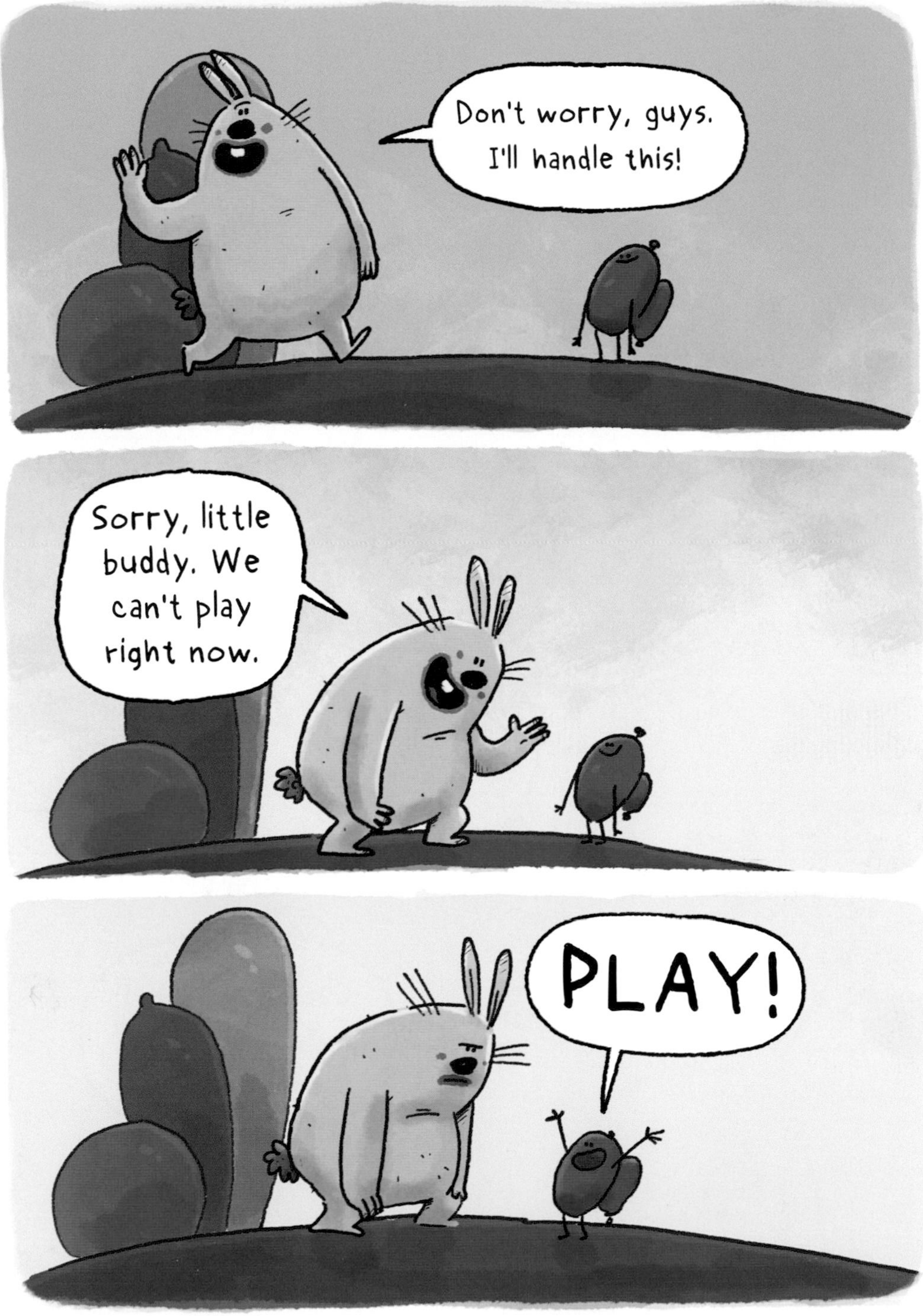
Don't worry, guys. I'll handle this!
Sorry, little buddy. We can't play right now.
PLAY!

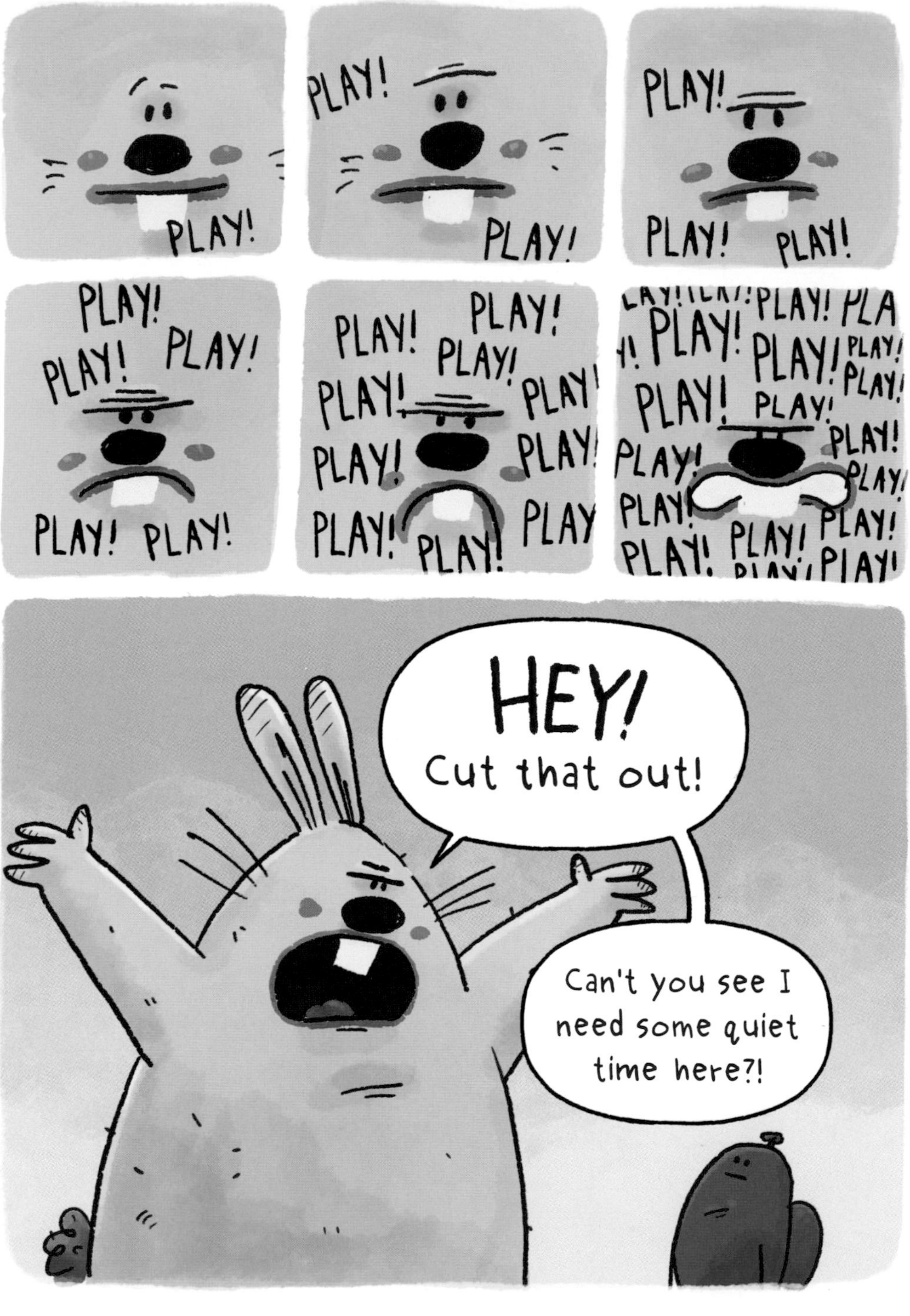
PLAY!
PLAY!
PLAY!
PLAY!
PLAY!
PLAY!
PLAY!
PLAY!
PLAY!
PLAY!
PLAY!
PLAY!
PLAY!
PLAY!
PLAY!
PLAY!
PLAY!
PLAY!
PLAY!
PLAY!
PLAY!
PLAY!
PLAY!
PLAY!
PLAY!
PLAY!
PLAY!
PLAY!
PLAY!
PLAY!
HEY! Cut that out!
Can't you see I need some quiet time here?!

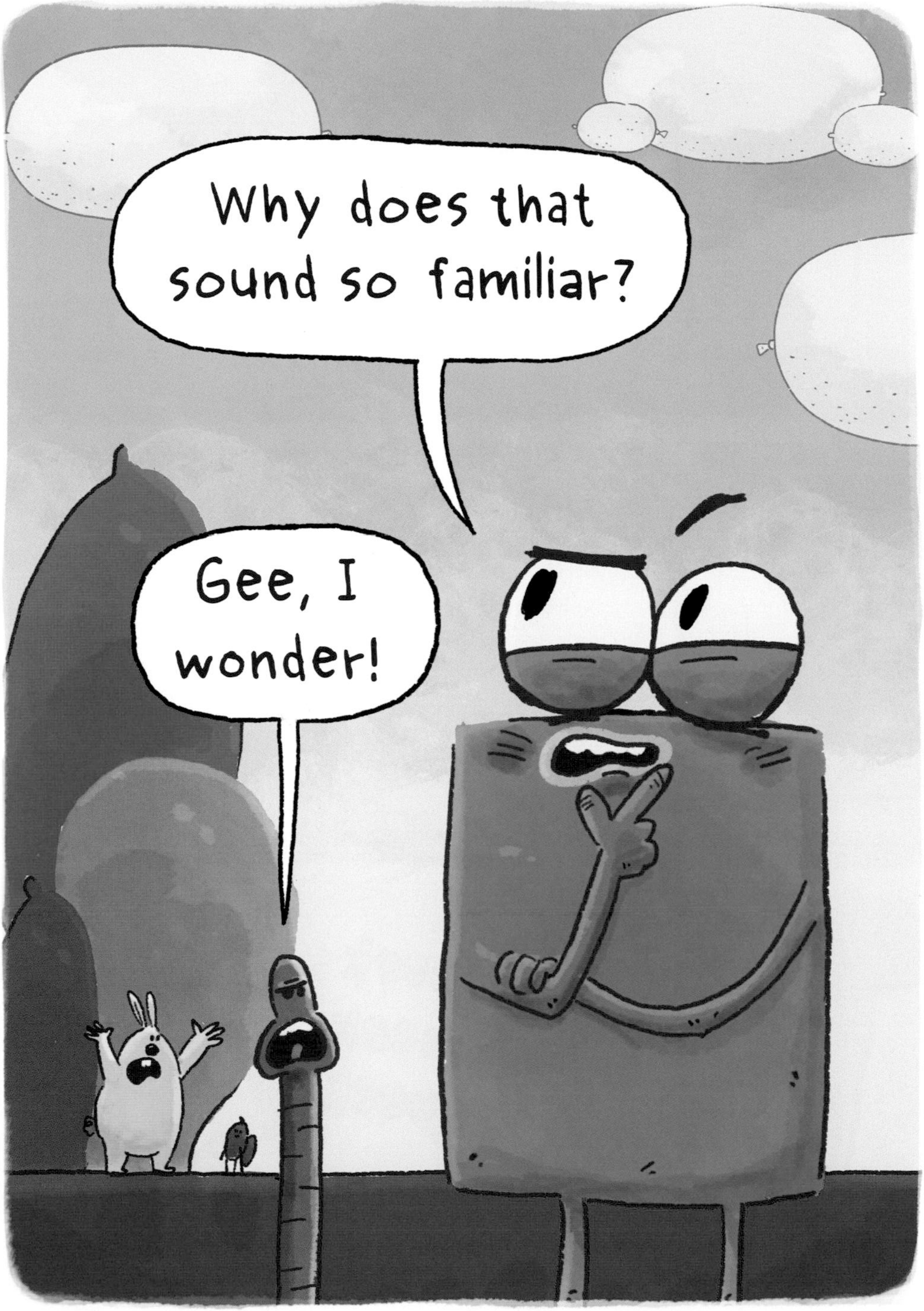
Why does that sound so familiar?
Gee, I wonder!

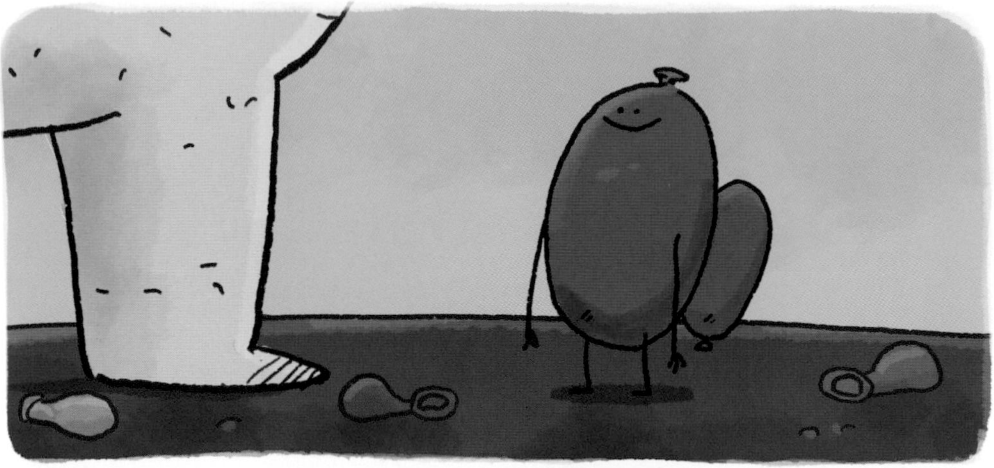

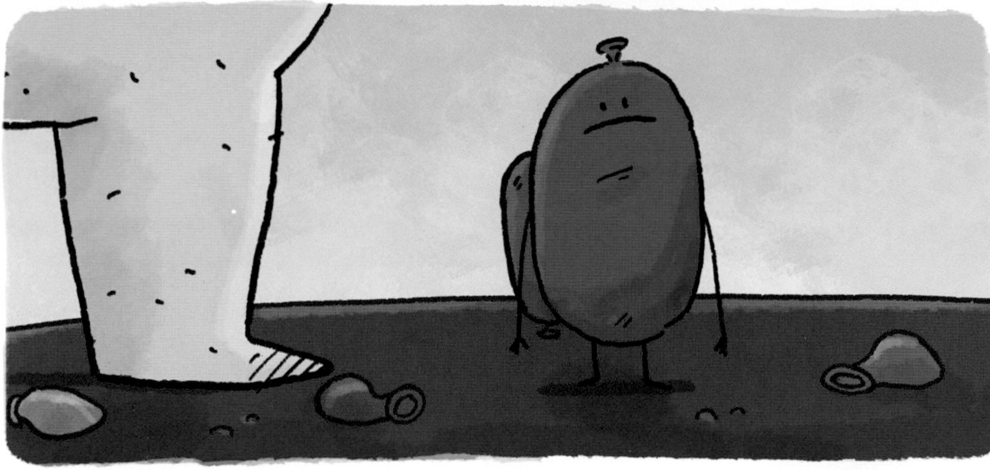

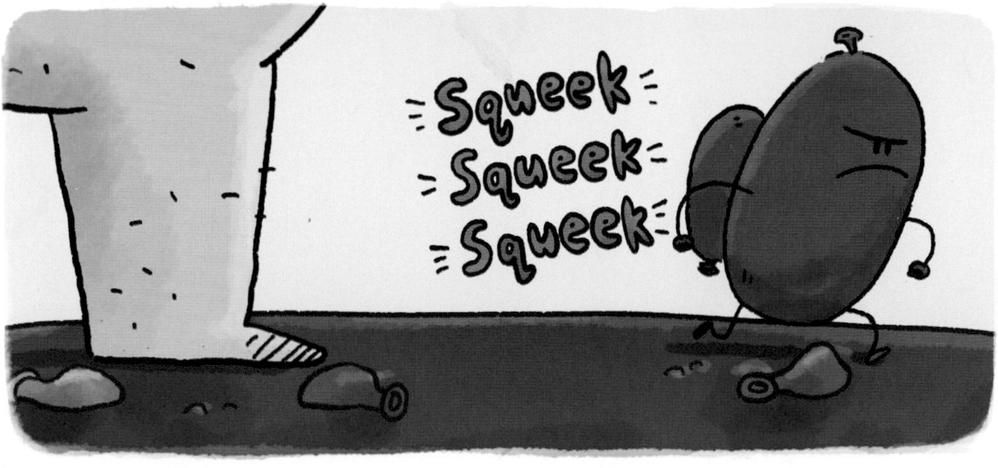
Squeek
Squeek
Squeek

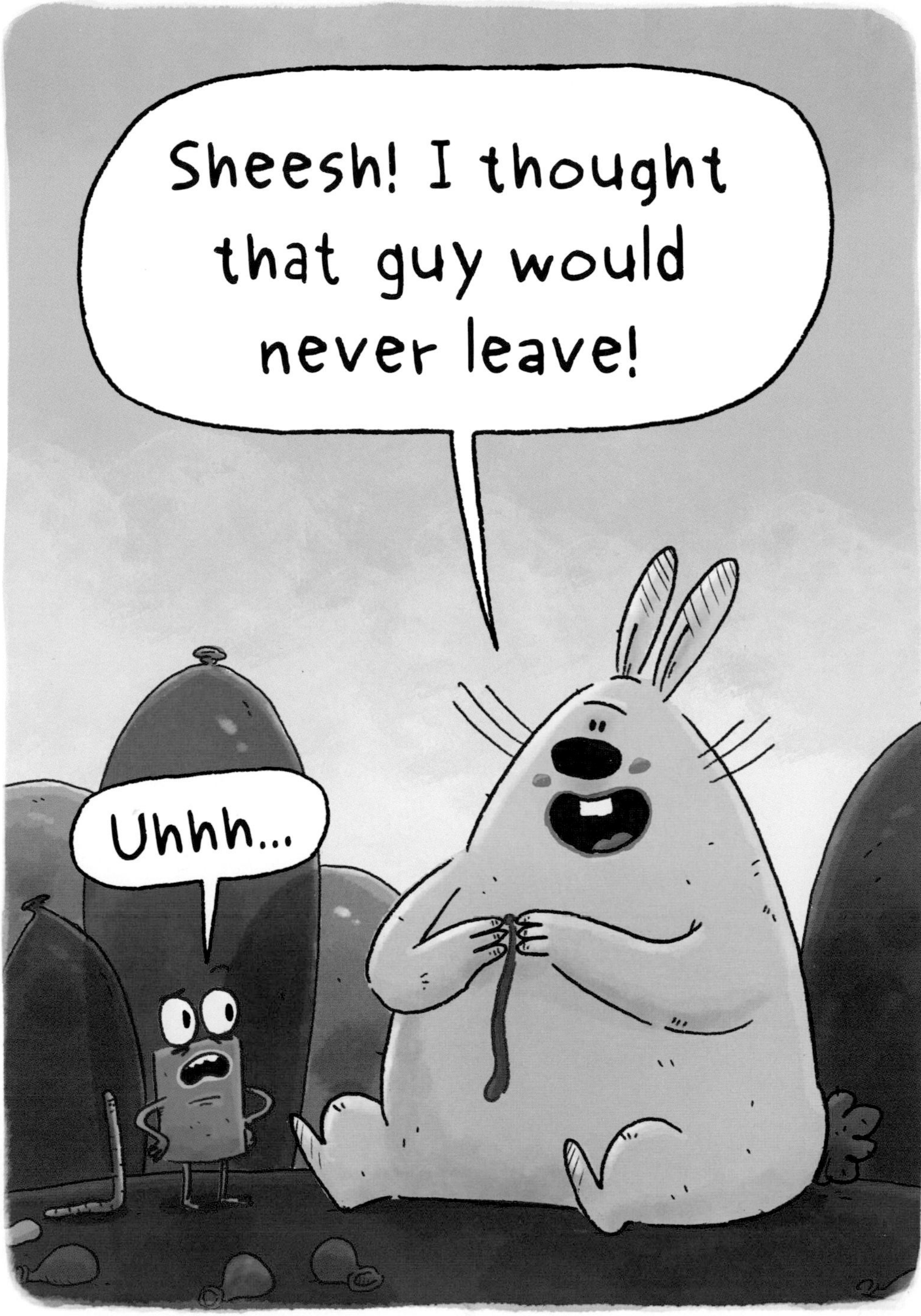
Sheesh! I thought that guy would never leave!
Uhhh...

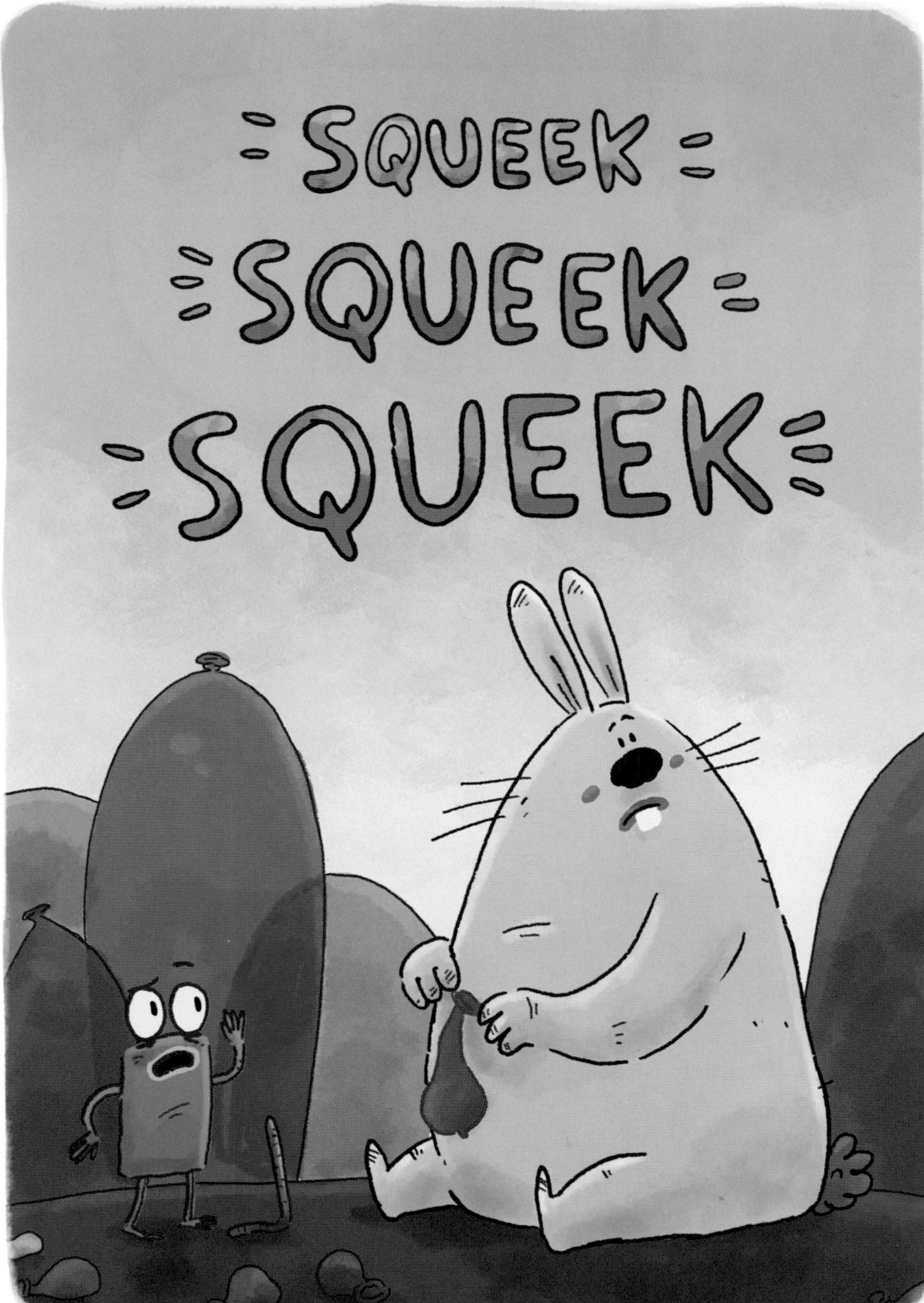
SQUEEK
SQUEEK
SQUEEK

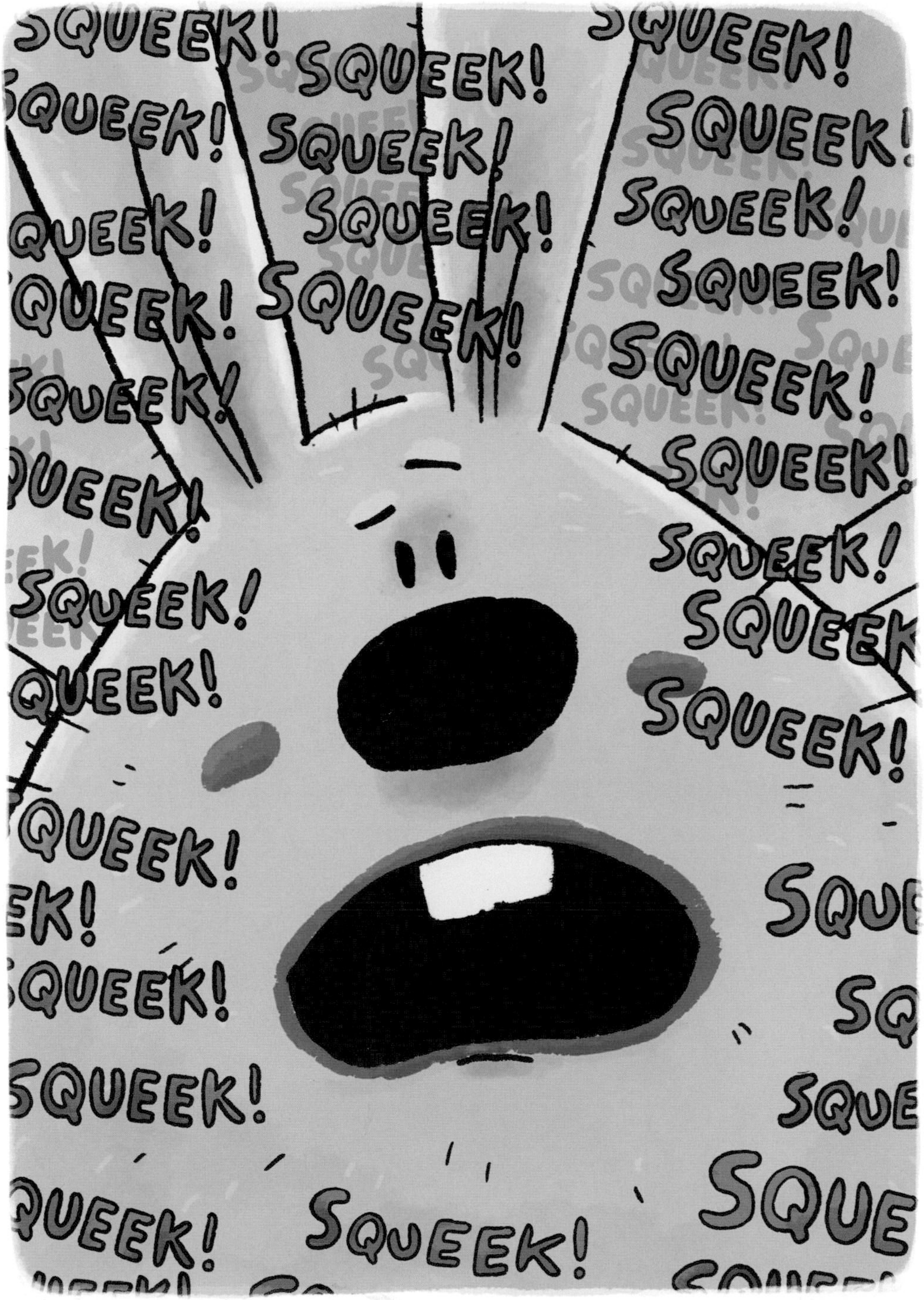
SQUEEK!
SQUEEK!
SQUEEK!
SQUEEK!
SQUEEK!
SQUEEK!
SQUEEK!
SQUEEK!
SQUEEK!
SQUEEK!
SQUEEK!
SQUEEK!
SQUEEK!
SQUEEK!

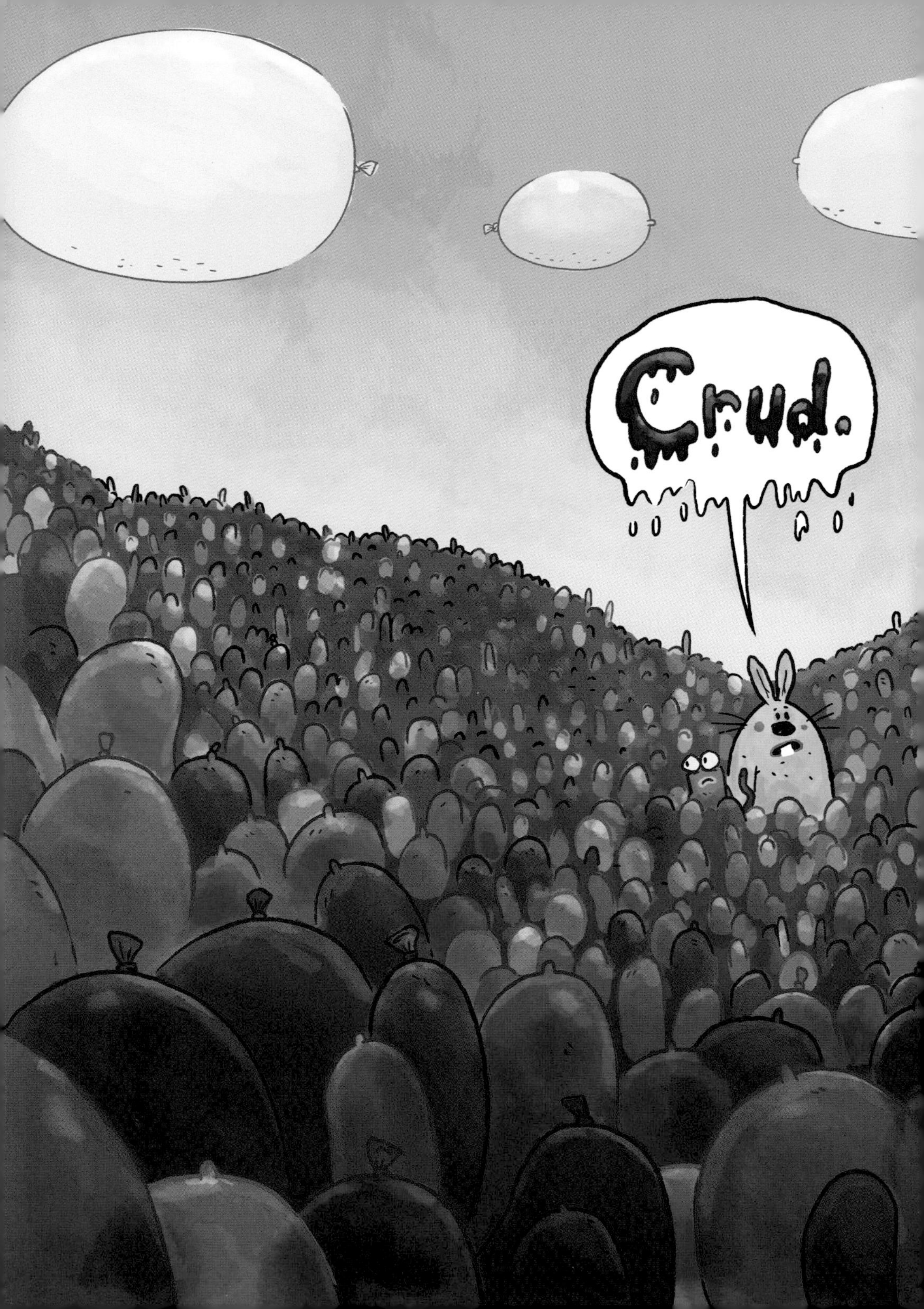
Crud.

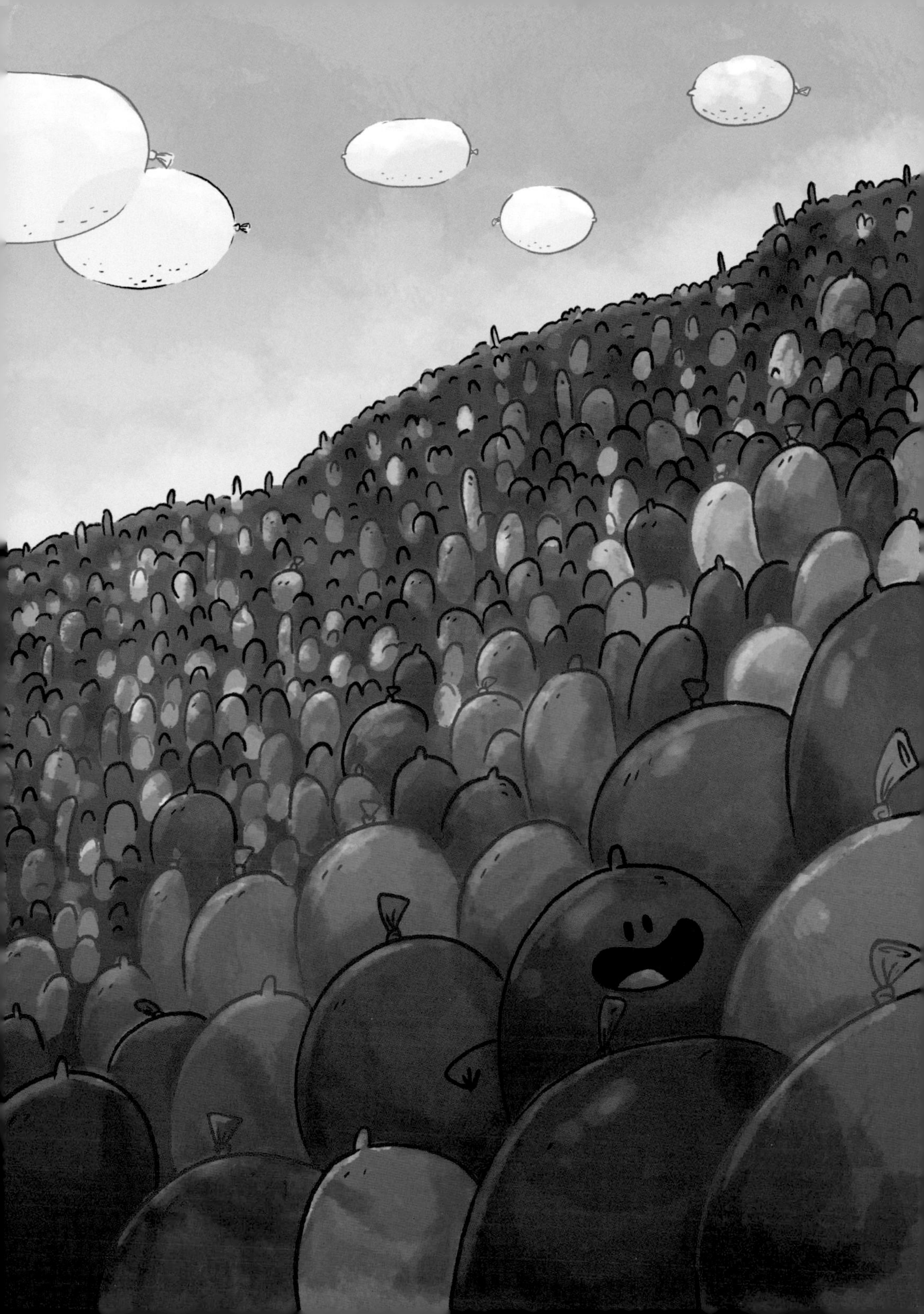

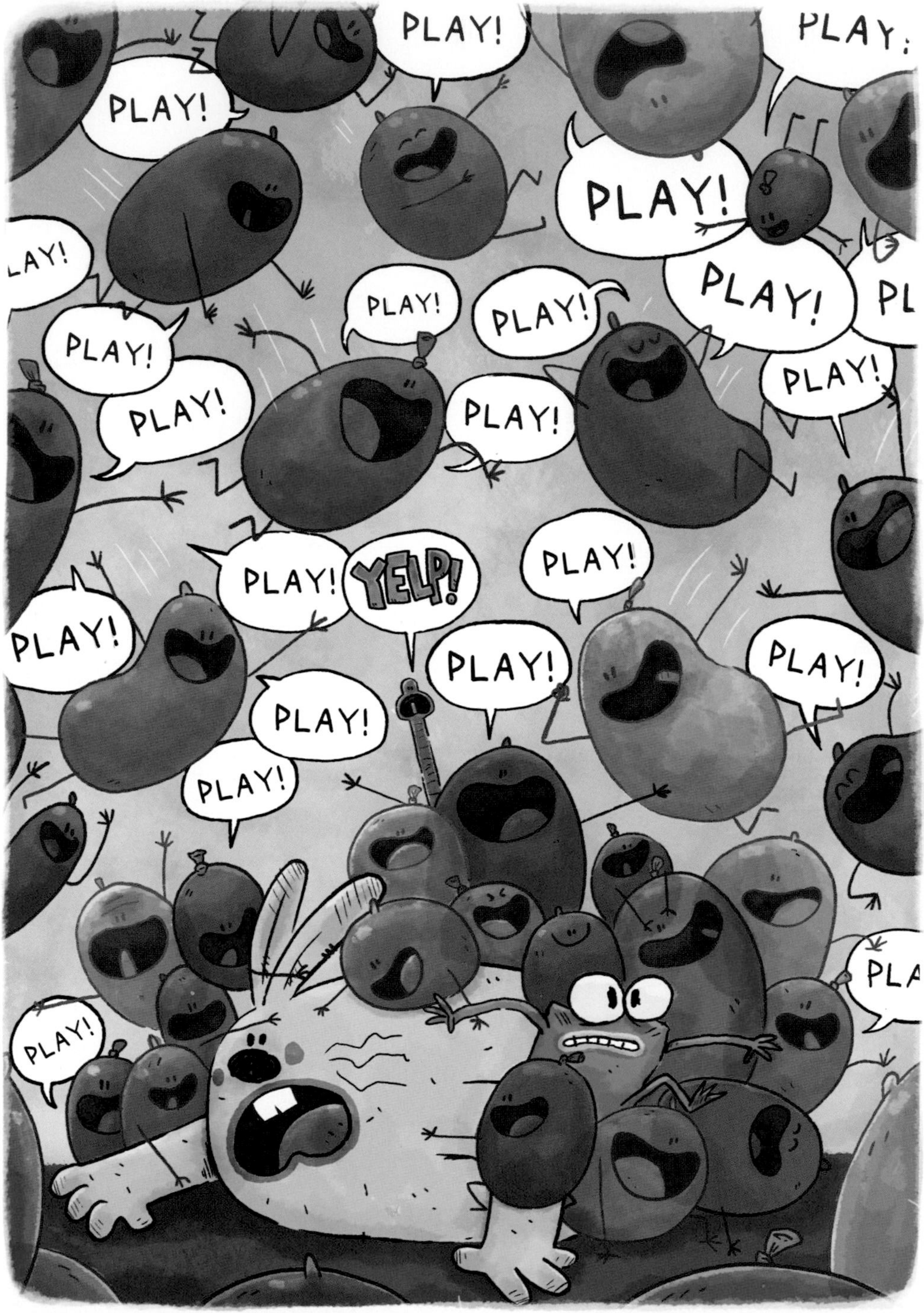
PLAY!
PLAY!
PLAY!
PLAY!
PLAY!
PLAY!
PLAY!
PLAY!
PLAY!
PLAY!
PLAY!
PLAY!
PLAY!
PLAY!
YELP!
PLAY!
PLAY!
PLAY!
PLAY!
PLAY!
PLAY!
PLAY!

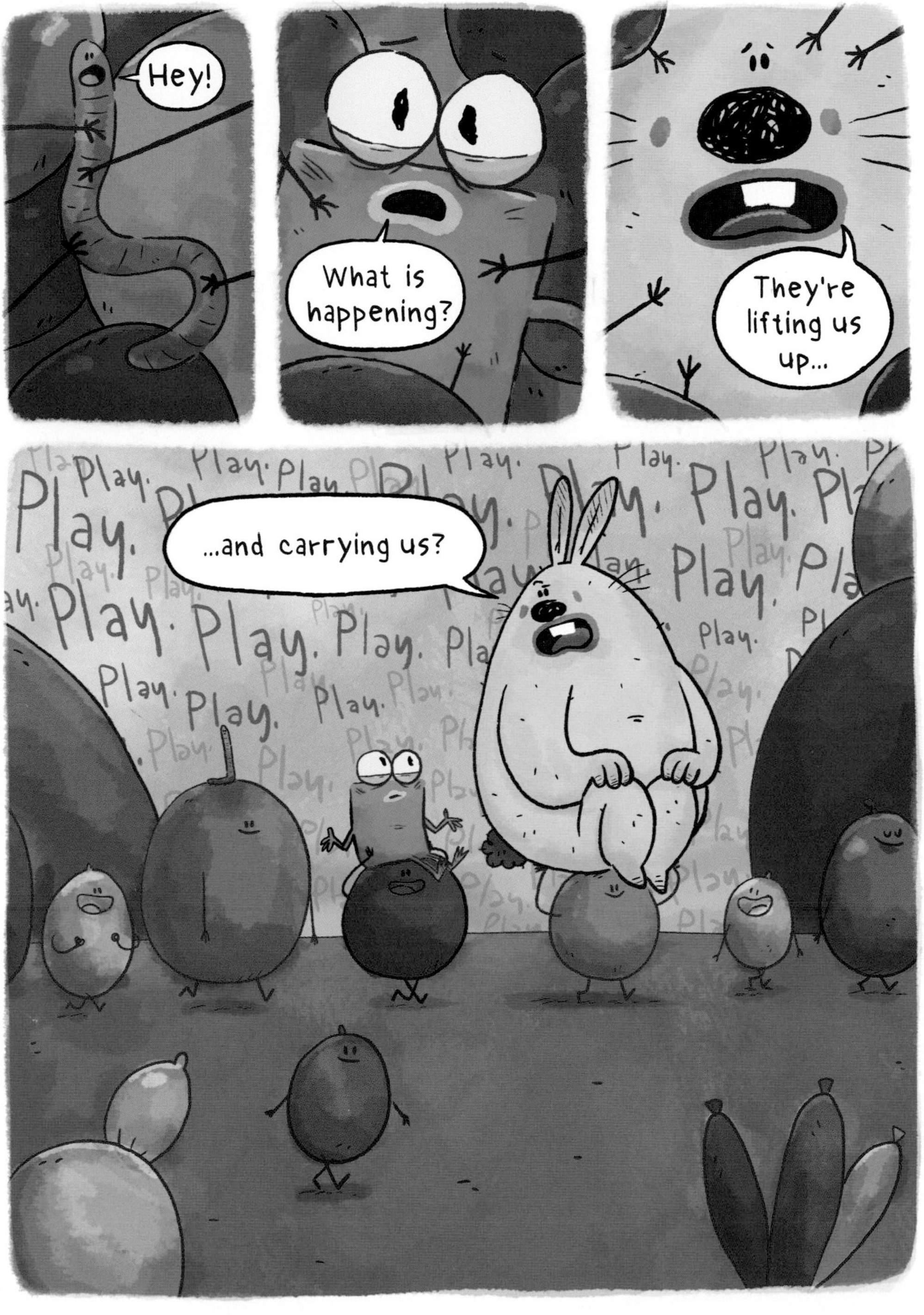
Hey!
What is happening?
They're lifting us up...
...and carrying us?
Play. Play. Play. Play. Play. Play.

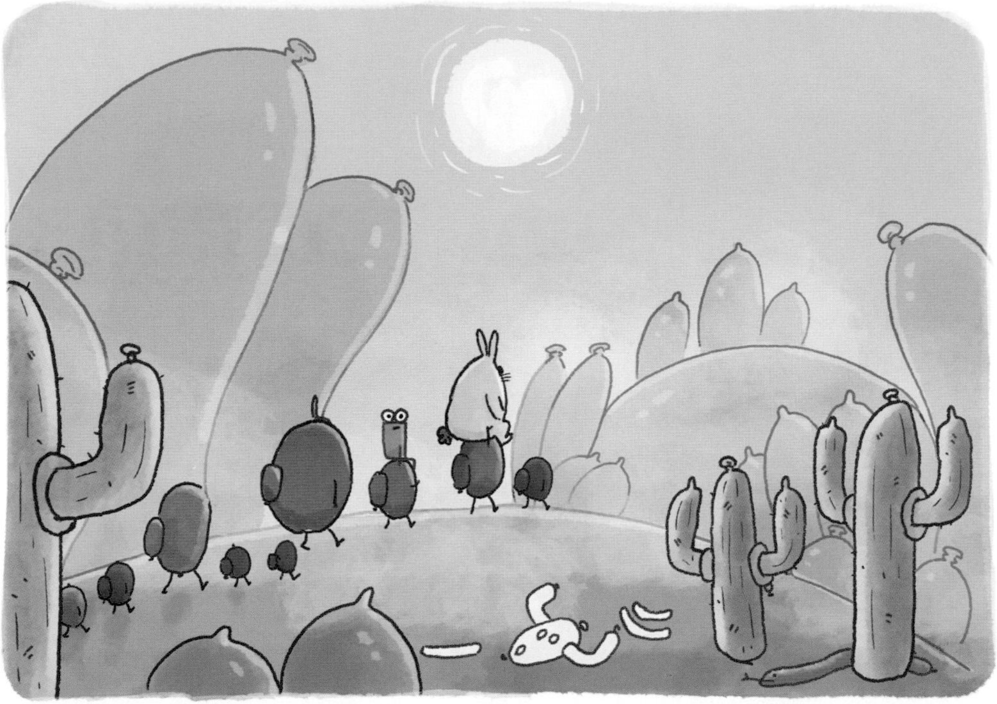

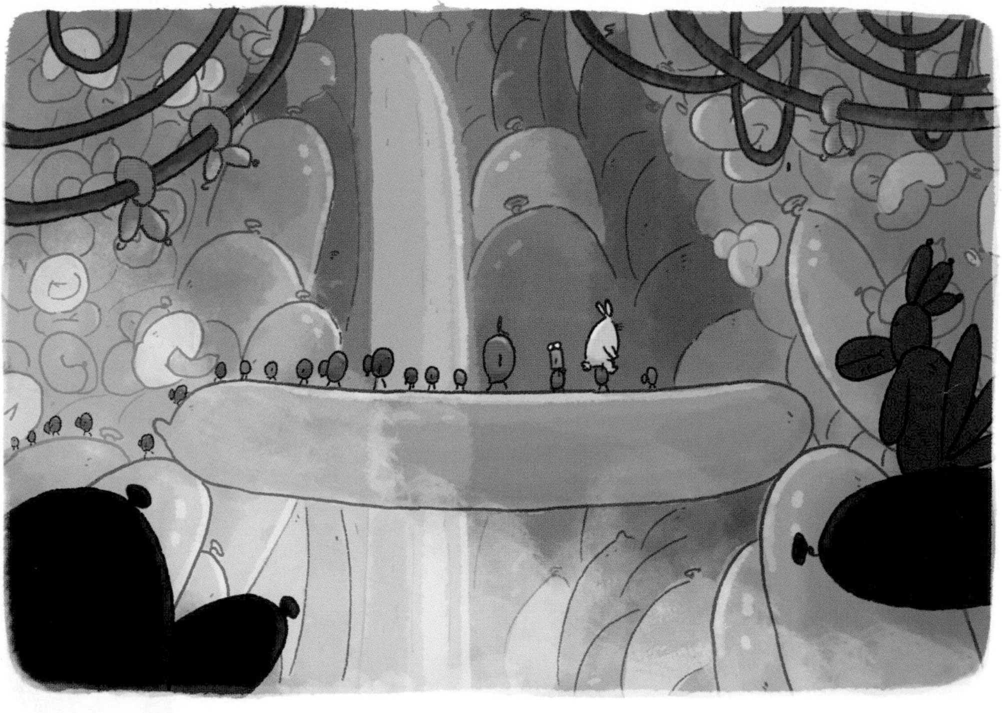

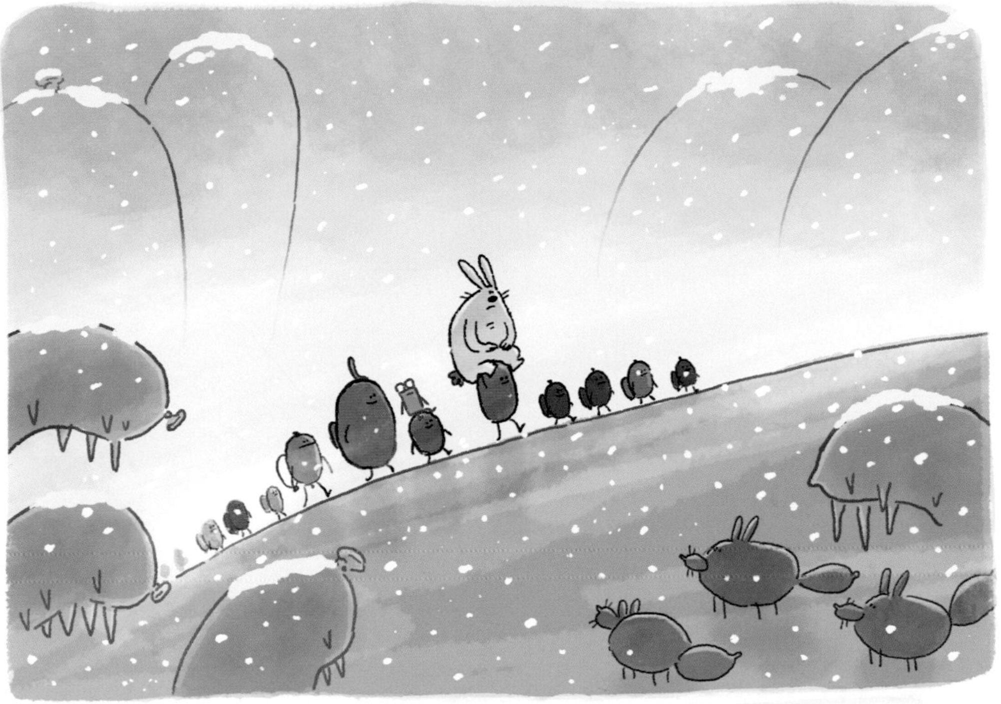

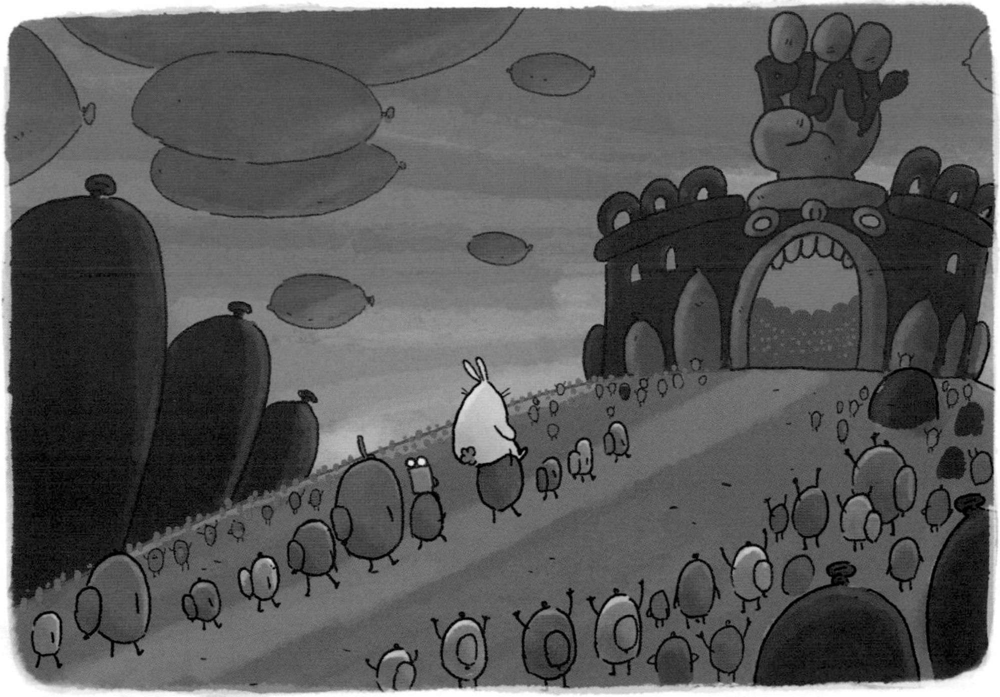
PLAY

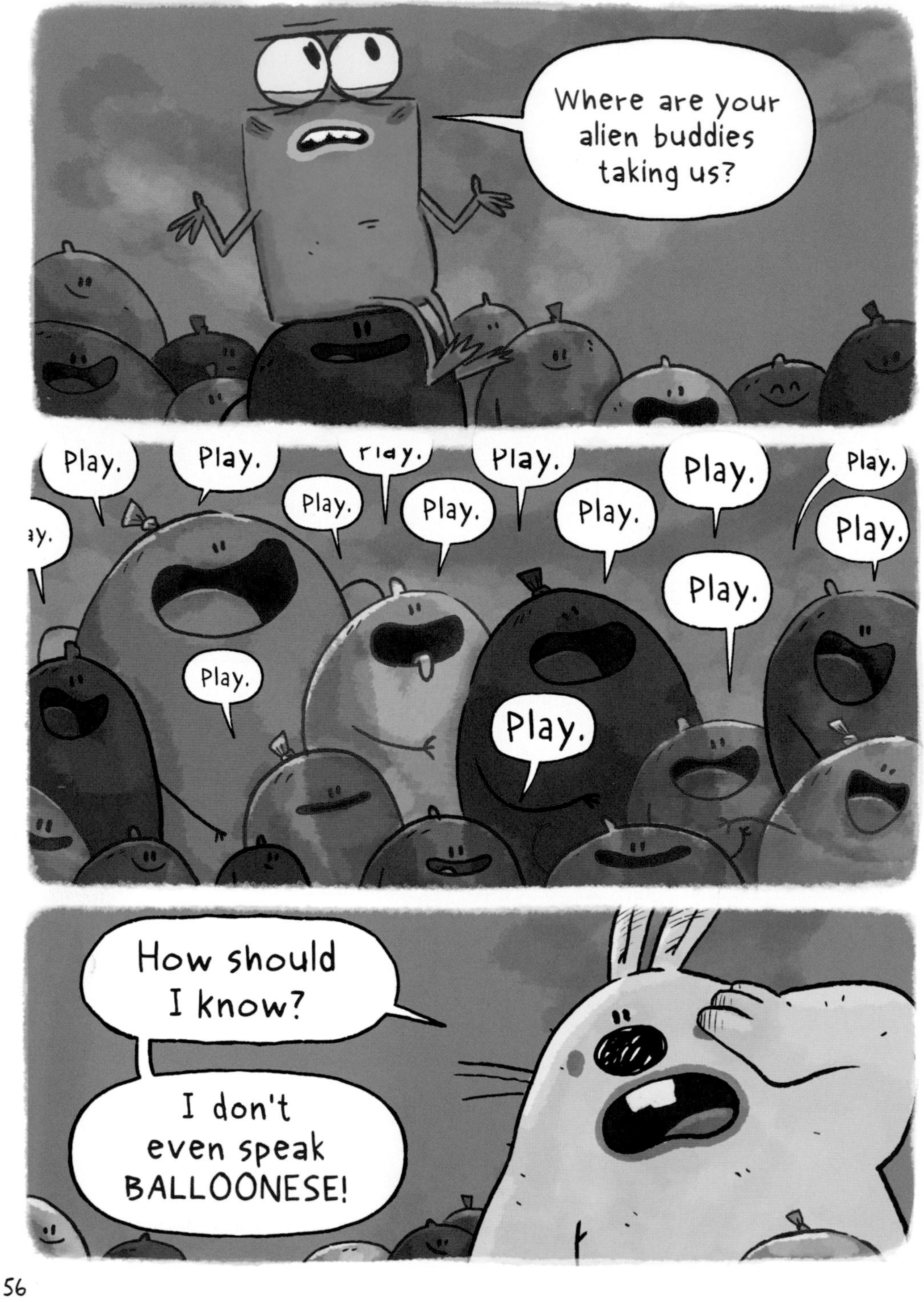
Where are your alien buddies taking us?
Play.
Play.
Play.
Play.
Play.
Play.
Play.
Play.
Play.
Play.
Play.
Play.
How should I know?
I don't even speak BALLOONESE!

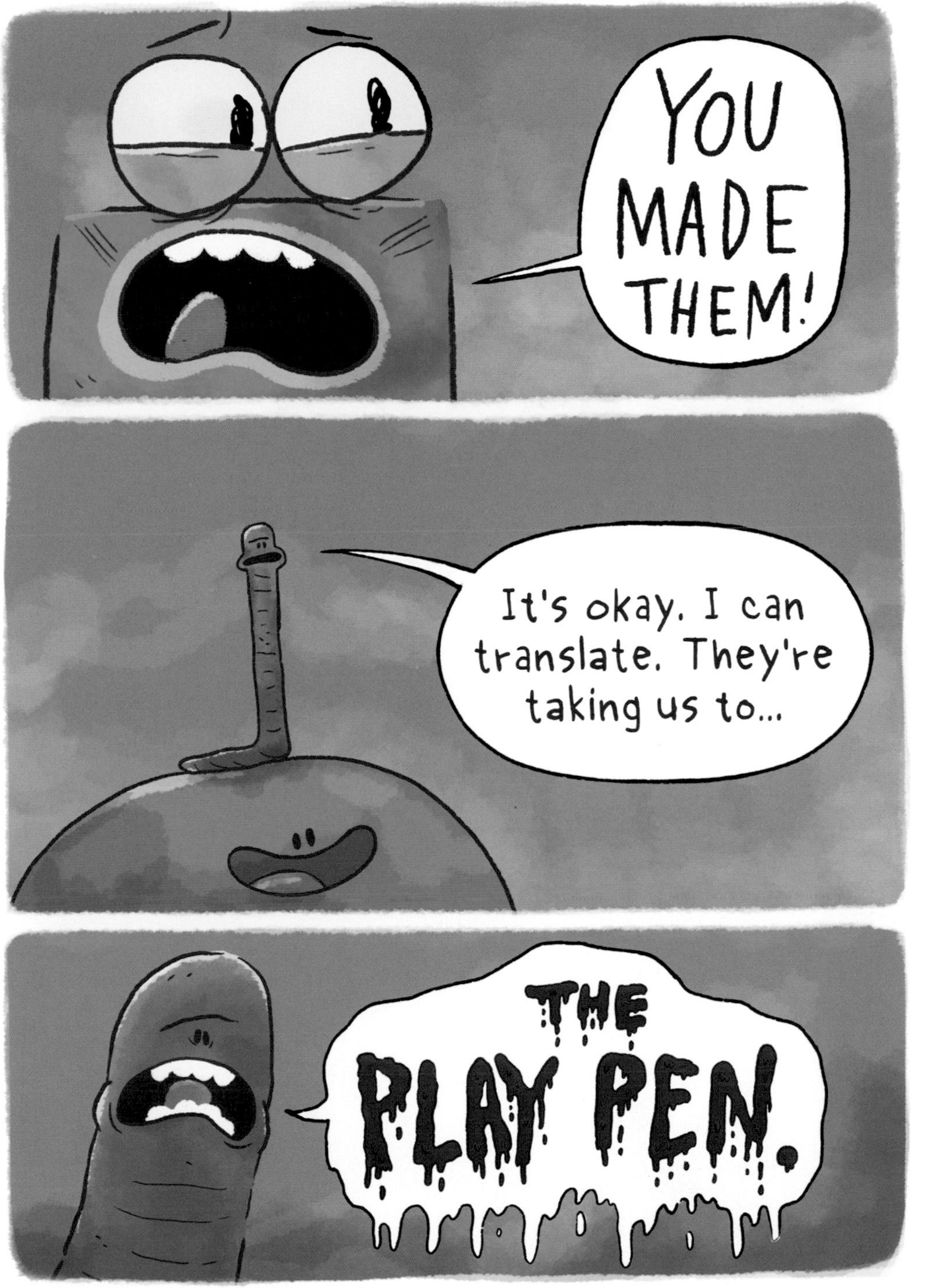
YOU MADE THEM!
It's okay. I can translate. They're taking us to...
THE PLAY PEN.

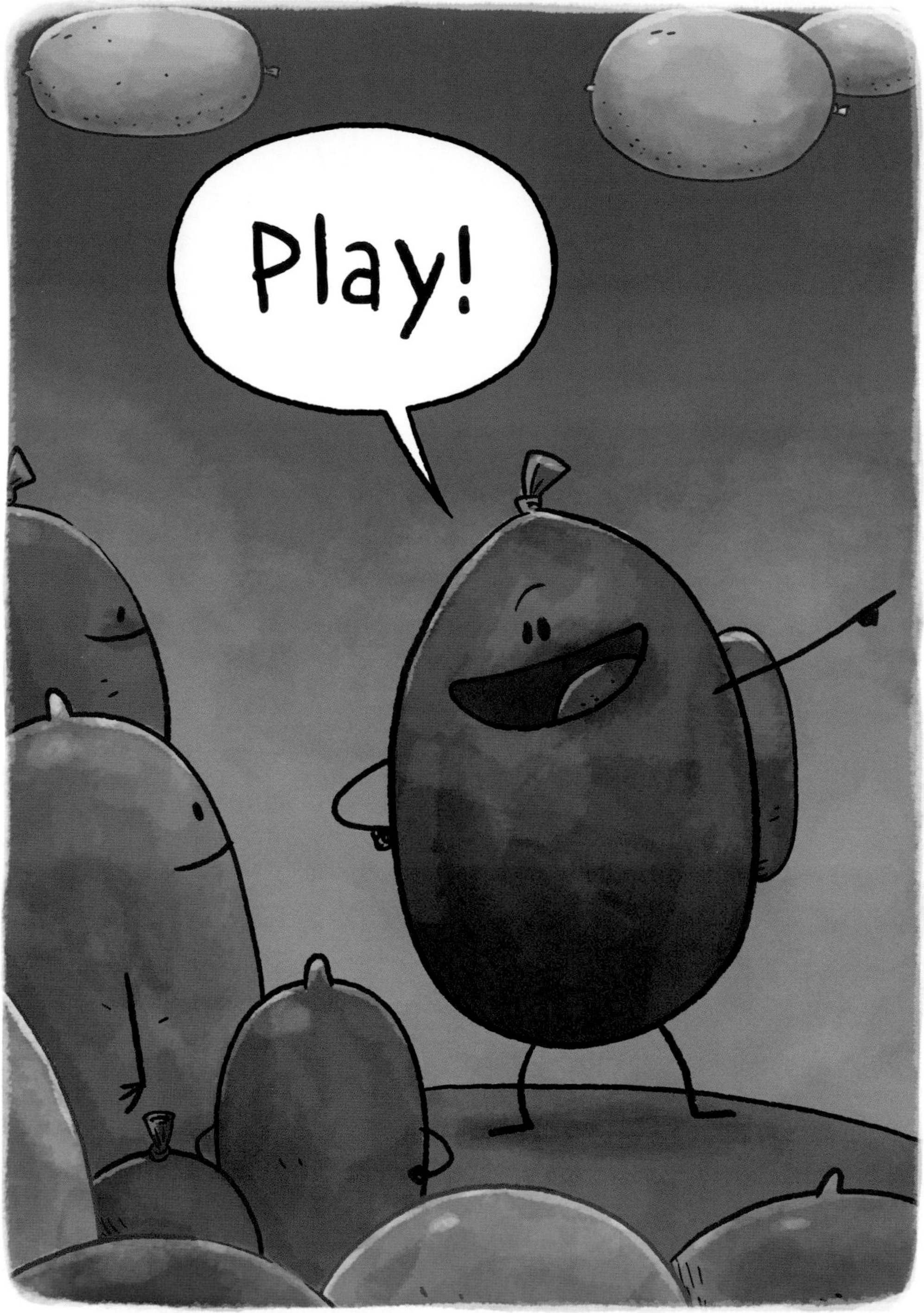
Play!

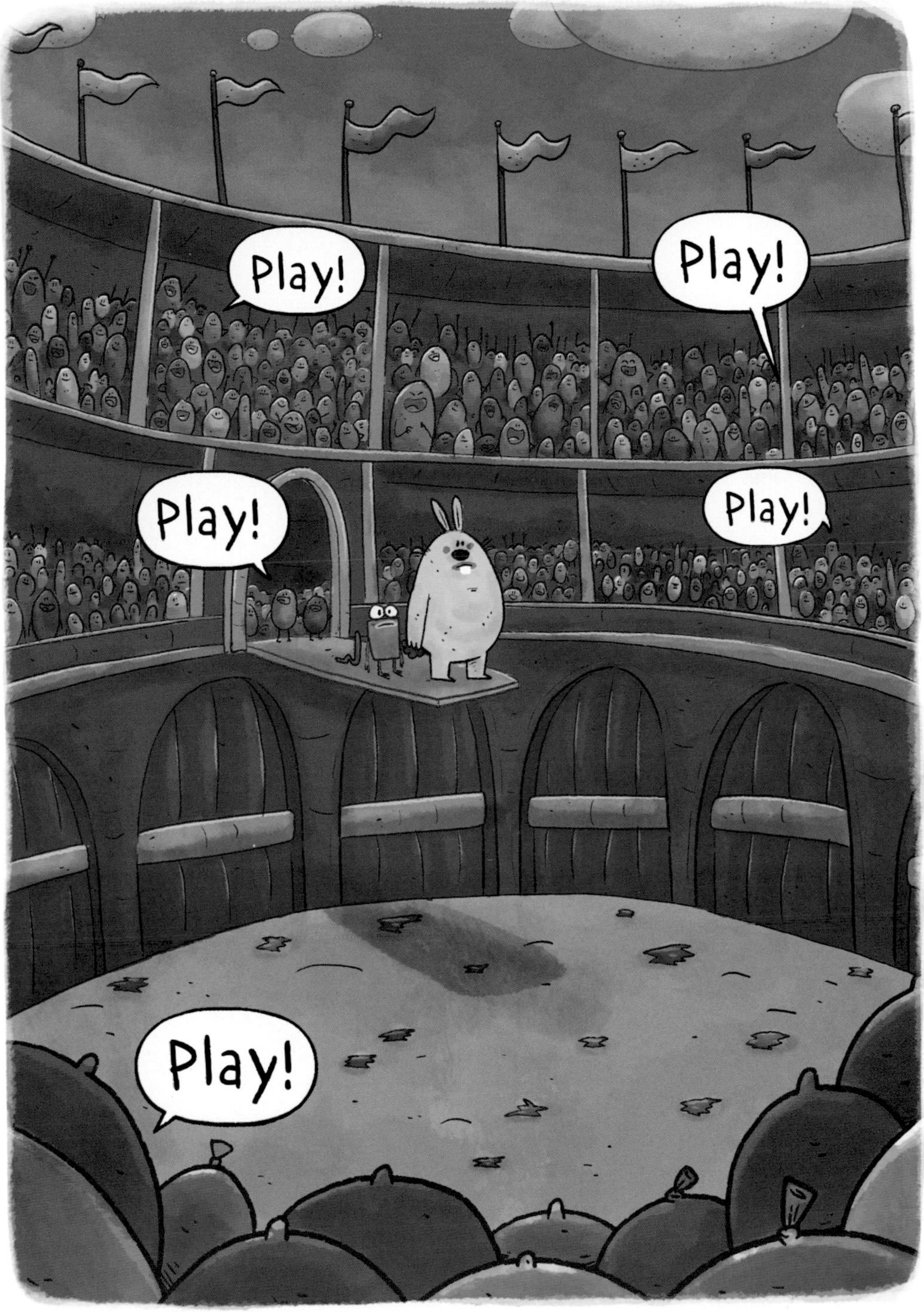
Play!
Play!
Play!
Play!
Play!

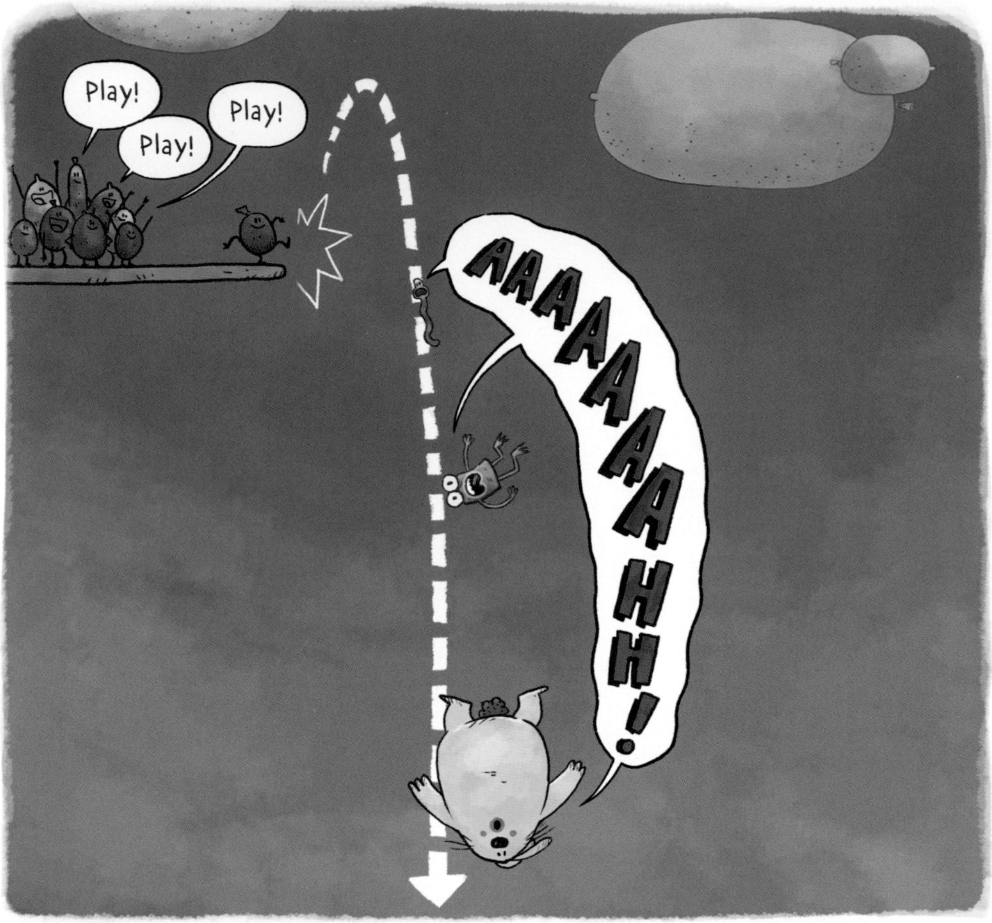
Play!
Play!
Play!
AAAAAAAAAAHHH!

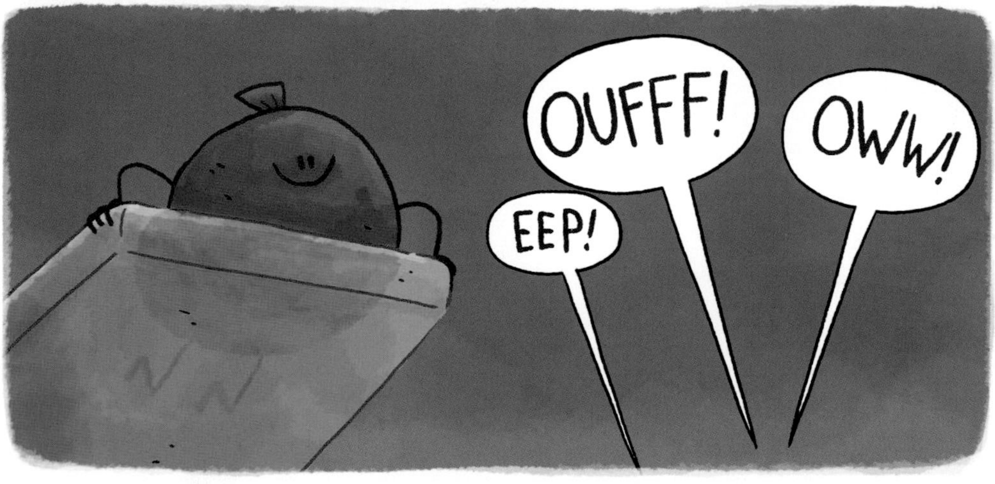
EEP!
OUFFF!
OWW!

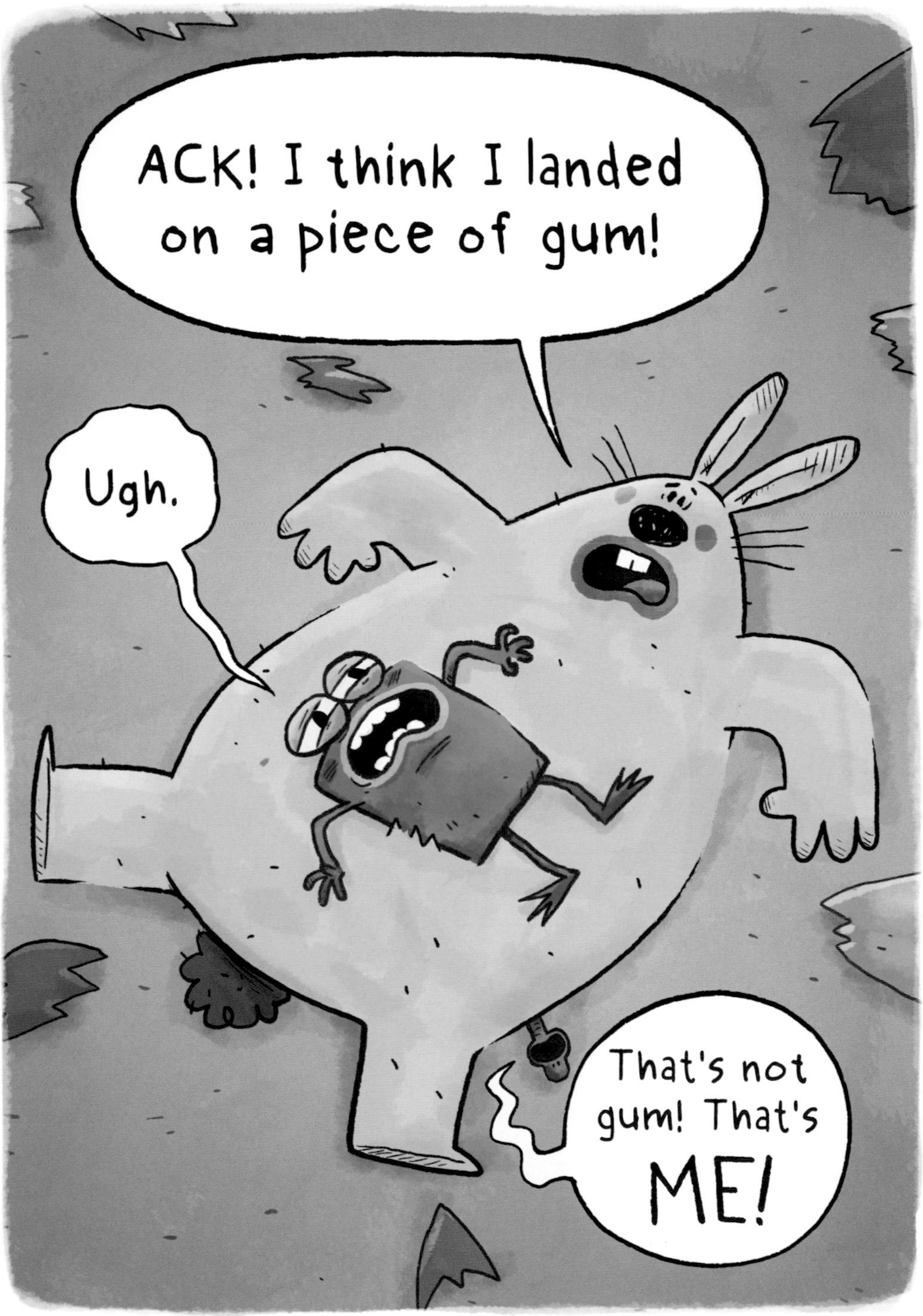
ACK! I think I landed on a piece of gum!
Ugh.
That's not gum! That's ME!

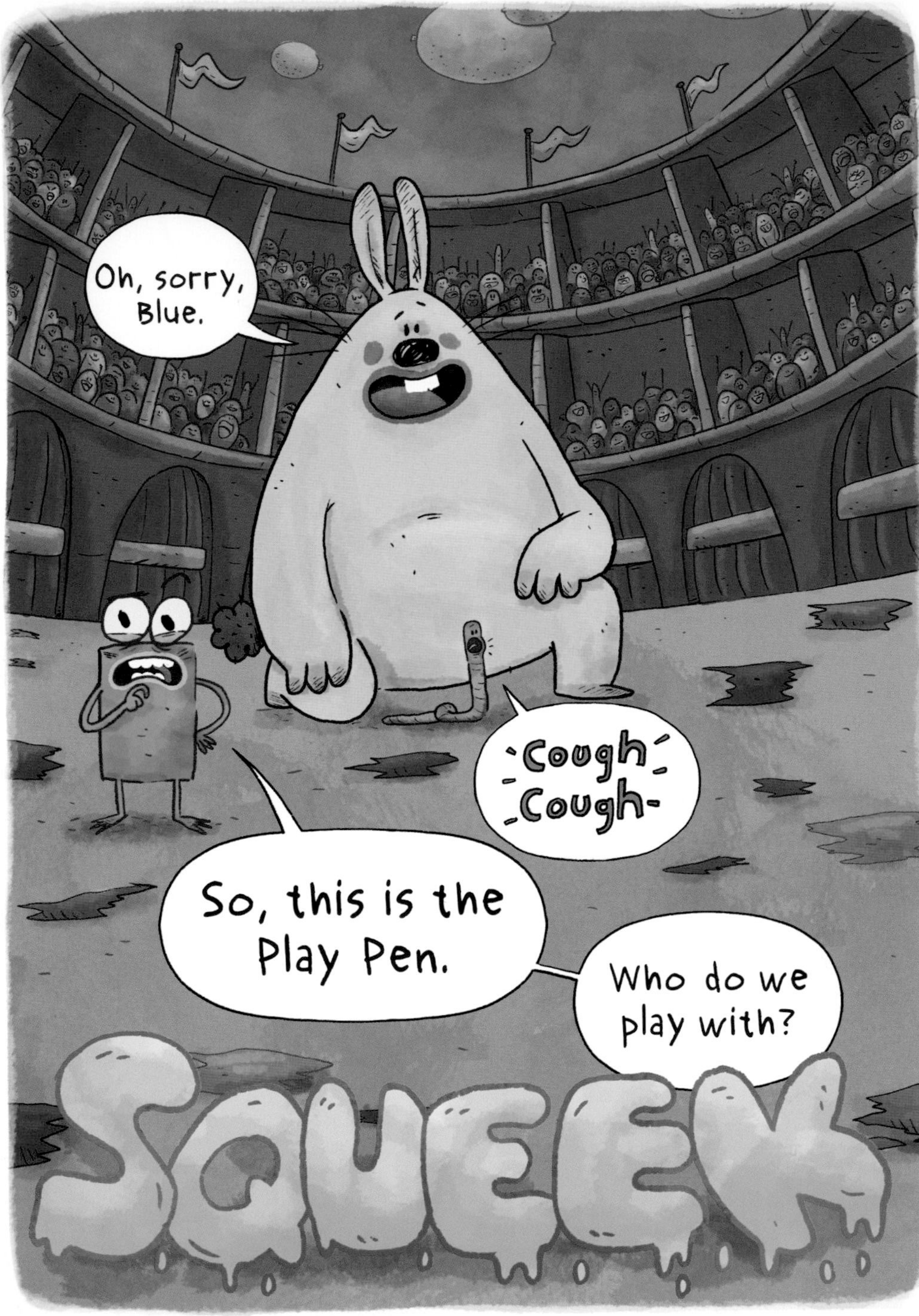
Oh, sorry, Blue.
Cough Cough
So, this is the Play Pen.
Who do we play with?
SQUEEK

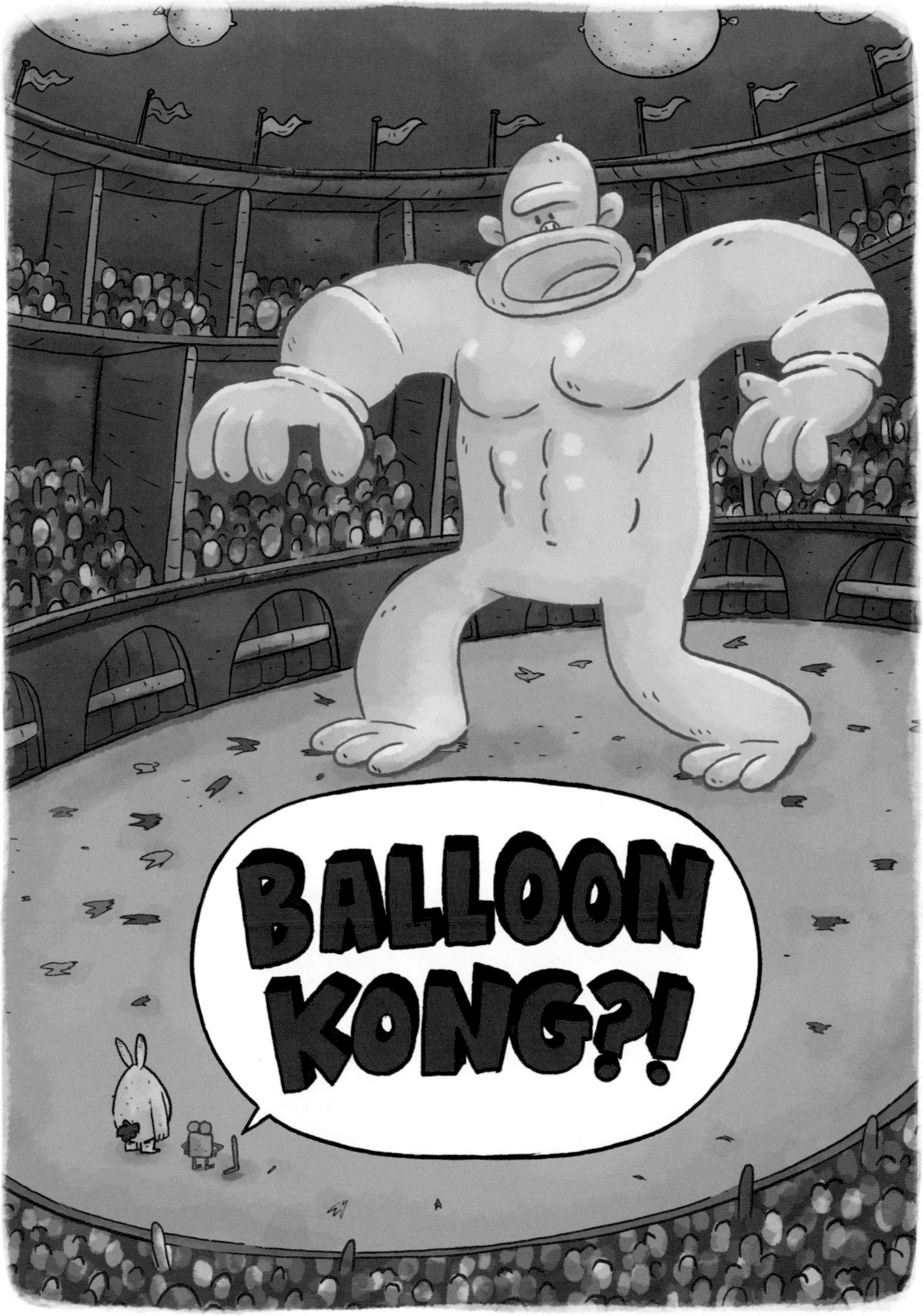
BALLOON KONG?!

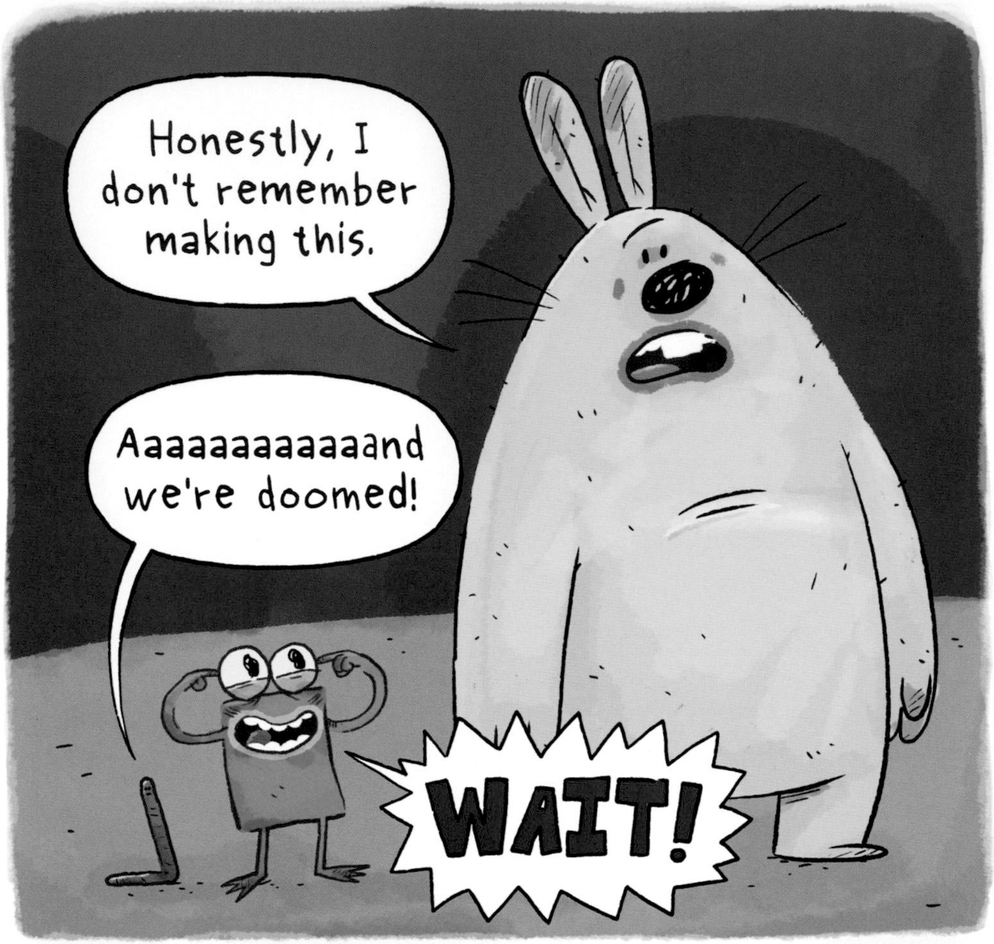
Honestly, I don't remember making this.
Aaaaaaaaaaaand we're doomed!
WAIT!

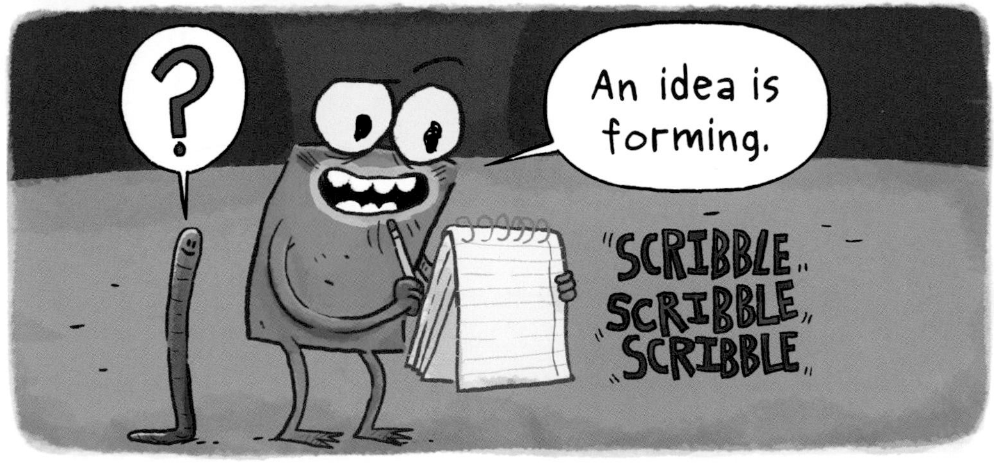
?
An idea is forming.
SCRIBBLE
SCRIBBLE
SCRIBBLE

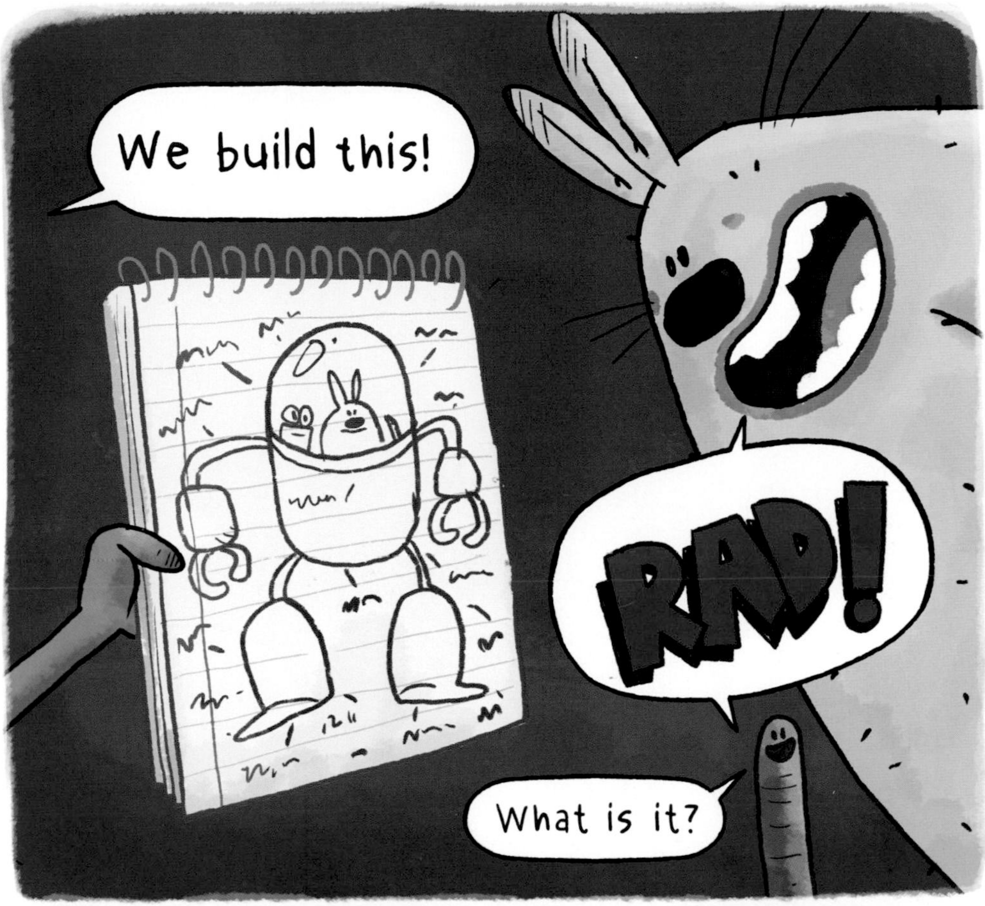
We build this!
RAD!
What is it?

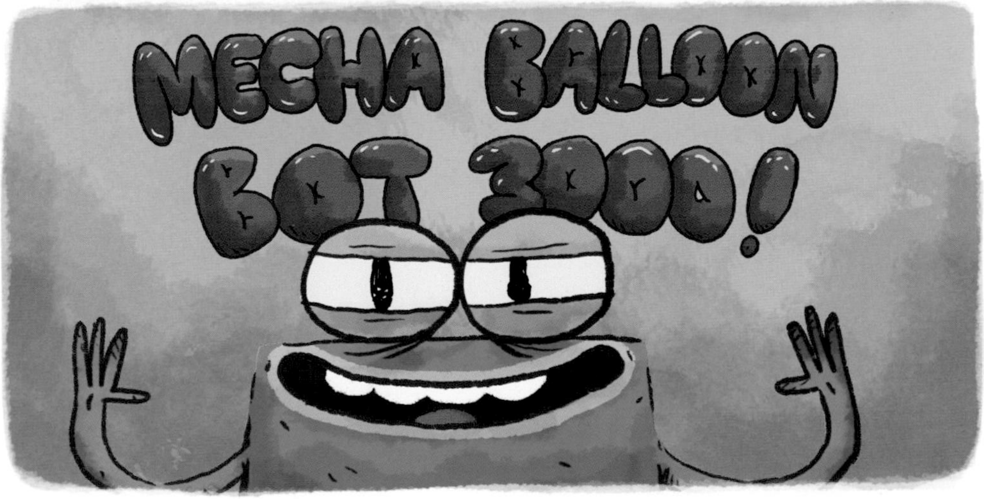
MECHA BALLOON BOT 3000!

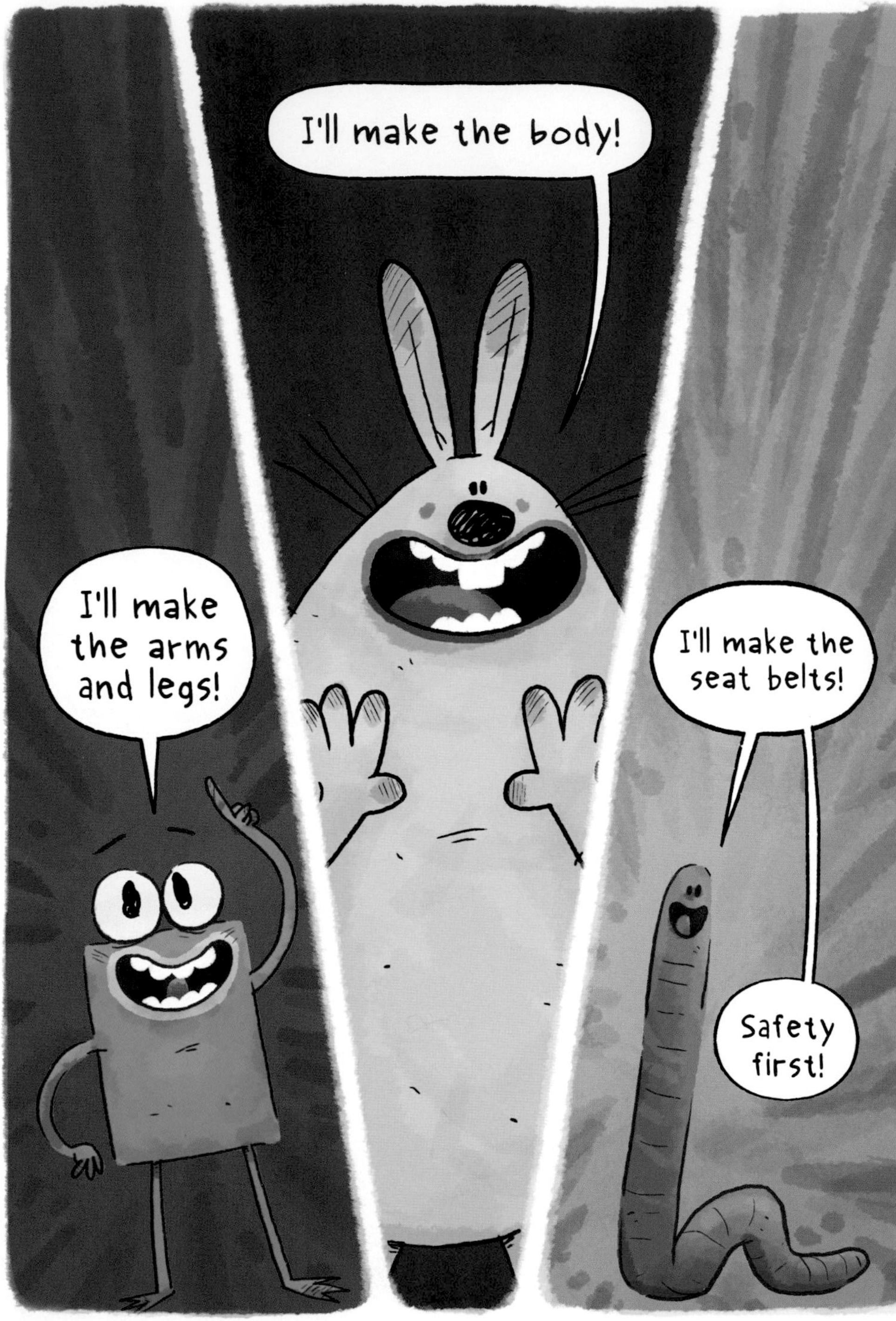
I'll make the body!
I'll make the arms and legs!
I'll make the seat belts!
Safety first!

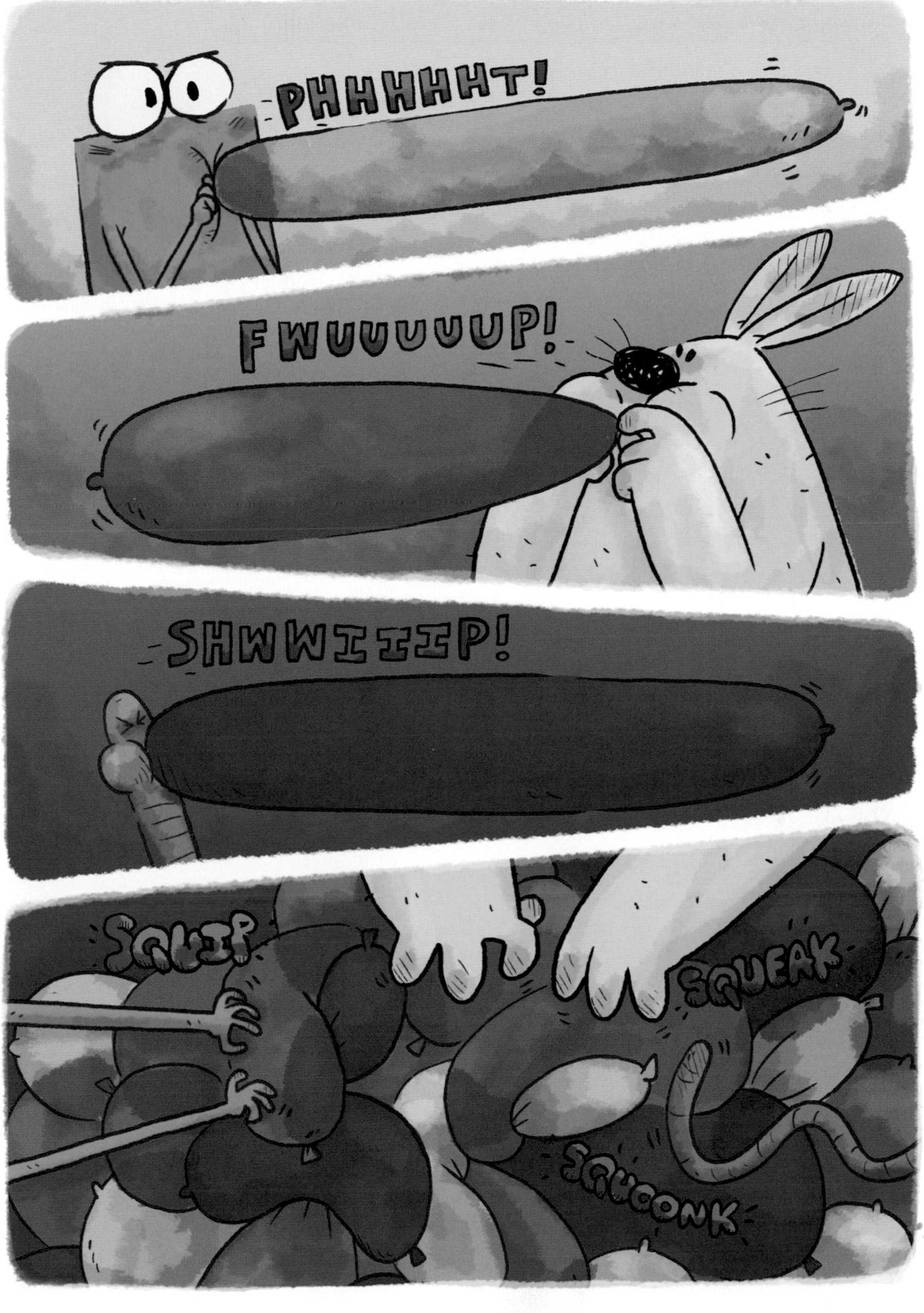
PHHHHHT!
FWUUUUUP!
SHWWIIIP!
SQUIP
SQUEAK
SQUOONK

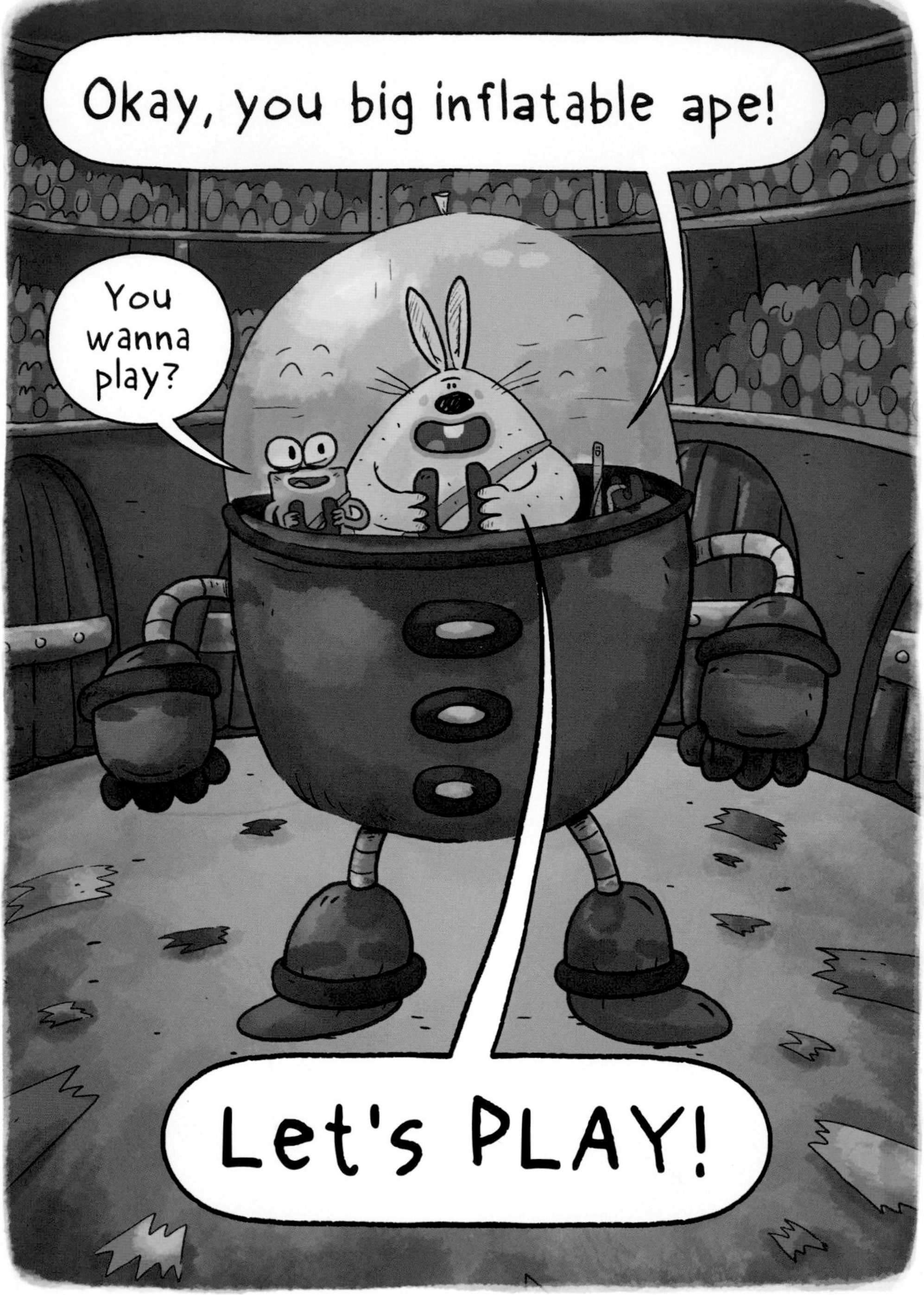
Okay, you big inflatable ape!
You wanna play?
Let's PLAY!

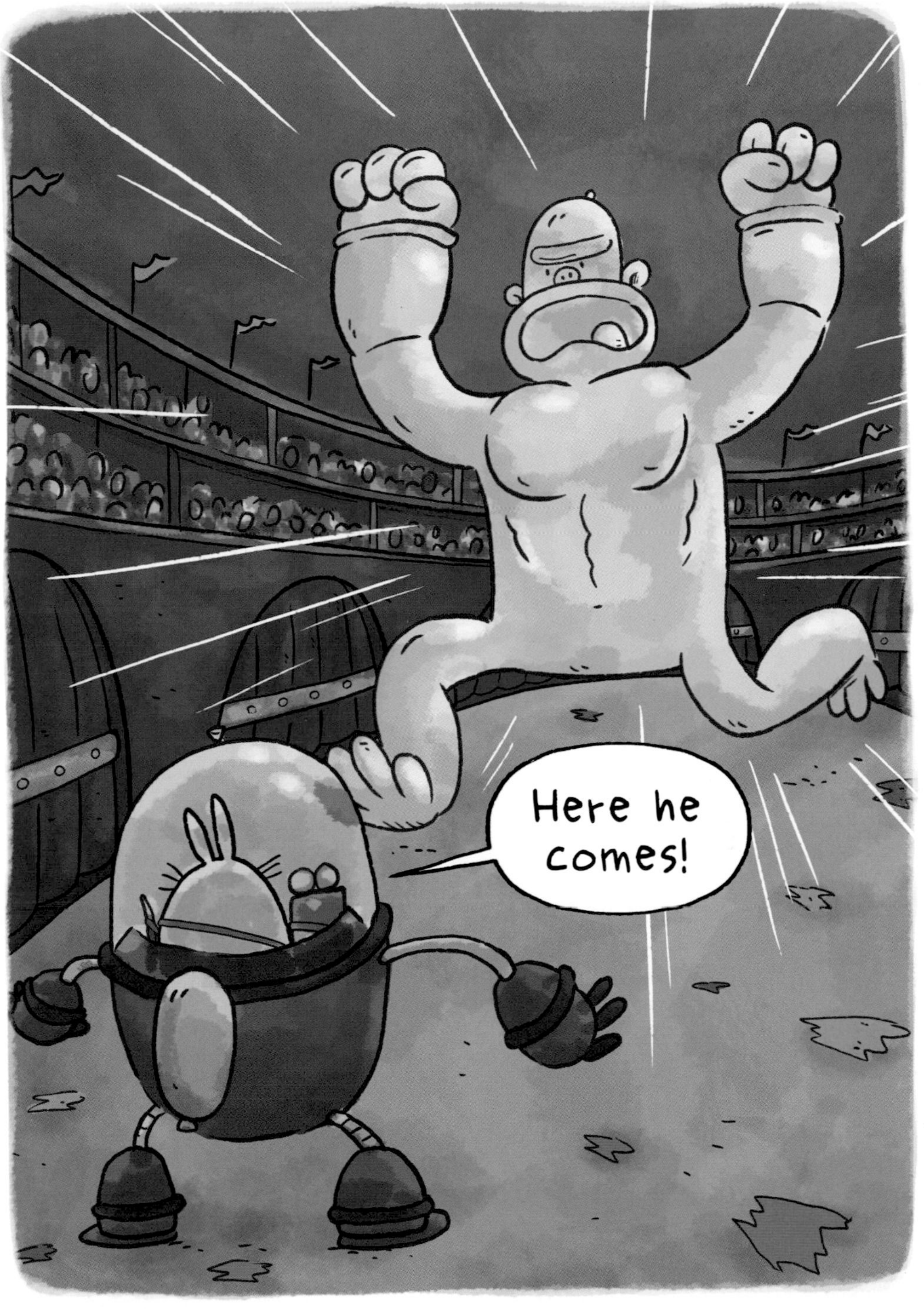
Here he comes!

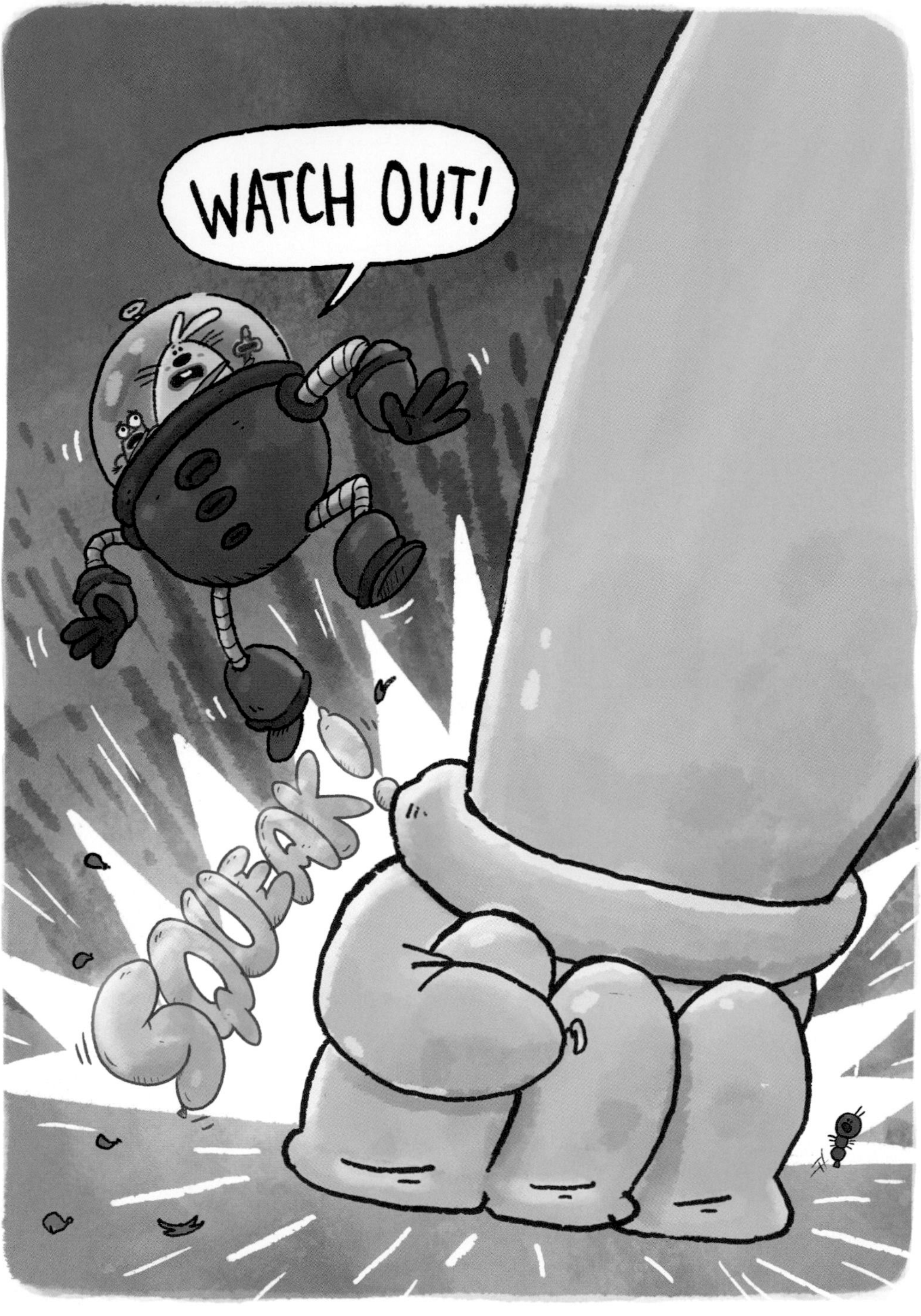
WATCH OUT!
SQUEAK

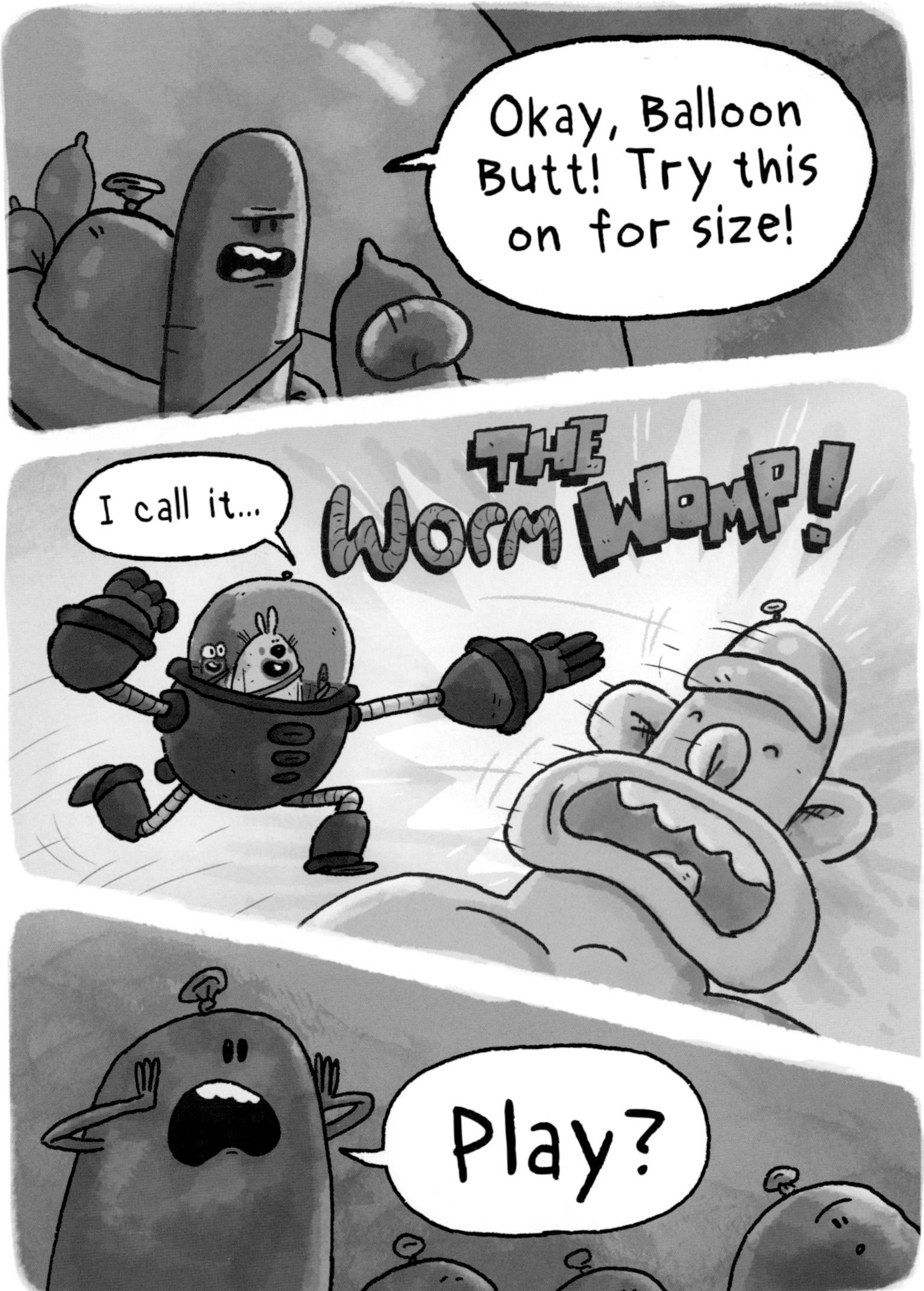
Okay, Balloon Butt! Try this on for size!
I call it...
THE WORM WOMP!
Play?

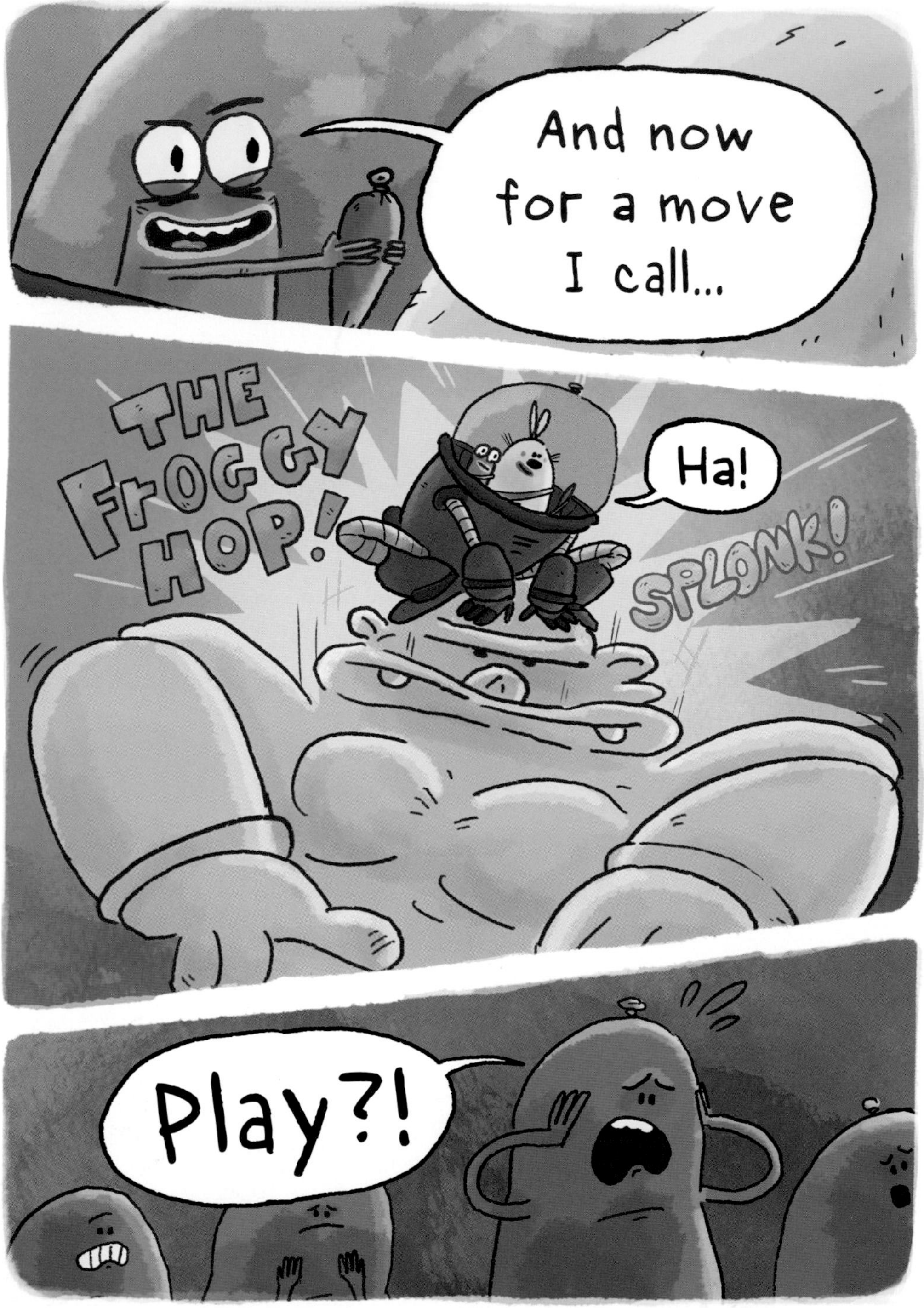
And now for a move I call...
THE FROGGY HOP!
Ha!
SPLONK!
Play?!

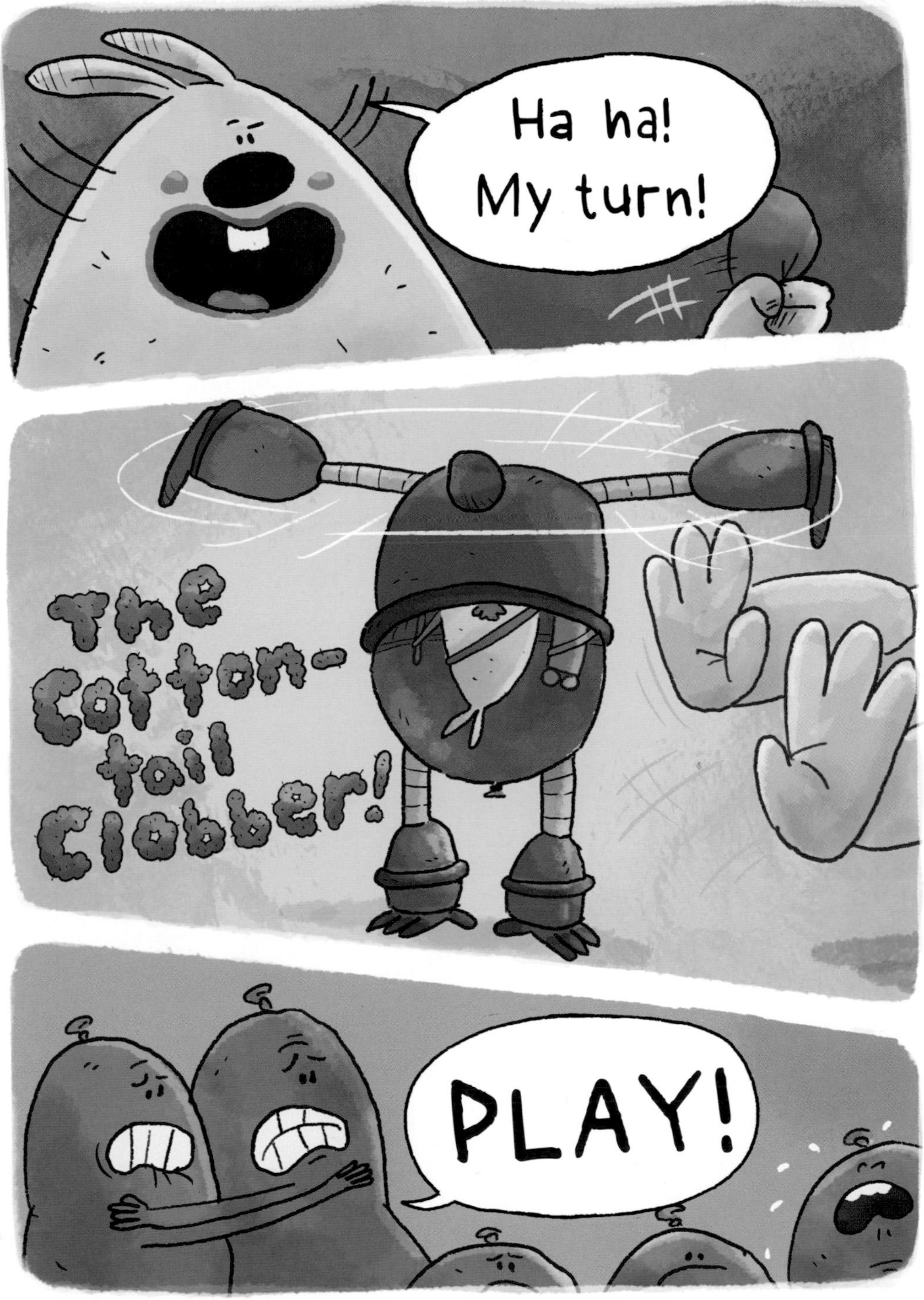
Ha ha!
My turn!
The Cotton-tail Clobber!
PLAY!

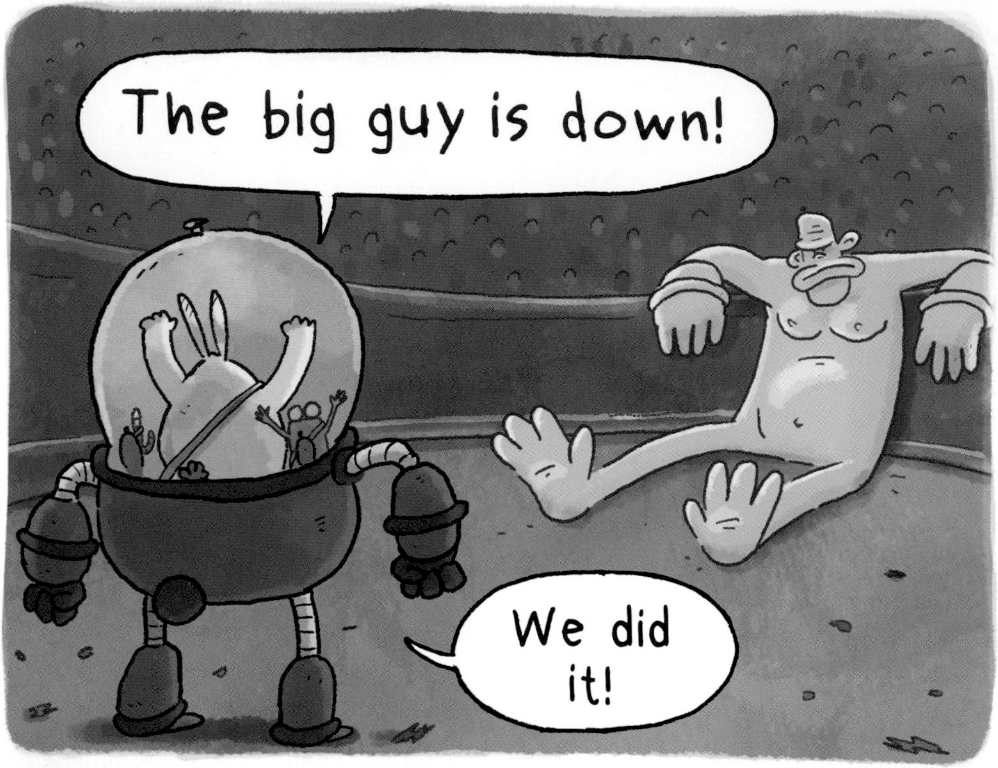
The big guy is down!
We did it!

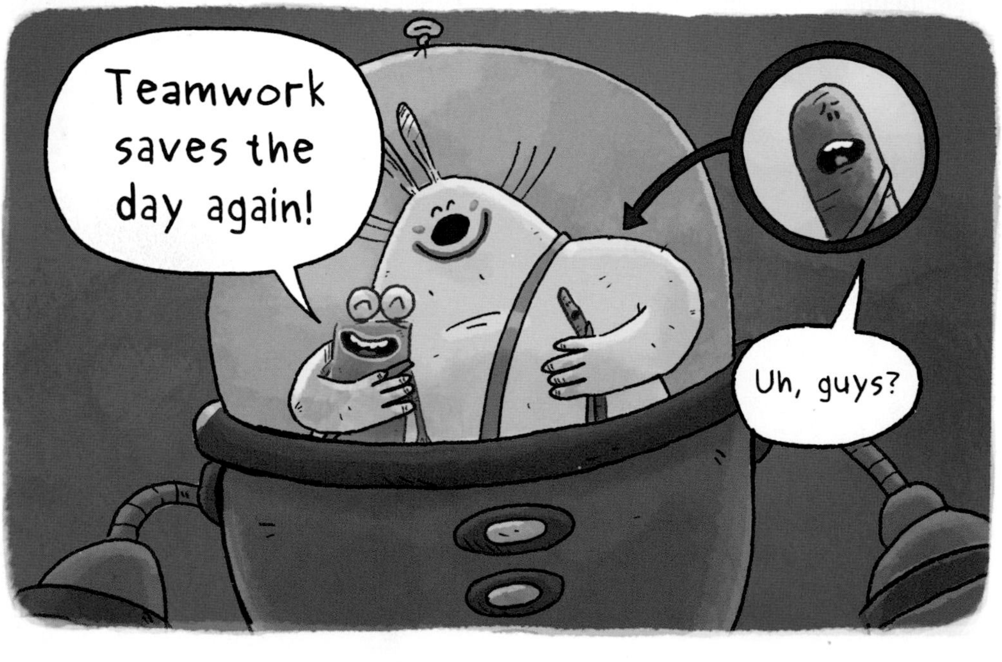
Teamwork saves the day again!
Uh, guys?

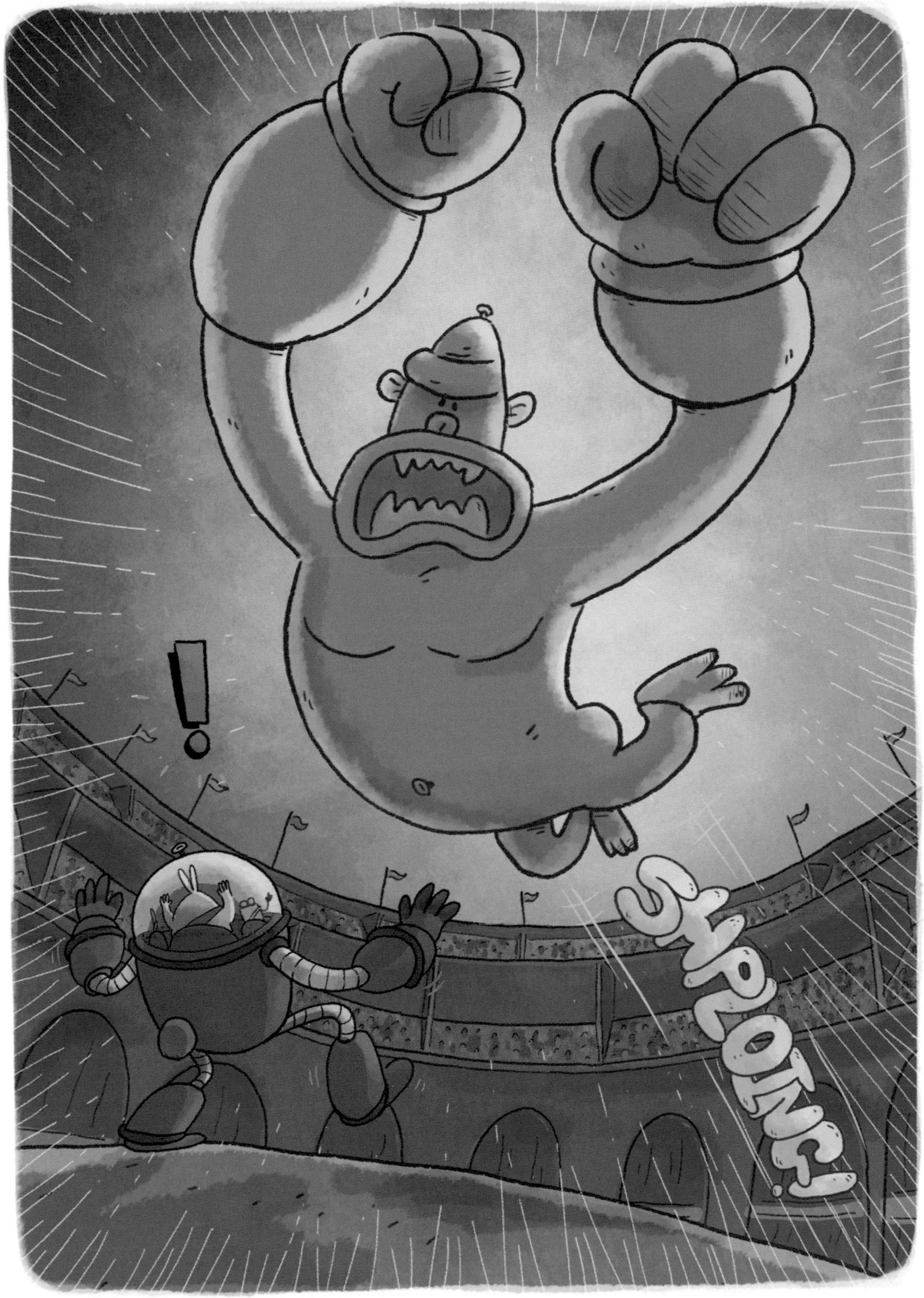
!
SPROING!

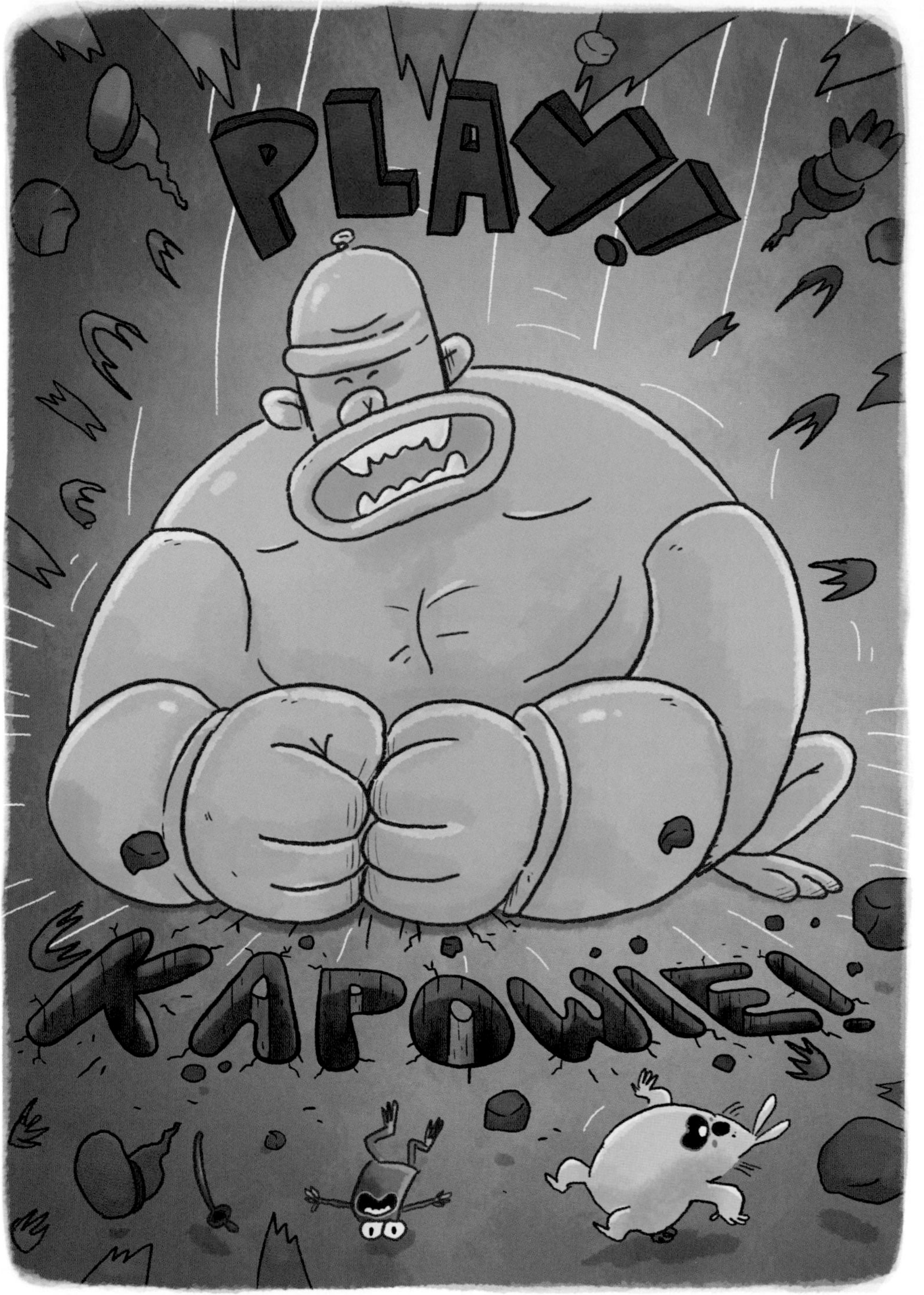
PLAY!
KAPOWIE!

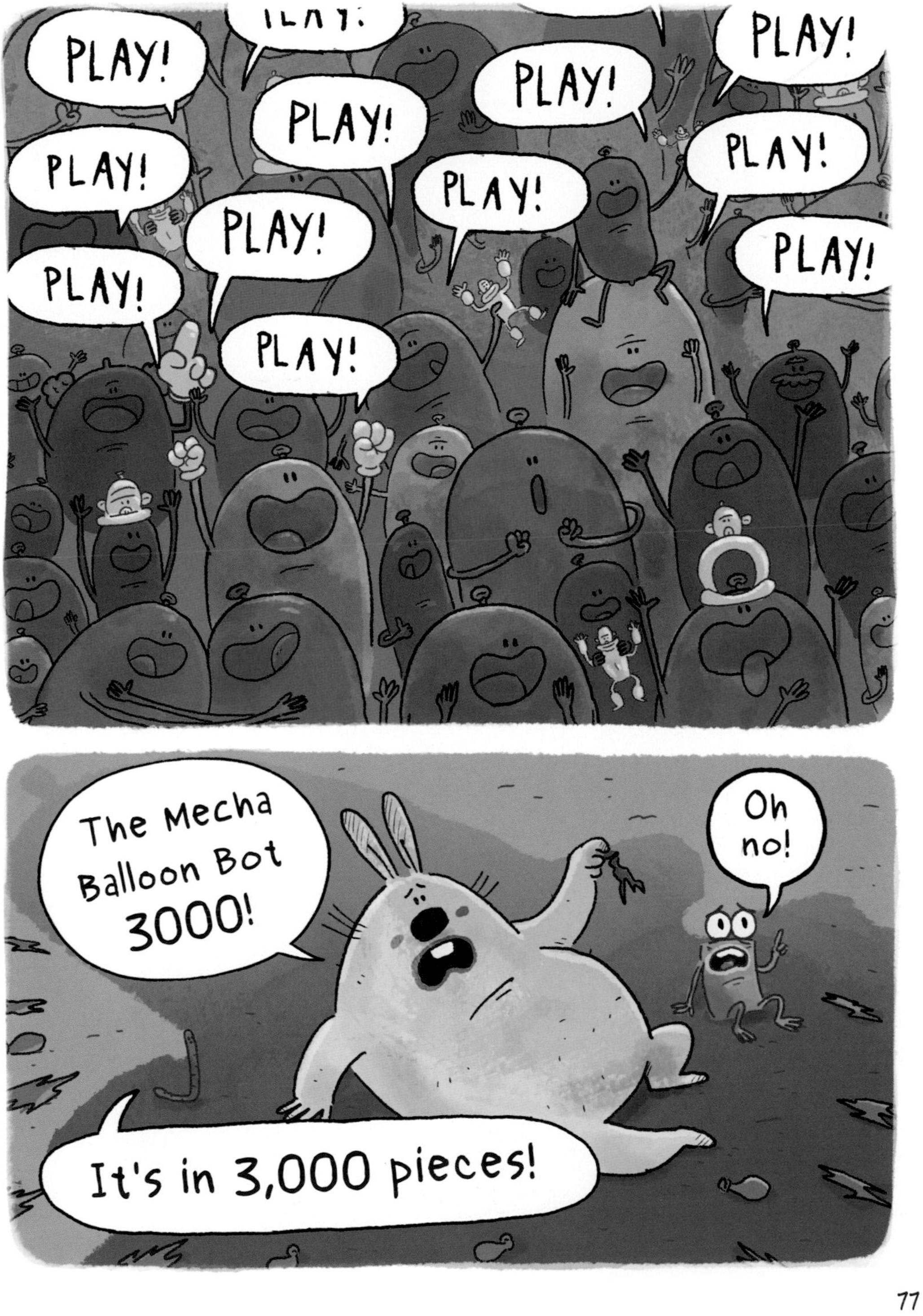
PLAY!
PLAY!
PLAY!
PLAY!
PLAY!
PLAY!
PLAY!
PLAY!
PLAY!
PLAY!
PLAY!
The Mecha Balloon Bot 3000!
Oh no!
It's in 3,000 pieces!

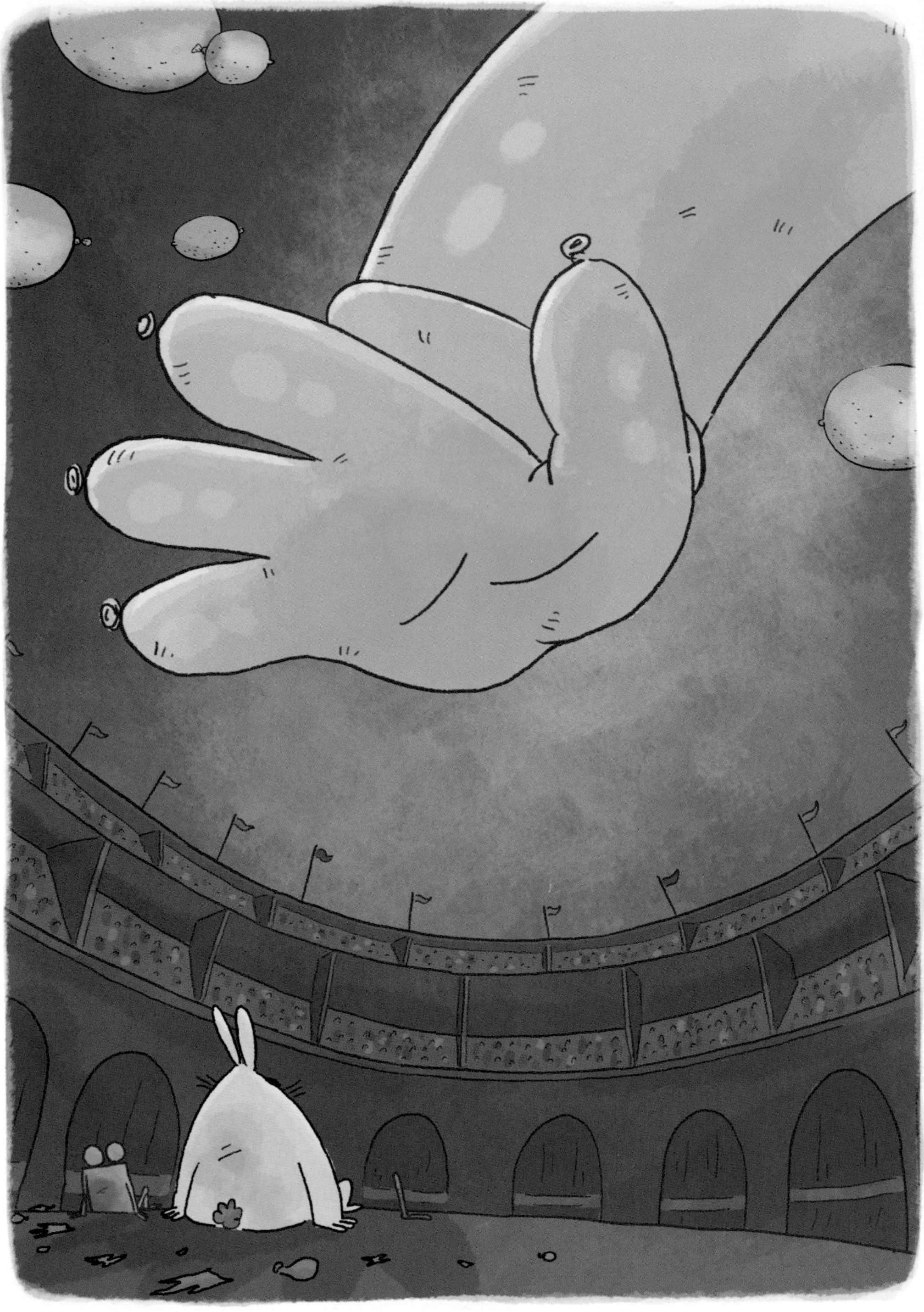

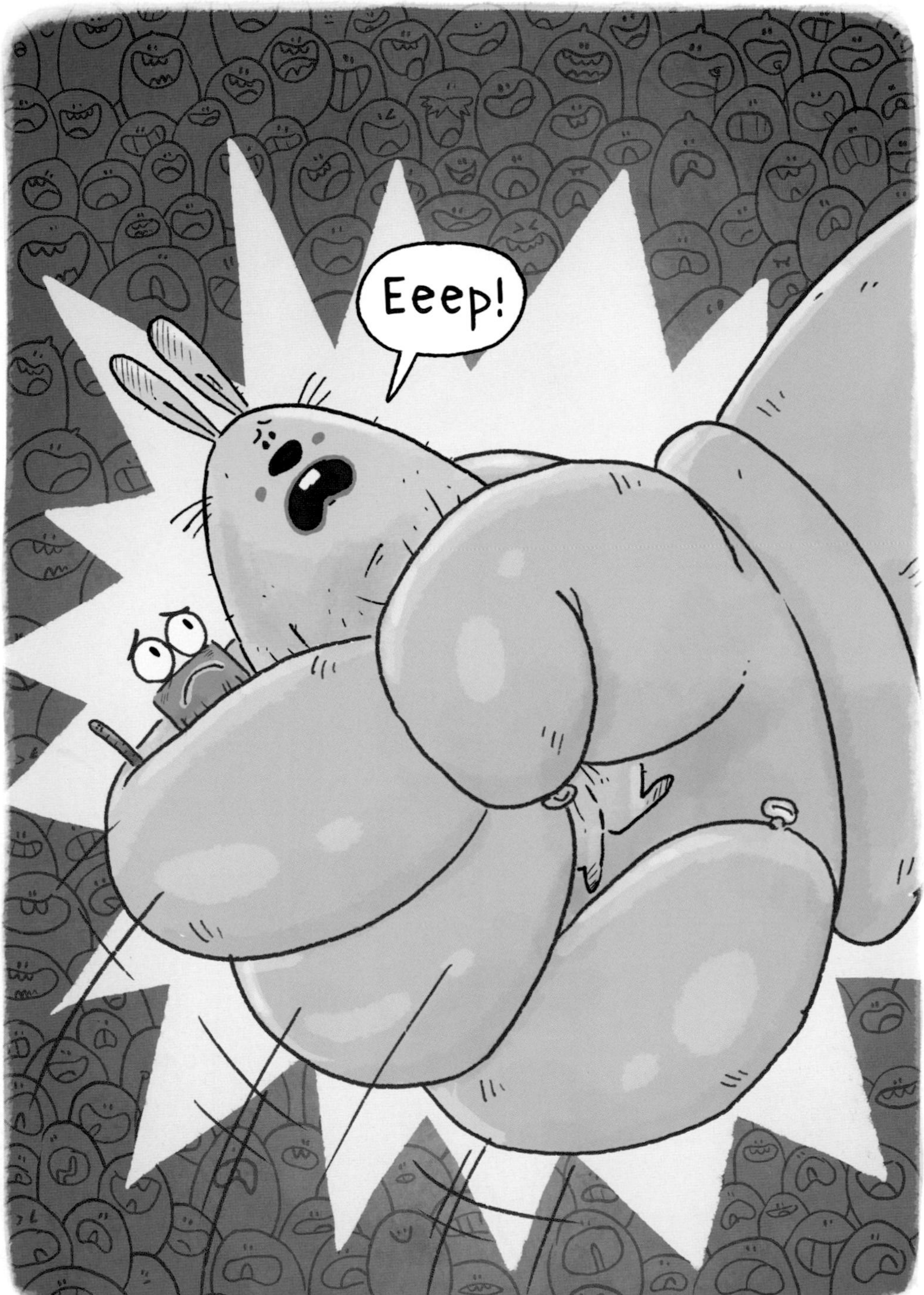
Eeep!

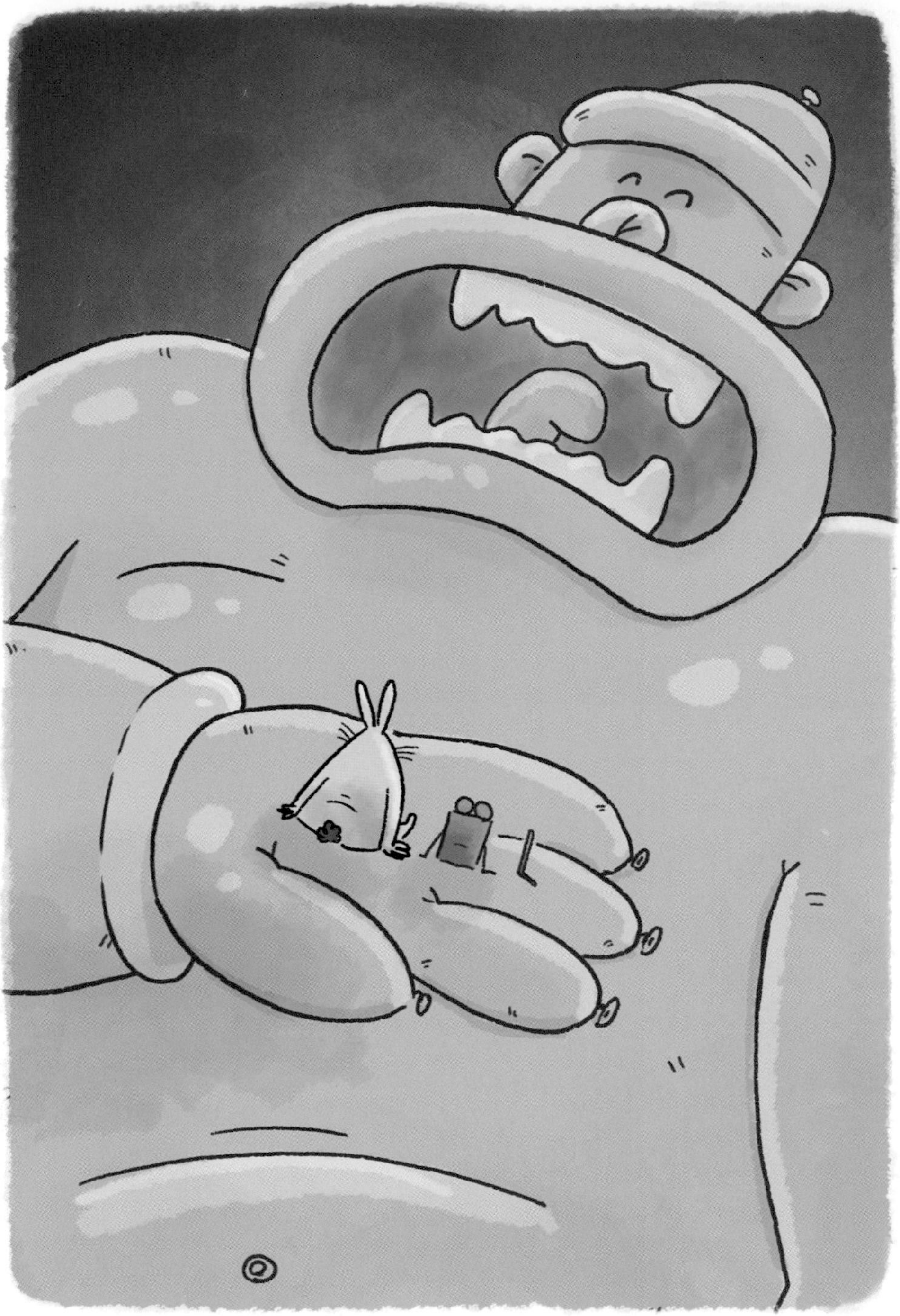

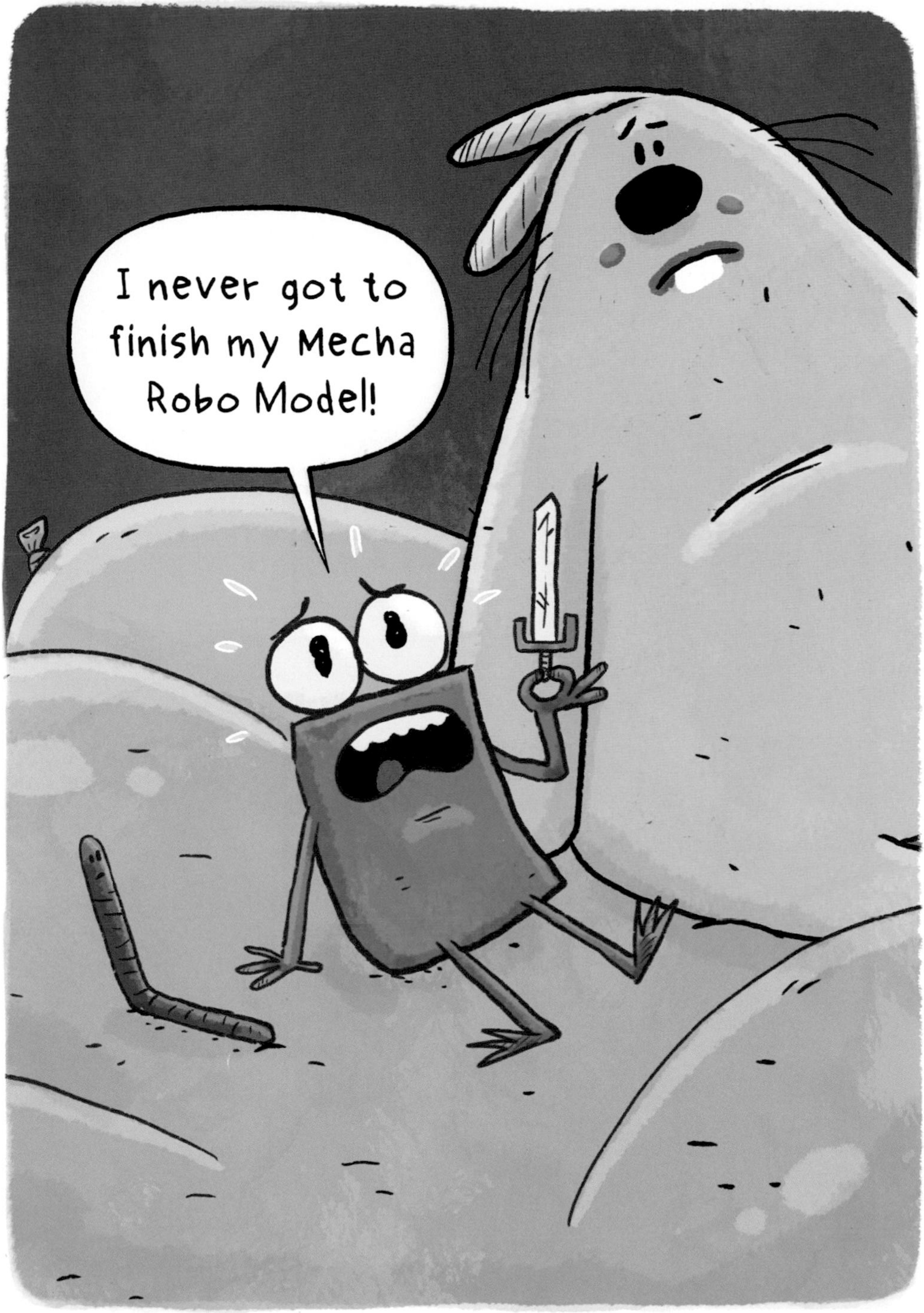
I never got to finish my Mecha Robo Model!

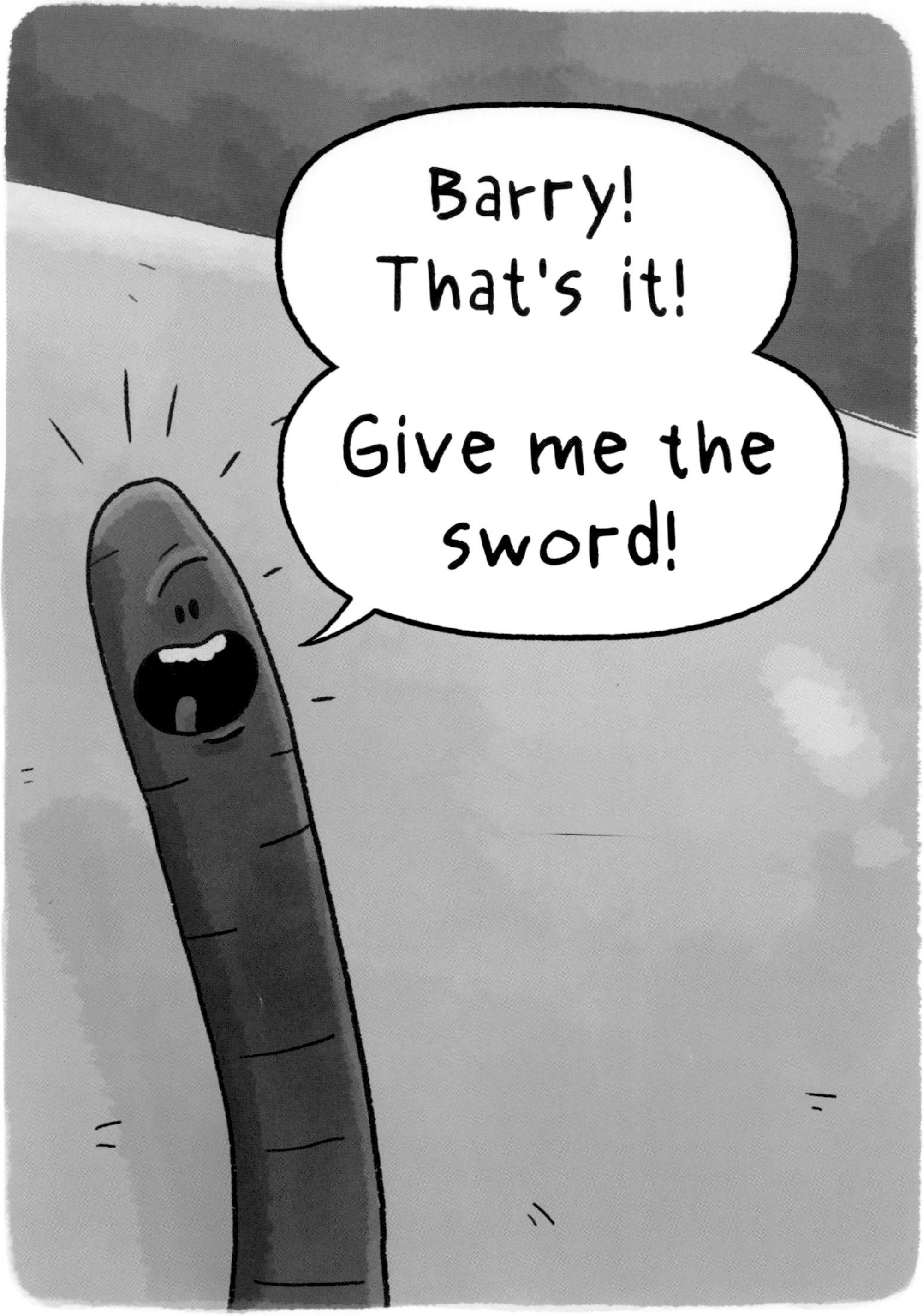
Barry! That's it!
Give me the sword!

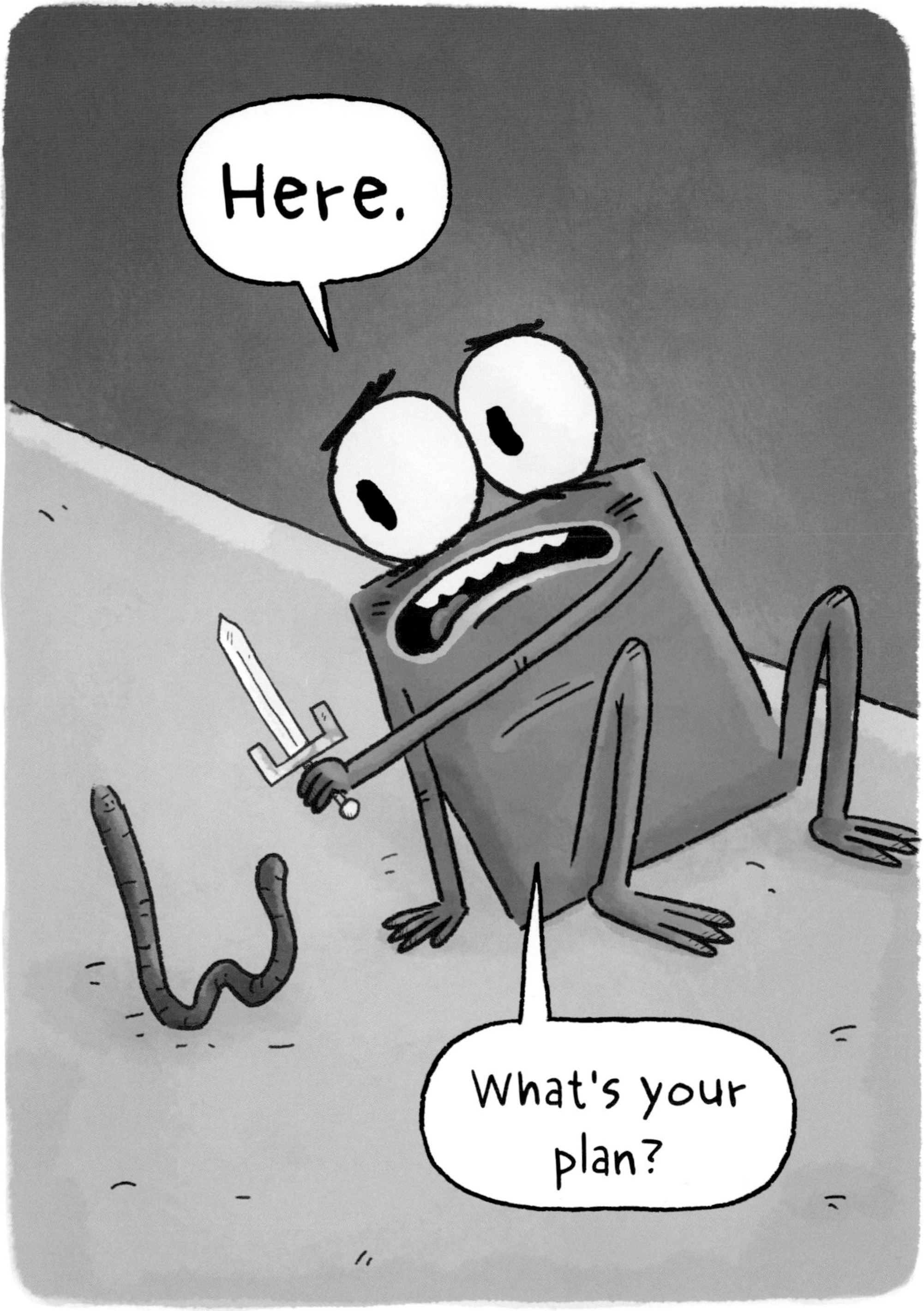
Here.
What's your plan?

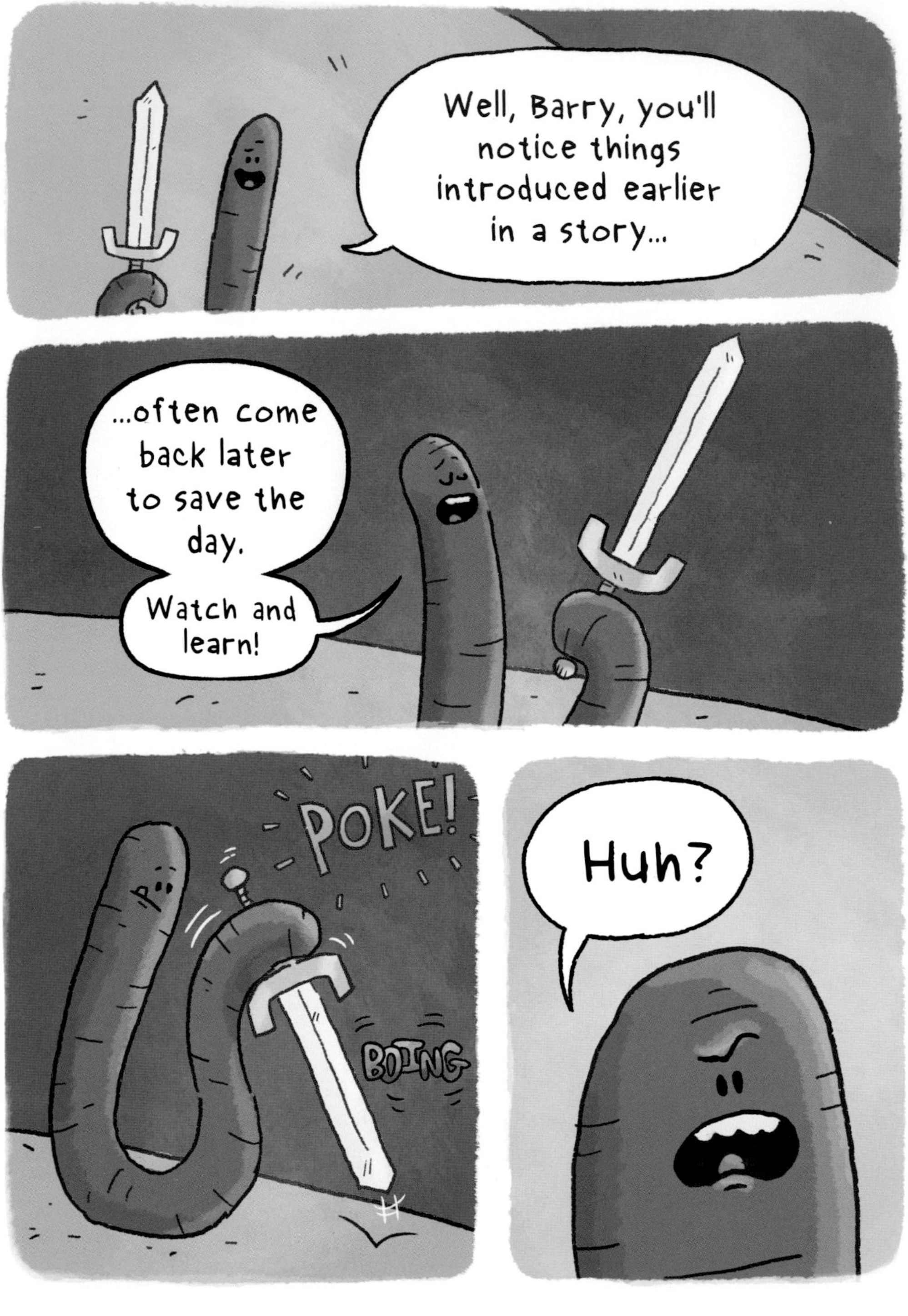

Well, Barry, you'll notice things introduced earlier in a story...
...often come back later to save the day.
Watch and learn!
POKE!
BOING
Huh?

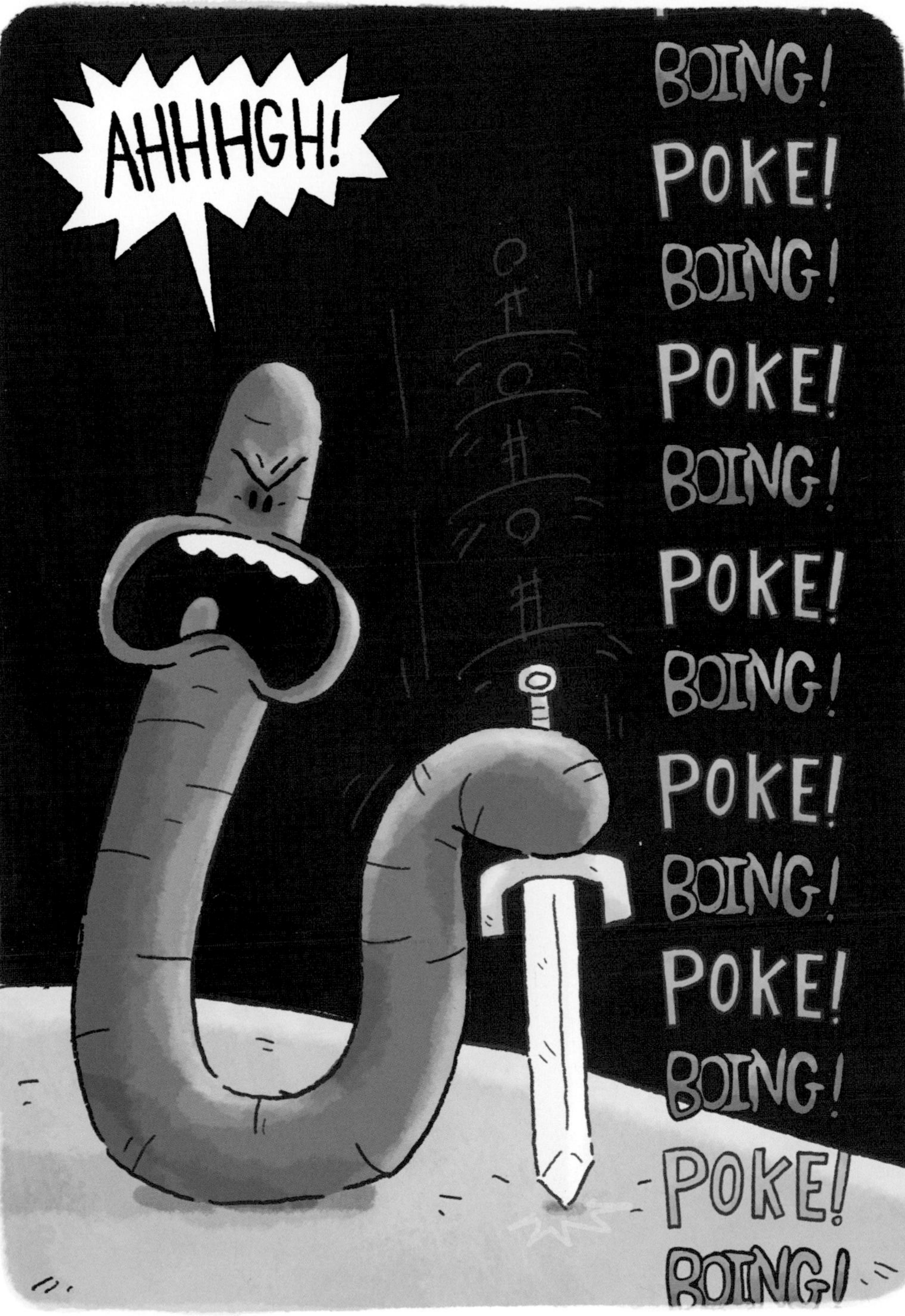
AHHHGH!
BOING!
POKE!
BOING!
POKE!
BOING!
POKE!
BOING!
POKE!
BOING!
POKE!
BOING!
POKE!
BOING!

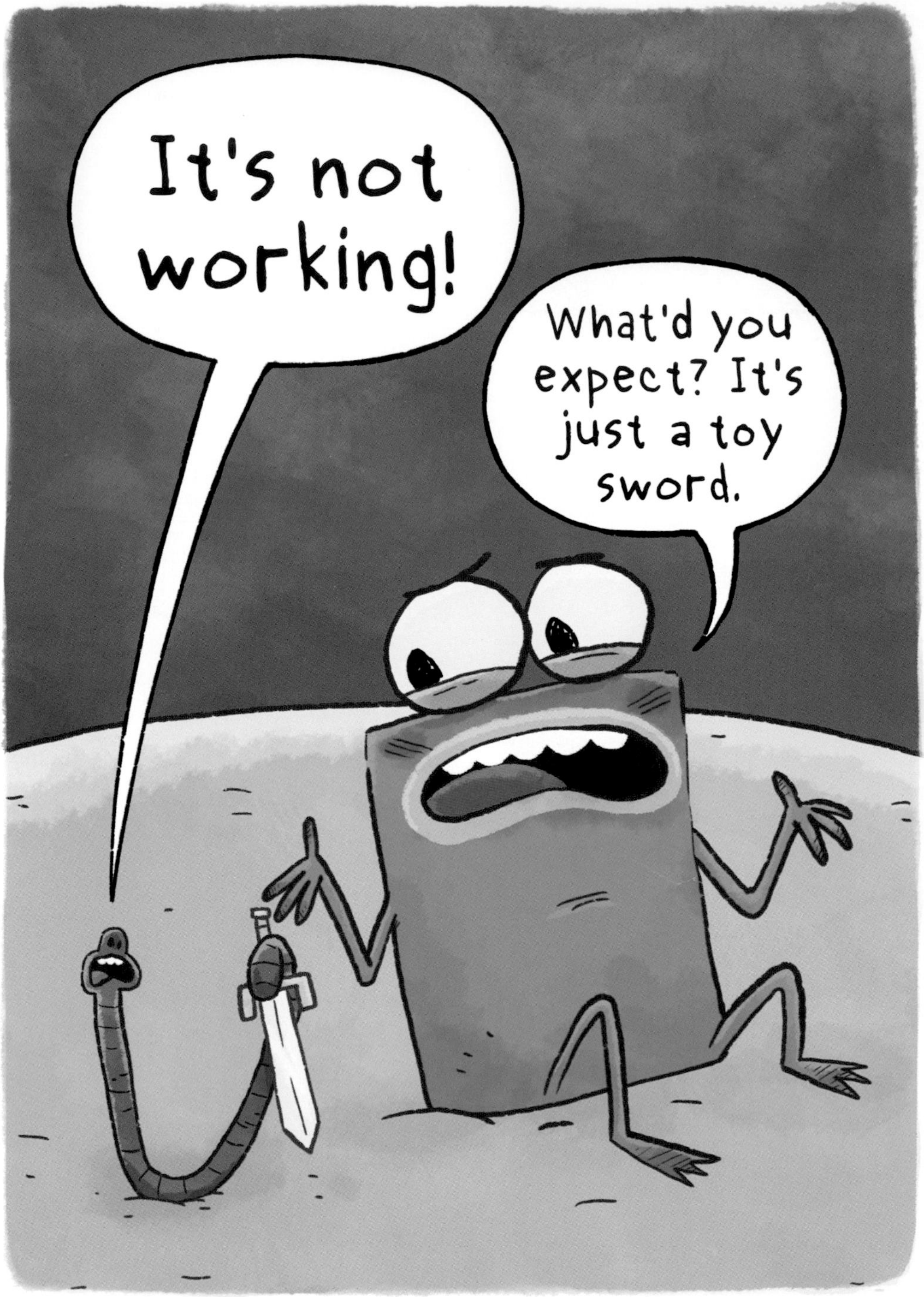
It's not working!
What'd you expect? It's just a toy sword.

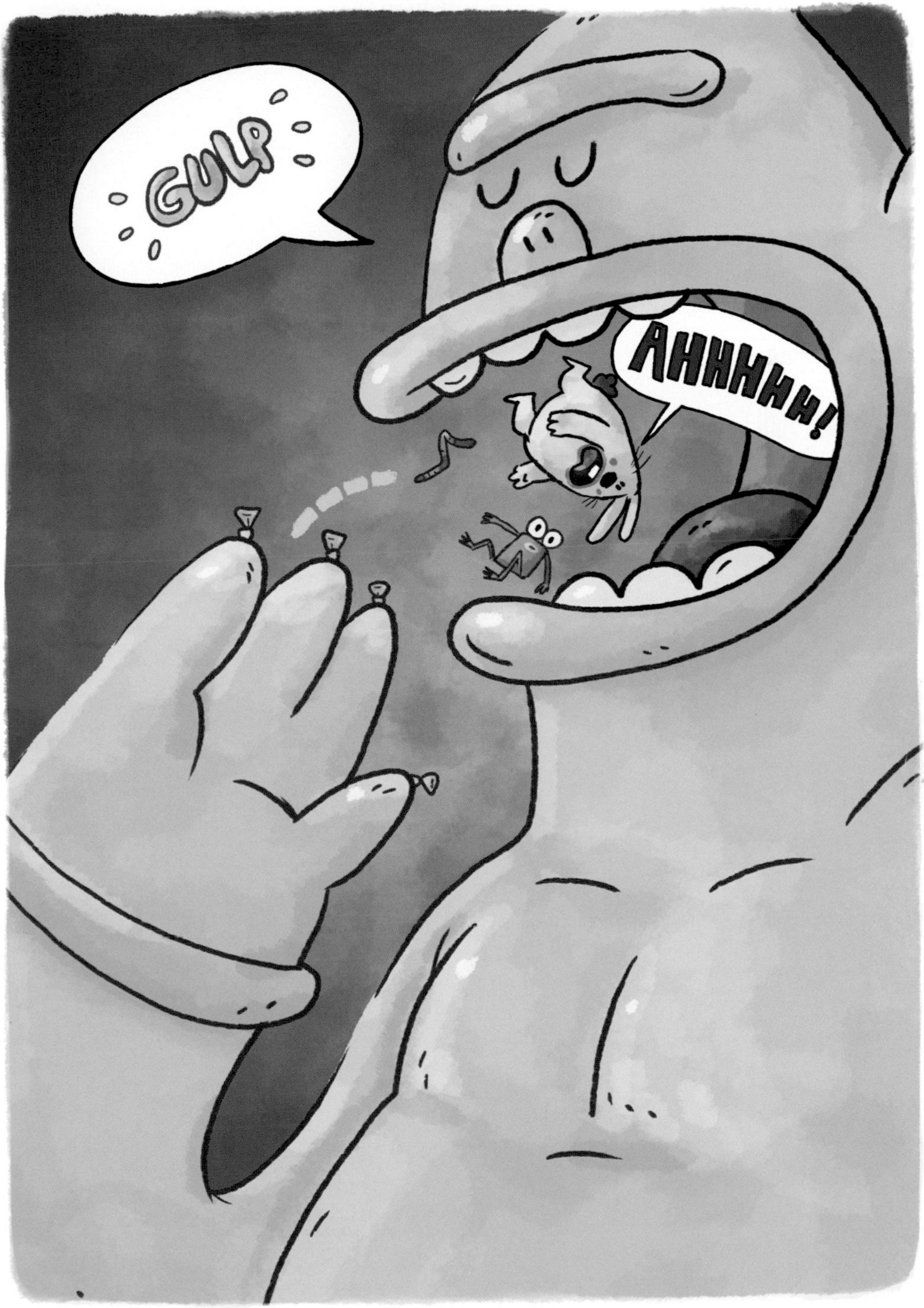
GULP
AHHHHHH!

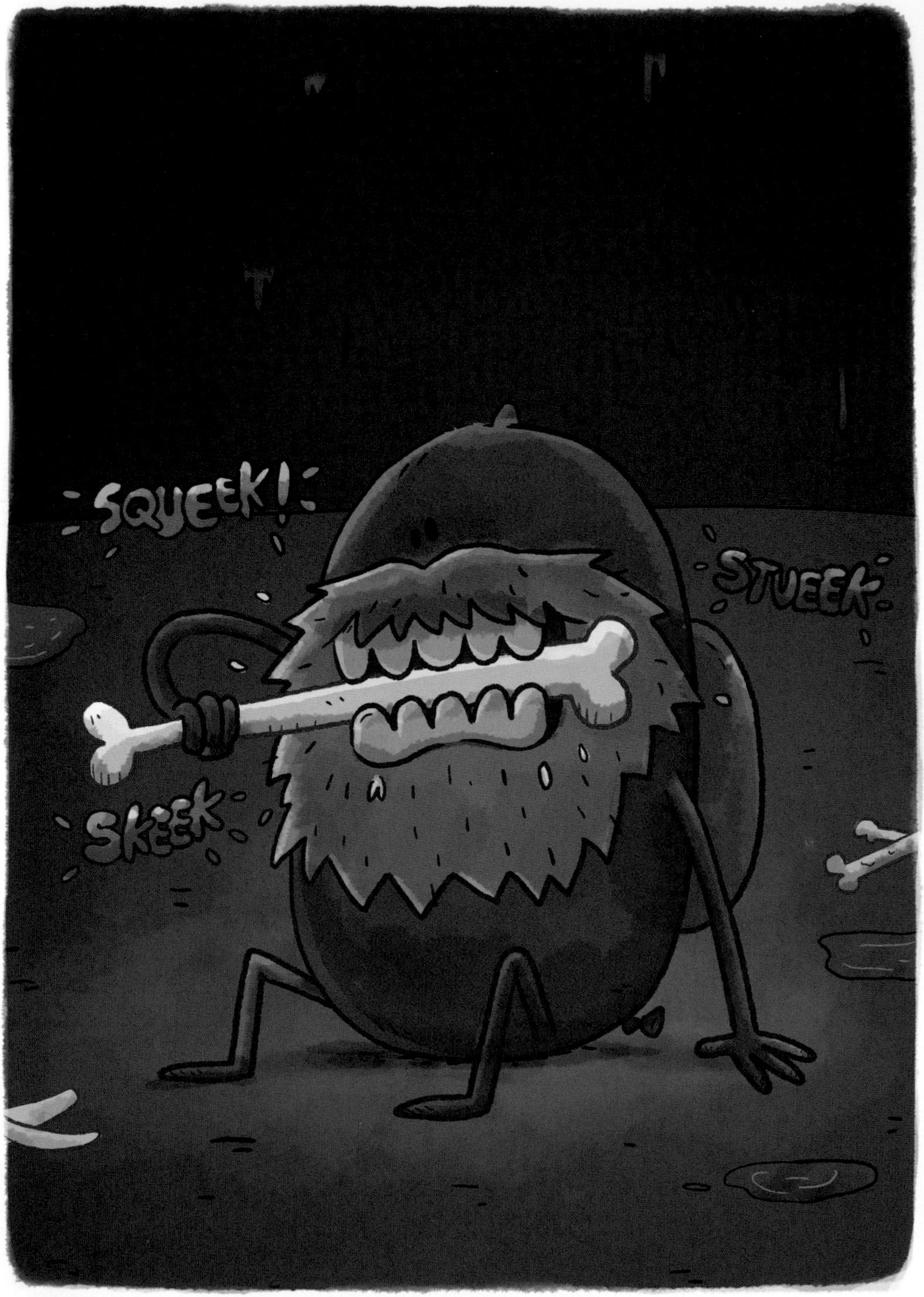
SQUEEK!
STUEEK
SKEEK

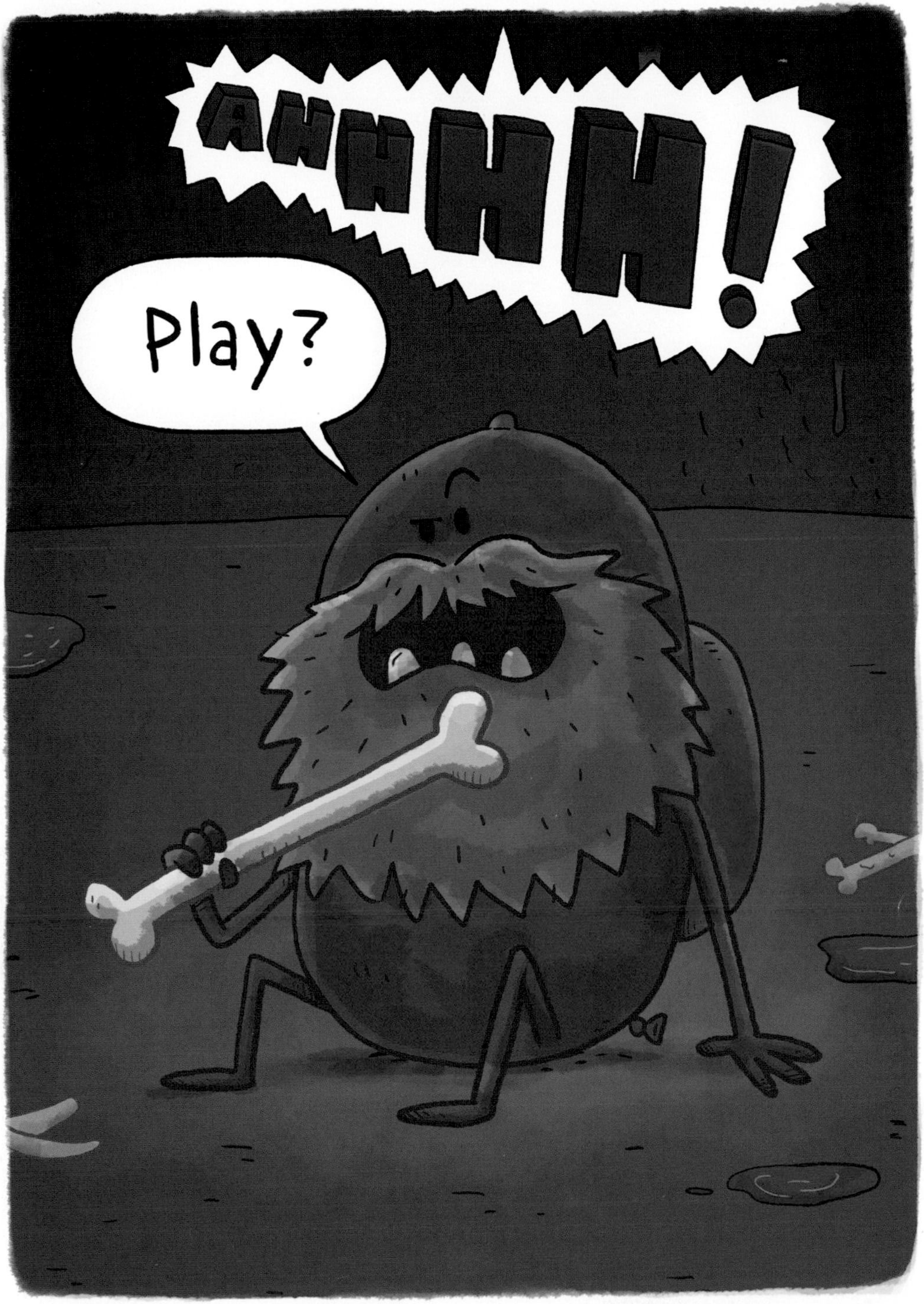
AHHHHH!
Play?

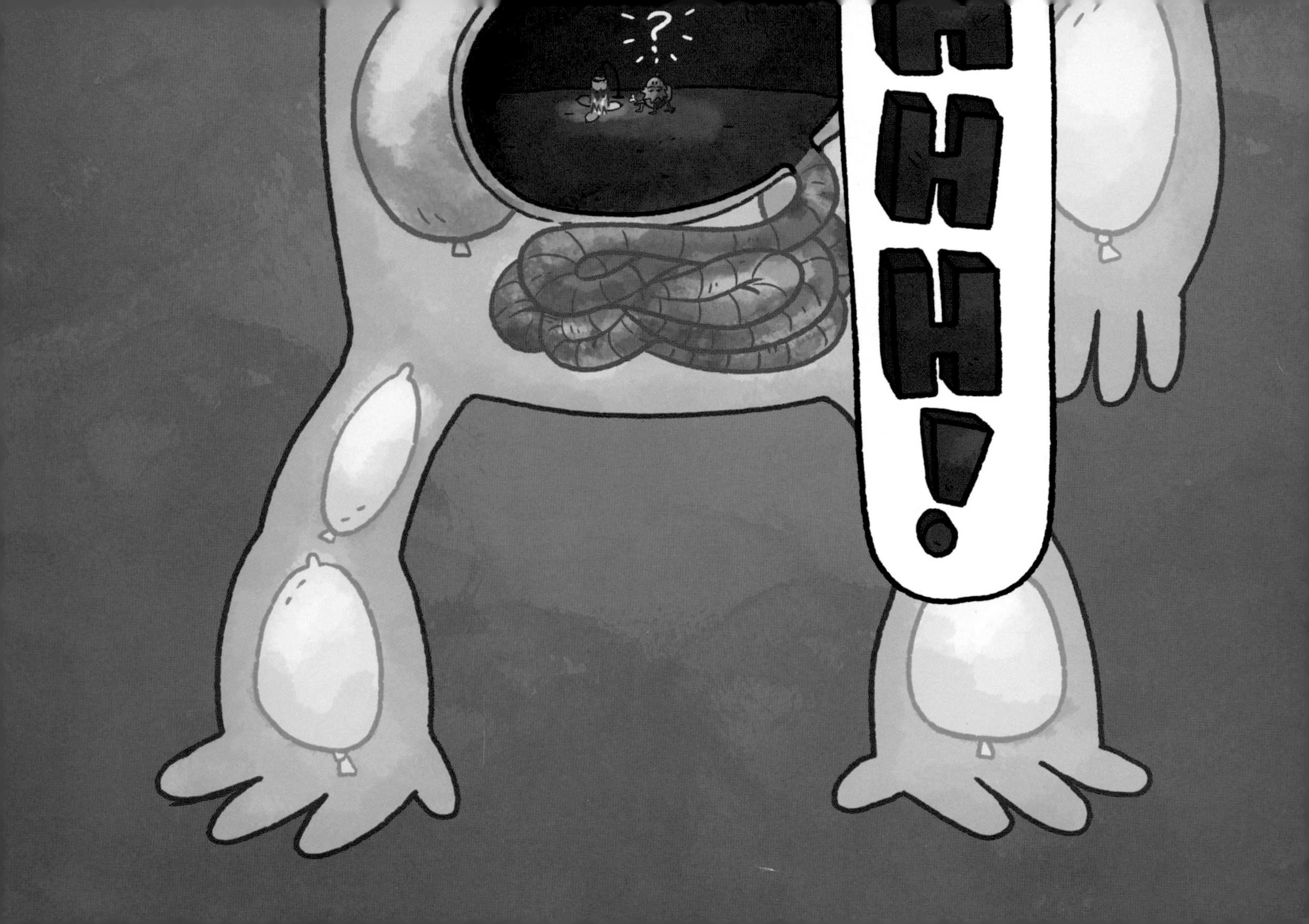
?
HHH!

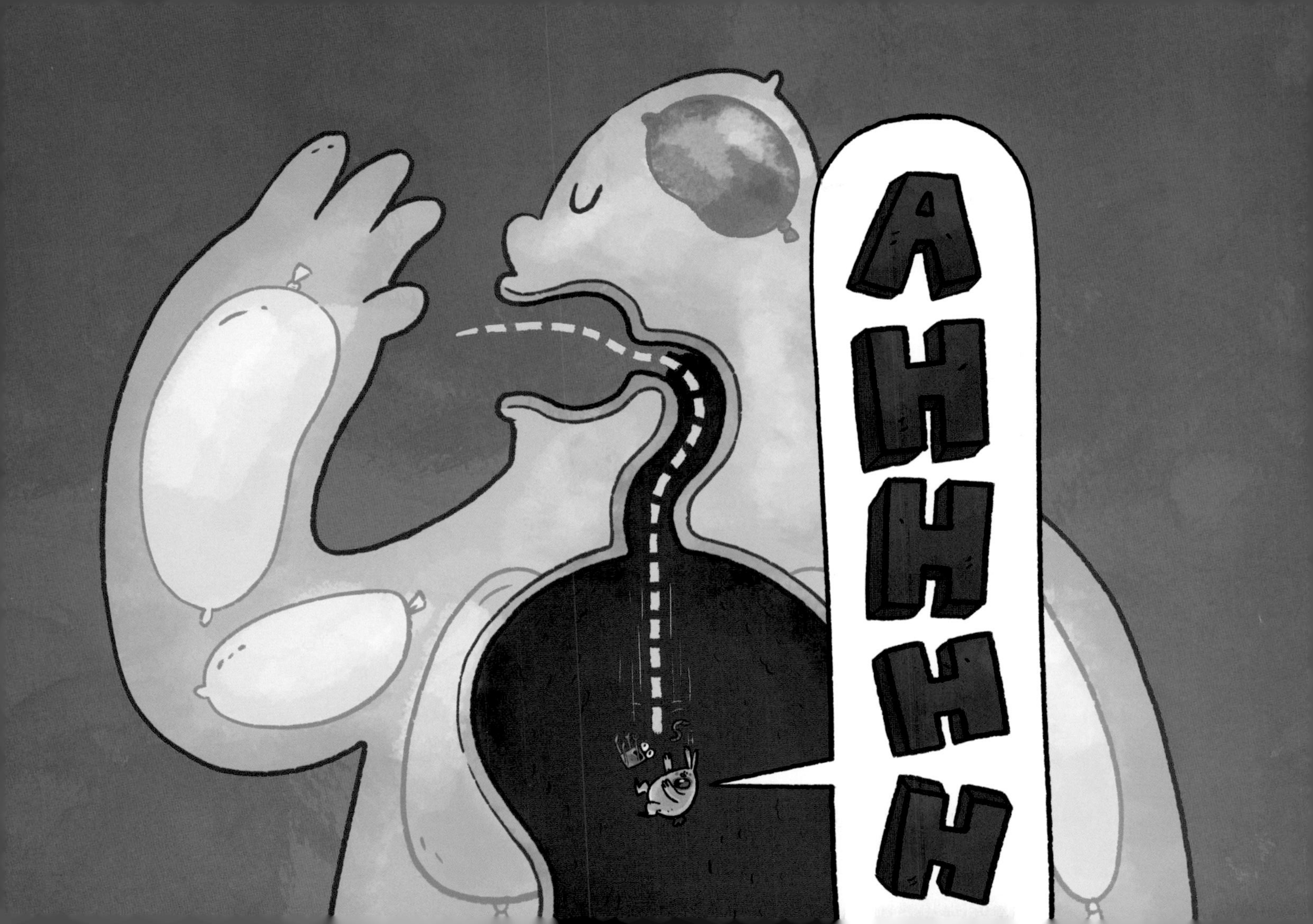
AHHHHH

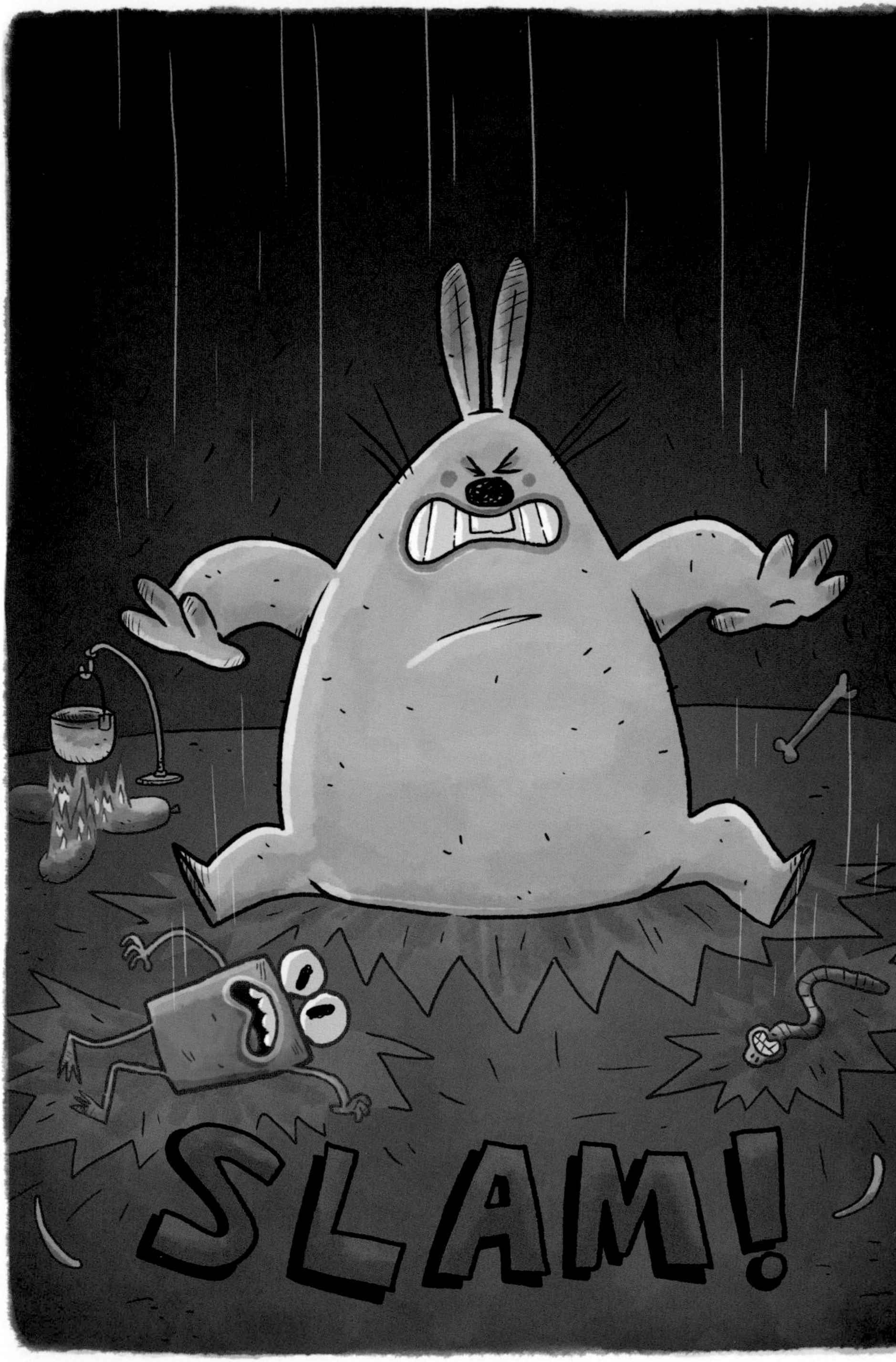
SLAM!

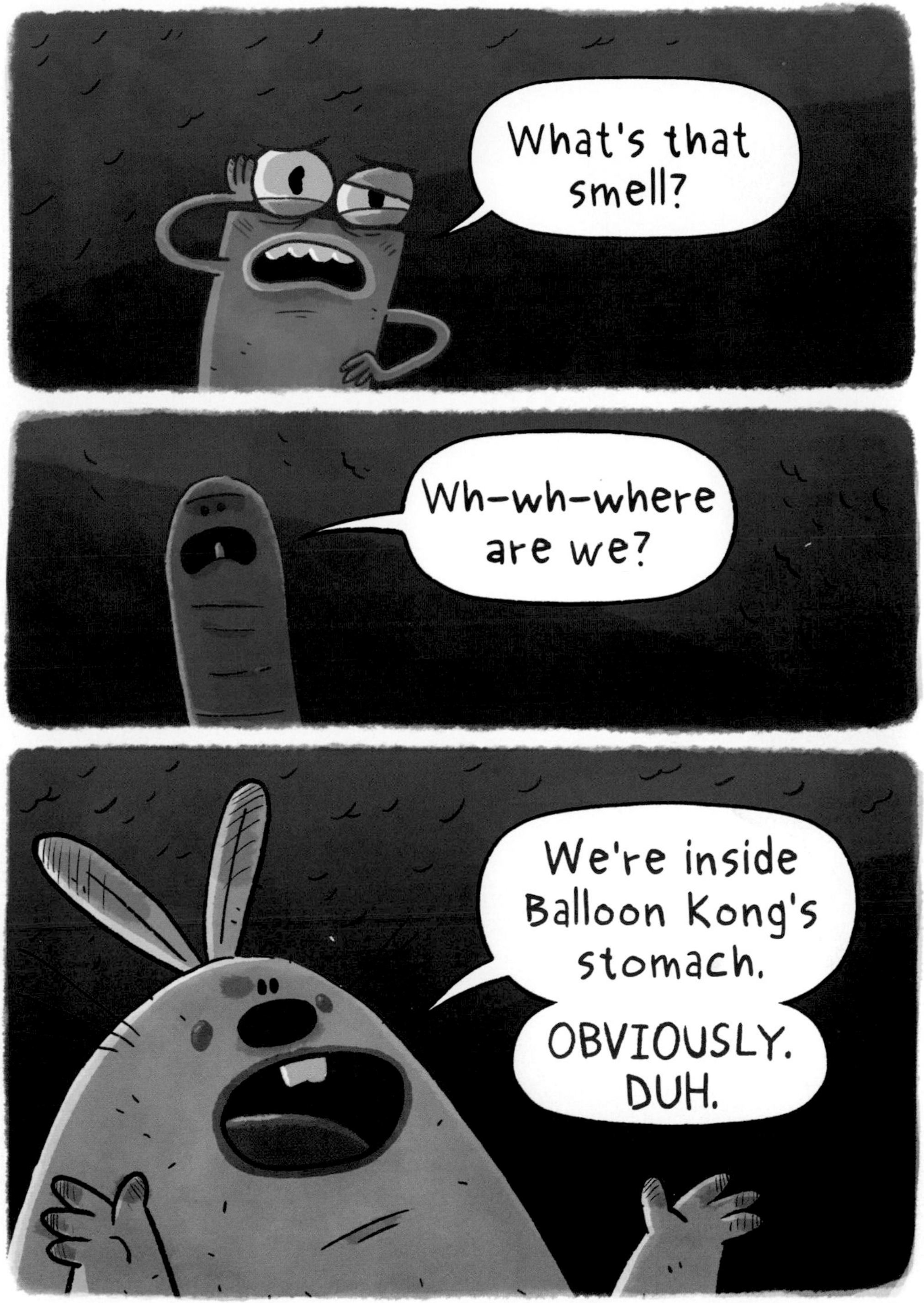
What's that smell?
Wh-wh-where are we?
We're inside Balloon Kong's stomach.
OBVIOUSLY. DUH.

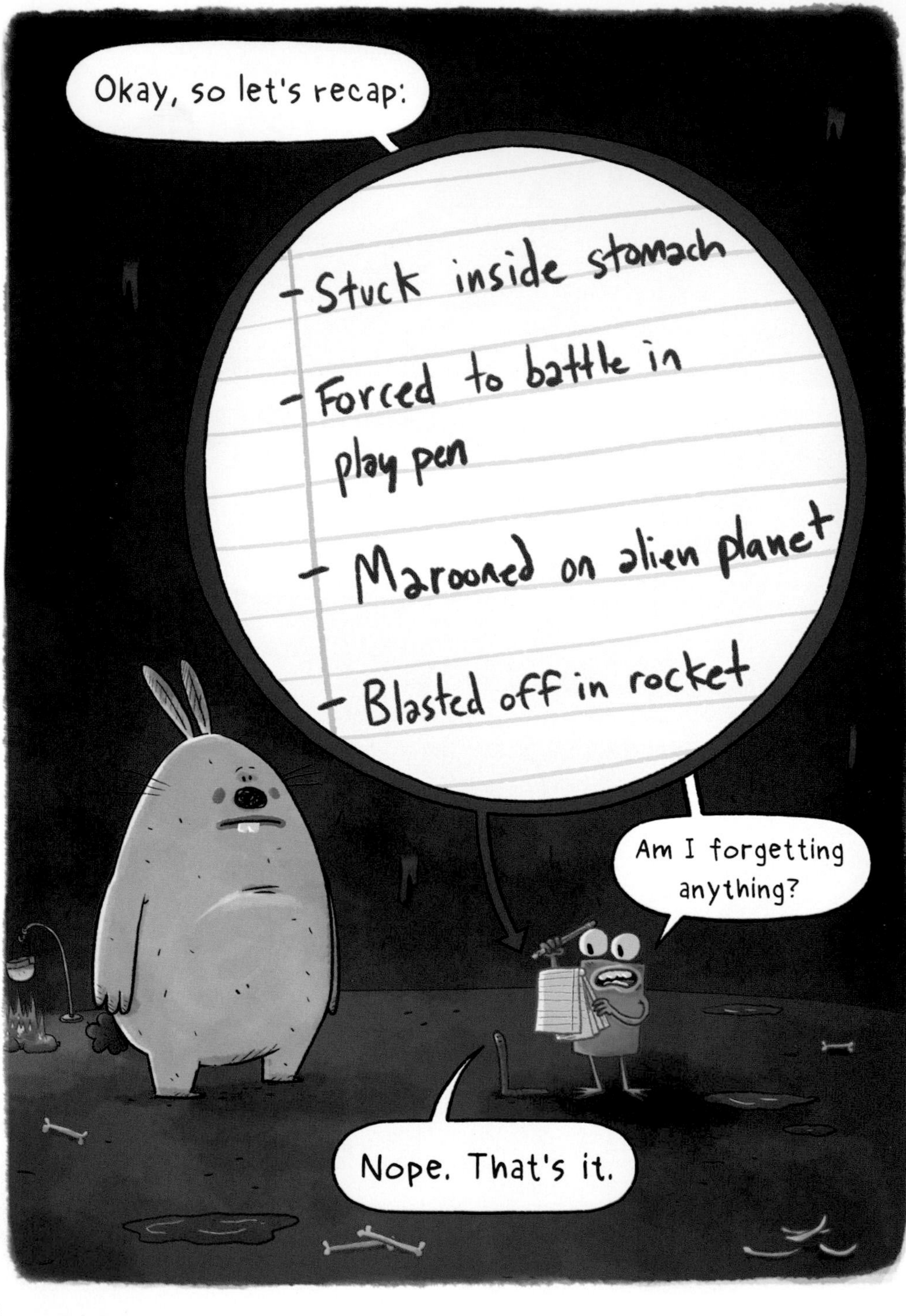
Okay, so let's recap:
- Stuck inside stomach
- Forced to battle in play pen
- Marooned on alien planet
- Blasted off in rocket
Am I forgetting anything?
Nope. That's it.

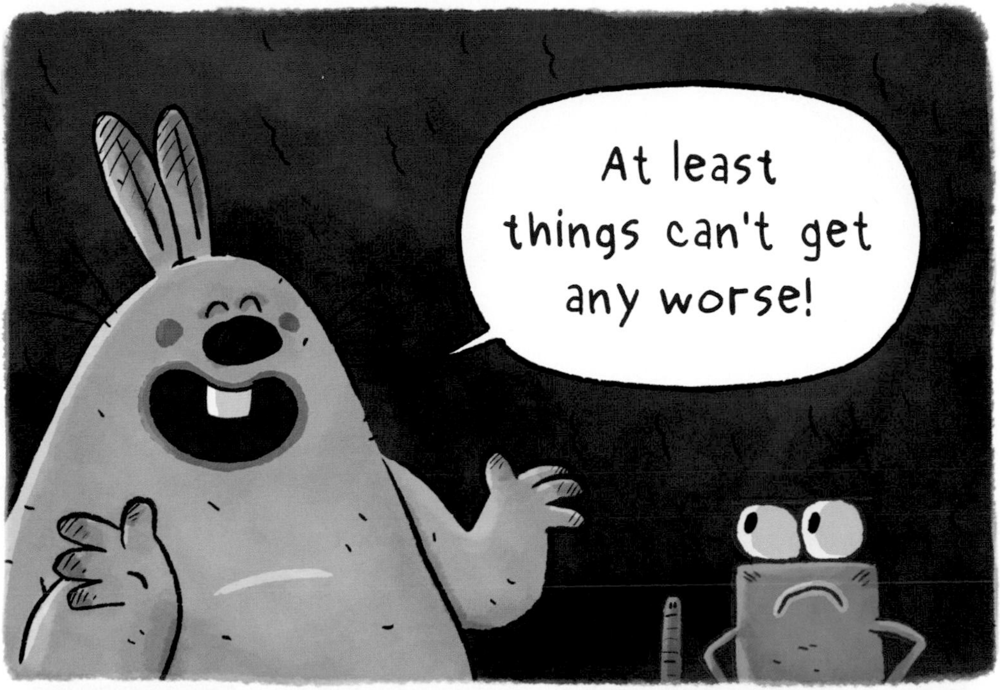
At least things can't get any worse!

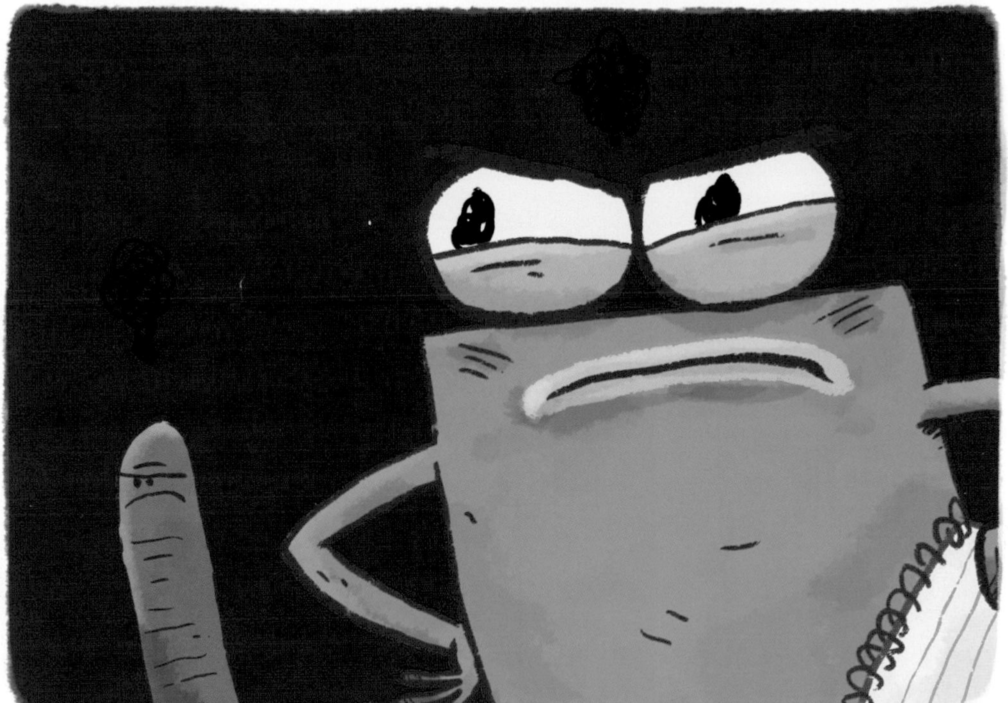

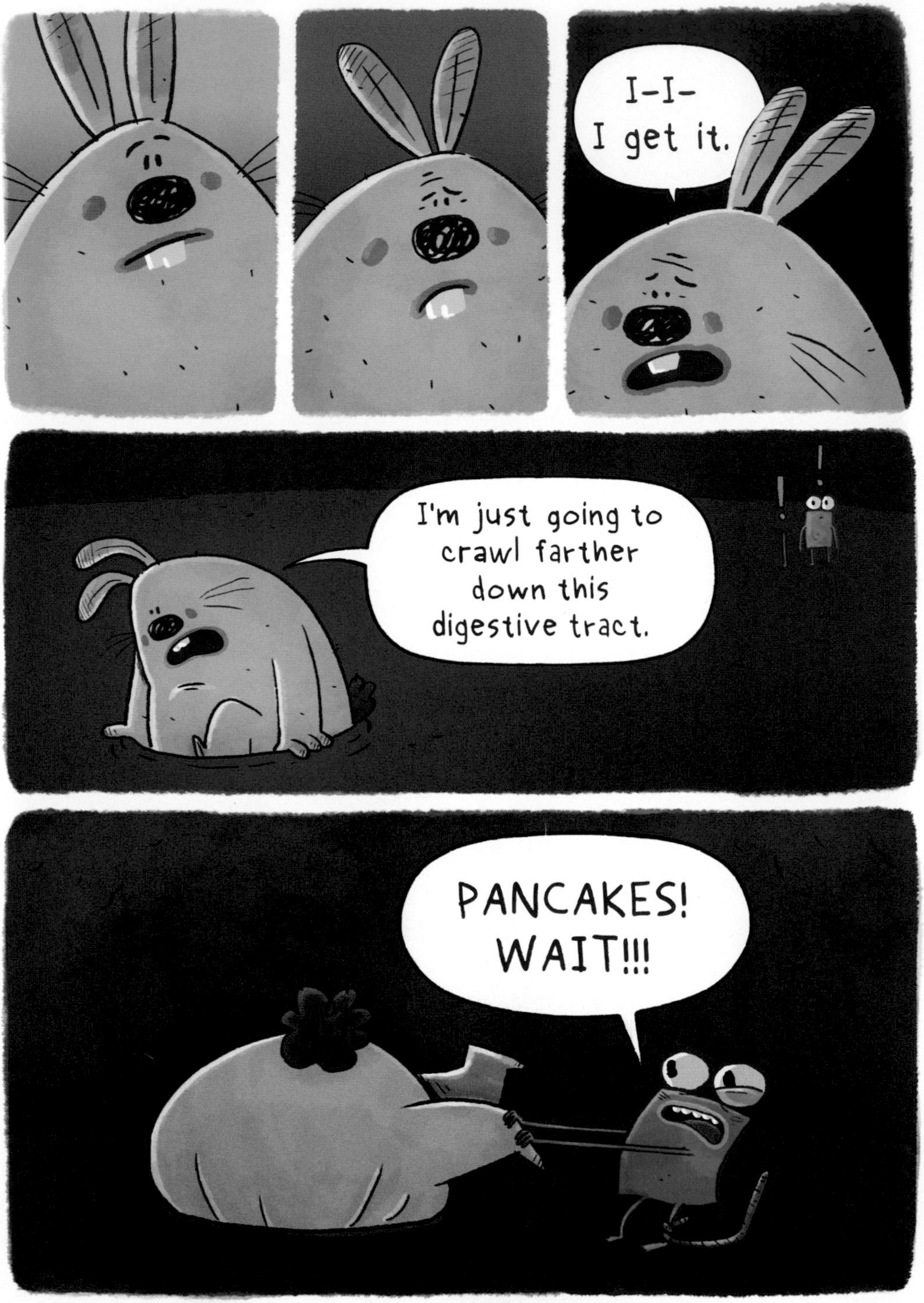
I-I-
I get it.
I'm just going to crawl farther down this digestive tract.
!
!
!
PANCAKES! WAIT!!!

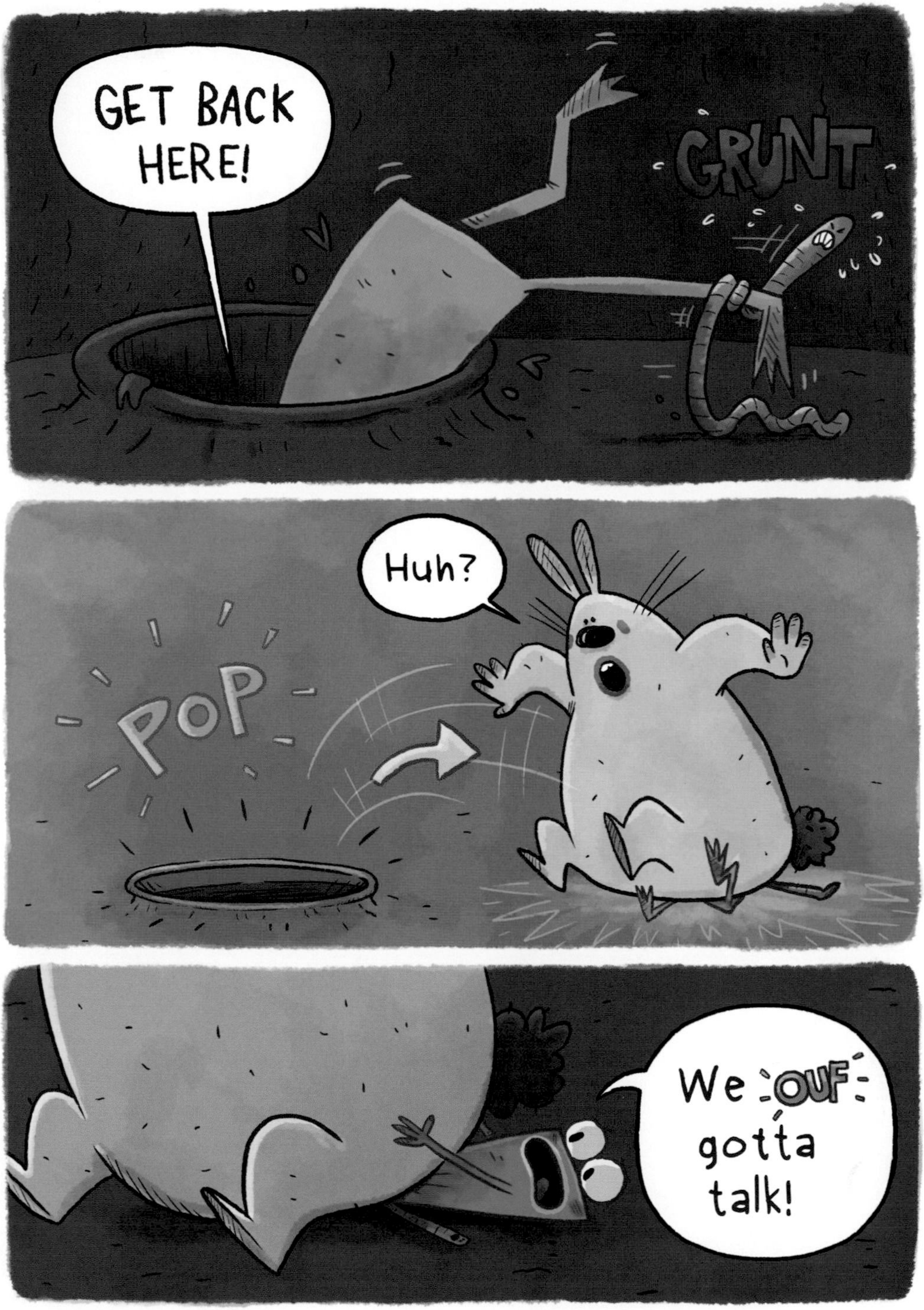
GET BACK HERE!
GRUNT
Huh?
POP
We OUF gotta talk!

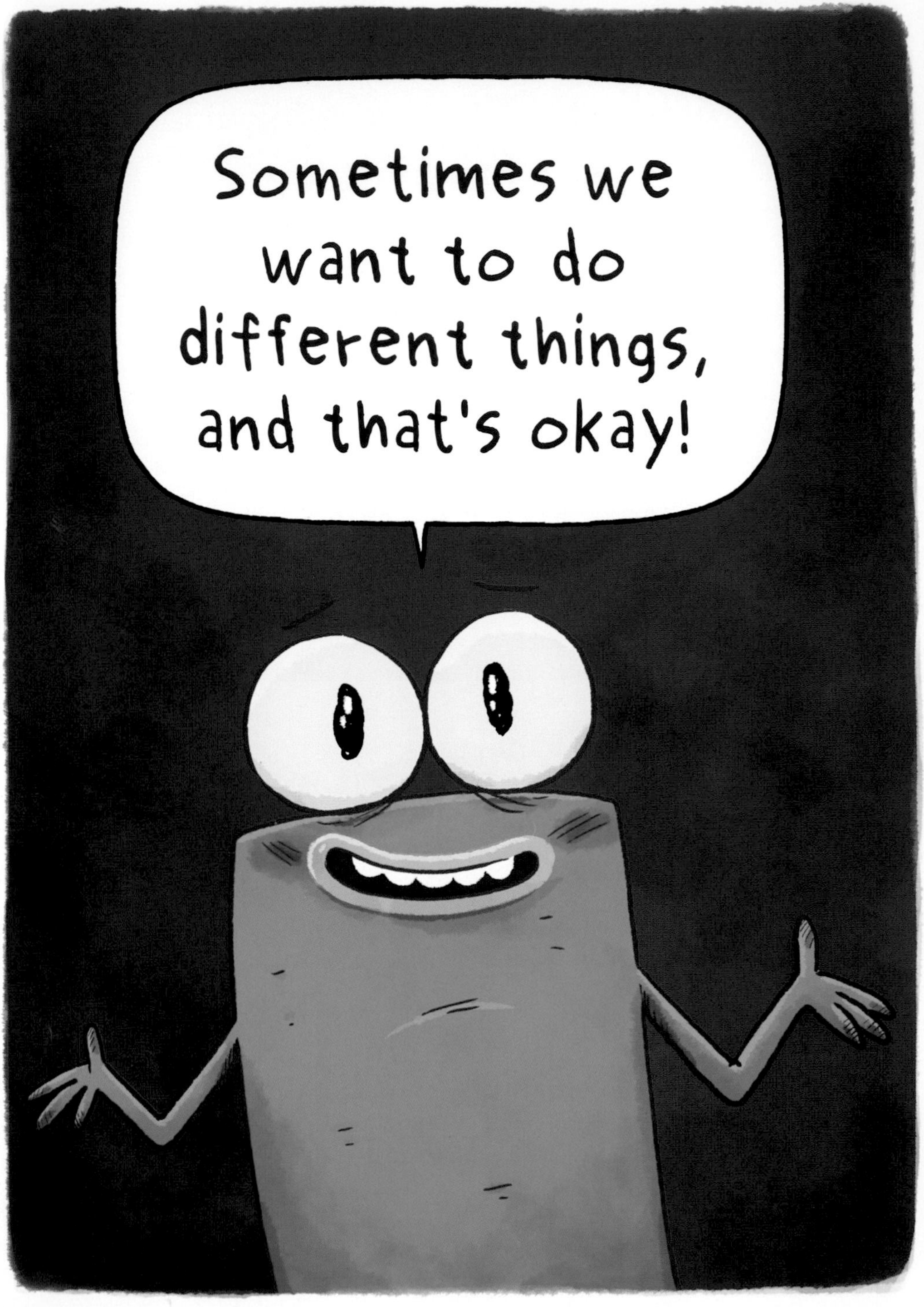
Sometimes we want to do different things, and that's okay!

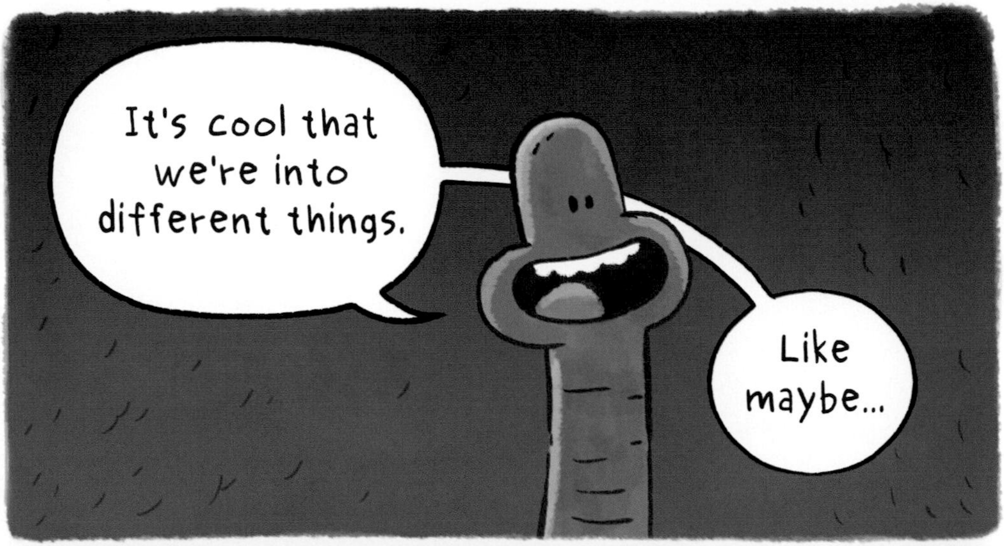
It's cool that we're into different things.
Like maybe...

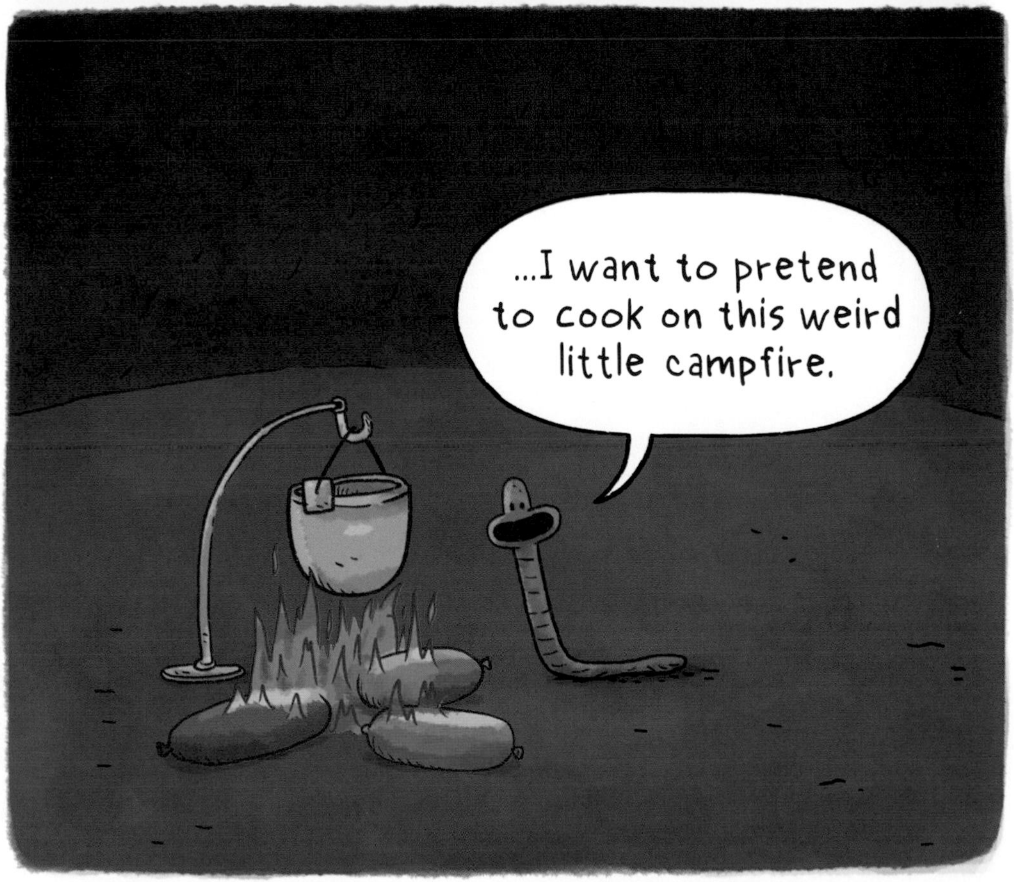
...I want to pretend to cook on this weird little campfire.

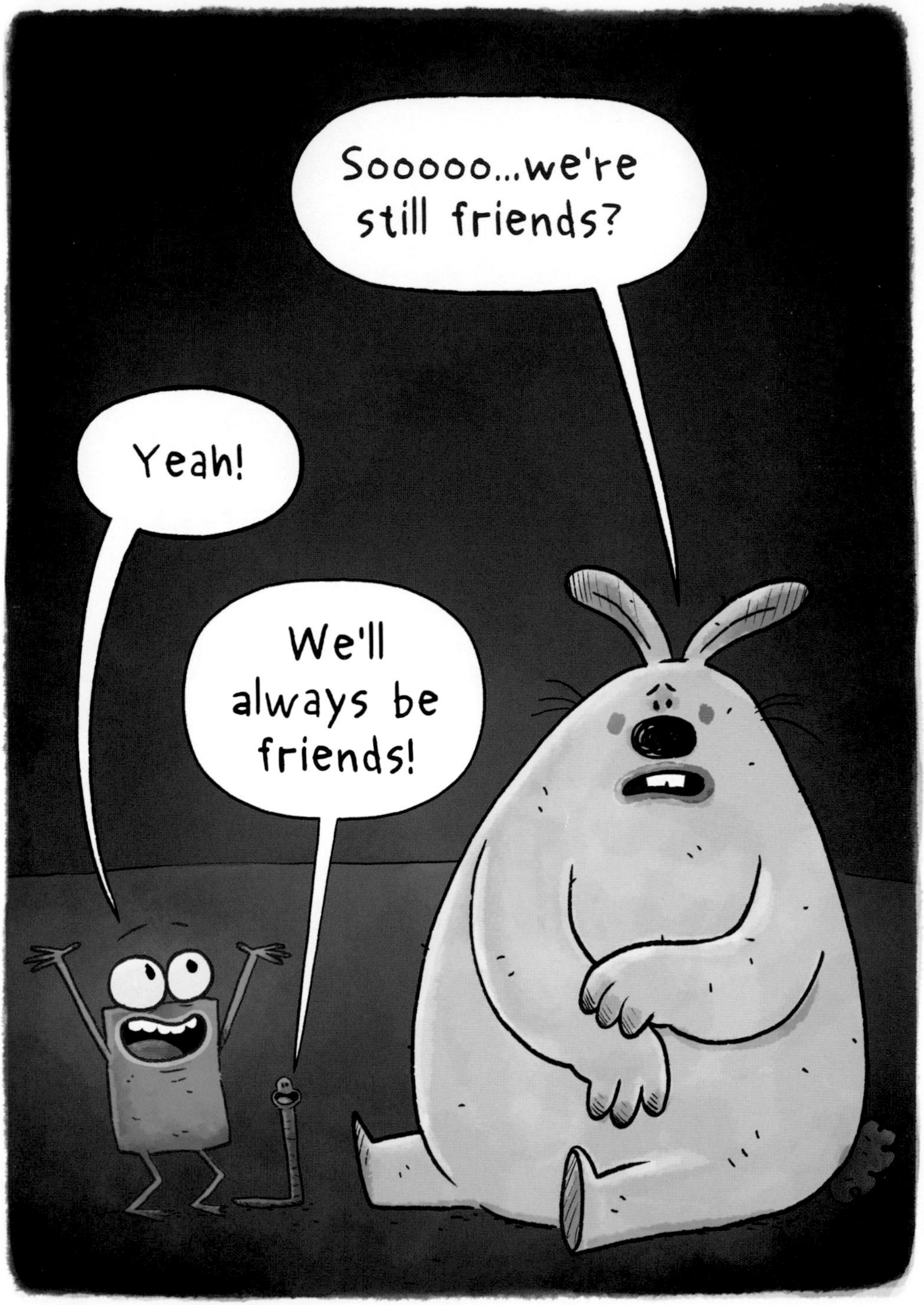
Sooooo...we're still friends?
Yeah!
We'll always be friends!

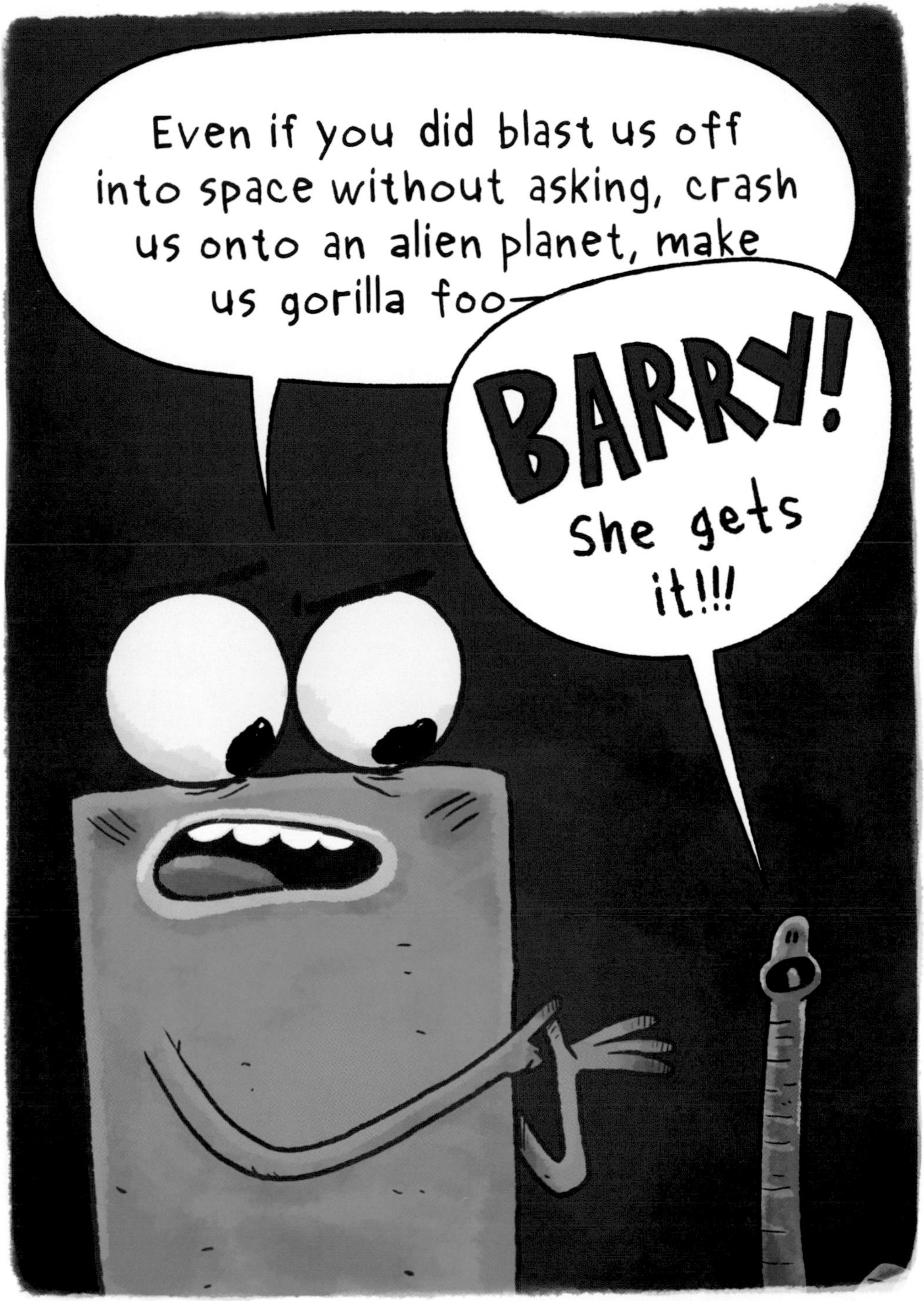
Even if you did blast us off into space without asking, crash us onto an alien planet, make us gorilla foo—
BARRY! She gets it!!!

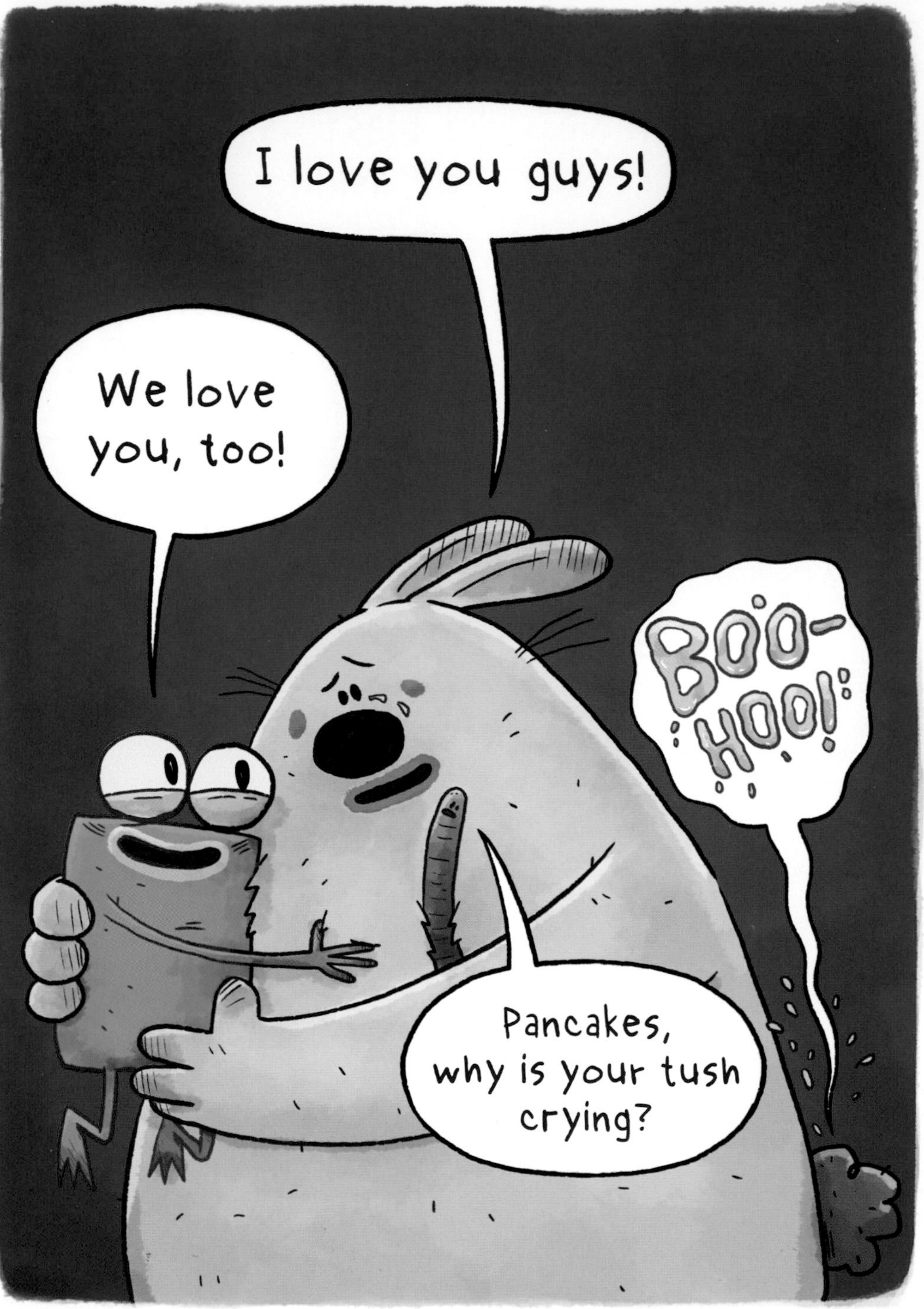
I love you guys!
We love you, too!
BOO-HOO!
Pancakes, why is your tush crying?

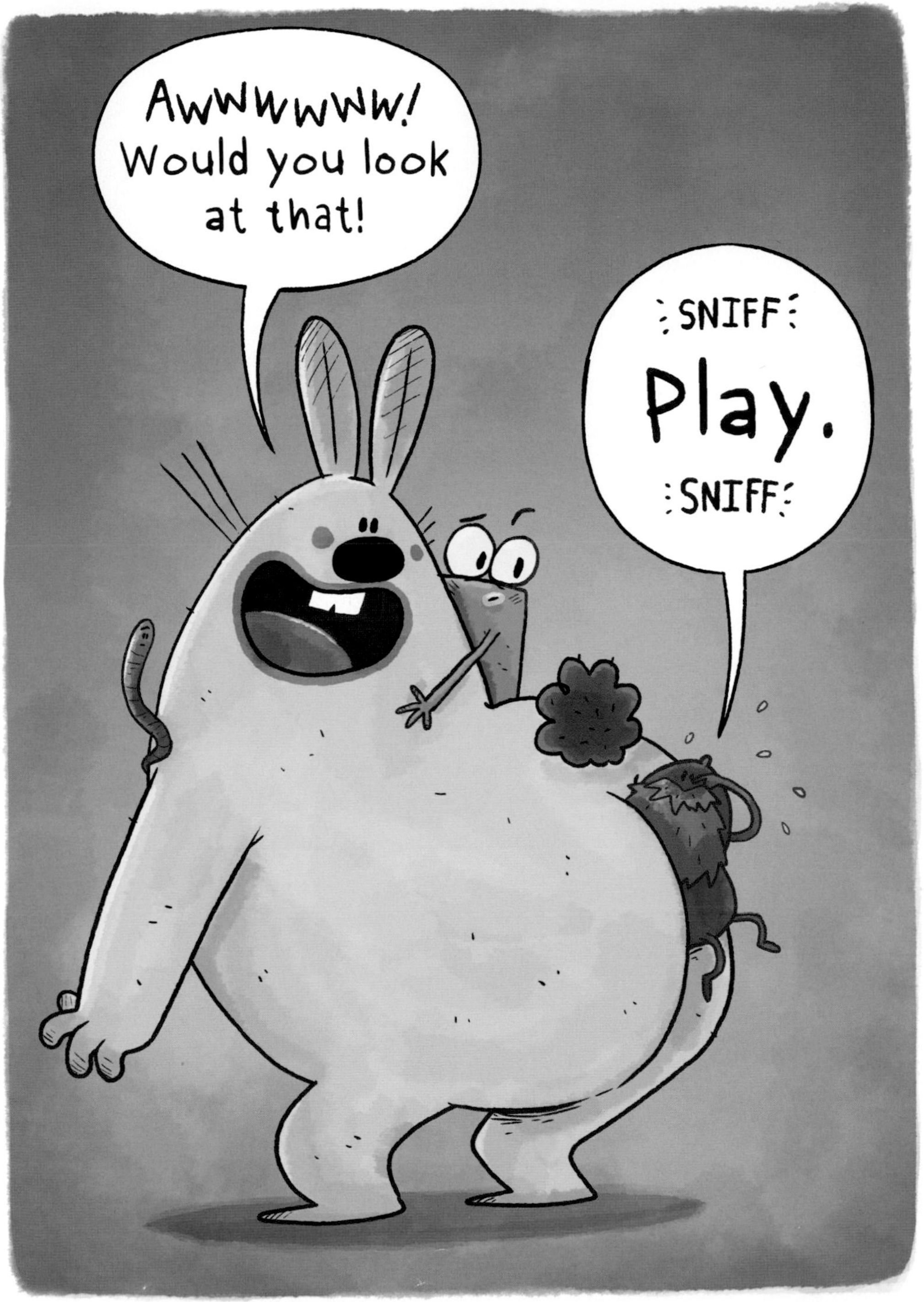
AWWWWWW! Would you look at that!
SNIFF
Play.
SNIFF

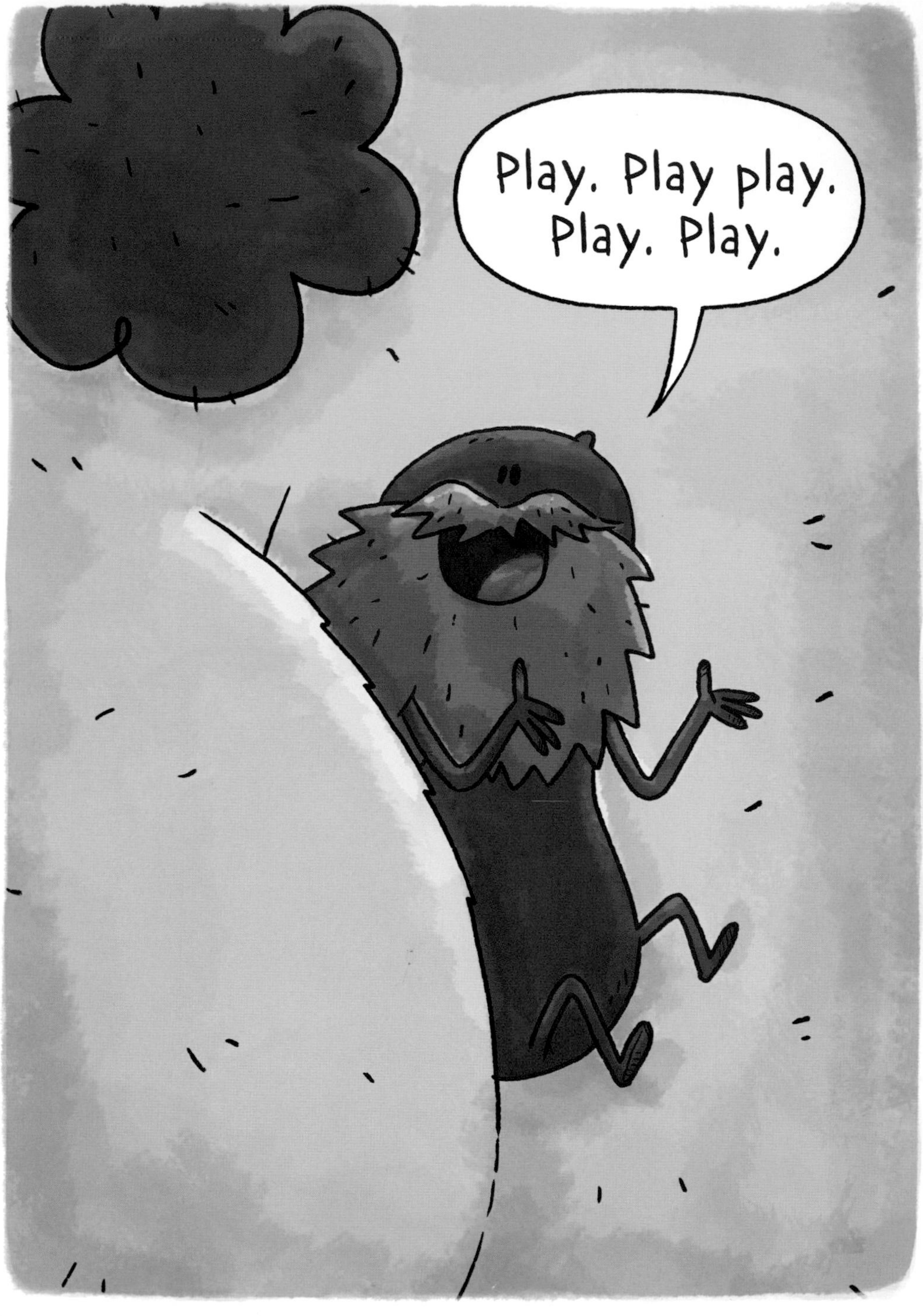
Play. Play play. Play. Play.

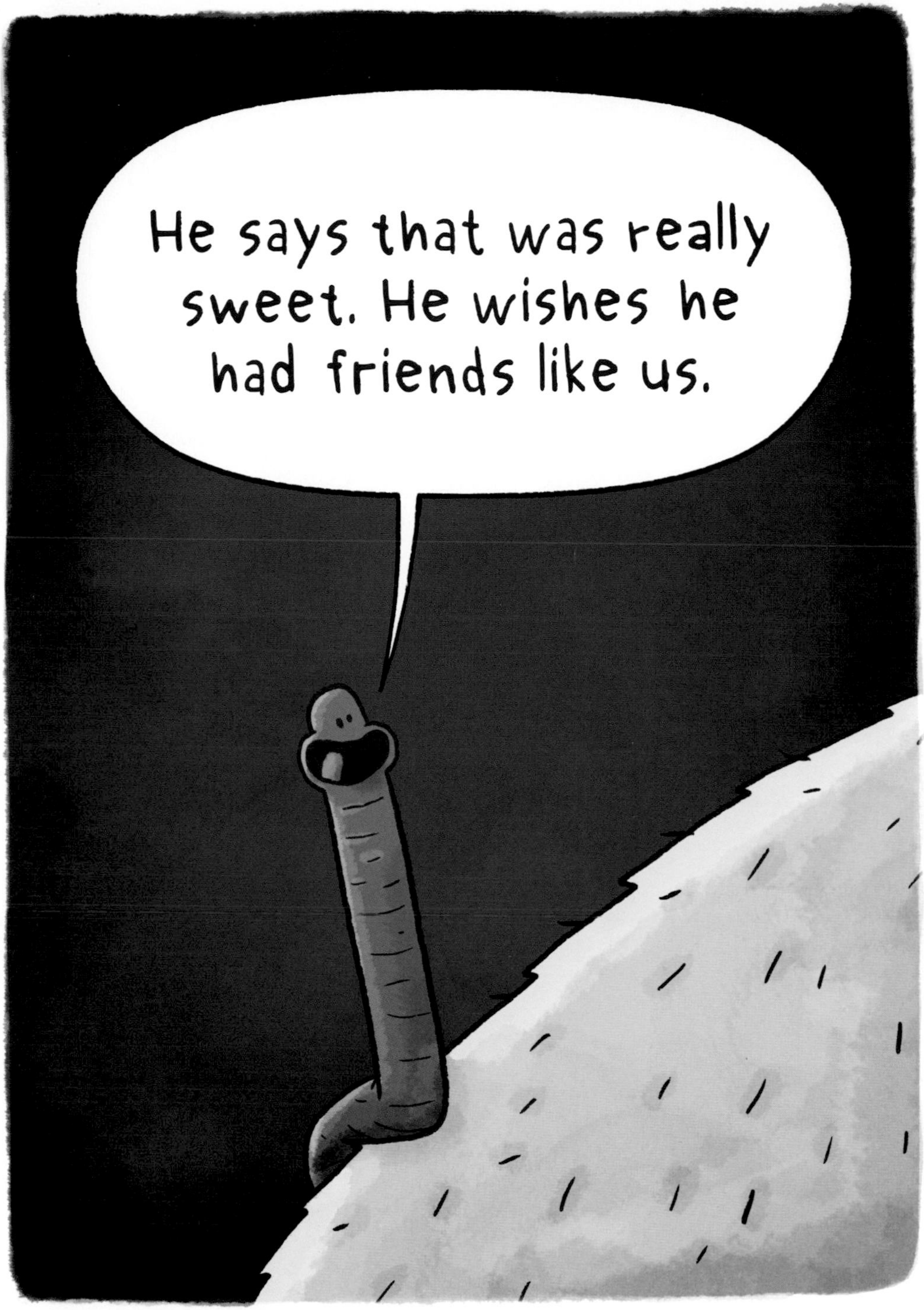
He says that was really sweet. He wishes he had friends like us.

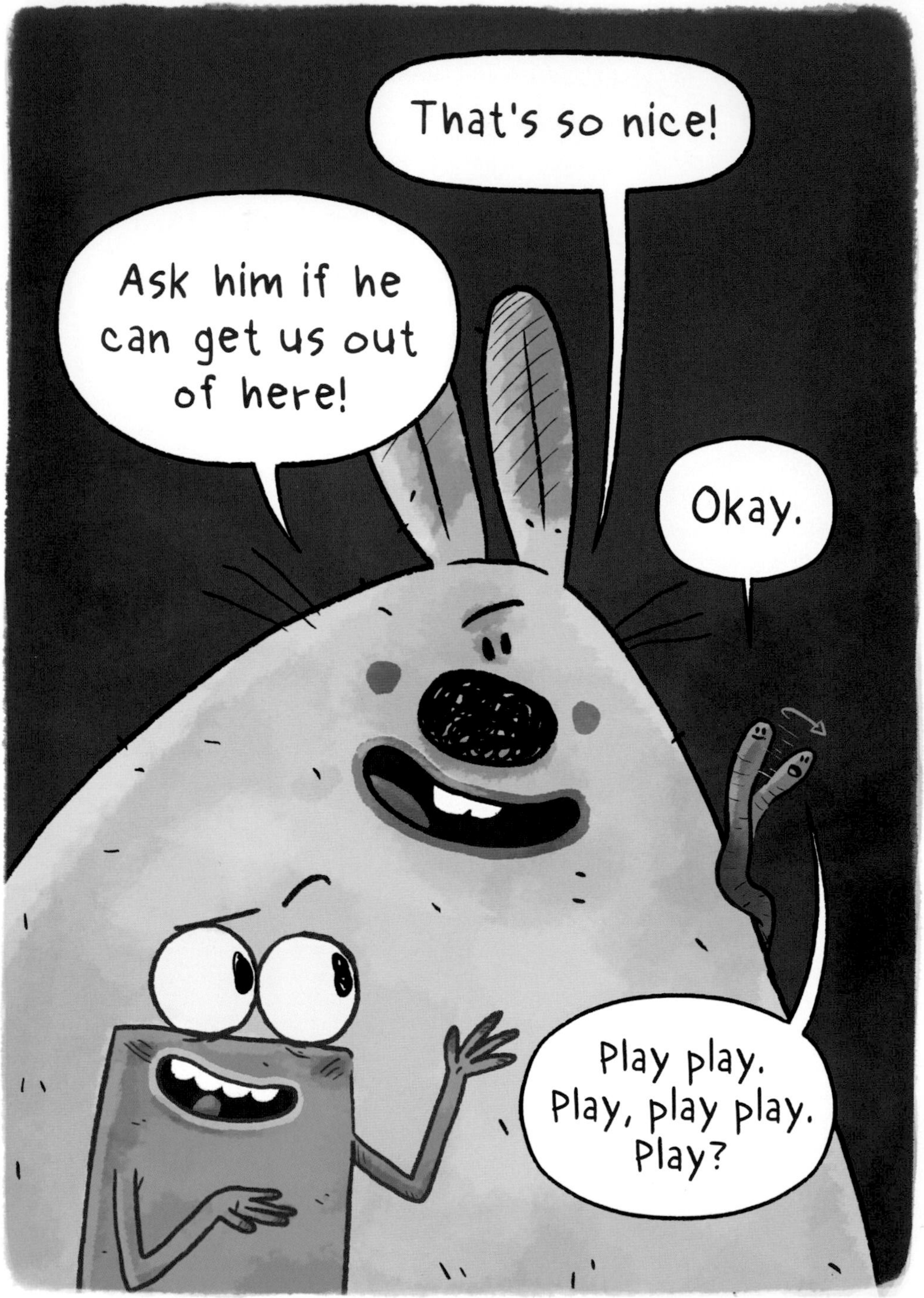
That's so nice!
Ask him if he can get us out of here!
Okay.
Play play. Play, play play. Play?

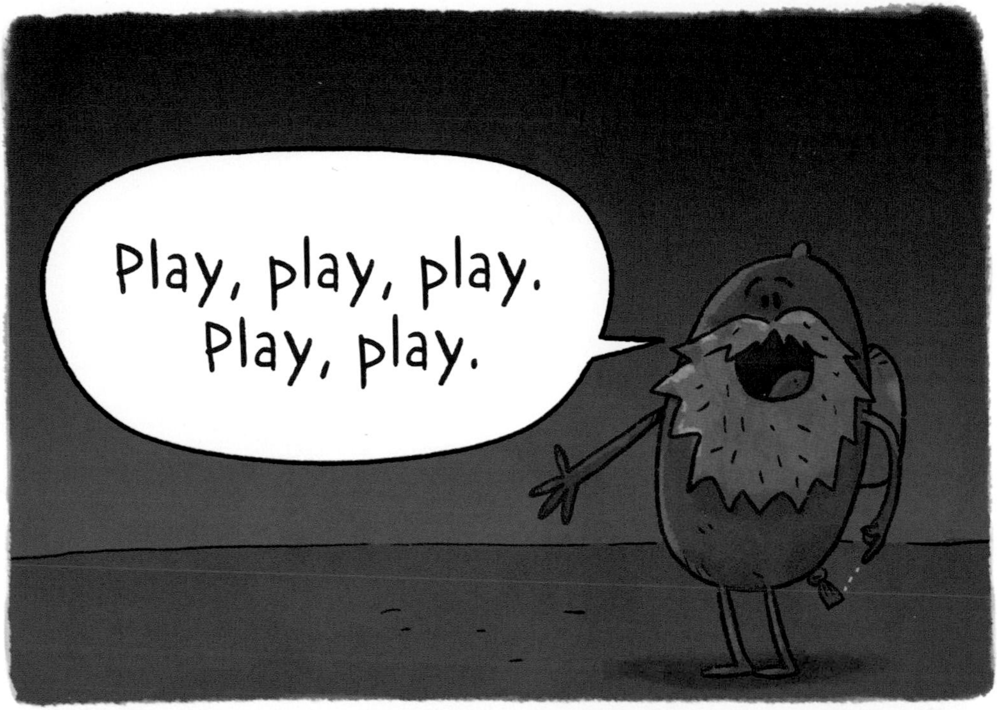
Play, play, play.
Play, play.

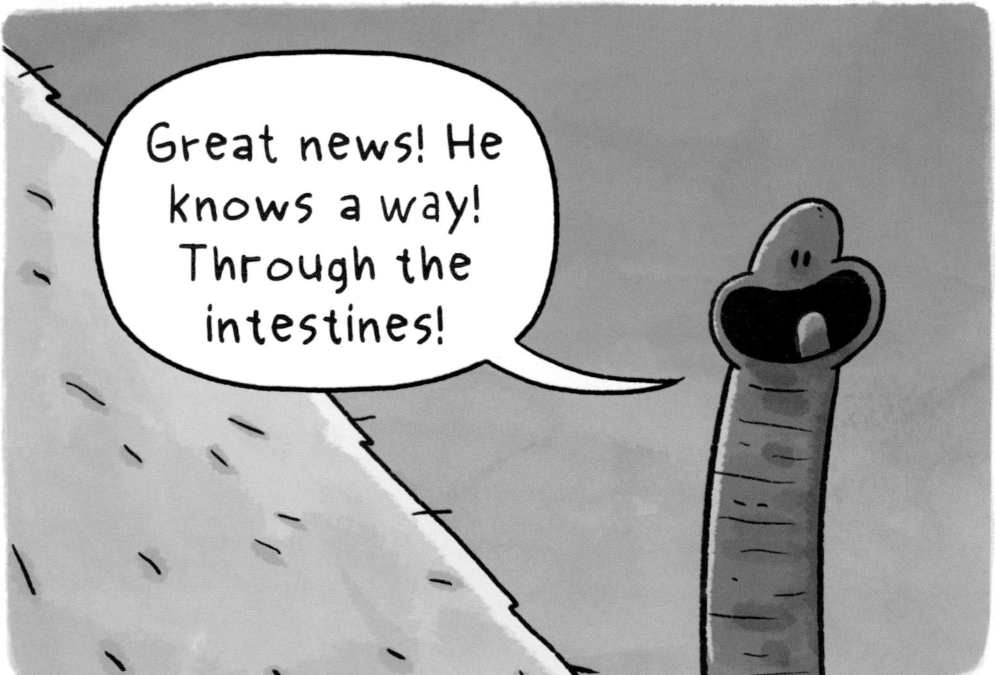
Great news! He knows a way! Through the intestines!

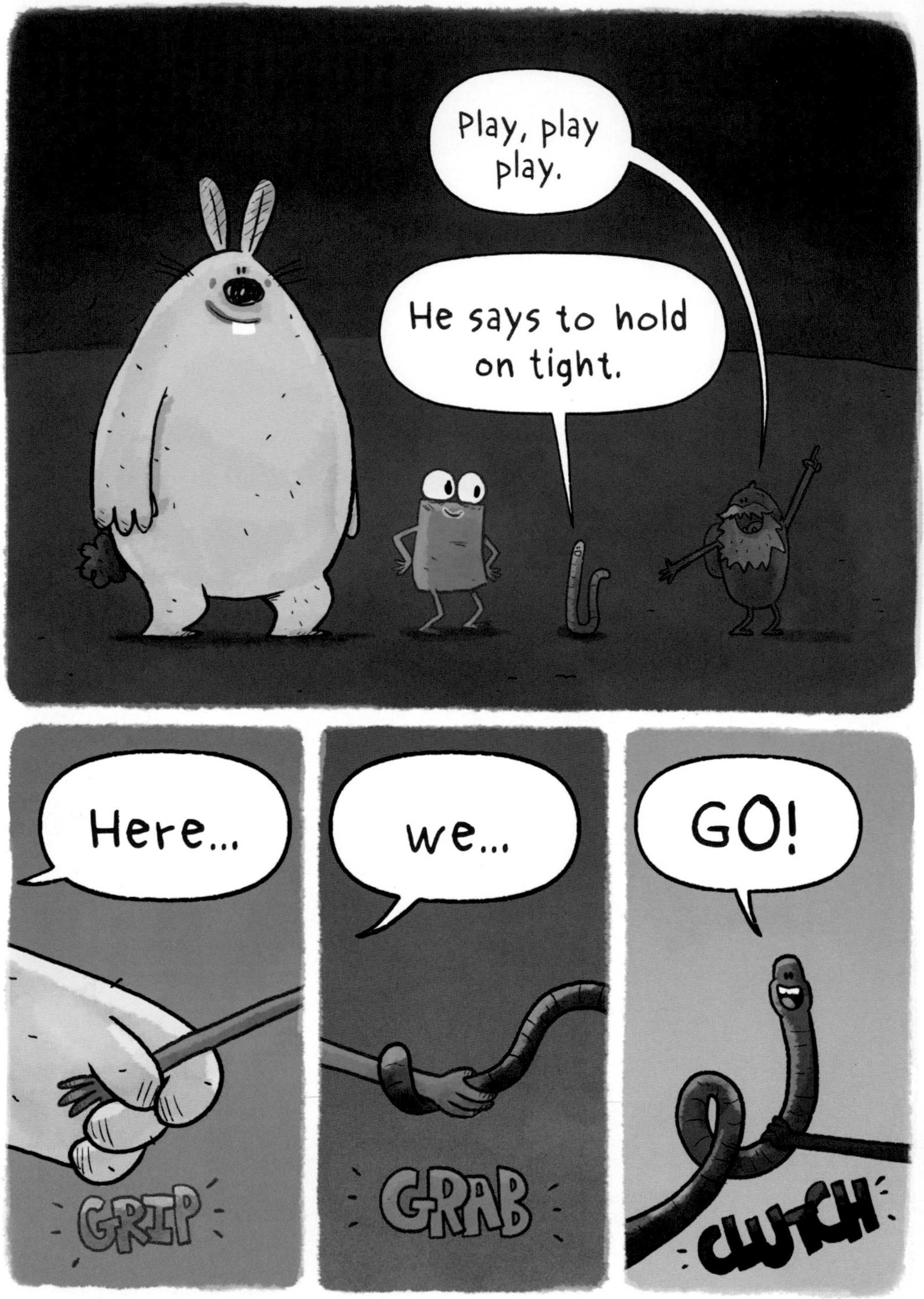
Play, play play.
He says to hold on tight.
Here...
GRIP
we...
GRAB
GO!
CLUTCH

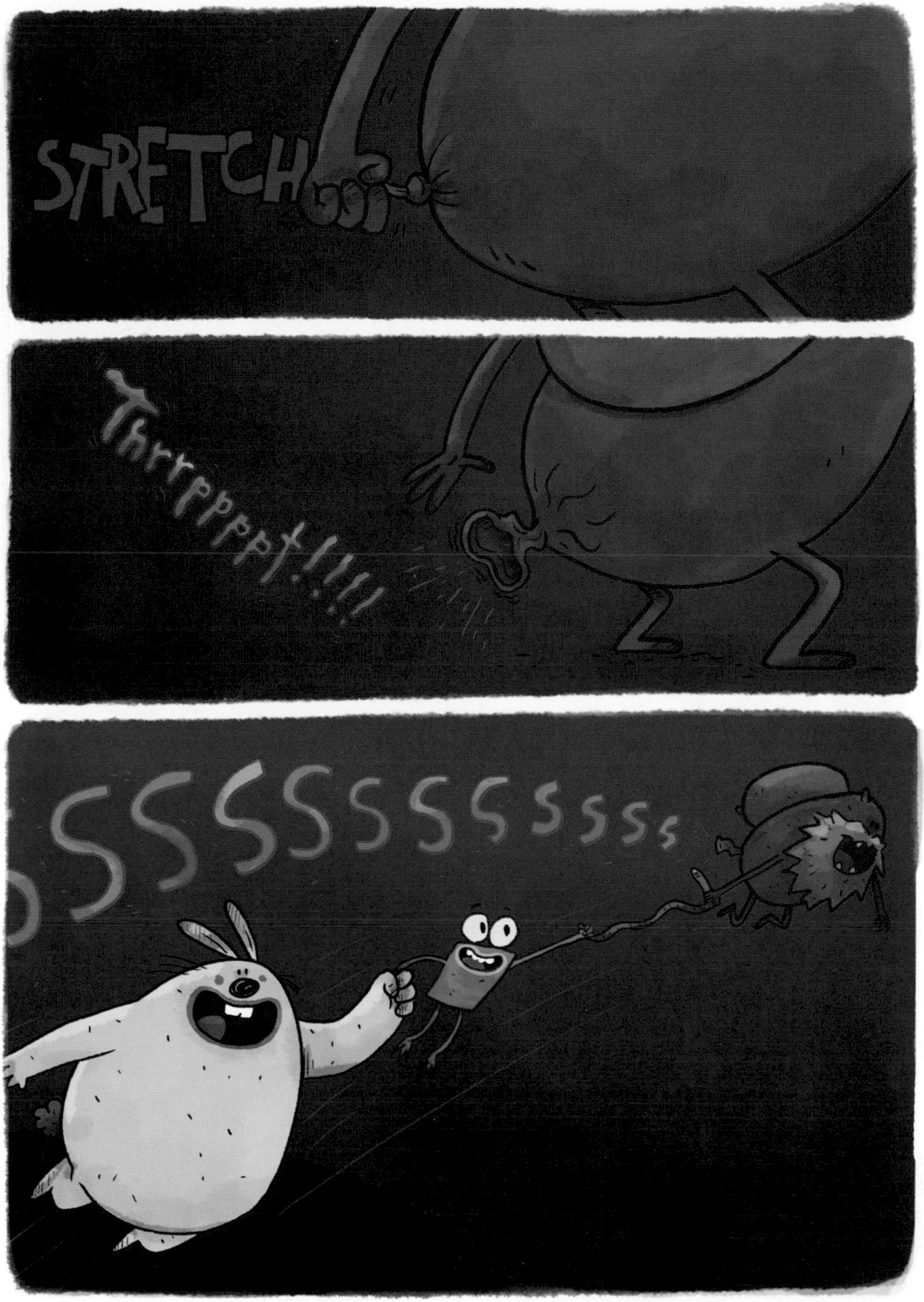
STRETCH
Thrrpppt!!!!
SSSSSSSssss

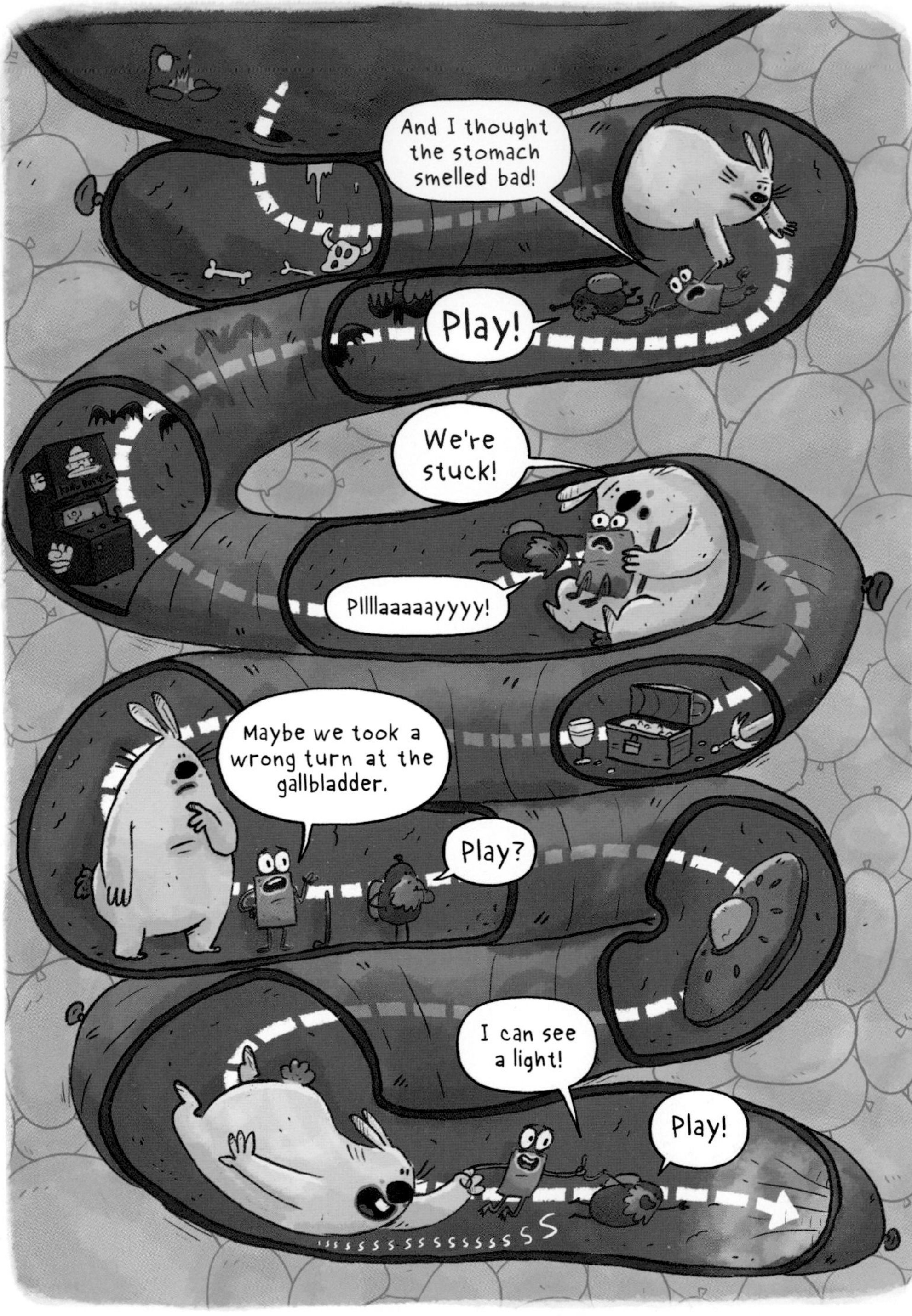
And I thought the stomach smelled bad!
Play!
We're stuck!
Pllllaaaaayyyy!
Maybe we took a wrong turn at the gallbladder.
Play?
I can see a light!
Play!
ssssssssssssssSS

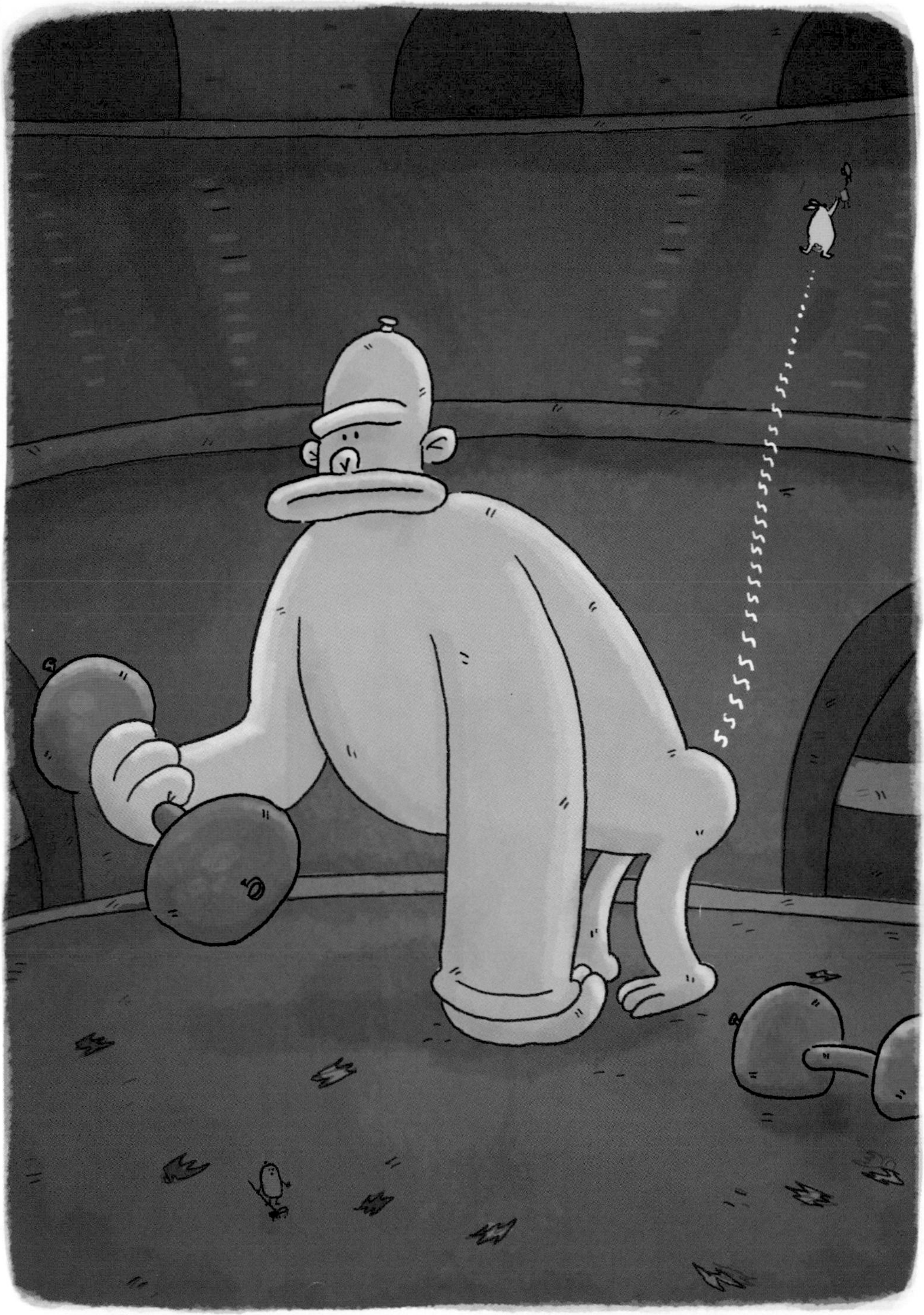

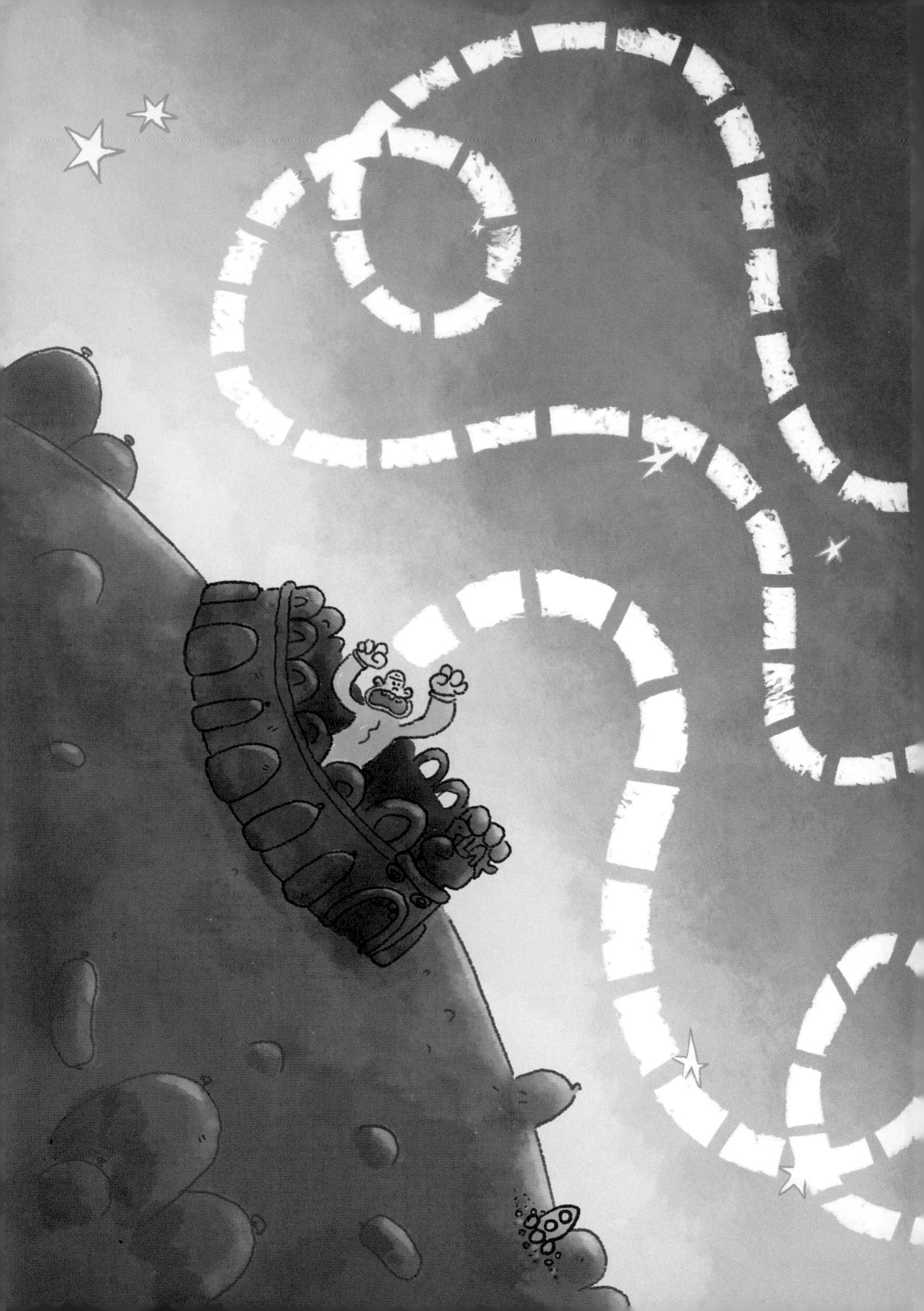

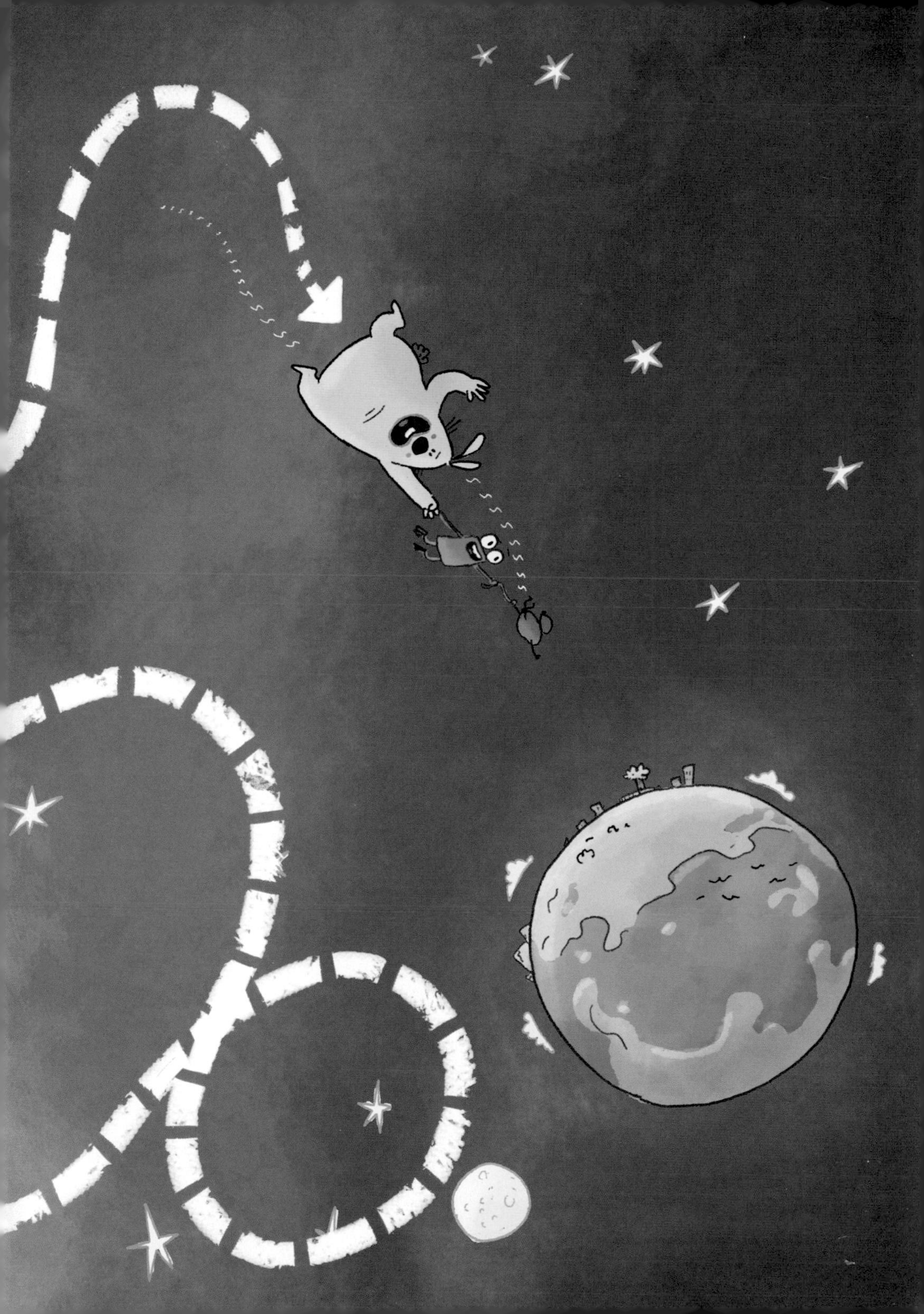

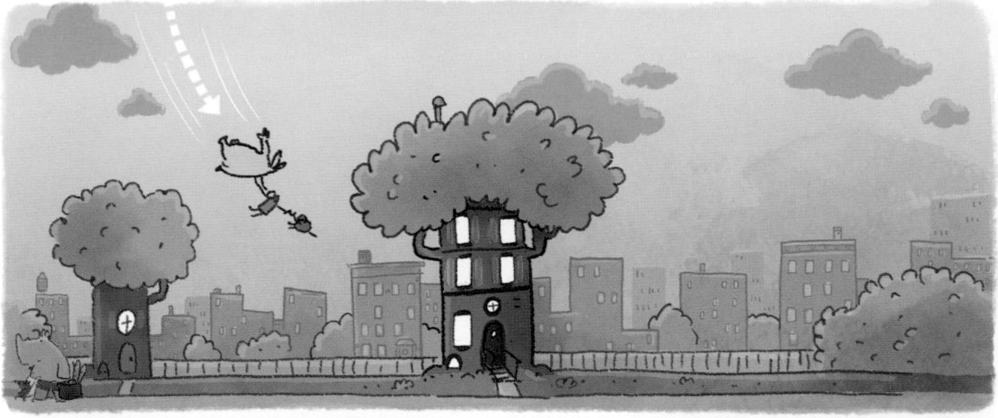

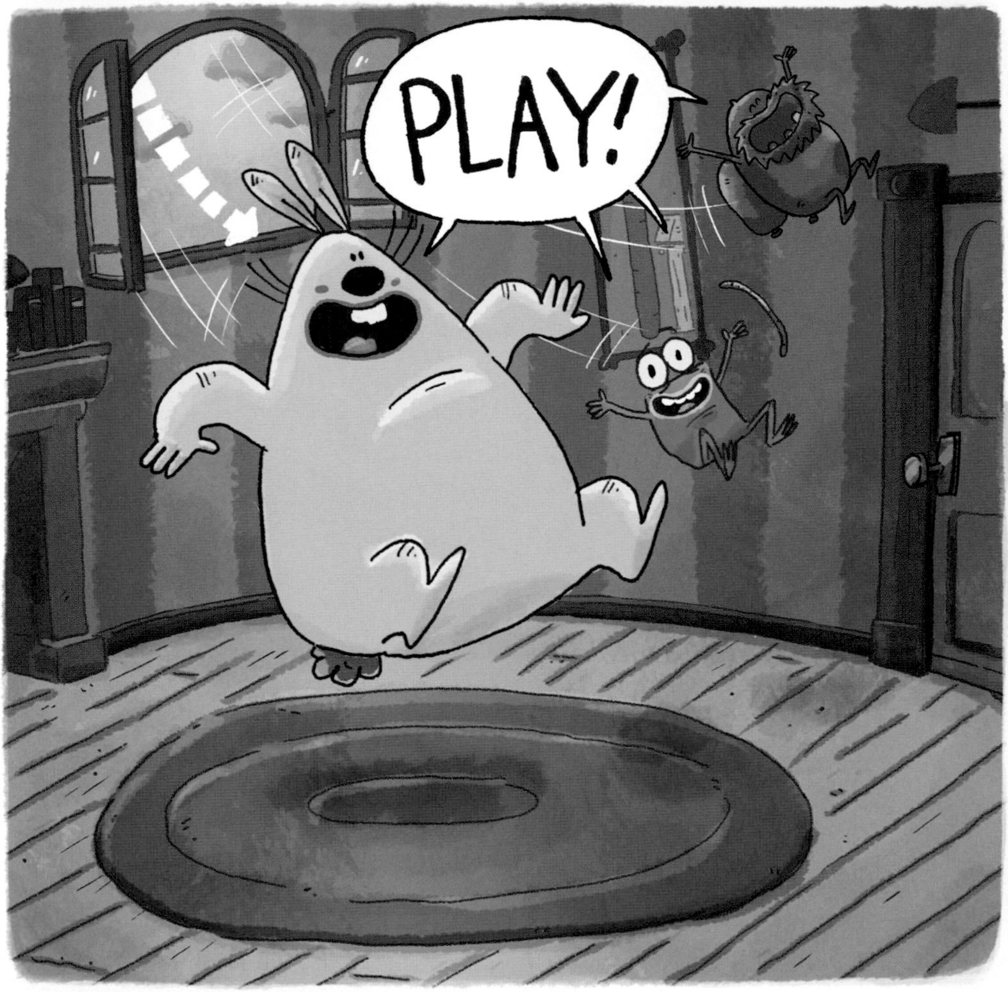
PLAY!

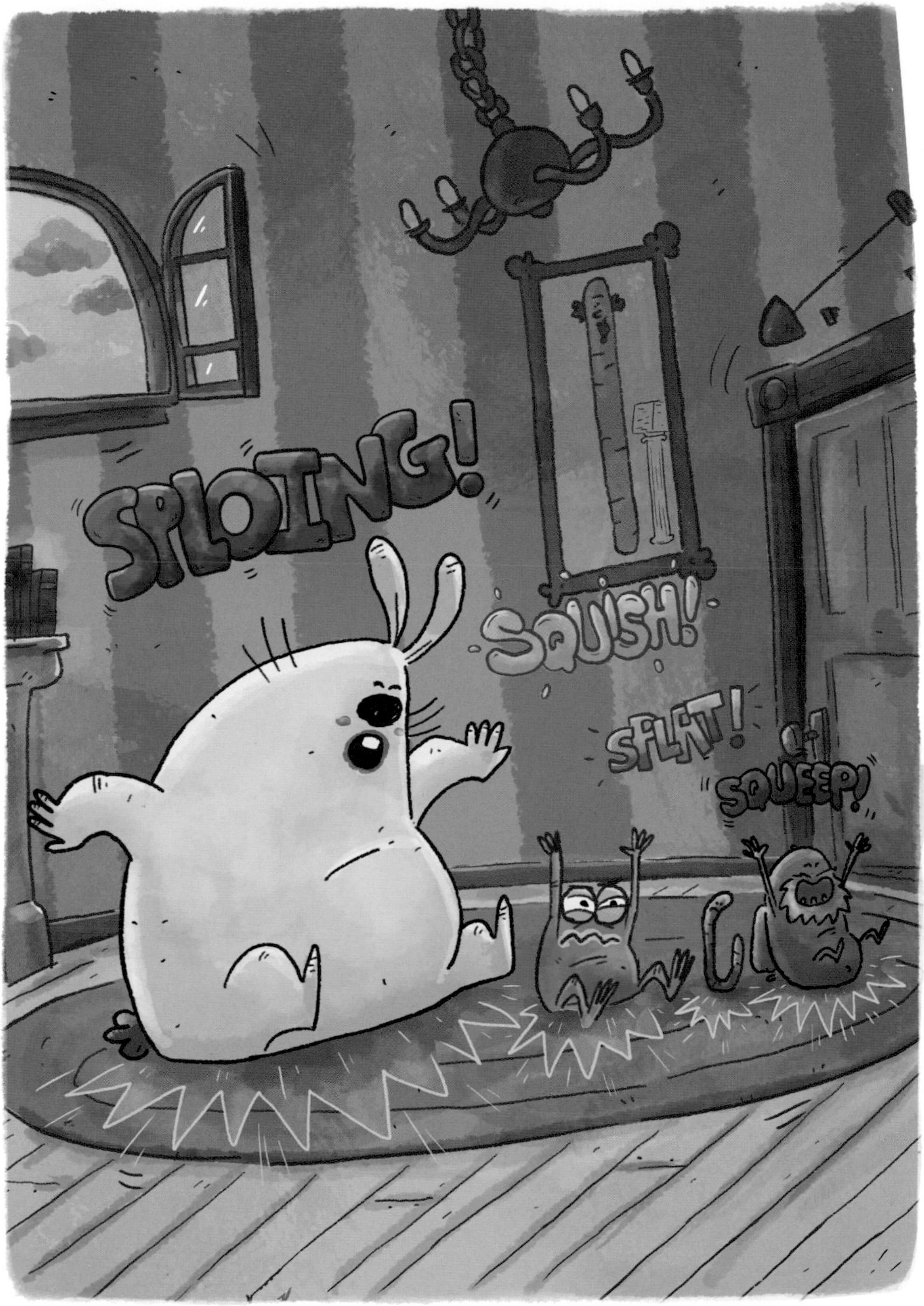
SPLOING!
SQUISH!
SPLAT!
SQUEEP!

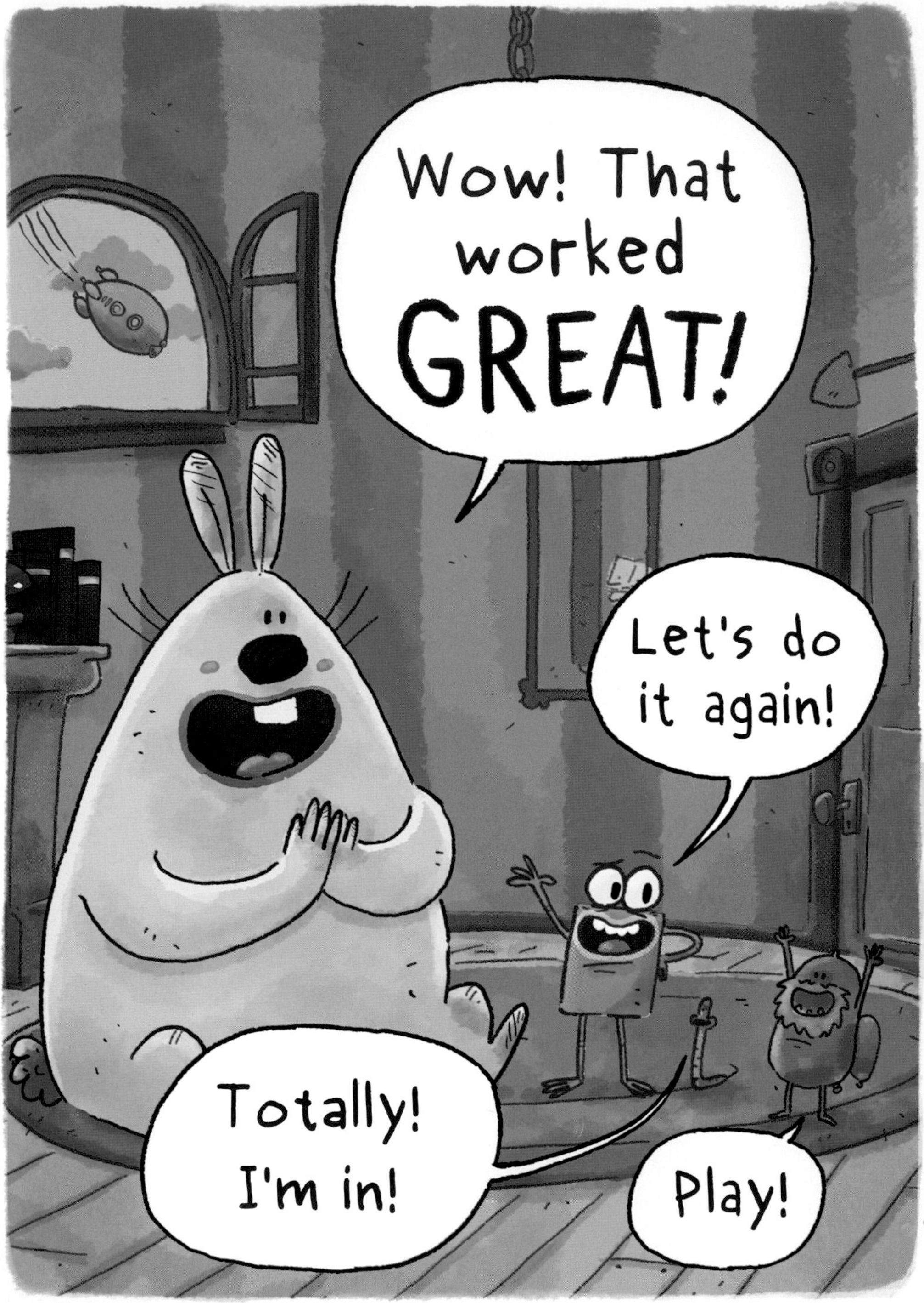
Wow! That worked GREAT!
Let's do it again!
Totally! I'm in!
Play!

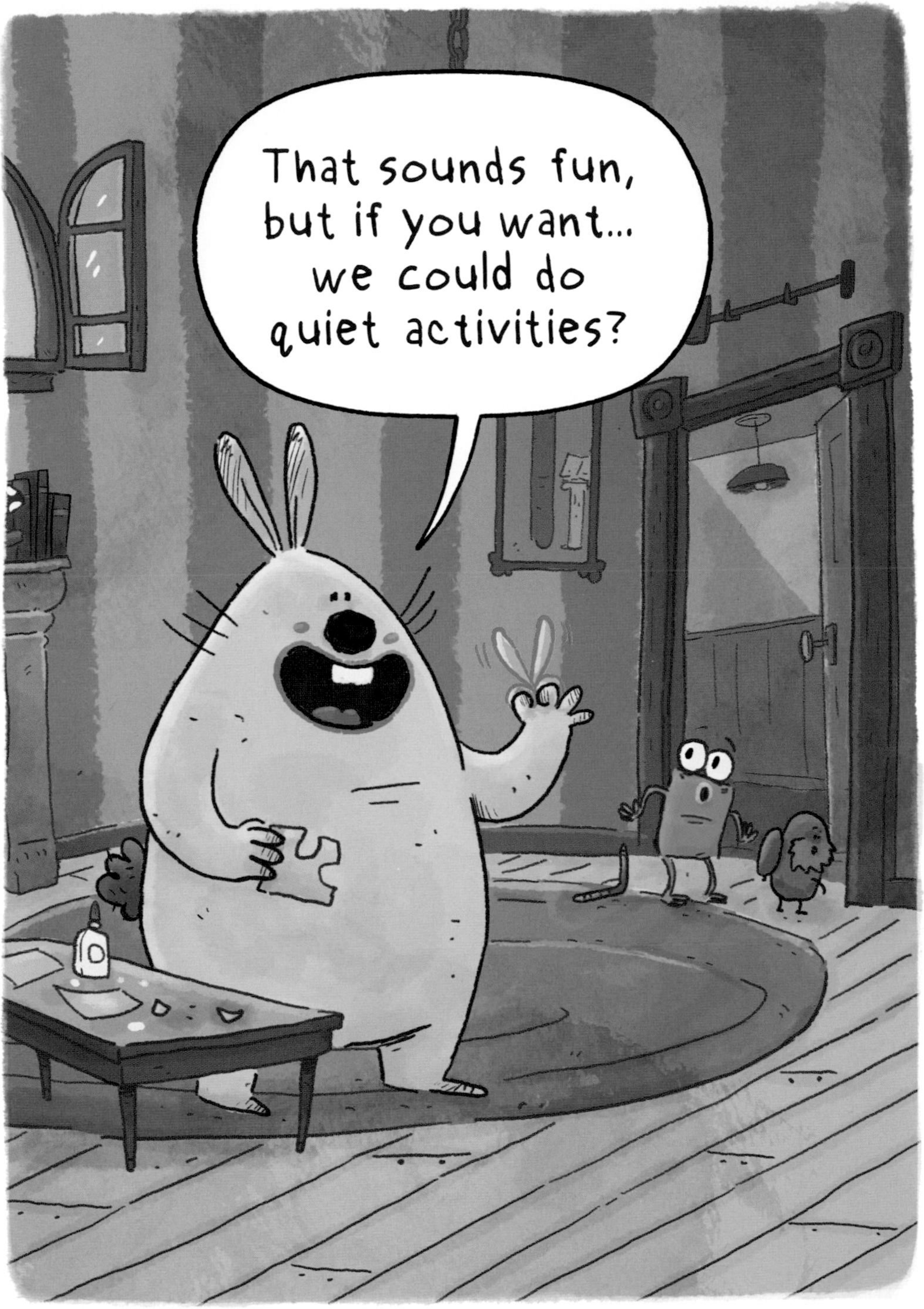
That sounds fun, but if you want... we could do quiet activities?

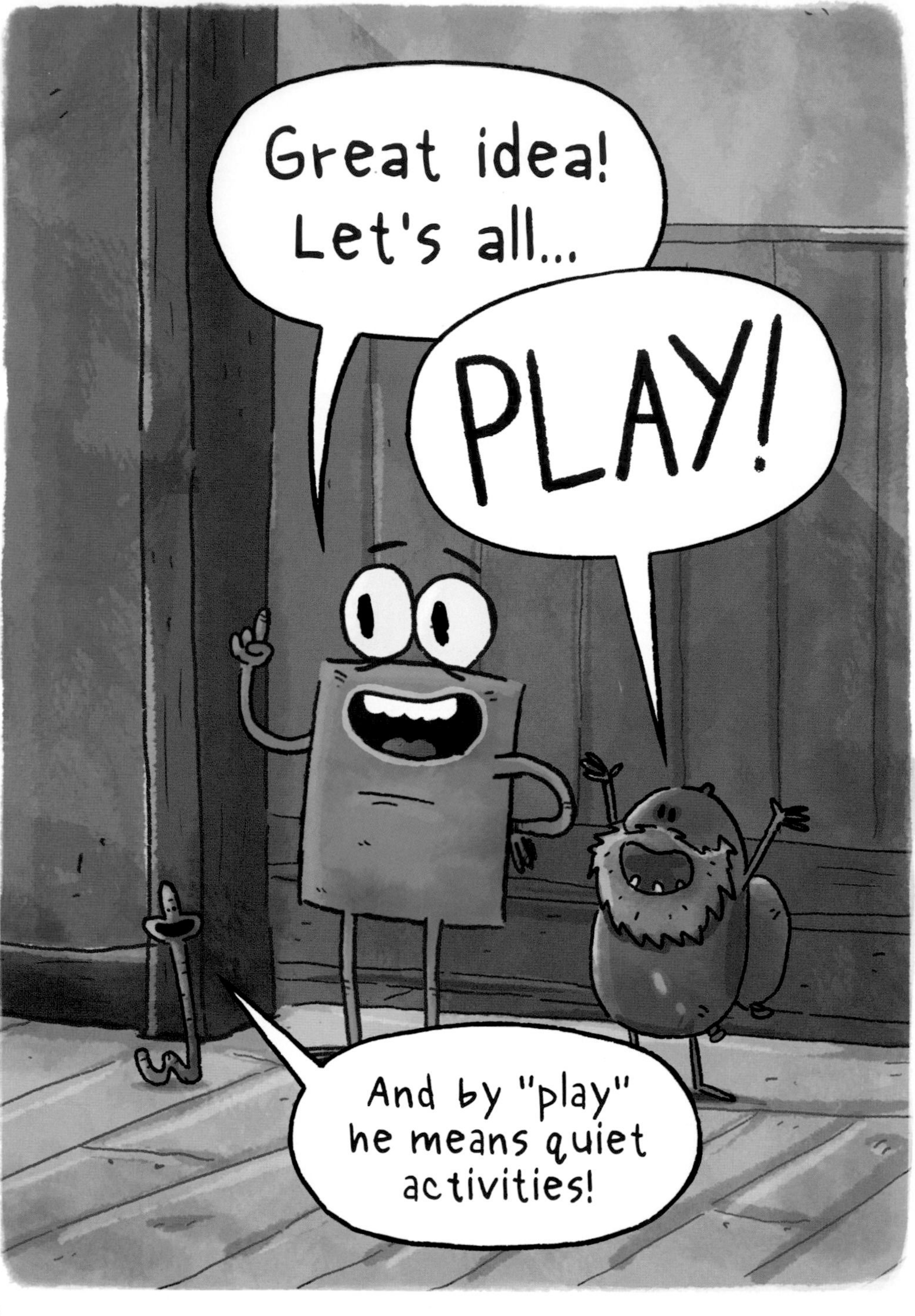
Great idea! Let's all...
PLAY!
And by "play" he means quiet activities!

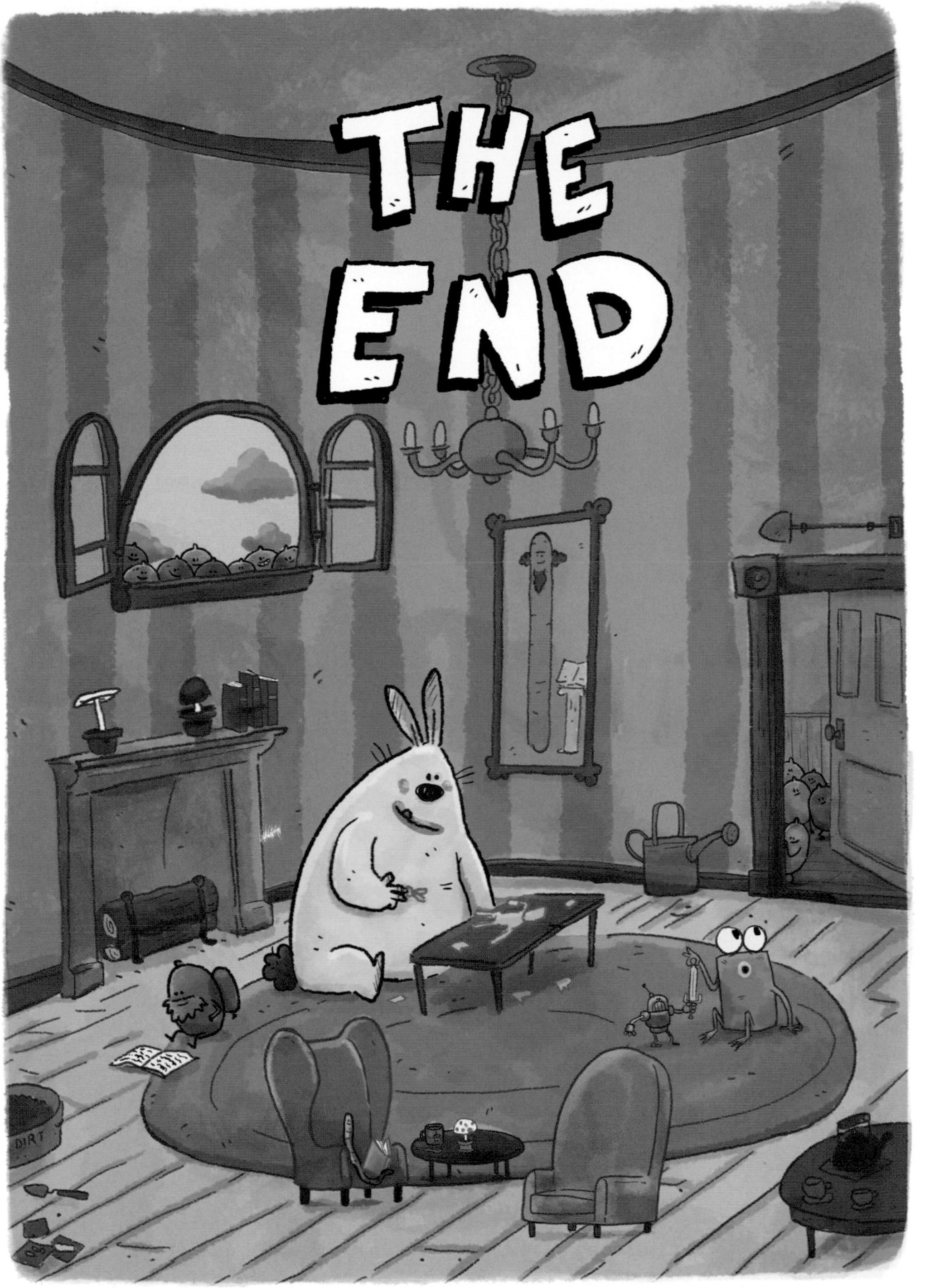
THE END
DIRT

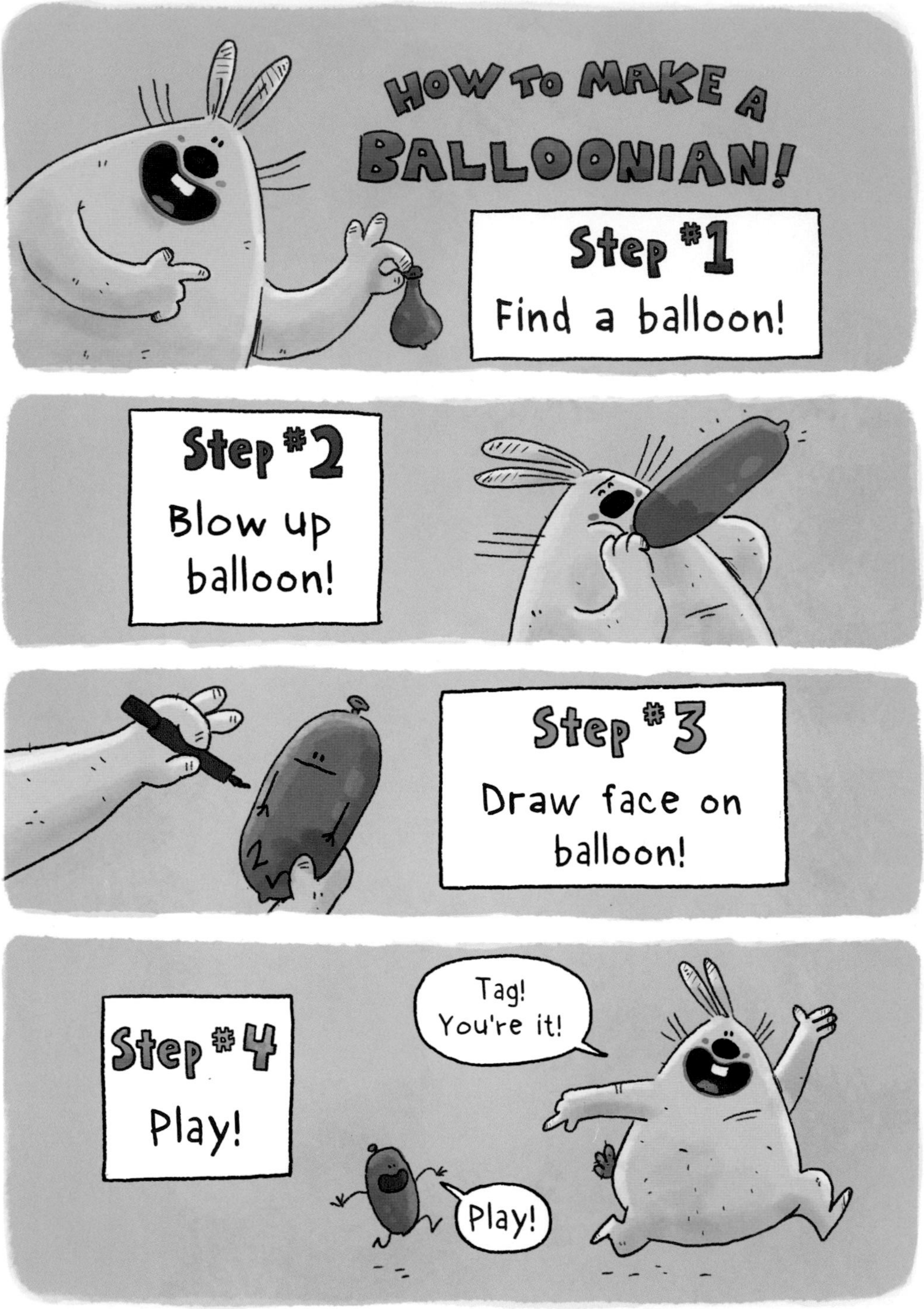
HOW TO MAKE A BALLOONIAN!
Step #1
Find a balloon!
Step #2
Blow up balloon!
Step #3
Draw face on balloon!
Step #4
Play!
Tag! You're it!
Play!

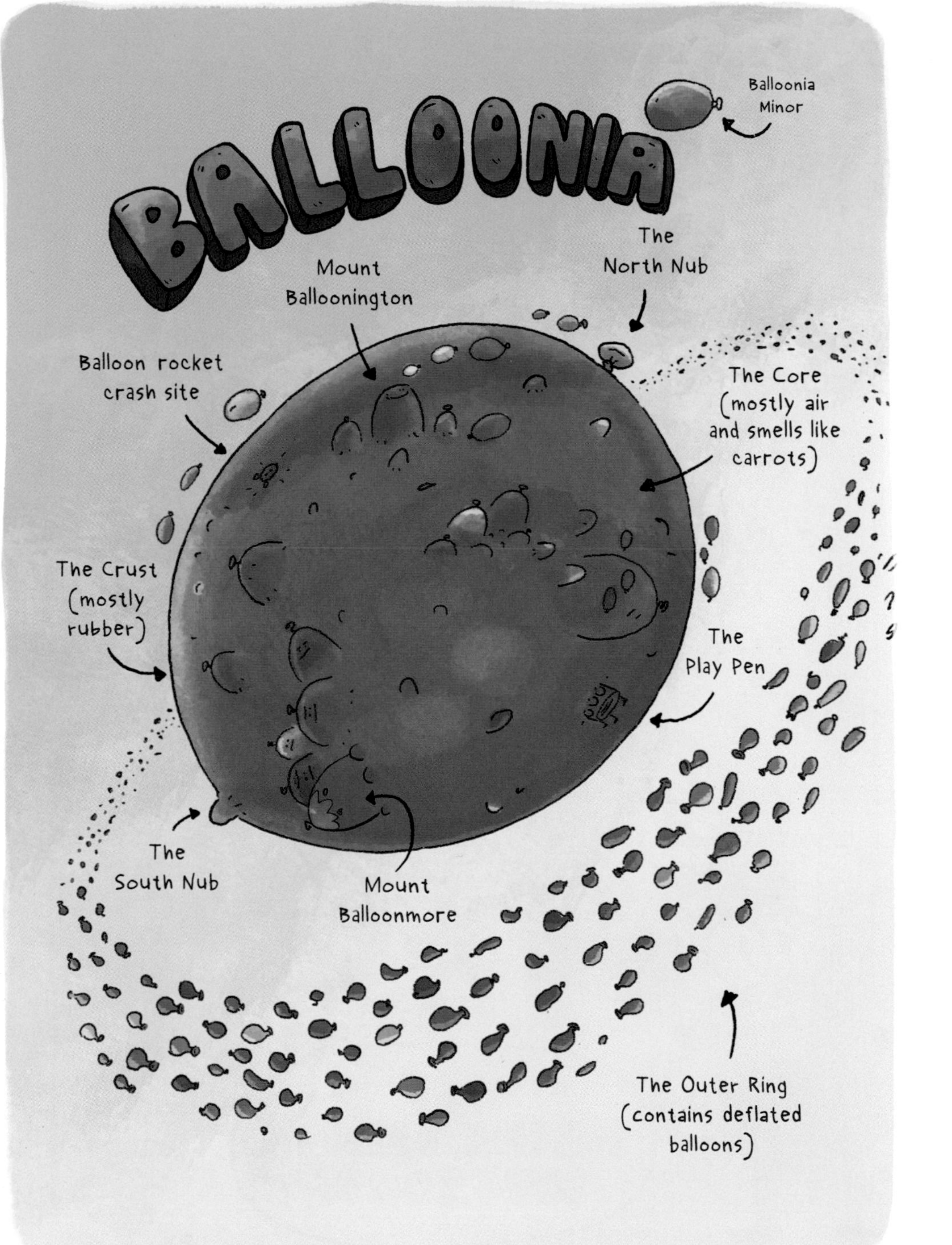
BALLOONIA
Balloonia Minor
The North Nub
Mount Ballooningston
Balloon rocket crash site
The Core (mostly air and smells like carrots)
The Crust (mostly rubber)
The Play Pen
The South Nub
Mount Balloonmore
The Outer Ring (contains deflated balloons)

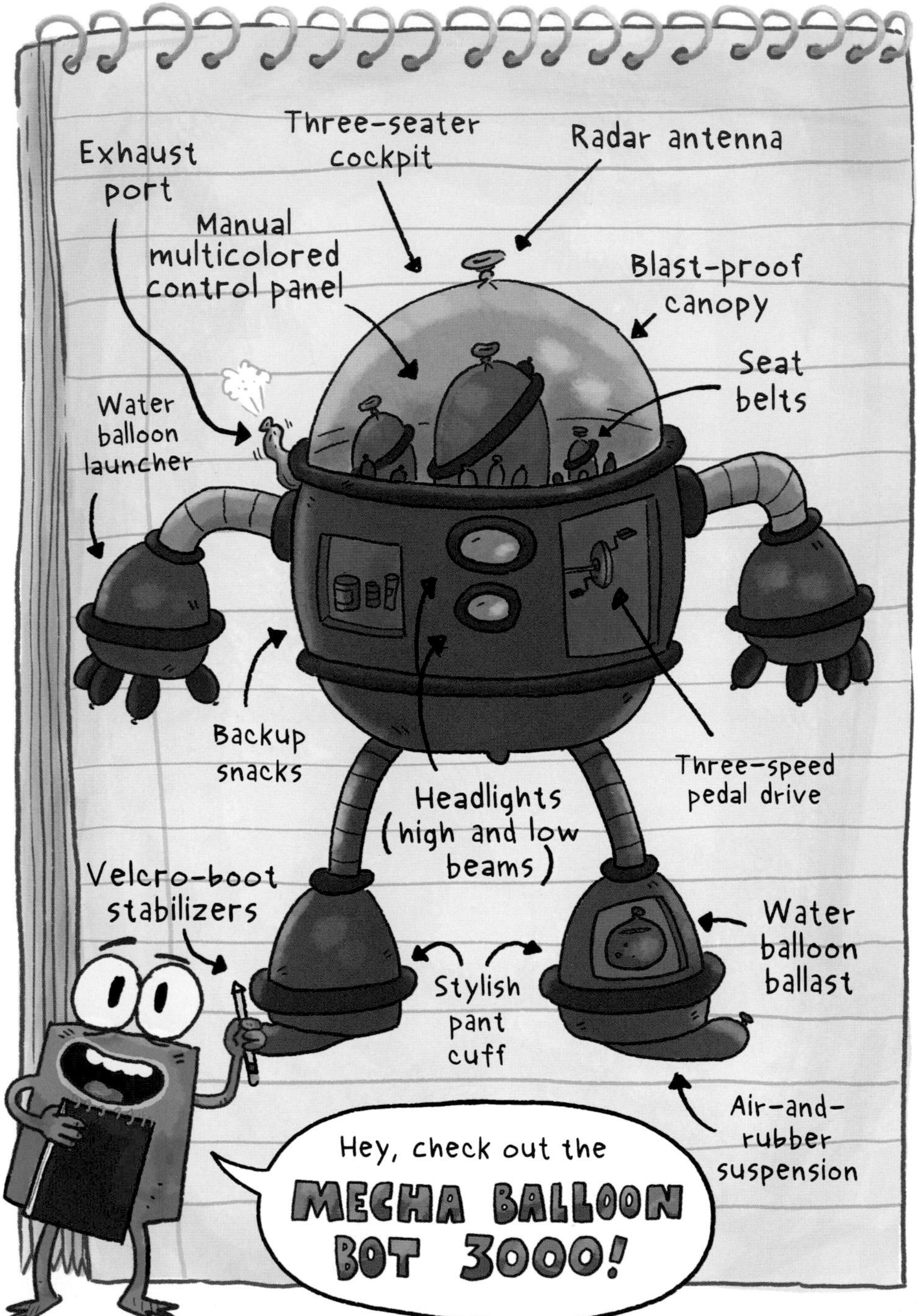
Three-seater cockpit
Radar antenna
Exhaust port
Manual multicolored control panel
Blast-proof canopy
Seat belts
Water balloon launcher
Backup snacks
Three-speed pedal drive
Headlights (high and low beams)
Velcro-boot stabilizers
Water balloon ballast
Stylish pant cuff
Air-and-rubber suspension
Hey, check out the
MECHA BALLOON BOT 3000!

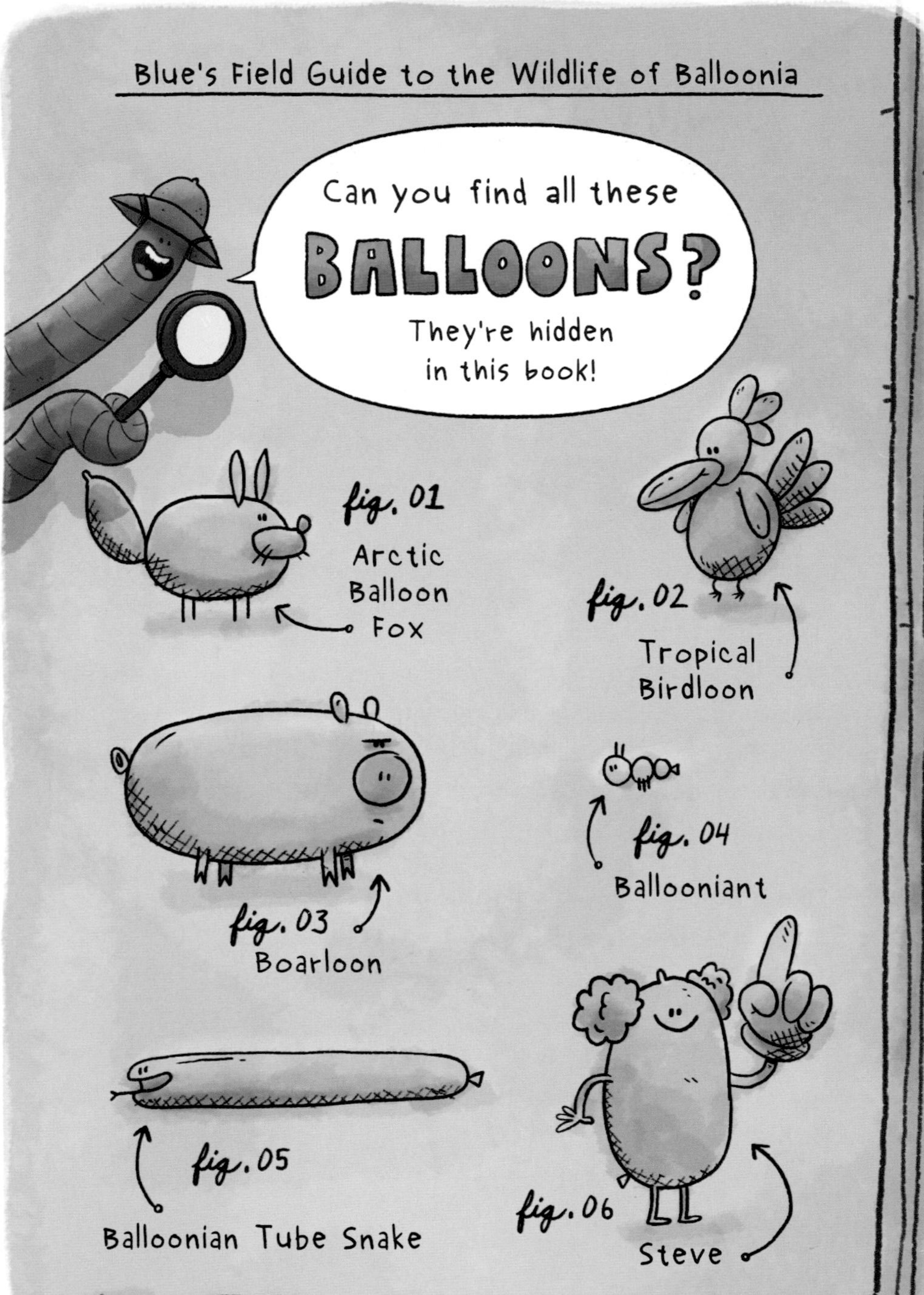
Blue's Field Guide to the Wildlife of Balloonia
Can you find all these
BALLOONS?
They're hidden in this book!
fig. 01
Arctic Balloon Fox
fig. 02
Tropical Birdloon
fig. 03
Boarloon
fig. 04
Ballooniant
fig. 05
Balloonian Tube Snake
fig. 06
Steve

About the Authors

Jason

Dan

Dan & Jason go back. Waaaaay back. They got their start drawing and writing stories in what feels like the early Jurassic period, also known as the '90s, when they were making comics in the back of their high school art room. Annnnnd they never stopped!

The acclaimed cartooning duo live, breathe, and eat comics and animation. *Escape from Balloonia* is their second Blue, Barry & Pancakes book. They love writing and drawing these stories more than anything else in the whole wide world, and they really hope you like reading them. They make everything together!
They think it, write it, draw it, mix it, bake it, and serve it together. Teamwork!

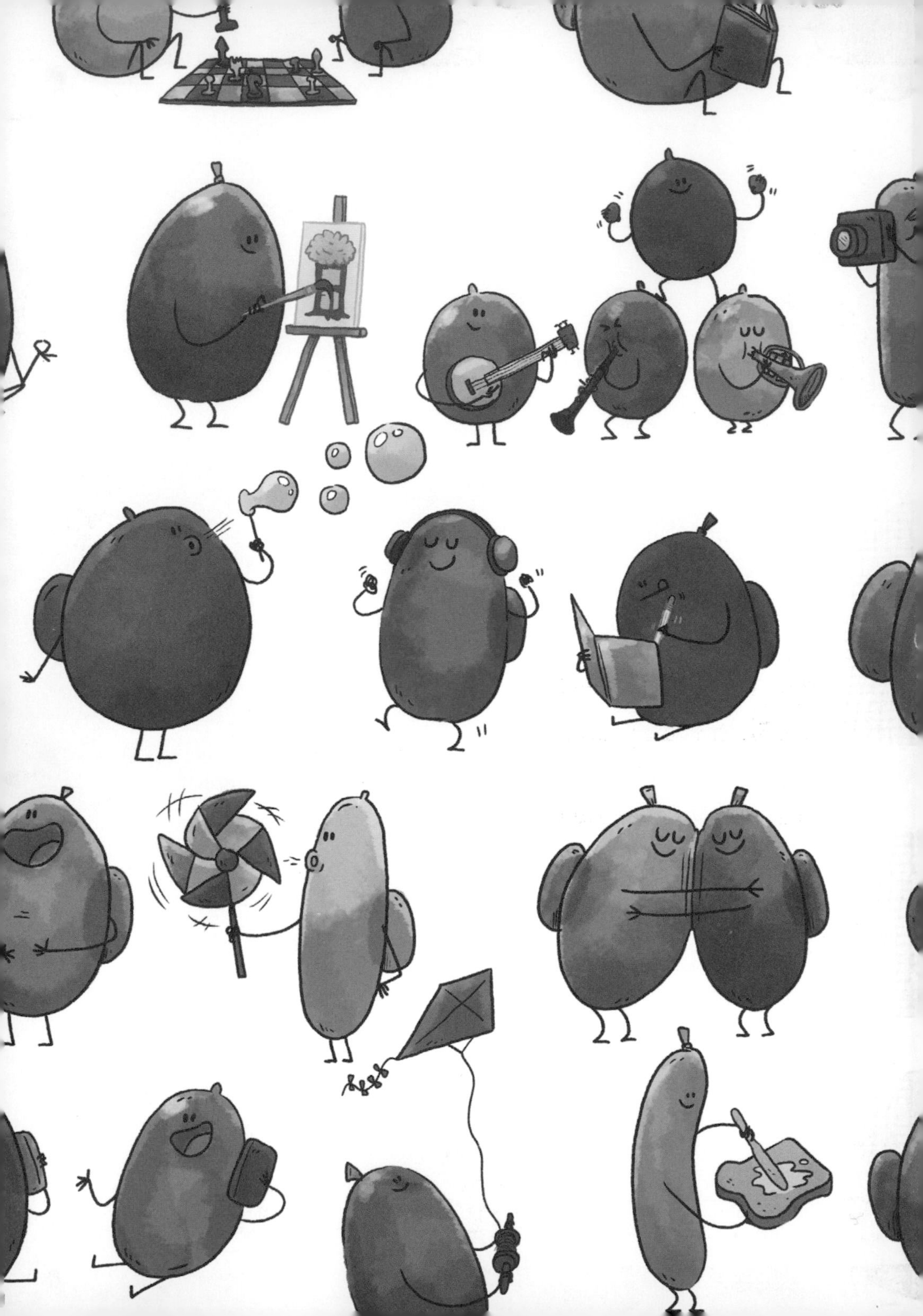